BULLY NATION

By

MARK T. SNEED

This book is a work of fiction. Names, characters, places, and incidents are products of the author's imagination or are used fictitiously. Any semblance to events or locales or persons, living or dead, is entirely coincidental.

Copyright ©2020

Second Edition

ISBN: 978-0-578-68061-3

DEDICATION

*To my mother, family and friends that continue to inspire,
encourage and challenge me to be a better person,
even when no one is around.*

THANK YOU

To the various lines that continue to thrive despite the lack of resources, equipment and education.

We carry our future on our backs.

Table of Contents

Chapter One.

Day Five.

With two days left in the challenge, there were easily a dozen or so hopefuls roaming the island seeking targets. There was no one on the streets. Walking on the streets on Day Five was an instant ticket to a dirt nap, Ralphie mused. The challenge was always won by the person that made the least slipups. The challenge had begun with nearly sixty battlers trying to be the champion 120 hours ago. Nearly three-fourths of the contenders were gone because they had made one miscalculation. One misstep in the challenge was enough to end the challenge hopes for three-fourths of the combatants.

Trying not to make any goofs that day was the reason that Ralphie had found a place to hide before heading into the Poppy art gallery. Initially, Ralphie had thought to rush Robert Nesta, the artist, on the streets but hesitated. He imagined attacking the Poppy on the street and him having some weapon that put his archaic croquet mallet to shame. That would have been a deadly error. So, he waited. When Robert Nesta had decided to enter Cosson Hall Ralphie had been faced with another decision. Should he attack the Poppy before he entered? Should he wait?

Ralphie, fifteen-year-old, thought all this as he tried to envision what was the next step now that Robert Nesta had entered Cosson Hall. The fifteen-year-old sat and listened to the sounds of the challenge just on the other side of the broken wall. There was sporadic gun fire in the distance, like two weeks after the Juneteenth celebration when kids found the last stash of firecrackers and lit them. There were one- or two- gun shots but not like in the first few days of the challenge.

He knew he was going in Cosson but still Ralphie sat and played out what he was going to do once he got inside the circular building. Ralphie envisioned climbing to his feet and preparing to run/crab walk across the space, checking in all directions, to the entrance of Cosson Hall. He would have his croquet mallet at the ready.

Knowing that Cosson Hall was circular he would enter and go right, staying low and looking for the Poppy that had beaten the undersized Jax. Ralphie hoped to find Robert Nesta on the first floor and catching him off guard and ending him in a few minutes. While he thought and rethought crossing the expanse between him and Cosson he watched the sun edge toward the rooftops of the buildings that made the island semi-habitable. At least, that was the plan.

One hundred yards from Ralphie stood the towering circular Poppy claimed building. The building was the largest standing structure on Pandemonium Island. It stood seven stories tall but was in a state of decay. Half of its edifice from the seventh to the fourth floor was open to the elements on the eastern side of the circular building. Ralphie tried to recall if there was any building that was taller than three stories on the island. He did not know, but he was certain that Cosson Hall was the tallest building on the island.

He recalled a video he had seen of the interior of Cosson Hall. It was featured on the Pandemonium Challenge website. It was one of the places to see when on Pandemonium Island. The Poppies, the artists of the Remains, decorated the circular building with various art from the lobby up to the seventh floor. At least, that was what Ralphie remembered from the video. Cosson Hall was something of a Poppy hajj. Every Poppy that entered the Pandemonium Challenge went to Cosson Hall. That was a good and a bad thing.

Looking across the space between the building where he sat and the entry to Cosson Ralphie thought he should just climb to his feet and walk to the entrance and put hands on the smaller nutbrown boy, with the mushroom cloud of black curls on his oval head, carrying his backpack and duffel bag, who seemed to move faster and be oblivious to the dangers of the challenge as he walked from the eastern part of the island to Cosson Hall. He had stopped twice to adjust his supplies. He carried the duffel bag that everyone had been given and his backpack. The duffel bag looked still packed like it had been on the launch. The second time he had stopped he was just a block from Cosson Hall. Of course, Ralphie did not know that was where the Poppy was headed at the time.

Ralphie had not clocked how long the Poppy had been in Cosson Hall but he felt that it had been longer than normal. So, Ralphie decided that he had to go in and find the boy that had bested the dinky Jax. Ralphie checked his digital map reader and took another five minutes to commit to the idea of entering Cosson Hall.

If there was one constant in the challenge it was that Poppies were drawn to Cosson like moths to a flame. Because everyone knew Cosson Hall was where every Poppy went, everyone with ill intentions headed there as well. As a result, most Poppies got flatlined either going or coming from Cosson. Getting got was what Poppies did in the challenge, especially near Cosson Hall.

Like clockwork, Poppies appeared on the island, ran for their lives, just like everyone else, rubbed out a few here and there and then they, the Poppies, were knocked off, like clay pigeons. In the challenge, burning the eight Poppies was like shooting fish in a barrel, knowing that every challenge they were all going to eventually head to Cosson Hall. It was their weakness.

Luckily, for the Poppies, all the lines knew the same information about each line and the lines inclinations. The Trads liked to move more than hide out or camp. The First Gens were hiders. The Second Gens liked places with electrical equipment and the water. The Boomers were more likely to be out of doors than indoors. The Innovators, well no one knew what the Innovators inclinations were as they had only had two competitors before Pandemonium Twenty-Three. For the Millers, the pundits said, that the craftsmen were drawn to all of the old manufacturing plants and factory structures. Ralphie did not agree. He did not agree because the pundits were wrong but because he did not want to feel predictable.

Ralphie thought about the above and knew that everyone in the challenge knew the same things. Few camped out at Cosson Hall for fear that another line might sight and target them waiting for an unsuspecting Poppy.

Inside one of the crumbling structures that made up Pandemonium Island, just one hundred yards from the cylindrical building known as Cosson Hall, Ralphie hunkered down. He had followed Robert Nesta for two blocks and plotted out the simplest and most painful way to dead the smug artist, who did not even seem to care that the island was filled with pre-teens and teens armed to the teeth all with ill-intentions towards each other. Ralphie had intended to end Robert Nesta one block before Nesta ducked into Cosson Hall but hesitated. That hesitation had allowed Robert Nesta to elude Ralphie when he believed he had enough nerve to end the boy with a black mushroom-like haircut.

Ralphie had targeted Robert Nesta, he rationalized, to set things right. At least, that was what Ralphie believed. All he had to make things right was his croquet mallet. He had carried his backpack because it had everything he needed. The croquet mallet was his offense and defense. That was enough. Yet, Ralphie hesitated. The fifteen-year-old squeezed his lips together and twisted them on his chocolate face.

He had followed Robert Nesta and prepared to beat his brains out but had failed when the chance presented itself. Instead, Ralphie had ducked into the crumbling building and hoped he had not been seen by the boy he was following. He was such a coward, Ralphie decided. All he had to do was get close enough to Robert Nesta and swing his croquet mallet. That would have been enough. Yet, he had not been able to close the distance needed to put Robert Nesta in his lethal arc. He had hesitated. Had he had second thoughts? Did he doubt his abilities?

Robert Nesta, the Poppy, had strolled to the entrance of the gigantic building and, for the first time since Ralphie had followed him, turned around and looked to see if anyone was following. Ralphie had frozen and backed into the shadows of the closest building to regroup and rethink his next steps. Immediately, Ralphie thought that Robert Nesta was playing some twisted game of cat and mouse and that Ralphie was the mouse being played with.

Had Robert Nesta known all along that Ralphie was following him and now waiting for the Miller to enter to cut off his head? Ralphie was unsure suddenly. Perhaps, Robert Nesta had rigged a few booby traps in preparation for the inevitable attack from Ralphie and others in Cosson. Ralphie's mind reeled with all the nefarious possibilities suddenly before him. He concocted a belief that Robert Nesta was one of those spiders that baits his trap with things that his prey wants only to turn the table on them in the end. Ralphie imagined just getting close enough to the entrance and a trap snapping and whipping him into the dark to be devoured by Robert Nesta. The longer that Robert Nesta remained in the building the wilder the ideas that sparked and germinated in the fifteen-year-old's mind.

He recalled that on Day One of the challenge the gun fire was thick and continuous. Day Two the gunfire was still steady but by the second night the rapid-fire sound of shooting slowed. Day Three, the gun fire seemed like someone was shooting off small packs of firecrackers more than gunfire. Each day, after that, the gunfire lessened and Ralphie imagined that those with the gun were choosing their targets better and conserving bullets. Or, that was the logic.

"You know how it is," the dwarfish Jax had explained the night before the challenge. "The first day knobs are shooting at everything that moves. They get a new toy and want to show it off. They probably kill more people by accident that day than any other on purpose." big-eared and puny Jax laughed. "If they could shoot mosquitoes or fireflies, they would that first day," Jax joked. He smirked at his own comment. He added, "Day Two the knobs are still gung-ho and shooting at anything that moves. Lots of innocent bystander shootings that day. Day Three it gets quieter than those first few cowboy days." Jax grinned at Ralphie. "Those knobs couldn't find their ass with both hands are done and gone. By the end of Day Three the ones that can are left and if they have burpers, they ain't doing pot shots. They are the real deal bad boys and girls. They are smarter. They aim and shoot. They ain't just tossing lead." the round headed Jax noted his cocky I-know-more-than-you-do smile in Ralphie's memory.

On the digital map reader Ralphie eyed the clock counting down in the left-hand corner of the reader. Ralphie had made it to 127 hours. 127 hours. Ralphie bit the bottom of his lip recalling that 96 hours marked the beginning of Day Four. 106 hours into the challenge and the shrimpy Jax was still in the game. Day Four Jax was cracking jokes and talking about vampires and werewolves and movies. 13 hours later, 140 hours in total, Ralphie paused and tried not to get maudlin.

"By Day Four the only ones pulling a burper are grave diggers. Day Five, most have run out of ammo or are using it like snipers," Jax, Ralphie's best friend in the challenge, explained 24-hours prior. "Day Six and Seven are going to be the quietest days. Anyone with a loaded burper in the last 48 hours is going to wait until the last possible moment to whip it out and aerate someone. They got to make every shot count. The challenge is all about surprises."

Ralphie recalled the whole stupid conversation from Jax, the jokester. Jax loved to talk. Jax, a foot shorter than Ralphie, had made it through the first four days and were planning on making it to Day Five or more when things went incredibly wrong.

He closed his dark brown eyes to the thought of Jax and his goofy smile and his wild streak being gone and without warning realized he had no control of what came next. The emotions connected to his memories of Jax gripped his heart and tore at his insides and rushed from Ralphie's eyes. He tried to close his eyes and stop the inevitable and think of anything but the loss of his friend as packs of boys and girls, in groups no larger than three or four, passed by looking to end him and anyone in their way.

The Miller peeked over the edge of the masonry and toward the front of the round building that looked like an old-fashioned totem pole Ralphie had seen in history tomes. At the bottom of Cosson Hall was this angry face with six floors of broken windows above it, the Miller youth mused. His musings were distracted by the sound of gun reports to the east. The gunfire was just a handful of cracks of noise in the distance. There was no danger to Ralphie, he knew.

For a moment, Ralphie found himself thinking of Juneteenth, just a month ago, and his great night in the park with Bailey Beaumont. That night had been magical. It had begun oddly with too much attention being paid to Ralphie by too many people he did not know. He had gotten a chance to see and talk with Baldwin before running into Jax the jokester and Zeke and Tee. Then he had spent the lion's share of the night with Bailey and her lyrical laughter and enticing beauty. The whole night had been capped off by

Bailey and Ralphie dancing and afterwards watching the Remains hourlong firework show.

The gunfire sounded again on the island and reminded Ralphie that he was not in the Remains but in the challenge. He snapped back from the memory of dancing with Bailey Beaumont and Juneteenth and all the glitz and glitter of that night.

Ralphie shook his head. He hated that he was prone to daydreaming. It was definitely a weakness.

In the Pandemonium Challenge daydreaming could eliminate Ralphie just as easily as being caught by a bear trap. The challenge was cutthroat and the ultimate survival contest. One blunder in the challenge could be the last flub anyone made. It was fierce and humbling to be bettered by tweens and teens any day. It was doubly embarrassing to have that humiliation televised across all of the Remains.

He was not impulsive or prone to what many called: spontaneity. Ralphie was deliberate and thoughtful. He was not rash. His teachers all admired his clear thinking and decisiveness. Yet, he had failed to follow through on his numerous opportunities to smash in Robert Nesta Scott's head when he followed him.

"We got 48-hours," someone crowed. Ralphie tensed at the words. He pressed against the wall and craned his head to see who had spoken. Through the crack in the wall he saw a horse-faced boy, the color of dark chocolate with shoulder length finger thick twisties, dressed in a blue and speckled green hoody, blue jeans and camouflage green combat boots.

"Just two days."

"Right, and we made it to Day Five," Ralphie heard someone, other than the horse-faced boy, growl. Ralphie turned and looked to the left and through a broken piece of wall that gave a view of the space between his hideout and Cosson Hall. Just to the left of Ralphie stood a cocoa brown girl, dressed in the dark blue and the forest green of a Boomer, resting an evil looking medieval weapon on her small shoulder. The weapon looked like it should have been in a museum more than at the challenge.

The milk brown girl seemed comfortable with the weapon that looked like the baby of a double-headed axe and a weighted pole. At the base of the weapon was this ornately designed round and dimpled metallic ball the size of a grapefruit. The girl was dressed similarly to the dark boy, in blue jeans and camouflage combat boots. She moved on incredibly small feet, Ralphie noticed. He also noted that her hair was in four gigantic Afro puffs on her small, round head.

"We made it to Day Five and now all we have to do is survive for another forty-eight to claim the prize," rhymed the dark boy that loomed over the girl. He was a little taller than the girl with apple cheeks and thin features. Of the two, he seemed closer to the hideout where Ralphie hid. The boy was dressed in Boomer hoody, jeans, combat boots and a single baseball glove. He was taller than the girl with gold teeth and carrying a double-headed battle axe. On his thin hips hung a cow boyish handgun that looked like it should have been in a Western museum more than in the challenge.

The girl with the four Afro puffs lifted the heavy halberd off her shoulder and swung it slowly and expertly in a full 360° circle at chest level and on the 450° the halberd slammed into a pole near a building on the other side of the street from Cosson Hall. Wires were attached to the pole and snapped free to dangle from the building and pole as the pole clattered to the street below. The halberd was heavy and dangerous in the right hands and sliced through the utility pole like it was rice paper.

Simultaneously, the boy, carrying the double-headed battle axe, jumped out of the area of the pole fall. He skidded to a stop on the opposite side of the wall where Ralphie was hiding. The battle axe slammed into the wall with a loud and deadly thunk. Dust rose and fell slowly in front of Ralphie as he held his hands over his mouth and cried.

"Rosa, you super-duper cray cray," the boy laughed.

"Cray, cray," laughed the girl. The pair laughed and ran westward. As quickly as they had appeared, they were gone.

"Think I'm downsizing. I ain't no lumberjack. Think I rather have the burper," the boy said, allowing the battle axe to fall on the ground beside him, just on the other side of the wall from Ralphie.

"Your funeral," the spunky girl insisted.

"Always my funeral," the boy laughed as he pushed away from the wall.

The voices were replaced by silence.

"Always my funeral," Ralphie thought.

In the seconds of silence Ralphie tried to quiet his emotions and regain his composure. For the tenth time Ralphie wiped at his dark eyes knowing that the action was futile and would have been easier if he were able to remove the memory of his best friend from his mind. Ralphie was crying because of how stupid and smart Jax was simultaneously. Jax had all of this weird information about almost everything in the walled Remains. He and Zeke loved talking about the challenge and strange things that happened in and out of the Remains. They loved being Millers and loved to talk about the other lines compared to the Millers. Jax was the only person, Ralphie knew, who knew all twenty-two of the challenge winners' names and lines.

Thinking about Jax made Ralphie smile and cry at the same time. It was the two-sides of Jax that elicited that response. Jax was the class clown. He tried hard to be the center of attention. Yet, he was this sad kid who lived with his aunt and her three daughters because his mother and father had died unexpectedly.

"I have goals man," Jax was always saying. "I am going to be a treasure hunter or get in the challenge and win and become legendary. Everyone will know my name. They will name buildings after me. I will make everyone proud of me."

"But you don't have to go to the challenge to make people recognize you," Ralphie tried to explain to Jax.

"Don't have to," Jax had noted with a tilt of his head. "Never said that, Ralphie. Thinking about getting in the challenge and showing the Remains what having a real Miller in the challenge can do. It is the easiest way for me to use all this knowledge," Jax had pointed to his temple. "I know so much about the challenge. All I have to do is get in the game and become legendary."

Ralphie knew he could not change Jax's mind about the challenge. Worse yet, Jax had convinced Zeke and Tee to sign up and commit to putting their hand in the machine and trying out for the Twenty-Third Pandemonium Challenge.

"Everyone thinks that the challenge is all about the burpers," Jax noted in his comical way. Jax would flex and make his eyes big while pursing his lips just to make Ralphie laugh. "Most of the toughs and winners ain't used a burper. There might be a few but just 'cuz they shooting don't mean squat if they can't aim." He paused and sucked in his lips.

Ralphie wanted to laugh at the memory of Jax but tears fell instead. He was crying because he could not push down his feelings for his kooky friend, who knew everything about anything in the challenge, and nothing at all. Ralphie was crying because he had not been able to save Jax from himself.

"Don't you worry about getting removed," Ralphie asked seriously.

Jax laughed off the question. Ralphie got serious at Jax's reaction.

"What you want me to worry about something that might happen in July when it's just now February," Jax said tilting his head to the left and studying his friend.

Ralphie was shocked into silence in the memory. It wasn't February any longer. It was now July. Ralphie felt a catch in his throat.

"Yeah, no one wants to be termed. But the fact is we live in the Remains. We ain't going to live forever. We could die from the toxic air. We could die from the poisons in the genetically modified foods that we are eating." Jax paused, thinking. "There's a bunch of choices, but as the great philosopher Alfred E. Neuman once said, "Life has a way of rewriting plans to make men look like fools."

"What?"

"When the fighting gods tire of your fight, then there's nothing you can do to stop the end from coming."

"Fighting gods," Ralphie questioned. "You believe in fighting gods?"

"How else can you explain the fact that no Miller has won the challenge in nearly thirteen years?"

Ralphie could not explain it. The Millers were hard working and resourceful. They should have won at least one or two challenges in a decade of fighting for the Pandemonium Challenge crown.

Ralphie closed his eyes and found himself replaying the fateful moment when he and Jax had entered one of the numbered buildings on the island and come under fire.

"The fighting gods are punishing us, Ralphie. They have been punishing our line for years. We have angered them somehow. They have figured a way to snatch victory from us every year. It doesn't matter that we are the best and most prepared line every year," Jax noted.

Day Four, when Jax had reminded Ralphie of the fickleness of the fighting gods and their desire to keep the Millers from winning, the very same gods directed Jax and Ralphie to the numbered buildings on the northside of the island.

"Jax, you know that the numbered buildings are death traps," Ralphie reminded.

"The fighting gods are guiding us today," Jax noted.

Ralphie was about to respond. Jax raised a hand. He closed his eyes and tilted his egg-like head to the sun as if he was listening to the air. Ralphie marveled. Was he listening to an unheard song on the still wind? Jax put a finger to his lips and entered the numbered building.

Ralphie knew that Jax entered the building hoping to catch someone off guard. They squinted in the darkness of the building and Ralphie was hyper-aware. Jax had only walked in one hundred paces when the pair found themselves prey to an unknown hunter. Three shots rang out and Jax and Ralphie were forced to scramble for cover.

Jax, being Jax, tried to show that the gun fire was just pot shots.

"They couldn't hit the ground with both hands," he smirked and stood up in the dark interior of the warehouse that they had entered looking for "easy" targets.

"Are you crazy," Ralphie breathed, not wanting to give away his position. But Jax stood up, despite being shot at by someone that neither had seen. Standing up was fool hardy. What was even more foolish was Jax lifting his right arm, the one with the arm rocket, and trying to shoot into the darkness at an invisible attacker.

Jax fired three marbles into the dark hitting nothing but hearing the shooting stop and gaining confidence.

"I think I know where this knob is," Jax winked, before being shocked into silence.

The fourth or fifth shot that afternoon spun Jax around like a top and the look on Jax's face was a mix of surprise and shock. Ralphie recalled that the shot had stolen Jax's voice. He did not scream. He did not cry out. It, the shot, seemed to come out of nowhere. Where it landed Jax, Ralphie was not sure. All Ralphie knew was that Jax was still spinning like he was dancing to music only he could hear. When Jax stopped spinning he dropped his left arm and the arm rocket fell silently to the ground, suddenly useless.

Witnessing the shooting Ralphie had wanted to scream, run or grab Jax-- pull him to safety--but he did none of that. His mind ground to a stop. Instead of doing anything he just watched, stunned into silence.

The second to last shot hit Jax somewhere in his back and drove him to his knees. Silent and mouthing wordlessly things that Ralphie could not determine. Jax was wounded and would not give up but Ralphie saw that he did not fight either. The last bullet seemed as if a gigantic invisible hand had slammed Jax to the ground. In Ralphie's mind, then and there he felt there was no such thing as fighting gods.

Ralphie hated that memory most of all, giving in and giving up on Jax. There was Jax on his knees, blood dripping from his wordless mouth, holding his side, silent and frozen in time. Jax mouthed something but Ralphie could not make it out. He did not want to make it out. There was nothing that he could do.

It was as if the world had fallen away and there was no wind, street noise, gun fire or any other sound allowed in the gigantic warehouse then. Ralphie was desperate and paralyzed. He found that he could not scream, move or do anything but watch.

Jax, though dying, struggled. Jax looked up and there was this anguished look on his face as if he had slammed his hand in a door. Tears were in his eyes. Ralphie watched as Jax tried to push himself up and stand.

The final shot came out of nowhere and tore through the side of Jax's head and he was suddenly lying on the ground unmoving. His body fell and before it struck the ground Jax had been removed from the challenge. Blood pooled around the wound. His arm rocket slingshot clattered on the debris of the warehouse space and landed just inches from Ralphie. He had been removed.

The fifteen-year-old tried to stop the water works but it was like trying to stop the rain from falling or the wind from blowing. Tears fell unchecked and without words. They seemed to be waiting for Ralphie's memory to come before they welled up behind his eyes. Ralphie tried to close his eyes and stop the tears and the memories of Jax but it was impossible not to think of Jax at that very moment.

Ralphie lowered his head and tried in vain to control his emotions. He pressed against the pillar of the structure for support and covered his mouth with his hands. Ralphie wanted to scream. Ralphie wanted to run out of the structure and into the deadly embrace of whoever was suddenly in the streets.

The fifteen-year-old wiped at his eyes thinking that by doing so he might stop the tears, but the tears eked out from under his hands. Tears flowed. The tears sought the cracks of his shut eyes. Ralphie opened his eyes and the tears continued. Tears spilled.

Ralphie wiped at his eyes. He tried to slow his breathing and regain his composure. He wiped at his dark eyes in a futile attempt to control the uncontrollable. Ralphie had suffered some cuts and bruises in five days of running, fighting, being shot at and nearly stabbed at least a dozen times. Yet, he was alive. He was breathing. His body ached all over as if he had been in a mosh pit with a dozen enforcers. Yet, none of that compared to the hurt of his friends being removed. The fifteen-year-old felt the loss of Tee and Jax deeply. Well, he felt the loss of Jax deeply.

His heart hurt. There was pain, physical pain that hurt and there was this emotional pain that seemed to stretch on forever. It was a pain that was not going to ease if his body felt better or another hurt took its place.

So, he wept and wept and wept and when he thought he was finally done weeping he wept some more. Tears poured out his red rimmed eyes. Tears spilled down his chocolate brown cheeks.

Ralphie did not know how long he cried. He did not care. He cried because he had suffered a loss.

The emotions behind the tears came at their own volition. Ralphie had no control over the beginning or the end of the memories that triggered his tears. The tears seemed to have a mind of their own. It was his emotions and memories of Jax that had brought him to the entrance of Cosson Hall. He had decided that he would avenge Jax by taking out Robert Nesta Scott. Jax and Robert Nesta had fought prior to the challenge and Robert Nesta had mopped the floor with Jax. Jax had bragged time and time again if he got a chance, he was going to pay back Robert Nesta in the challenge.

He hated that he cared so much about Jax. Others had been flatlined in the challenge that he knew but it did not affect him. Jax's foolish finish irritated Ralphie. He did not have to be cheesed. He got cocky. Jax had thought he was bigger than the challenge despite the challenge being bigger than everyone in it.

"Damn it, Jax," Ralphie croaked, and immediately he clamped his own hands over his mouth. He had not intended to say those words, let alone to say them loud enough for someone to hear. The thoughts of Jax derailed his thinking. Ralphie closed his eyes tightly behind his hands.

"Drop kick," someone screamed and laughed just on the other side of a wall where Ralphie cried. The two words and chilling laugh that followed froze Ralphie. There was a silence and then a metallic sound like that of a something crashing into a wall.

Ralphie wiped at his eyes and twisted around to peek over the empty windowsill as a boy with a machete flashed by. Ralphie saw through blurry eyes two figures dressed in the signature Golden Bear hooded sweatshirts, jeans and blue and gold combat boots walking and kicking at trash they stumbled on. The boy with the machete was hacking at anything that he could hack at and not damage the blade. The other boy, just ahead of the boy with the machete, was carrying one of those baseball bats that had barbed wire wrapped around its head.

The closer Ralphie looked the more details he saw. The two wore Second Gen gear. The hooded sweatshirts were distinct in their Golden Bear dominated design. Ralphie pressed into the darkness, watching the Second Gens looking for victims.

"Hey, Bear, you see anyone we can gut," the taller of the two Gens asked.

Ralphie did not speak. Ralphie did not move. He simply listened and waited.

"Naw, man, there ain't no Poppies around anymore and I ain't going in that art deathtrap. If they ain't out they must be cheesed. They got to be maggot hotels already." Bear suggested,

Not Bear turned and stopped. "We should head to the sky bridge and see if there is anyone stupid enough to try and reach the supply dump," grinned the smaller of the two Gens.

Not Bear had a broad smile and high cheekbones. His hair was shaved on the sides and only a crown of twisted nappy hair sat on his shiny round head. The second boy stepped closer to Frankie.

"The supply dump is the real death trap," Bear noted.

"Yeah, but people do stupid things every day," the second boy noted.

"You ain't too stupid, Dre," Bear grinned.

Dre beamed and toed the ground like someone embarrassed. Bear jerked his head and he and Dre moved. Bear led. The boys walked to the end of the street and turned left and disappeared.

The street once again became quiet. Day Five of the challenge had cut down the competition from nearly sixty to less than twenty, Ralphie calculated. Twenty people on the island trying to beat the breath out of each other was no easy task. There were all these places to hide. There were infinite places to wait and ambush the unsuspecting. Those that hid were forced into the open by the challenge committee. The committee did not allow hiding. There was too much money at stake to let people hide in the challenge. Everyone was outfitted with a camera and every four hours everyone's location was available on the map reader. Regrettably, the challenge was not a game of wait and see but find and destroy.

The committee would broadcast locations if someone was in one place too long. They also were in control of the bracelets on each contestants' wrist, which was able to generate a significant electrical charge to motivate the unmotivated to move. It was all very technical and scientific.

The challenge was never what it seemed, Ralphie realized. When there was no one on the streets it was possible that someone was scoping someone stupid enough to walk on the street. The committee liked hand-to-hand, but they did not frown on sniping. If someone was stupid enough to walk around, in plain sight, thinking there was some sliver of safety on the island then they deserved what they received.

In the twenty-two challenges before this one Ralphie had seen people do stupid things that no one would have done if they had one iota of what his father called: common sense. For Ralphie that common sense was another way of saying self-preservation. There were death traps on the island. Going to them was suicide.

Numbered buildings, in the challenge, were death traps. The supply dump was suicide by stupidity. Walking in the open was suicide. Making a bunch of noise was definitely suicide.

Quiet was not safe in the challenge. Silence was the absence of audible movement, not peace in the challenge. If someone wanted safety, then they needed to find a place where no one would find them and pray that when they slept no one found them and slit their throat.

Ralphie knew all this just like everyone did that loved and watched the challenge every year. It was one week of stupid people doing stupid things and paying the consequences of their stupid decisions for all the Remains to see. It was unscripted high drama. It was the basest form of entertainment.

"At 1800 hours, here is the sixth report for Day Five of the Pandemonium Challenge: There are only nineteen contestants that remain in the challenge. The Pandemonium Challenge wishes to remind all of the loss of the following contestants from the last six hours: Joyce Bryant Battle, Tina Turner Bennett, Isaac Hayes Moore, Aloysius Price and Ali Washington."

Ralphie listened to the list and registered the official names of two people that he had come into the challenge with; Tee and Isaac. They were Millers like him. They were suddenly out of the challenge.

By his calculations, that meant that of the eight Millers that had started, there were now just Zeke and Ralphie still in the challenge. There was only six hours left in Day Five. Zeke and Ralphie only had to make it two more days to get to Day Seven.

He liked Tee, when she was being nice. Ralphie lived down the block from her. They walked from the educational facility every day. They were… sort of friends. Hearing her name made Ralphie try to dredge up the last good memory of being with Tee. She had bandaged his shoulder a day ago, he recalled. Then, when she was bandaging him, she had been nice.

Isaac was someone that Ralphie knew in the halls of the Leathern Apron, the Miller educational facility middle grades. He knew Isaac more as the second to Dame, the leader of the other group of Millers at the Leathern

Apron. Ralphie tried to think of a good memory of Isaac and all he could find was of him co-signing everything that Dame uttered. He was a cling-on more than a person, Ralphie thought.

The fifteen-year-old tried to imagine how Tee and Isaac had been caught. The thought made Ralphie...sad. He struggled with a feeling for Tee. She was someone he knew from the compound and neighborhood, but she had changed. She was not the same person he had first met. Isaac was an appendage, an extra limb for Dame and no feeling came up after hearing his name mentioned.

Although he knew it was meaningless Ralphie tried to think of the last time that he had seen Tee or Isaac. Tee was with Gina braiding each other's hair, probably, and switching loyalties and breaking Zeke's heart in the process. Jax surprisingly was trying to be sympathetic. Isaac was in the hideout where they all had hid and he was sitting on the floor watching Zeke, Jax and Ralphie grapple with Tee and her newfound friend.

All that had happened days ago. All that was beyond Ralphie. He had come to the challenge to battle and nothing more. All the melodrama and who liked who was meaningless to Ralphie. The idea of how Tee and Isaac had been lullabied was just an exercise in Ralphie's mind to stall before heading to Cosson Hall. It, how either had been lullabied was a fruitless effort to consider. The challenge was a constant war of traps, lies, betrayal, violence, misdirection and attrition. Mental, physical and emotional bloopers were the cause of most sleepy time endings. That was what Ralphie wanted to believe, at least. It was all that he wanted to consider.

So, Ralphie climbed to his feet and decided that he had to do something. After a deep breath he moved as stealthily as possible across the street to Cosson Hall. He paused just long enough to steel himself for whatever awaited him. Entering the gaping maw of Cosson Hall, Ralphie held his croquet mallet at the ready for any attack.

The Cosson Hall was dark and no matter where the sun was it was on the island. There was no electricity on the island and no lights. So, Ralphie flipped on his mini flashlight and watched as the penlight beam cut through the darkness. The light beam was precise and Ralphie had to adjust the beam to broaden and take in a three-foot swath of area.

Ralphie made his way as quietly as possible around the seemingly endless circular first floor of the Cosson Hall. The first floor had a theater that dominated the main area but was trashed. The chairs had been torn out and what remained of the space was the orchestra pit and stage. Stage curtains, torn and useless, hung from the rafters. The auditorium and first floor were covered with graffiti. Well, not exactly graffiti. Graffiti was the quickly sprayed tagging of JDs that wanted to be legendary but ended up being vandals, at best, Ralphie mused. In Cosson Hall there was no such thing as something done mindlessly. The art was detailed and thoughtful and at times 3-D or reminiscent of famous classic art with a twist on it. On the first floor, as Ralphie walked, cutting the darkness with his flashlight, he noted that the floor was covered from floor to the ceiling in some of the most interesting, creative and inventive art Ralphie had ever seen.

Ralphie was not an artist by any stretch of the imagination but the art that he saw was remarkable. On the first floor and in the lobby, there were art pieces, mostly spray painted, that reminded Ralphie of the artwork that he had seen in history books. There were the blocky, abstract human figures that reminded Ralphie of Jean Michel-Basquiat mixed with Jacob Lawrence and other notable artists for some reason.

There was a jumble of brightly painted splotches in one corner and on the far side of what had been a window was the delicate painting of a couple on a playground that Ralphie could have sworn he had seen in a history book. The image was simple and riveting in its simplicity. The image was of two faceless girls on a playground, one girl wearing a white dress and the other a black dress. Behind the girls was a half-demolished wall and behind that calm water and a mountain.

Ralphie wanted to stop and try and understand what the artist was trying to say with the art, but he heard noise above him and refocused and returned to his hunt for Robert Nesta. He focused. Looking left and right Ralphie headed left in the curved interior of Cosson Hall.

At the first-floor staircase there were painted stairs and Ralphie found himself engulfed in more art. Some of it seemed just splashes of paint but like on the first floor he was surprised to find in the jumble of competing art there were dynamic pieces that stood out from the rest like a giraffe from pigs. Ralphie could not help but study the art.

In the stairway, halfway to the second floor, there was a 3-D sculpture that sat in a recess on the wall of the stairway. The art stopped Ralphie in his tracks. The image and sculpture were of a harp. Yet, this harp was made of fifteen graduated choir singers that made up the fifteen strings. The harp was the arm and hand of God, Ralphie supposed. At the head of the harp, in front of the tallest singer, stood, crouched a man holding a placard. Ralphie had never seen anything like it before.

"Look at this," Ralphie heard himself say despite his desire to remain silent. He rubbed the back of his neck. The statue was three times taller than Ralphie's five-foot four-inch height.

Ralphie climbed the steps, grabbing the painted spiraling railing that rose toward the second floor and studied the 3-D sculpture noting that it was made up of various pieces of trash that he had seen all over Pandemonium Island. The bulk of the harp was made from honey brown PVC pipe. The strings, Ralphie noted, were real wire. The faces were a combination of papier-mâché and paint. The whole thing was remarkable.

"Somebody had a lot of time on their hands," Ralphie added in a whisper, more to himself than to anyone else.

Ralphie wanted to laugh at his own stupidity. He had fallen prey to the overwhelmingness of the challenge. In that continual ultra-violence, there was splendor and absurdity to be found in the challenge. The challenge always featured all this brutality but simultaneously, in that brutality, there were moments of incredible, fleeting beauty. It was the schizophrenic nature of the challenge.

Just when things were at their seemingly most frenetic and insane there were moments of tranquility and beauty. It was as if the process that created incredible pressure also birthed diamonds. In video after video Ralphie had noted that the chaos of the challenge created these tender and fleeting transcendent moments of beauty. The same was true in Cosson Hall. Yet, playing tourist and doing stupid things got you removed, in the challenge, as quick as a giant rat bite gave you rabies. That was the challenge. No second chances. Stupid ended most. Trying to be the baddest on the block flatlined many. The challenge was never the same challenge and the challenge was subtle. Not everyone that came into the weeklong battle was prepared. The challenge did not distinguish. It was without mercy.

"You might think so," a voice breathed from behind Ralphie and he spun around and swung the mallet in the direction of the voice. The mallet slammed against an empty space that seemed to be just darkness in the staircase but was in fact an alcove that Ralphie had not noticed.

Chapter Two.

The machines.

100 days before each challenge seven silver flatbeds emerged from the Central Government parking lots. The flatbeds were distinct in that they all displayed the Pandemonium Challenge committee chevron on their doors that looked a lot like the old emoticons: peace and rockets. Each flatbed sported a canvas cover that was strapped securely over the bed. Everyone and anyone in the Remains knew what was under the canvas covers.

Seven trucks left from the Central Government parking lots and each had a specific destination. They moved methodically from the walled Central Government island into the Remains proper. The walled city within the walled Remains sat in the center of the Remains and had methodically constructed seven boulevards that led to the seven distinct lines.

There was the eastern route that was named after the innovator Robert Abbot that led to the Makers compound. To the west and the closest to Acid Bay was Alvin Ailey Boulevard and the Artists compound. Muhammad Ali Boulevard moved south from Central Government to the Traditionalist compound. James Baldwin Boulevard was the southeastern road to the First Gen compound. Mary McCloud Bethune Boulevard left the Central Government and made its way northwest to the Second Gen compound. Aretha Franklin Boulevard wound its way north to the farthest compound in the Remains, the Boomers compound. Sojourner Truth Boulevard was the northeastern road that led to the Millers compound.

The seven lines, each unique to itself, contributed to the Remains individually and collectively. The lines, seven in total, had grown after the flash and were the DeFacto city centers. The most influential line was the

Shakers, the Makers, the Innovators and any number of names that the teens coined for the richest line in the Remains. The most industrious line were the Builders or Millers. They had the distinction of building the Remains infrastructure. Construction was given whole heartedly to the Millers. They had in two decades built the great outer wall that protected the Remains. The Millers line had built 90% of the buildings in the Remains. The other 10% of the buildings were built cooperatively by the Millers and the other lines.

Technology, little that there was post-flash, in the Remains was thanks to the First and Second Gens. Robotic inventions were First Generation creations. Wireless innovations were Second Generation driven. Boomers were the naturalists of the Remains. They were the agriculturalists as well. The Boomers supplied the Remains with fresh food crops. In theory, the Remains worked together because each line was forced to rely on the other line.

The Poppies, artists, Creatives, were tasked with beautifying the Remains. The First Gens were given the task of robotic development. Second Gens were in charge of computer innovations. The Boomers were the naturalists and continually protesting against something and fighting for the environment. The Trads were the law focused line. They were the legal arm of the Remains. Lawyers, police and the military sprang from the Trads.

The Remains was a collective. Seven distinct lines held together by the Central Government and their desire to survive in a world that existed after the flash. No one line was superior to the other. At least, that was the idea. Of course, the practice proved harder than the theory. The theory, in the Remains, was that these seven groups of like-minded people would gravitate to each other with or without the Remains and help the entirety of the Remains with or without government and direction.

Yet, there was dissension in the Remains. The Remains was imperfect. There was still poverty. There was still crime. People cheated. People stole. People fought.

It seemed that after the flash people chose to be nicer and better than they had been before the flash. Murders were nearly non-existent post-flash. The Central Government had instituted enforcers and their presence had dampened many altercations that in the past might have led to bodily harm. Still, the government officials knew, there was still a need to release aggression. Thus, the Pandemonium Challenge, was created.

So, the silver trucks moving through the Remains said, without announcement, that the challenge was near. The fifty selected for the challenge would become Remains celebrities until the challenge got underway. Inside the silver vans were the machines that promised instant Remains fame and looked like old-school gumball machines but ten times bigger.

The machines would select eight names from each of the educational facilities in each division for the Pandemonium Challenge. The machines were incredibly large and bulky things and needed four men to extricate them from the trucks. There was a whole production once the gigantic machines were removed from the trucks. The four men that had wrestled the machine out of the van then had to dolly them to the central area of each educational facility.

In the Foundry, the educational center for the Millers, the masons, construction workers and laborers of the Remains, the arrival of the machines was celebrated like Christmas. There were lights strung up and the selected were showered with presents before they headed to the challenge. Every home was decorated with the names of the aspirants and lights. A traditional part of the challenge was the ceremonial lighting of the forge the night the challenge began until the end of the seven-day contest. Another tradition was to keep candles burning for the Millers that remained in the challenge. Often there were candles lit for very popular hopefuls all over the Remains.

Everything in the Millers compound radiated from the central forge. The Millers compound was centered around the large central forge where the eternal fire burned. The history of the forge was that after the flash it was the only thing still functioning. Thus, the central forge was seen as the heart of the Millers compound. The gigantic fiery maw that had at one time been a great furnace for one of the industrial plants was now just symbolic and sat a silent memory.

After the flash and creation of the Remains as well as the rise of the enforcers and the first repulsion, the Remains had become the only walled community in existence on the Acid Bay. Everything that had been before the flash was gone. It was as if the world pre-flash had been erased. Humanity was gone. All civilization, at least what was measured as civilization was gone. New York was a smoldering crater. Washington, D.C. had been bombed out of existence. Chicago had been decimated. Remarkably, there were some that had survived in the Midwest. Yet, the first winter had destroyed the few that had survived the flash. Denver had not sustained much damage somehow. Texas was a wasteland. The desert that stretched from Texas to California had reclaimed its grip and swept across cities burying them post-flash. In what was California there was finally a piece of the Golden state that broke off and sunk into the Pacific Ocean. Southern California had fallen out of contact after the flash and most believed that everyone there was cinders and ash. Yet, in Northern California, there was the Remains.

The Remains had been built in defiance of the post-flash world that greeted so many. There were stories, legends now, of the survivors battling monsters, creatures unimaginable, that were born on the back of the flash. The first repulsion had educated, hardened and given those that survived the resolve to create a plan that was just the idea of the Remains. Twelve individuals had sketched out a plan and Charles had been bold enough to put that plan into action. The outer walls were built first. The twelve towers were completed by the end of the first anniversary of the launch of human destruction by the handful of elected idiots.

It had only taken hours to destroy the seven billion that remained. The rich and famous had escaped to the stars, leaving the poor and unphotogenic to die on the smoking planet. Yet, the poor refused to die, like the planet, despite humanities best effort to blow them to smithereens.

In the aftermath of the flash people survived in spite of the best efforts of nations to kill everything. The post-flash world was nothing like the pre-flash reality. Things changed on what was once earth. There were things that seemed more suited for nightmares than the dark corners of the post-flash. Even with all the changes humanity attempted to find a balance. It was in all humanity, it seemed, to rebuild and live rather than surrendering and giving in.

Years had passed after the flash, and the second repulsion, before the outer and inner walls were completed and manned by the dedicated enforcers. The second repulsion had ended with the legends being named and the seven great towers labeled, honoring those that fought off the abominations that unsuccessfully tried to overrun the Remains. Remains hero names like: Browning, Dunn, Hall, Jenkins, Lewis, Massey and Truelove adorned the towers of the great walls. The enforcers rose and became Remain celebrities and after a decade of stability several of the Remains lines began to redesign and expand their lines compounds.

One of the first lines to do a redesign in the Remains was the Millers. They redesigned the forge that was surrounded by more efficient energy plants. Those plants regulated energy and power to all the 47,873 residents of the compound. Those four smaller furnaces worked tirelessly to be the source of fire and energy for the compound. Like the power and energy that centered at the four furnaces and moved from that central point so too did the city design.

There were twelve major avenues that led everyone in the Miller compound to the central forge and central meeting place of the Miller Fount. The Miller Fount was next to the central forge. The Fount was an empty fountain that had been a great fountain at one time in a small university. The Fount in the Miller compound was the loci of the compound. From the Fount everything radiated. The mayor's office and the compound government offices rested in the central forge's building. Yet, for the public, the fount was the unofficial center of the Miller compound.

In the Miller compound the design was similar to that of an old analog clock. In the center was the central forge and Fount. The twelve o'clock avenue which moved north, and south was Frederick Douglass Avenue. The one o'clock avenue was Garrett Morgan Avenue. The two o'clock avenue was Benjamin Banneker Avenue. The three o'clock avenue was Booker T. Washington Avenue. Ralphie lived off W.E.B DuBois Street. The four o'clock avenue was Lewis Howard Latimer Avenue. The five o'clock avenue position was designated as Elijah McCoy Avenue. The six o'clock avenue was Martin Luther King Jr. Avenue. The seven o'clock avenue was Madame C.J. Walker Avenue. The eight o'clock avenue was named Frederick McKinley Jones Avenue. The nine o'clock avenue position was held by Malcolm X Avenue. Of all the avenues it was one of the most controversial as many protested the name of the avenue. There was a constant debate on changing the name of Malcolm X to Malcolm Shabazz Avenue. The nine o'clock avenue was Dorothy Dandridge Avenue. The ten o'clock avenue was named: Josephine Baker Avenue. The eleven o'clock avenue was named: Thomas L. Jennings Avenue.

In the pathway to the central forge were the dozen statues to the history of Millers. Twenty-four unblinking eyes stared out into the pathway, ever vigilant, ever searching, just over the heads of everyone that walked into the Foundry's circular courtyard. Once in the courtyard visitors were greeted with post-modern art that seemed to suggest a time of industry with its blockish drawings and simple palette of colors. Thirty feet in the air hung the banner of the Miller's oath above the entrance to the three educational facilities.

Ralphie paused as he always did when seeing the oath. He looked at the words and quietly recited them to himself.

"Industry. Purpose. Product. We work. We dream. We produce. We design. We craft. We manufacture. We are Millers. We dream—but do not make dreams our master. We dream-- and will not make dreams our only plan. We produce – yet, we refuse to make our work our aim. We know we will meet with Triumph and Disaster and treat those two impostors just the same. We do not strive to hear the truth we've spoken, Twisted and made a trap for fools, Or watch the things we have given our life to, broken, But, if so, we shall stoop and build 'em up with our worn out tools: We are Millers and ours is what remains of the Earth and all that is in it, And—which is more—we shall shine and be a beacon; a testament of all that we have done."

Ralphie smiled broadly at the oath. Every Miller knew it. Every Miller had committed the oath to memory. It was a mark of intelligence how fast and accurately students could recite the oath. It was a short and poignant thing that united all the Millers, young and old.

In the shade of the thirty-foot banner Ralphie noted four men dressed in yellow coveralls positioned the gumball Pandemonium Challenge selection machine. In all the challenges and years that he had known of the challenge this was the first time that Ralphie had seen the machines being placed.

All four of the men wore bright blue baseball caps and sunglasses. On their hips were gun belts and pistols. On each cap was the distinctive peace symbol emoticon a plus sign and two rockets. Three of the workmen were adjusting the machine into place. The fourth worker, bearded and with his hat on backwards, was chewing something and watching the courtyard. The fourth nameless worker stared at Ralphie.

Ralphie waved awkwardly at the workman. The fourth worker lifted a hand and waved back.

Ralphie detoured toward the workers. The fourth worker, the guard, studied Ralphie as he got close. On the guard's hip was a gun belt and gun. As Ralphie got closer the fourth worker rested his hand on the gun butt.

With his free hand, the guard gestured for Ralphie to stop. Ralphie was less than twenty feet away. The three workers stopped and looked up, seeing the fourth worker with a hand on his gun.

"Everything okay?"

"Yeah, think so," the guard said. The three continued working. They were screwing the machine into the ground.

"Everything is cool," the guard breathed, never looking from Ralphie. He spoke clearly through clenched teeth.

Ralphie took another step.

"That's far enough, partner," the yellow coverall guard said, unsnapping the safety on his gun.

Ralphie stopped.

"I just wanted to know when the selection will begin," Ralphie attempted, stopping and watching the guard's hand on the heel of the gun hand.

The guard smiled smugly at the question.

"Oh, that's all? We don't know really. We the grunts. That information comes from people much higher than any of us."

Ralphie nodded and thought that this was the closest he had come to talking to anyone from the Pandemonium Challenge committee.

"Anything else, kid?"

"Why are you all," Ralphie stopped himself. He gestured as the nameless worker had. The worker followed the Millers gesture to his sidearm. The toothpick chewer smiled easily.

"Not everyone likes the challenge, kid. There are some lines that take issue with it," the dark man with the toothpick in his mouth noted. "We don't always know where we are going. It is a crap shoot which line we get."

"There's lines that have issues with the challenge," Ralphie said aloud.

"Yeah, go figure," the worker said.

The information was new to Ralphie and it took him a moment to digest.

"Anything else, kid? We got work to do," the toothpick chewing worker said.

Twisting his lips Ralphie paused. He studied the tall and angular man dressed in his baseball cap, yellow coveralls and combat boots. Ralphie wagged his chin, left and right; no. He nodded, twisted his lips, and turned and walked away.

Ralphie made his way from the entry to the Foundry to back of the facility and the soccer stadium of The Leathern Apron. There were easily thirty or forty people from the Foundry watching the game. On the opposite side of the field were nearly sixty people from the First Gen educational facility. Ralphie walked up the short set of stairs to the bleachers and pretended to watch the Miller Knights battle the First Gen Chargers.

Ralphie sat down and checked the scoreboard and noted that the Knights were losing. The clock was ticking down to the end of regulation time. Ralphie looked around and thought if he should ask how much penalty time remained. He saw a few familiar faces but chose not to engage them. Ralphie did not know the handful of faces well and opted out of talking to them at that moment.

The whistle blew and Ralphie checked the score again. The soccer game ended and not surprisingly the Millers were losing. They had a handful of minutes, Ralphie guessed, to lose a close game. Three minutes later the referee blew the final whistle and the game ended. The score was, he had to check, 3-1. All Ralphie knew was that Bailey had scored a goal a few minutes after he had arrived.

After the game, Ralphie made his way to the sidelines and the families and teams milling about. When he was on the sidelines with everyone else the teams were packing their bags and preparing to leave. Bailey was dressed in her First Gen soccer kit that had a silhouette of the goddess Minerva and an eagle across the jersey. Bailey had her black curls pulled up and into an Afro ponytail. She was sipping water from a water bottle and Ralphie noted that she was wearing the First Gen signet ring on her pointer finger that all the First Gens were given to identify them and distinguish them. Bailey was unlacing her cleats when Ralphie arrived.

Her teammates were laughing and talking when Ralphie waved timidly toward Bailey. There were several people around her. Bailey was laughing when she saw Ralphie in the thin crowd. Bailey upon seeing Ralphie moved to him, forgetting, for the moment, about her shoes.

"Good game," Ralphie smiled broadly, happy to see Bailey. The First Gen soccer player closed the distance between them quickly. She weaved effortlessly through the crowd with a big smile on her chestnut brown face.

"Thanks," Bailey sang, and without a word she was hugging him tightly. Ralphie was stunned and hugged Bailey back. He held her and straight away thought he smelled flowers. He giggled. There and then, there were all these thoughts in his head. He could smell her hair. It had the scent of honeysuckles in it, Ralphie noted. Bailey released Ralphie a little awkwardly. She brightened. "I didn't think you were coming."

"I said I was," Ralphie blushed, smiling as if it was his birthday. "As soon as I heard you were playing, I figured I could come by to see you." Ralphie paused, hearing what he had uttered out loud.

Bailey grinned. She looked at Ralphie, mischievously. The soccer player shook her head. "Stalker much," Bailey questioned.

He grinned and laughed. Maybe, he laughed a little too loudly. For an awkward moment there was a pause. Then Bailey grinned, a gentle and slow thing that began at the corner of her wide mouth and seemed to spread and make her lips part and show her teeth. Gone was the initial awkwardness replaced with Bailey's approving smile. She giggled as well.

He looked down and tried to recover. "You scored a goal." He added, "I was pretty impressed. I thought you were just someone that just liked running up and down the field. Who knew you could play?"

"Thanks again, Ralphie," Bailey beamed. She had a big, natural smile.

"You played...well," Ralphie repeated. There was a pause. "I know I'm not supposed to be happy you guys won or you scored against us but I am."

"Ralphie, you are—," Bailey Beaumont began with a smile.

"Beaumont," the First Gen coach called from the First Gen transport.

"Got to go," Bailey announced and frowned at those three words. She looked back at her coach and then back at Ralphie. Bailey dropped her soccer bag to the surprise of Ralphie.

Bailey again gave Ralphie a hug, without warning. Ralphie felt her squeeze him and he hugged her back. The scent of honeysuckle filled his brain and as quickly as Bailey had hugged Ralphie, she was grabbing her cleats and running toward the First Gen transport.

"Thanks for coming," Bailey grinned, scooping up her First Gen soccer bag and stopping to turn and smile at Ralphie. Bailey ran toward the transport. Ralphie watched as Bailey Beaumont ran to the transport and climbed aboard. Once on the transport Bailey spun around and waved to Ralphie.

Ralphie waved and watched as the transport silently pulled away from the soccer field and made a left to leave the educational facility. Ralphie stood waving until he realized that Bailey was gone. He looked down the paved street where the solar powered transport had been and disappeared.

Ralphie studied the sidewalk that was now deserted. He walked back across the Foundry courtyard and noted the gigantic machine sitting just across from the eternal flame. Ralphie took in the immenseness of the selection machine. The screen that would begin with all of the names in the Foundry and then thin it out to only eight names at the end was dark. Ralphie assumed that the Pandemonium Committee would turn on the screens of all seven monitors simultaneously. Ralphie walked close enough to see the eleven-inch gap that every hopeful was expected to put their hand in for scanning. It looked like a mouth, Ralphie thought absently.

The fifteen-year-old walked home thinking that this was the first year that he could compete in the challenge. Ralphie walked to think about things. His thoughts flitted from one thought to the next. The machine had arrived. He had talked to Bailey. Bailey had waved and smiled.

Ralphie walked and tried to think why he cared so much about Bailey smiling at him. He replayed the whole time with Bailey in his head. He found himself floating at the memory of Bailey turning and waving at him as she boarded the transport.

His phone buzzed breaking his thoughts of Bailey Beaumont.

Ralphie tapped his ear bud that connected to his phone. There were two long beeps that signaled he had received a message. He flipped over his wrist that had a rubber bracelet on it and the action activated a small LED light on the bracelet that projected a message on his forearm.

"Meet us at Donald's hill," the message read. It had come from Jax.

Ralphie checked the time and calculated how long it would take to get to the hill from the Foundry.

"Give me ten minutes," Ralphie said into the air to the message.

"See you there. Last one there buys a Yoo-hoo."

"Deal," Ralphie responded and began his speed walk for the exit of the auditorium. He figured, if he ran, he could get to the hill in seven minutes. Seven minutes was not a world record pace, but it was pretty fast, Ralphie imagined.

So, Ralphie ran. He ran and as he did the buildings blurred and the streets melted away to become just colors. The coffee browns of bricks, grays of steel and green of grass swam together into an earth tone soup on the way to Donald's hill.

In seven minutes and some change Ralphie came to a stop at the foot of Donald's hill. All around the hill were smaller hills of trash and debris in what the Millers called: The Reclamation. The Reclamation was hundreds of acres of trash.

Donald's hill sat in the biggest Recyclery in the Remains. The hill was the largest pile of trash the debris handlers had gathered from all over the Remains to be reclaimed at some point. The hill was actually seven hills of everything from mattresses to old transports piled thirty or forty feet high and covered with mesh to control any blow away. The First Gens had come up with some nanotechnology that was supposed to be in the process of breaking down Donald's hill, but the process took time.

Donald's hill was named after the hill that anchored the Reclamation. It was where most of the Remains teens and tweens congregated. There was a bright yellow and red plastic sign that stood defiantly on the hill that read:

Donald's. The sign had somehow survived all the chaos and destruction over the years and remained visible through the hill's reclamation. Ralphie climbed to the top of Donald's hill and found Jax sitting on a broken chair reading a scrap of a paper comic book. Zeke, the muscle was sitting on a metal beam that was sticking out of the hill that seemed to hang in midair. Tee, Zeke's girl, was studying her polished ice blue nails when Ralphie arrived.

"Were you already here when you called?"

Jax smirked his answer; yes. Zeke looked dully at the question. Tee just rolled her eyes in response.

"You owe me a Yoo-hoo," Jax noted.

Ralphie shook his head at Jax's trick. He had agreed to the deal. Ralphie didn't mind the trick. Jax was always playing tricks on people.

From the top of Donald's hill Ralphie could see the faint outline of the western wall that had been built to protect the Millers. Out of the blue Ralphie had a random thought about his cousin Dominic. His cousin was an enforcer on duty at Emmet Tills Road just a few miles from the Reclamation Center. The Reclamation Center was closest to the forbidden zone. That meant that Dominic was nine miles east of Donald's hill sitting on the six-foot-high wall and the eastern entrance to the Miller compound.

"You smell like flowers," Tee decided, breaking Ralphie's concentration and thoughts of his cousin. Tee turned her attention to Ralphie, curious. "How come you smell like flowers?"

"They delivered the machines today," Ralphie announced trying to ignore Tee. He smiled goofily and thought about the brief hug he had received from Bailey less than thirty minutes ago as he sat down and looked out over the Miller compound that stretched for miles in every direction.

"What," Zeke asked.

"How you end up smelling like flowers," Tee asked.

"They delivered the machines today, after school, and I was there," Ralphie deflected trying to ignore Tee's question and hoping that Zeke and Jax's curiosity about the challenge would supersede Tee's curiosity about Ralphie's remnant of Bailey on him. He looked at Tee out of the corner of his eye and she was studying him like there was an answer there. Ralphie continued, "I saw the Pandemonium truck. Four guys rolled the machine to the Foundry."

"They delivered the machines?" Jax nodded.

"You think that they up and running," Zeke asked no one in particular.

Ralphie was about to speak but before he could Jax spoke.

"Naw, they won't make it available for at least a week. They love the whole drama of getting people excited about it before they announce or get things started," Jax pointed out.

"Yeah, they like drama," Tee decided, eyeing Ralphie.

"Okay, you know what that means."

"We are less than a hundred days from the challenge. We have to get scanned. The machines will probably go live at the end of the week. So, by the weekend we should all be scanned and ready to rumble." Zeke declared that day.

"Hundred days or less," Tee noted.

Ralphie and Jax smiled stupidly at Zeke and Tee.

"So, we have a plan," Tee stated.

"We go to the Foundry and get scanned," Jax advised, shaking his head.

"Yeah, that's the first part. Then after we get scanned, we start to lay out ways to win the challenge. We need to make sure that we don't do the stupid things that knobs do," Zeke mused.

"Okay, Tee, you need to step up the survival kits. Things are in play."

"So, by the end of this month, the next two weeks, we should all be registered," Zeke announced.

"Everyone get registered as soon as you can," Jax added.

"Yeah, the countdown begins" Tee noted.

"We all about to become pre-challenge famous," Jax pointed out.

"Pre-challenge famous," Zeke laughed.

Ralphie just shook his head. Zeke and Jax were Pandemonium Challenge experts. They knew all the details of the challenge.

Ralphie thought about what the challenge experts had just said and suddenly thought: Was he ready for the challenge? Being a part of the challenge would change his life forever. He would be a Miller celebrity. Ralphie did not know how he would deal with people in the compound knowing him and watching his video. He did not know if he would be comfortable with that part of the challenge; the pre-challenge celebrity.

Registering for the challenge also meant that Ralphie would have to deal with his parents and Macy, his baby sister. His parents would lose their minds. They would be angry. They expected him to take over the construction company, Ralphie figured. He was the only son. They might be hysterical. They might threaten to disown him.

His parents were two question marks. They might laugh and say: Good riddance. Or they might forbid him participating. Ralphie paused and thought about that. His mother would be all emotional. She might cry. His father... would not cry. His father was this bull of a man that carried a pistol every day and managed a business that employed nearly five hundred people. He did not cry. Ralphie tried to imagine his father crying. He laughed at that idea. Knowing his father, he would either encourage or discourage Ralphie being in the challenge. His father was always very up or down.

His mother would cry. Ralphie knew that his mother would try and guilt him into reversing his decision. She might try and convince his father to use his significant influence on the Pandemonium Challenge committee and remove Ralphie's name from the challenge contest.

Ralphie tried not to think about his father. His father was this bigger than life character that had built Reynolds Construction from nothing to one of the most reliable and called upon construction companies in the Remains. His father was a Remains legend. He was unquestionably a real-world superhero. Every day, he helped make the Remains better. It was the thought of his father being disappointed that Ralphie feared the most. He never wanted to disappoint his father. He had sacrificed so much for Ralphie and Macy.

Macy might cry. Macy would not care. She was nine and all about goofy movies and unicorns. Knowing his sister, the way that he did, Ralphie imagined, that it was a crap shoot as to how she would react upon hearing that Ralphie was in the challenge.

Zeke broke Ralphie's train of thought with a directive.

"Okay, we meet back here at the end of the month and then we'll begin to really plan our strategy to win the challenge," Zeke stated breaking Ralphie's thoughts.

"Right, we'll meet back here at the end of the month," Jax repeated.

Tee rolled her eyes. Ralphie grinned. He also secretly dreaded the idea of the next two weeks. Registering was one thing. Signing up for the challenge was a big deal but it was just a step in the process. The challenge was the prize, Ralphie believed. Yet, there were all these things in between the registration and acceptance and the challenge.

Ralphie did not want to be pre-challenge famous. He preferred to be anonymous before the challenge began. He knew that was not possible. There was too much money involved in the challenge for anonymity. People had to wager. People needed to know who they were betting on. Ralphie, if accepted, would be a name and odd to bet on, nothing more.

Of course, in the Remains, betting was not just blind. Everyone wanted data. Everyone wanted a video or videos. So, Ralphie tried to steel himself for the inevitable, if selected.

Selecting meant possibly being called for video. Video meant selection. Selection meant publicity. Everyone in the Remains would know those selected because of the videos.

So, though Ralphie knew he was supposed to register he had to admit he was reluctant. He dreaded the publicity. He looked forward to the challenge and being in the challenge but not the lead up.

Fourteen days doesn't seem a long time unless you are on a schedule. Ralphie after the last meeting on Donald's hill intended on going to the machine and registering. He had woken up and went to the Foundry and that morning found that there were easily three dozen knobs milling around talking about registering and daring each other to place their hand in the machine. Ralphie hated the puffery. Everyone there, that morning, wanted an audience. They were all attention seekers. If they registered and made it to the challenge, they would be nothing more than cannon fodder. At least, that was how Ralphie saw it.

The arrival of the machine made everyone in the Foundry suddenly brave. The machine and registration dominated discussion. Ralphie listened and tried to discern who was prepared and who was just looking for attention. Based on a straw poll, everyone at the Foundry was going to register for the challenge. No one was scared. No one feared the challenge.

For a full week Ralphie was confronted by the knobs wanting attention for being near the selection machine. Just being near it gave the knobs clout. They could loud talk, laugh and joke in front of the machine to the amusement of everyone in the Foundry paying attention.

"Hey, knobs, are you registering or just posing for pictures," some derided.

"Posers," some said.

"Punters," others sang.

The knob quotient shrank. No one in the Foundry wanted to be labeled a poser or punter. The knobs found other places to loiter.

Still, there were crowds of people standing around and waiting to document those that registered. At lunch, it was the worse, as everyone in the Foundry was there and noting anyone and everyone brave or stupid enough to walk toward the machine. If there was a time when there were less people by the machine it was when the bell rang for the end of the day and hundreds headed home. There was still a small smattering of knobs there, but they diminished the closer it got to four in the afternoon.

Each day, Ralphie imagined that he would walk up to the machine at the end of the day when there were fewer eyes to witness his brave act. Yet, he hesitated. A week had gone by and it was nearly the end of the second week when he got the message to meet at Donald's hill.

Two weeks later, fourteen days after the machine had been delivered the quartet were on Donald's hill again. Zeke and Jax beamed having registered for the challenge. Ralphie slowly trudged up the hill knowing the interrogation that he was heading into.

"Did you register?"

"No," Ralphie admitted.

"Why not?"

Ralphie tried to come up with something that did not make him seem lame but all he could say was the truth.

"There were just too many people watching the machine, you know? I didn't want people all in my business, like that."

"They are watching because just registering is a big deal," Jax explained.

"Yeah, I know but I just—," Ralphie began.

"What's the delay," Tee asked, appearing beside Zeke, and studying Ralphie.

"You backing out," Zeke asked.

"No, you know that Ralphie is not backing out," Jax defended.

Ralphie thought of explaining but he held his tongue. He did not speak. He did not have to when Jax was defending him.

"You need to step up, Ralphie," Zeke teased.

Ralphie did not respond.

"Ralphie will register," Jax noted. "He ain't backing out. He'll get it done this week."

Ralphie chuckled at Jax's defense. It made him appreciate his goofy friend. Jax, for all his flaws, and he had many, one good thing about him was his loyalty.

Perhaps, because of Jax's loyalty and defense of Ralphie's not registering Ralphie woke up with the desire to register as soon as possible. He woke and headed to the Foundry with one goal in mind; registering. He intended to register before school but too many people were there to watch or stop or question him. He tried at lunch but there were too many there talking about the names swirling on the gigantic monitor above the gumball machine. After instruction Ralphie had hoped that all the Miller students would have left, like usual. Of course, they loitered.

"Hey, Ralphie, what you doing," asked Tina, one of the Millers he knew from wood shop class. Tina wore glasses, was curvy and smart and prone to gossip and talking in class. Ralphie might have talked to her a handful of times.

"Nothing, I was just leaving," Ralphie admitted and left Tina near the great machine that would select the participants for the Pandemonium Challenge.

The next two days were just like the first day that Ralphie had decided to register for the Pandemonium Challenge. There was always someone around the machine. There were always groups there at lunch. Even after school students just stood and talked waiting for someone to register.

That same night Ralphie had gone on the Pandemonium Challenge website and reviewed the video of the day the machines were delivered to the various educational facilities. He studied the details of each educational facility. It intrigued Ralphie how different each facility was compared to the Foundry.

For the Innovators, AKA the Movers and Shakers, the central educational facility was found in the center of their compound, in what was an old college near the Eastbay hills. It was a sprawling compound. The educational facility sat in a main courtyard of the facility under the clock tower that sat at one end of the serenity pool that pointed toward the main educational building that had a magnificent and majestic golden "M" on the steeple of the highest roof. The educational facility of the Innovators sat in the prestigious public college school of Letters and Science long ago. The college had been abandoned after several biological incidents at their laboratories and eventually reclaimed by the Innovators to insure their lines future and the future education of their children. The Innovators lived in the spacious abandoned buildings that had once housed the various disciplines of the college.

The Innovators, per their name, were the brightest in the Remains. They were also the richest line in the Remains. The Innovators held the most power, as a result. In the Remains Central Government, the Innovators determined most laws and were leaders of the Remains judicial system. They were influential in the judicial and legislative branches of the Remains.

Innovator's children were nicknamed: Brats. They had all the newest fashions. They wore real gold and diamonds while the other lines wore gold-plated jewelry and cubic zirconia. Brats distinctive Shaker wear was a three-stone diamond pendant that they wore around their necks. Their logo was an inventive embroidered design that resembled a reimagined blue and gold trimmed Superman logo.

At the Law and Order educational facility, AKA the Traditionalists or Trads, there was a thirty-foot representation of Lady Justice created out of what appeared to be marble, but no one believed was marble. The thirty-foot statue stood on a round platform in the midst of a ten-foot wide pool. The statue looked just like Lady Justice, blindfolded, holding a scale in one hand and a sword in the other. The Trads lived by rules and made rules and laws for the Remains. Most Trads wore a pin of Lady Justice on their clothing.

The Trads loved order. They were Central Government workers mostly and populated the Remains legislation branch. Half of the judicial system that oversaw the legal system were Traditionalists.

In the First Gen campus, the machine was wheeled to the central building courtyard. In the courtyard there was a terraced flower bed that was perpetually planted with the sweetest smelling flowers still alive in the Remains and the Disjointed Sovereign Surviving States. The First Gens were what was similar to the pre-flash Silicon Valley. They, the First Gens, were all given signet rings to note their membership.

The First Gens continually found unique ways to use technology that was not invasive or pushed up against privacy laws put in place by the Trads. The First Gens had attempted and failed to improve the wireless abilities of the Remains. Their failure with wireless had ushered in a new wave of technology from the line in robotics and miniaturization. They concentrated on the vast field of robotics. They created dozens of household robots for the Remains. They were responsible for the robo-creatures that patrolled the exterior of the wall and monitored the dead zone where enforcers had died. The robotic innovation helped the Remains with the most distasteful tasks. Thanks to the First Gens there was a robot sewage line cleaner.

At the Second Gen were the Information Technology guys. They rewired the Remains. They created or reawakened the InterWeb. Their campus, where Brandon White and Dianna Thomas had r the Remains, the great machine was placed at the foot of the Zen garden. The Zen garden was a sprawling stretch of land in the middle of the campus. The garden was bordered by imported sand that was maintained by mini stone moving robots. At the Zen garden, that was near the central building, students gathered and showed off their badges that resembled pre-flash police badges. The Second Gen every morning would reflect and meditate and quietly talk, before heading to their instructional pods.

The Artists, AKA the Poppies, compound was a mishmash of styles and colors. The Poppies wore hoodies with a clock patch design on their shoulders. The clock patch design tied in with the Poppies overall clockwork patch design in their compound. It, the machine, sat on a tree lined walk that featured over twenty-five sculptures of artists that had inspired students throughout the years. In the middle of the path was a circular intersection that lead in eight directions. In that nexus point there were four benches that had been crafted to go together or be separate and individual. The machine, though only there for one month a year, was always spray painted and graffiti covered by the time it was removed. There, in the nexus, the four men wheeled the gigantic machine.

The Boomers, who were in the northern most part of the Remains, were more agrarian and rural than the rest of the Remains lines. The Boomers were farmers mostly. Their compound was surrounded by blackened Redwoods and sat on the northern edge of the Remains in the rolling hills of what most called the Headlands. It, the Headlands, stretched from what had once been the edge of the destroyed entrance to the once functional Carquinez Bridge that had collapsed nearly a century ago and was never fixed or replaced.

Ralphie had never been to the Innovators, Second Gens or Boomers complex. Few, that Ralphie knew, had been to the Boomers complex. It was remote and more natural than the other lines. The educational facility was ensconced in the northern most section of the Boomers compound, some noted. It was surrounded by a thick ring of blackened Redwood trees. All Boomers had a wolf headed ring with the blackened Redwood trees in the background. The facility itself was located in a gentle decline to a cavernous entrance to the underground educational complex. Most of the Boomers complex was underground. The great machine was placed at the mouth of the entry to the cavern.

That night, a Wednesday night, Ralphie went to sleep and dreamed of that cavern in the Boomers compound. In his dream, Ralphie had woken against one of those blackened Redwood trees disoriented. He looked around, in his dream, and noted that though he was in a forest there was no birds or animals chirping or scampering about. It was eerily quiet in the Boomer compound in his head. Ralphie imagined that every forest was filled with the sounds of nature. Yet, in his dream, it was just the opposite and that unnerved him.

In the dream, just a hundred feet from him stood the open maw of the cavern to the Boomers compound. Despite his fears, in his dreams, Ralphie found himself moving forward toward the cavern. It was as if it had a magnetic pull on Ralphie. The closer he got the more he wanted to turn and run. In his head, he knew that whatever was in the cavern was nothing good, but he could not stop his body from moving forward. In his dream, Ralphie found himself at the entrance to the cavern.

On Thursday, Ralphie woke up and looked around to find himself in his bedroom. The dream had ended and returned him to his home and his bed on the second floor of his parents' home in the Remains. It was early. Ralphie had woken up earlier than usual and dressed and prepared for school. He left the house in the dark and walked to the Foundry with one goal in his mind. Without any fanfare or encouragement Ralphie walked into the Foundry and instead of heading to the Leathern Apron walked to the Foundry's central gathering point. Ralphie entered the quiet and deserted facility and walked up the slight ramp past the statue of the worker that featured so prominently where Millers congregated, as well as on everything that they wore.

Under the Miller's oath, where just 17 days before he had watched the men place the great machine, he stood. The machine sat defiantly on the southern side of the central forge so that all could see the results of anyone's attempt to be selected. In the Foundry anyone brave enough to register would be listed on the great wall and become line legends just for registering for the Pandemonium Challenge. It was an even bigger honor to be selected to participate in the challenge.

So, with all of his reluctance, that late May morning, before classes began, Ralphie stared at the great maw of the machine. He looked around and was happy to see that there was no one to witness his registration. He placed his hand on the glass screen and watched as the greenlight of the scanner moved back and forth and identified him.

The machine was a biometric scanner and immediately on the screen in front of Ralphie appeared his full name: Ralph Ellison Reynolds. His age, fifteen, was there as well. Beneath those entries were the names of his family members. Beneath that was a question.

"If these are correct, press: Yes. If any information above is incorrect press: Start Again."

Ralphie pressed: Yes. He was prompted to insert his Miller dog tag as identification to verify his identity. The machine also did a retinal scan. The whole process took less than two minutes and Ralphie was registered for the Twenty-Third Pandemonium Challenge.

"Ralphie, you going to be a part of the challenge," Chelsea Underhill tittered, suddenly next to him. She was this banana-hued beauty with curly hair, big bronze eyes, a slightly hooked nose and a broad smile, framed by thick kissable lips. She was only thirteen years old. Her family had lived in England, a long time ago, when there was an England.

With the flash what had been England had disappeared. Terrible things had emerged from the smoking crater of Europe and chased those that survived for other regions. Chelsea and her family had abandoned the ruins of Europe and walked across the suddenly empty Atlantic Ocean on their way to the Dissolved Sovereign States. They walked for two months before finding the Remains. Somehow, Chelsea and her family kept the twangy pre-flash English accent.

Ralphie knew all this from the short banana skinned teen. Yet, as he looked at her, he did not respond. He figured that Chelsea had seen him register. So, there was no real need to answer.

"Good luck," Chelsea called.

The bell rang and school began, and for the entire day he avoided everyone and their gazes. He saw people talking and pointing at him. Ralphie tried to ignore them.

Most kids congregated at the cafeteria and when he arrived, he sat at a table with kids he did not know. Ralphie scanned the cafeteria for Jax or Zeke but did not see them, that moment. He resolved himself to just fade away into anonymity. That anonymity was personified in Ralphie sitting at the unpopular table because the kids did not speak to him.

That lunch, Ralphie could hear the rumblings and see the glances and kids staring. He was immediately uncomfortable. Fearing for his life he chose to have lunch in one of his teacher's rooms.

Miss Garrett had finger thick braids on her head. She was a whip thin woman with big glasses that magnified her dark eyes and narrow nose. Her thin shoulders held her thin neck and slightly praying mantis like triangular head. Miss Garrett was Ralphie's History teacher. Ralphie arrived to find Miss Garrett sitting in the darkened room eating her lunch.

"Is it okay to eat in here?"

"Sure?"

With that he sat in the rear of the room and did not speak.

"Ralphie, are you okay?"

Ralphie nodded.

"Is there something wrong?"

Ralphie shook his head.

Miss Garrett stopped her nibbling on her food she had for her lunch. Ralphie looked up from his hiding place and watched as Miss Garrett, still behind her desk, studied him silently. Ralphie did not speak. He knew that she expected him to say something but Ralphie did not speak.

Miss Garrett sipped at her water bottle.

"I heard that you registered for the challenge. Is that true?"

Ralphie closed his eyes. He considered bolting. He could just climb to his feet and walk out the door. There had to be quieter places to hide. Perhaps, Ralphie thought absently, he could go to the gym. He could hide in the locker room. Ralphie, looked at Miss Garrett and her praying mantis like head and for an instant, thought of going to sit in the bathroom until lunch was over.

"Ralphie, is that true?"

Ralphie nodded.

Miss Garrett tilted her praying mantis like head and studied Ralphie for a long moment, silently. She nodded and sipped at her water bottle.

"Well, good luck," Miss Garrett said and that was all he had to deal with from his teacher, that lunch.

After lunch he had three classes to suffer through. He had science. He had math. He had art. Of the three he liked math. He hated science. He tolerated art.

Miss Morris was Ralphie's science teacher. They spent the entire period talking about possible solutions to de-Acidifying the Acid Bay. The Acid Bay had been a freshwater resource pre-flash but had become acidic and deadly to all animals daring to drink or swim in the toxic soup. Ralphie sat with Lionel Webster, Sade Thompson and Luther Webb; his lab partners.

"I heard that you registered," Sade Thompson said when the four were supposed to be discussing the Acid Bay. Everyone at the table waited for Ralphie's acknowledgement or denial. The bell rang. He left without a word.

At Math class Ralphie tried to be invisible. Thankfully, Mister Davis did not ask students to work in groups. Students were asked to review for the Friday test. So, Ralphie sat and tried to avoid the stares and looks from his classmates. The fifteen-year-old instead of being drawn into a futile conversation with classmates concentrated on his work or pretended to. When David Kincaid tried to get Ralphie's attention he ignored him. He pretended to be engrossed. Ralphie looked to his teacher.

Mister Davis looked sick to Ralphie. He could always tell. Right before the class let out Mister Davis sneezed and Ralphie figured that his Math teacher would be absent either the next day or Monday.

"Feel better, Mister Davis," was all that Ralphie said the whole class as he left the classroom.

"Ralphie, heard you signed up for the challenge," someone said in the hallway but Ralphie ignored the comment.

"Who do you think you are Reynolds," called another voice in the hall as Ralphie weaved through the bodies in the gauntlet that was passing period. Ralphie moved as if he had blinders on. Suddenly, he was at the door and class of Mister Fields, the art teacher.

Ralphie dreaded the art class because it was more loosely organized. Students were responsible for work and as a fifteen-year-old he was expected to end the year with an artist's portfolio. But, overall, the art class students were given more freedom to create their dozen art projects in various mediums. There were check-ins throughout the year to finish projects.

Ralphie had completed eighty percent of his projects and was working on a pen and ink drawing of his baby sister when he walked in after registering. In class, Ralphie found his supplies and drawing and sat at the art table with three others; George Lawrence, Bessie Tucker and Erica North.

"I heard that of the possible scrappers there are never really more than a dozen people that register at any one facility," George Lawrence noted.

"Is it true, Ralphie," Bessie Tucker asked. "Did you register?"

Ralphie did not respond.

"Ralphie, didn't register. He ain't got the stones to register," George Lawrence opined.

"Don't know about his stones," Erica North snickered. "I think that he's just the type to register."

"What you mean?"

"I mean, he's the guy that you wouldn't expect to register for something like the challenge and," Erica North said, noticing that she had paint on the back of her hand. "He might be the one to win."

Bessie stared at Ralphie.

"He's just the guy that would tell everyone that he registered and find out he was really eyeballs deep in cow poo," George Lawrence laughed.

Ralphie did not respond. He did not need to speak when the others were caught up in their own debate. Ralphie just listened and watched the clock.

The bell for dismissal rang. Ralphie and the others left art class. At the end of the school day Ralphie got a message to meet on the bleachers of the soccer field. Ralphie walked to the soccer field and was surprised to find that besides Jax, Tee and Zeke were four other Millers.

"What up, Ralphie," Jax crowed then frowned. "You ghosting me?"

Ralphie shook his head.

"What gives? We heard you registered all late and dramatic," Tee crowed.

Ralphie looked at Tee but did not reply.

"This is—you know everybody? They signed up for the challenge with us."

"The way I see it this is our team for the challenge," Zeke noted.

"We need to prepare for the challenge if we are all going to be in it. We need to know our enemies and our allies," Dame, the thickly muscled cashew skinned teen concluded from behind an oily and slightly pimply face and braces.

"We can't be the first team exed out," Gina stated.

"We won't be the first to be exed out," Jax scowled. "We got some serious talent on this team," Jax, the joker of the group, noted.

Maddy and Tee shook their heads.

"Why did you sign up for the challenge," Jax asked Isaac.

"I signed up because no one I know been out of this compound," Isaac admitted.

"Seriously," Ralphie stated.

"Ralphie," Jax tried.

"People go to the other compounds every day," Ralphie added before he could stop himself.

Jax shook his head. Isaac looked at Ralphie through thin brown eyes. Gina smirked at Ralphie's comment. From the looks on Maddy and Dame's face Ralphie had not made friends. He had in one word offended the other four Millers.

"Not everyone gets to go to other compounds, Reynolds," Tee spat.

Ralphie winced at Tee's announcement of his last name. He knew that most in the Remains were born, lived, worked and died in their compounds. Few, very few, traveled outside of the compounds. Of course, there were exceptions.

Ralphie knew most in the residents in the Remains did not venture far from their compounds. They might have to go to Central Government which was centrally located so that all the lines only had to cross one of seven bridges to the moated and ancient looking walled city within a city. The reasons for going to Central Government were usually legal, financial, or judicial.

Each compound contained all that any resident needed. There were schools in each compound. There was industry in each compound. Businesses, big and small, existed in all the compounds. In each compound there was a central area where most of the line met when celebrating or meeting about important issues. The town hall idea was perfected in the compounds. News was fed to all compounds through Central Government.

Few had the luxury of travel from one compound to another like Benjamin Reynolds, Ralphie's father. Benjamin Reynolds worked in various compounds through his construction company; Reynolds Construction. Reynolds Construction was one of the largest and most respected construction companies in the Remains. Benjamin Reynolds worked all over the Remains. His family, as a result lived all over the Remains.

The first five years of his life were spent in the Foundry. Then his father was asked to oversee a project in the Poppy compound. Ralphie traveled everywhere with his father. When he turned five, he lived in the Poppy compound. His memories of that place were vague but colorful.

Ralphie had lived in the Poppy compound for a year. The Poppy compound was a technicolor explosion of every color and artistic medium. There were statues, paintings, murals, sculptures, films and photographs dispersed throughout the compound. Every surface was a canvas in the Poppy compound.

After the Poppy compound Ralphie had been in the Trad compound. It was a very black and white, steel and concrete, compound. That stay had been only for a year and a half. It, the Trad compound, was so different from the Poppies compound. The Trad compound was so ordered. The streets were straight lines. The parks were green squares of space. Things were so ordered. Trads should have been clock makers. The streets were clean and beautifully drawn from one end of the compound to the other. Everything in the Trad compound began at the compound center and moved away from the city hall to the compound outskirts. In the four quadrants of the compound there were four parks for the children. In each park there was a climbing structure, a swing set, rocking horses and a slide. Those green spaces are what Ralphie remembered fondly.

Ralphie had left the Trad compound and followed his father to the First Gen compound. He lived in the First Gen compound for nearly five years. The First Gen compound was different as day and night from the Trads, Poppy and Miller compound. In the First Gen compound there were robots. There were robots that were sent out to clean the streets. There were robots to remove trash. Overhead, in the First Gen compound, flew drones that monitored the compound from north, south, east and west. In the compound all of the First Gen residents slept comfortably as a result of the drones flying overhead.

The Reynolds moved back to the Miller compound and been there for nearly four years. In those four years he had become close friends with Tee, Jax and Zeke. They were his closest friends in the Miller compound.

As Ralphie recalled all this he looked at Gina and Ralphie knew that he had crossed a line. He was not better than anyone, he rationalized. The words he had used had made him sound like a snob. The idea made him shrink. Should he apologize? Should he say something? He sheepishly looked at Isaac, the Miller sidekick, who seemed unconcerned about Ralphie.

"The way it rolls out is they select the first batch, then they video them, then they get another group for the next batch and it is all very hush hush. No one really knows who was selected until they release the videos. The videos are the official announcement to the Remains that those people are in the challenge. Then the betting starts and sometime after that we get scooped," Jax noted changing the subject and saving Ralphie.

"So, when do you think we get interviewed?"

"Don't know," Jax admitted. "I don't think that they like to give all the details to the challenge all the time."

"I'm more curious how many are going to be in the challenge this year," Gina smirked with a smirk, cutting her eyes at Ralphie.

Ralphie lifted his hands in surrender. He grinned at the girl with her diamond shaped face and pointy chin.

"Well, seven compounds, eight contestants each," Zeke calculated.

"Minus the Shakers," Jax pointed out. "Those rich bastards never participate."

"When you have last names like Lafayette, Newman, Jenkins or Buchanan then the rules do not apply to you."

"Haves and have nots," Isaac blurted.

"We are definitely the have nots," Zeke decided. "But if we win, we will remind those other lines that we are essential to the Remains," Zeke concluded.

"More essential than the big box warehouse stores and bicycles," Dame stated behind his braces.

Jax sidled up to Ralphie and whispered into his ear: "Think Gina likes you."

Ralphie shook his head.

"Seriously," Jax joked.

Ralphie allowed his eyes to reflect his sudden curiosity, thinking of Gina.

"I know what you're thinking," Jax joked, again with a smile. "You got this thing for that First Gen girl. That is a dead-end relationship if there ever was one and it is mostly in your head."

"Jax, I don't have time for this," Ralphie attempted.

"Is it because she is…thick?" Jax moved his eyes to Gina and gave a slight smile.

Ralphie shook his head and punched at Jax. He was slightly embarrassed. He pulled on his earlobe, nervously.

"You can't be a weight shamer," Jax chided, all at once serious.

"I ain't a weight shamer, Jax," Ralphie boomed defending himself.

"That girl got curves, man. You know she does not miss a meal," Jax joked.

Ralphie refused to continue the conversation. Instead, he thought about the upcoming challenge. He climbed to his feet and headed toward the Foundry exit. Tee, Zeke and Jax followed after their goodbyes.

Jax was the first to catch up with Ralphie.

"You being all sensitive all of a sudden," Jax laughed. He put his arm around Ralphie's shoulder and smiled all big and goofy.

"I ain't being all sort of nothing," Ralphie replied shrugging Jax's arm off his shoulder. He studied Jax coldly. Jax feigned hurt. Ralphie sucked at his teeth and did not speak for a long moment.

"Come on man, you know that I was only kidding. You and Bailey are a match made in heaven," Jax joked. Ralphie cut his eyes at his friend. "Don't be that way, man. I was only kidding. I mean, there are plenty of fish in the sea."

Tee and Zeke caught up with the pair just then. Ralphie thought about what Jax had said. He did not disagree. There were plenty of fish in the sea. Yet, he did not want all fish. He paused and for the first time Ralphie thought that he might have feelings for Bailey other than as a friend. The idea shocked him in its newness. Ralphie was not sure how to handle the idea so he submerged it, drowned it in the business of the day.

He paid attention suddenly to the conversation that Tee, Jax and Zeke were having. They were talking about the four other Millers.

"The way I see it Isaac is a Klingon," Tee noted.

"Robin, for sure," Jax agreed.

"Dick Grayson, War Machine, Doctor Watson," Tee continued, with a sly smile.

"I mean if he was Damien Wayne, then I wouldn't be all concerned," Jax stated.

Zeke looked at Tee and then Jax. Jax grinned awkwardly and fell silent.

"Gina is the comedian," Tee said.

"Yeah, maybe, but she isn't that funny," Jax noted.

"You would say that as our resident jokester," Tee smiled looking at Jax. Zeke nodded at that comment.

"Madison is the cute and confused one," Jax noted.

Zeke studied Jax seriously. Tee snickered.

"What?"

Zeke brooded and did not speak. He walked on with his arm around Tee's shoulder. Jax tried for the next couple of blocks to figure out what he had said to upset the bullish teen.

At the busy intersection that led to the Estates Zeke pulled up. He stopped Tee. Jax and Ralphie stopped and waited.

"See you tomorrow," Zeke said, releasing Tee. Jax and Zeke exchanged an elaborate handshake and finished with a fist pound and smile. Ralphie nodded to Zeke as Zeke walked away. Zeke walked across the busy W.E.B.DuBois Avenue and toward the central roundabout and toward Josephine Baker Avenue.

Tee watched Zeke walk away and Ralphie and Jax began their walk toward the Estates. The three walked on silently. Ralphie knew that anytime that Jax was quiet he was concocting a hairbrained idea. He dreaded the new topic of discussion that his fast friend was about to offer.

"You know there are seven lines and seven lines are given the opportunity to participate in the Pandemonium Challenge."

"We all know that," Tee rasped. Ralphie waited.

"What I don't understand is why no one in the Remains seems to bat an eye at the fact that Innovators chose not to participate."

"Rich people have options. We don't," Tee screeched.

"Don't seem fair."

"A lot of things ain't fair. You ain't no baby, Jax. You know that already."

"I know that, but I figured that in the Remains there was supposed to be," he paused, thinking of the right words. Jax twisted his lips on his face. "Fairness."

"You ain't that stupid," Tee laughed.

"What you mean?"

"Ain't nothing fair," Tee pointed out. "We live in the Remains and there is a tenth of the world population in space heading for God knows where. They put in plans long before the flash. Right? They are heading toward… trying to terraform planets but we aren't in the loop. We didn't get no choice in that. That wasn't fair. Why ain't you talking about that?" Tee said, moving her head left to right and poking out her lips.

Ralphie watched as Jax fell silent.

"The Remains was built to create something better," Jax began.

"All you talk about is nonsense. We have heard all the tinfoil crackpot theories already. Why aren't you talking about things that matter," Tee breathed exasperated. "There are giant rats, dogs and all sorts of things that the enforcers are tasked to protect us from that we don't talk about," Tee seethed.

"For fear of causing mass hysteria," Jax pointed out only to receive a death stare from Tee.

"There are the monsters on the other side of the wall that continue to try to get in here. You ain't talking about that. Those idiots that hid in crypts before the pre-flash and thought that when everything was over, they would come out and be loved and cherished and restart this whole thing over again are missing. But you ain't talking about that or how our government is better or worse." Tee paused thinking. "We got real problems in the Remains and you want to ask why the rich are rich and how come the rich don't take part in a Remains distraction."

"The challenge is not a distraction," Ralphie protested. "It is the one thing that makes sense in the Remains. In all the craziness of the Remains and the lines and the routines the challenge makes sense. There is no politics in the challenge. There is nothing but survival and outwitting and outlasting everyone set against you."

Jax smiled broadly. Tee did not smile. She seemed genuinely stunned by Ralphie's words. Ralphie pursed his lips to stop himself for saying anymore.

"Check out my boy," Jax beamed. "He quiet but when he got something to say he going to say it."

Tee studied Ralphie carefully. She reluctantly gave him a slight smile

In that moment, Jax stepped a little closer to Tee and beamed at the walnut brown girl wearing a pre-flash baseball cap that had been from one of the pre-flash football teams. She was dressed in jeans, sneakers and a black and white blue and gold California state seal imprinted hoody.

"What you trying to do, conspiracy boy?"

Jax raised his hands in surrender.

"Thought we were having a moment," Jax smiled coyly, awkwardly.

"Yeah, no," Tee smirked.

"It felt like a moment," Jax attempted.

"Oh, and since you are being sane for a minute. You always talking a bunch of nonsense. There are no aliens in the Remains. There are no secret tunnels. There is no Illuminati. We ain't got time for that. If you are going to talk then talk about solutions." Tee concluded. She looked at Jax with open contempt. "Oh, yeah, don't nobody believe there's still white people around either."

Jax seemed offended. He took a moment to recover. He looked at Tee. "Well, never said there were aliens," Jax said calmly. Tee was staring daggers at Jax. He continued, slowly. "There are secret tunnels. The treasure hunters don't want everyone down there. Me and Ralphie been down a couple of them. Ask him," Jax said looking to Ralphie.

Ralphie non-enthusiastically nodded. Jax, emboldened by Ralphie added: "The Illuminati was wiped out by the flash. And I never said that there were white people around. I was just asking where they went," Jax said. He quickly added, "Oh, and by the way, I don't think that where they went is relevant to this conversation." He concluded dismissively.

"Then why you thinking that things are suddenly going to be fair or different because we are living behind two twenty-foot-high walls?" Tee asked. "There are still things that are worse outside the walls than inside."

There was a silence that built between Tee and Jax. Ralphie did not dare to step into the arena of the professional debaters. They were in a league of their own.

Tee and Jax loved to argue. Jax loved to irk Tee. Tee loved to show how smart she was. If Tee wasn't crushing on Zeke, Ralphie believed that she would have been with Jax despite her protests.

Jax turned on Lewis Latimer Drive and blew a kiss to Tee and Ralphie. Tee scowled. Ralphie just shook his head.

Ralphie watched Tee, his neighbor, head down the street without another word. Tee had changed Ralphie realized. She had been this sweet and friendly tomboyish girl when he first met her half a decade ago, but something had changed her. She was now this mean girl that was always trying to be … mean. She liked to talk down to people. She liked embarrassing people. It was as if she had become someone unrecognizable.

Tee walked on never looking back never talking to Ralphie as she made her way to the top of the street where they both lived. Her home was at the top of Elijah McCoy Avenue. Ralphie's home was kitty corner to her house, on the opposite side of the street.

Ralphie watched Tee walk up her walkway to her porch and go to the front door. Ralphie shook his head as he mounted the front porch steps.

"Bye Ralphie," the fifteen-year-old mumbled under his breath, turning to see Tee open her front door and enter without turning around or looking toward him. "Bye Tee. Have a good day. See you tomorrow," Ralphie whispered in Tee's voice, again under his breath, as he opened his own front door, knowing that no one heard him.

Chapter Three.

Ritual.

The Pandemonium Challenge was a Remains ritual. There had been twenty-two challenges, and each had topped the other with intrigue, deception, backstabbing, alliances and love triangles, quadrangles and rhomboids. In the challenge there were no givens. Anyone could win. The underdog was only the underdog in name alone. Everyone was the underdog. Rarely, did a favorite win the challenge. It was a war of attrition and the last one standing was crowned the champion of the challenge.

"Once again, the Boomers take the coveted crown of the Pandemonium Challenge this year with winner Andrew Young Lloyd being the sole survivor of the seven-day contest," Dan Fleming announced.

As an annual ritual, there were expectations, rites, ordered steps and a plan, to the build-up to the Pandemonium Challenge. Before the challenge began boys and girls from all the lines that made up the Remains, as young as fifteen and no older than fifteen, were selected for the seven-day ordeal.

Yet, the selection did not begin with the announcement of the year's hopefuls. The challenge was one of the most highly anticipated events in the Remains. It, the selection, and the challenge itself was debated for ten months before the announcement of the year's contestants. Prior to Juneteenth and the announcement of the fifty plus or minus names of those being publicly broadcast.

"The Twenty-Third Pandemonium Challenge will have to be some kind of special to top this year's challenge, is all I have to say," reported Zora Ashcroft.

"The best part of the challenge is that it is always going to be better than the year before. It has to be. In its very nature the challenge cannot go backwards," Reggie Hightower explained.

The selection was a year-long process that began almost immediately at the conclusion of the previous challenge. the Remains prepared for the challenge mentally, eleven months before the announcement of the official contesters to participate in the first week of July.

The challenge would barely have ended before everyone in the Remains had taken a collective breath over the intrigue, subterfuge, backstabbing and unexpected twists of that year's challenge had offered then the critics began speculating. There was immediate conjecture, hypothesis and debate over which line would crown the next year's Pandemonium Challenge winner.

At the end of the previous year's challenge the obvious questions would be offered. Who did you fear the most? What was the hardest part of the challenge this year? What surprised you the most in the challenge? Where was your favorite safe spot on the island? When did you know that you could win? Were you ever worried that someone else might win? Why did or didn't you upgrade your weapon? How did it feel to be the challenge winner?

While the challenge winner was interviewed, sometimes from a hospital bed, the critics pointed out their own thoughts on the strengths and weaknesses of the year's talent pool. Few were satisfied with the challenge outcome. Everyone had an opinion. There were always line disappointments. They went on and on about the lack of effort from the Poppies and Gens.

"Half of the seven lines are more cannon fodder than combatants. If you add in the Shakers, that is four of the seven lines," Joe Chapman, one of the Remains commentators stated in the studios of the Remains Interweb.

"Did you see the same challenge that I saw," barked Eric Knight from another fancy studio on the Interweb. He was one of the more popular commentators of the challenge. In the studio that day was Michael Cooper, one-time enforcer and now commentator, Serena Taylor, a Remains politician and commentator and James Nelson, a Remains legendary commentator.

"The problem with the challenge is that we forget about second and third place," James Nelson noted.

"This year a Boomer won, and everyone knows that," Michael Cooper pointed out.

"Lloyd won this year and that is good for the Boomers, but you know that it wasn't a marshmallow fight. This was a hard-fought battle," Eric Knight noted.

"But they forget that on day seven in the last few hours there were still three other lines vying for the crown."

"I thought the Trads had a chance earlier in the day," Serena Taylor noted. She added, "They were extremely close to winning with Arthur Ashe Wilson," Serena Taylor admitted.

"My money was on Wilson Pickett Matthews of the Second Gens. I mean that kid was mean and motivated," Michael Cooper mentioned.

"Me, I was leaning toward the girl, Gladys Knight Westbrook, from the Millers to take it before Andrew Young cleaned house," James Nelson admitted.

There were always a number of jaw dropping events that happened every challenge. After that and sometimes during that debriefing of that year's challenge there were inklings and suggestions of which line was more likely to win the following year's challenge.

Some equated the challenge to the fanaticism of team sports before the flash. Some likened it to incredible amounts of money generated in football and baseball of the twentieth century. The Pandemonium Challenge was nearly a religion for most lines. There were some fans that could list all of the winners in the twenty-two years of the challenge and their running odds of winning. There were some fans that could name the top five combatants year after year, going back five-ten-or fifteen year. The challenge brought out experts in the challenge. Some experts suggested that the challenge was skewed toward the strongest members of whatever line participated. Of course, those experts were laughed at and scorned. The challenge was never that simple. True, some winners were big bruising hulks from the lines of hardworking men and women, but the winners of the challenge had also come from the lines less likely to dominate a physically demanding seven days.

The challenge was unpredictable and annually without clear or distinct winner every time it began. There were always near winners from each line that infuriated the lines and gave hope to those same lines each year. Winning the challenge was the penultimate achievement but being in the top five gave hope and inspiration to the lines for the next challenge.

It was as if the near wins, in the challenge, that was incredibly brutal and mentally draining, suggested that had things transpired in another way might have changed the outcome of the challenge. Those lines that had nearly won the challenge hoped and dreamed of their line member being crowned champion of the Pandemonium Challenge. The near challenge champions were gristle for the grinder to chew on and discuss from the streets to the highest offices in the Remains.

So, even with the challenge beginning the second week of July each year, the unofficial beginning of the Pandemonium Challenge came, unofficially, at the conclusion of the previous year's challenge. As the year's champion was crowned and made a Remains celebrity those that had witnessed the challenge began to prepare for the next year's challenge.

The Pandemonium Challenge was unique as a competition. Unlike most contests it did not have defending champions. No one wanted to participate in the ultimate battle of wits and skills more than once. The cost was immeasurable. The challenge itself was brutal and physically and mentally grueling.

The physical aspect of the competition was like no other contest in the Remains. The enforcers, the elite of the Remains, did not have a life and death gauntlet that they had to survive to become enforcers. The mental aspect of the challenge was always downplayed, but by the sixth- or seventh-day favorites made mental slips that they would never have made earlier in the challenge. Those mental misjudgments usually were the causes of defeat of most in the challenge.

The attraction of the challenge, to the viewing public, was the inevitable unraveling of those that appeared bulletproof. The unpredictable nature of the event held everyone that watched enraptured. It was not scripted. It was not canned. It was real. It was fly-by-the-seat-of your-pants, balls out action from the launch until the final day and crowning of the champion.

Twenty-two years ago, the challenge had begun modestly in an underground stadium and had only twenty-one contestants. The twenty-one warriors had only the basics of weapons and by the second day become one of the largest Interweb events in the Remains. That inaugural event crowned a lanky Trad boy named: Craig Robinson Benning, Pandemonium Challenge champion. He was the first challenge champion. Benning had won with a little luck and a whole lot of brutality.

Benning had never hidden. He had faced everyone that thought that he was an easy target. He had begun with a baseball bat. He had broken that wooden weapon after the third attack and upgraded to a machete. Craig Robinson Benning had lost his machete in the head of a First Gen who had thought that a sword was a better weapon against a machete. Benning had fashioned a pair of num-chuks out of two pieces of polished wood, fifteen-inches in length and attached by a length of chain and two screws drilled into the top of the wooden pieces.

Craig Benning had destroyed three adversaries, a Miller, a Boomer and a First Gen, who had dared face him on his way to his final showdown. The final fight had been between Benning and a Boomer named: Louis Armstrong Streeter. Num-chuks versus a single solitary fire axe? Streeter was no slouch. He had been impressive with his rage and axe. When Benning and Streeter faced off the bets reached nearly two million credits.

The battle had been in a shell of a building that faced the Acid Bay. It was one of those moments in combat that are talked about for its intensity and seemingly perceived underdog. Streeter was the bruiser and killer. He had attacked. Benning had been ready. The fight did not take long.

As a result, the anticipation for the next challenge grew. The fascination with the challenge grew. There was nothing on the Interweb like it. It grew from that initial underground event to be a Remains most watched and bet on activity ever. It was one of the most anticipated seven days of the year.

Because of its popularity a government building that had been used for motor vehicles was converted to house the Pandemonium Challenge and their hive of tirelessly working committee members. The committee was tasked with the creation of the seven-day event that nearly ground the Remains to a standstill every year. It was bigger than any event in the

Remains. The amount of money created by the Pandemonium Challenge demanded the attention of the Remains government.

The Pandemonium challenge was the biggest and most lucrative thing in the Remains. The money generated in the official betting of the Pandemonium challenge was nearly fifty percent more than any one-day event in the Remains. It generated, legally, in seven days, nearly one billion credits a day and paid out twenty million credits in various forms throughout the weeklong challenge.

There was an incredible amount of money exchanged in the seven-day contest. Of the 314,159 residents in the Remains there was a spike in interest in the challenge that dwarfed everything else on the Interweb. Everyone in the Remains watched the challenge. The statistics suggested that every year at least one person bet on the challenge in some form or other. The Pandemonium Challenge committee never seemed to run out of ways to wager on the seven-day event.

There were hourly wagers which paid the lowest amounts. There were one-day wagers. There were two-day wagers. There were three-day wagers. There were seven-day wagers that promised to pay out six figures from the vast treasury of the Pandemonium Challenge committee. The lure of making fast cash was an incredible enticement for most.

Beyond the money-making element of the challenge there seemed to be endless debates over the challenge from every quarter of the Remains. Everyone, it seemed, had an opinion of the challenge. Competitors were instant celebrities. Everyone knew the twenty-two challenge champions. Combatants were endorsed and given opportunities to display name brand clothing, but few cared. The flashy items offered were always on display from the families of the combatants. The participants did not seem as concerned about wearing the latest and greatest as they prepared to face off with people driven to eliminate them from the competition.

With the lure of celebrity and swag for their family, pre-teens, tweens and teens prepared themselves for the ultimate rite of passage in the Remains. Everyone that participated walked through the fire of a challenge like no other. There was nothing like the Pandemonium Challenge. There was no real way to prepare for it but to prepare for anything and all things.

Those that volunteered were unusual pre-teens. They were unconcerned with the threats of elimination or being maimed or crippled. The reward of legendary status was enough of a draw for every line to offer up their eight entries. The challenge list was always full.

So, all that being said, the challenge and those that decided to register for the challenge, as a result, became important in the Remains. It did not matter that the challenge was months away. It only mattered that the challenge was happening in July.

It did not matter that the unofficial beginning of the challenge began at the end of the last Pandemonium Challenge then three months later, in September, after three months of discussion and analysis of the previous year's challenge waned there was an introduction of the first public debate by those committed experts as which line seemed to be able to offer the challenge a notable and worthy challenge for the next challenge.

That one debate over the merits of the lines and participants, which was usually in December, brought the challenge official begin to just six months from its next launch. The discussion usually found one line pitted against another for various reasons. There was always the discussion of the top five from the year before and their chances of repeating that success. There was also the belief that one line was better than the other.

Listening to the endless discussions about the challenge most agreed which line had no chance. Innovators were never in the discussion. There was never any Shaker in the challenge. The Poppies were not real threats. They seemed more interested in making their artistic hajj to Cosson Hall and dying there.

There were few that believed in the Gens, even though two challenges ago one First Gen had made it to Day Seven only to be steamrolled by the Trad that had faced off with the eventual winner. There had been two Millers that had made it to Day Six and one to make it to Day Seven. The Miller had faced off against the Boomer that had won the challenge. Those five lines were given chances to win the Twenty-Third Pandemonium Challenge, but most leaned toward another win by a Boomer, or at least a Trad.

There was no objectivity on the Interweb. There was always discussion about which line was the strongest. In the last half decade, the one line to dominant the challenge was the Traditionalists. They had won three of the last five challenges. The Boomers and The Second Gen had each won one challenge in that same amount of time.

Any discussion of the cherished challenge was scrutinized and dissected and analyzed over and over again by the fanatical lines. The critics were ruthless. The numerous pundits, that seemed to know everything about anything based on the challenge, did not hold back. They shot first and asked questions never. There was no filter on those that brought up the loved and hated Pandemonium Challenge or line superiority. When those issues were floated on the Interweb it was as if chumming the water for shark.

The Interweb was vicious. It was at best a hive of angry hornets. The Interweb was, at worse, a pack of ravenous wolves. Bullies, anonymously, slammed anyone and everyone that offered a different perspective. Lobbing up an opinion on anything, by anyone, opened that person up to ridicule and derision. It was on the Pandemonium Challenge Interweb that "bully nation" was born.

It, the bully nation title, came on a day where the simple suggestion by Stevie G, a First Gen, that the Gens had a chance to win a Pandemonium Challenge was lofted into the Interweb. Now, it is worth nothing that the Gens had never won or challenged for a win in the Pandemonium Challenge in twenty years.

The fiery darts that were launched at the innocent Gen supporter, after a challenge, were borderline racist, homophobic and misogynistic.

Those that dared suggest that the once powerful line of Millers had a snowball's chance of winning again after a near seven-year drought were laughed off the Interweb.

"The Millers are all over the board. They had a chance a few years ago, probably their best chance was when Shandle Woodley seemed on a tear those first three days," Carl Porter, the broad faced commentator noted. "Of course, Shandle was cut down like one of those trees near the silent woods when she forgot to check her six. All the hopes of the Millers went with her."

"The challenge gives, and the challenge takes away," Richard Wright Thomas, another commentator noted from some studio location.

Some, brave hearts, argued with the commentators online. the Remains Interweb was a marvelous tool to reach out to men and women throughout the Remains. There were pockets of humanity the post-flash world that every-once-in-a-while responded on the Interweb, but the Interweb was designed uniquely and specifically for the Remains residents.

"We know that all the ignorant races were eliminated with the flash, but you seem to be a holdout Trad," Flame Boy, an anonymous rude boy, announced from somewhere on the Interweb.

"You must be the Missing Link that everyone is still looking for. Is your momma a horse or dog Miller?"

"Damn, Deux, don't they have medicine at your compound?"

Those were seen as tame compared to the more insulting comments.

"Are you out of your green cucumber munching mind?"

"The Three Blind Mice can see that you and your line Juan, might be missing a few chromosomes. No sane person that hasn't been drinking from the Acid Bay, like you, gives the Gens a chance in hell to compete this year," FireFireBlaze, another Interweb critic, shot in those early Interweb days.

"Computer nerds? Fighting? Rather see paint dry," UberMan an Interweb troll fired.

"I feel sorry for the lines that have to fight the Juans, Deux or Poppies. They haven't put up a fight since they heard there was a sale on brushes at the art store."

"Fighting a Gen ain't worth the effort," announced OneTwoThreeKO, a Trad Interweb commentator.

"Fighting a Juan would be like fighting my blind baby sister, on a bad day, if I had one," explained a Boomer in a chat room on the Pandemonium Challenge website.

"You think that the computer chip line has a chance against real warrior types? Now, I know that they outlawed drugs in the Remains, but you must have a stash somewhere in the Deux compound to suggest that," fired an anonymous sniper in the same chat room.

"Your mama must have dropped you on your head as a baby, Poppy, and just to make sure maybe she did it again, just to make sure," another nameless tough boy opined.

The same fate rested on those that tried to offer up the Poppies who had never won a challenge in twenty-two years.

"Poppies are too worried about leaving a masterpiece than trying to win the challenge," Tupac Shakur Fuller, one of the Pandemonium Challenge commentators noted on his Interweb broadcast.

The critics, the finger pointers, never allowed a commentator to possess the air. They instead weighed in on the merits of the other lines that had not won a challenge in nearly a decade and noted their strengths and weaknesses. The Innovators were mentioned but never considered a serious contender as they had not offered more than one participant in the nearly two decades of the challenge.

Usually sixty to ninety days after the conclusion of the challenge, there was the appearance of the unannounced and unofficial Pandemonium Challenge countdown clock. The Pandemonium Challenge website was usually a place to see videos from the day, when active. After the challenge the website was usually dormant. The appearance of the countdown clock, when activated, signaled the true beginning of the year's challenge.

In the Remains, with the appearance of the countdown clock there was increased activity. It, the countdown clock, signaled activity, and that activity usually revolved around cleaning and sprucing up the inner walled city where the Central Government of the Remains resided. The Central Government was the only walled section in the Remains. The Innovators had the only gated line in the Remains.

When the Pandemonium Challenge banners were unfurled from streetlight poles it heralded the unofficial hundred days before the start of the challenge. 100 days before the challenge and things, for the players, began to be interesting. There were interviews. There were photo shoots. There were endless Interweb interviews.

Challenge contestants became Remains celebrities. Line celebrities found their lives amplified. Everyone in the Remains wanted to take pictures with the dark horses.

During the cleansing, what most called the sprucing up of the Central Government, the Remains enforcers systematically positioned street barriers and road dividers throughout the walled city in advance of the yearly protests against the challenge. The challenge was not embraced by all the Remains.

There were many that thought the challenge was barbaric and archaic and something that should be banned, like all gladiator sports. The protests were to be expected. The protesters were dramatic and dangerous. Many protesters dressed in costumes and wore masks of famous anarchists in history and espoused all sorts of politic against the challenge.

Well, every line participated, except the Innovators. The Innovators, the most influential and richest line, chose not to participate in the challenge.

In the twenty-two years only two Innovators had participated in the challenge. The two Shakers to participate was a contrary boy named: Samuel Cooke Newman and an evil looking girl named: Vanessa Williams Martin. Both entries seemed so unlike their elite line that everyone, upon seeing them in the challenge, wondered if the Innovators had screened their members and line sufficiently.

The contrary boy, Samuel Cooke Newman, who was in the Tenth challenge for nearly forty hours, was a spoiled brat who had wanted to challenge himself. Newman was extricated by a group of highly trained enforcers that invaded Pandemonium island in the late hours of the night, under the orders of the Shaker Chief Operating Officer, at the time, Peabo Bryson Newman, the cherished great grandson of Angela Bassett Newman and uncle of Samuel Cooke Newman.

Five years later, the evil Vanessa Williams Martin threatened everyone in the challenge and talked about leaking anyone that got close to her. She called Samuel Cooke Newman a female reproductive organ and dared anyone to test her. Vanessa Martin was this wide hipped girl the color of copper with shoulder length braids and all bad attitude. Everyone wanted to take her scalp but before anyone could she was out of the challenge. Martin had lasted thirty-four hours. She was removed from the challenge unharmed, transformed and changed. Gone was her evilness. After the challenge Martin dedicated herself to philanthropy.

The Twenty-Third Pandemonium Challenge was the exception. It had been eight years since a Maker had attempted the challenge. It was also the third time that a Maker would enter the challenge.

Chapter Four.

The Gathering Center

In the Remains, the year was measured by holidays and celebrations. Every school year began with the 1619 August Remembrance of the beginning of slavery. The first slavery remembrance in the Remains was called Angola 20. So, August 20-21st was honored as the dates of the Angola20.

Ten days after Angola20 school began in the Remains compounds. Everyone six to sixteen were mandated to an educational facility. The lines prided themselves in their educational products. Students were the measure of each line. The biggest employer was the Remains government. The government relied on the enforcers, their military arm, to serve and protect those in the Remains.

The first of September was reserved for the celebration of the enforcers. Enforcers were seen as real-life heroes. They were bad asses. They feared no one or nothing. They manned the outer walls. They manned the inner walls. They walked the various streets of the seven lines of the Remains. Enforcers protected everyone and everything in the Remains.

There was a Remains holiday in October to celebrate the memory of John Brown's raid. Halloween had been abolished in the Remains. There had been claims over and over that Halloween had initiated many pre-flash to devil worship. In the Remains, there was no devil worshipping allowed.

November was the traditional Thanksgiving celebration. In the Remains Thanksgiving was not about pilgrims or settlers but mainly focused on the Native Americans welcoming and the family tradition of thanks. It was a good excuse for good food.

December was the celebration of the ratification of the 13th Amendment and the unofficial remembrance of the death of John Brown. Christmas was celebrated in the Remains as were other religious holidays of the residents. Yet, Christmas by far was the biggest celebration and the traditional lighting of Christmas trees in the compounds was a big event each year.

The first of January, in the Remains, was not just a celebration of the New Year but also the enforcement of the Emancipation Proclamation penned by Abraham Ralphie. The beginning of January each year in the Remains there was a reading of the Emancipation Proclamation in the Central Government park. Thousands attended.

February and March were months without historical celebrations. There were the non-historical celebrations of Saint Valentine's Day in February. There was also Presidents Day which gave all students in the Remains a day off in the educational facilities but there was no official Remains celebrations those months. An official Remains celebration always had music, face-painting and fireworks.

April was the month of the celebration of the 14th Amendment. There was a one-day celebration. Seven artists from lines were given opportunities to be heard. It was a Remains staple.

May was the month of celebration of the 15th Amendment and the Supreme Court decision of Plessy v. Ferguson which essentially gave African American men the chance to vote. Like the celebration the month before seven artists from the lines were given the chance to be seen by the Remains as they displayed their talents.

Yet, in June, after all the educational facilities had let out for the summer, the annual Juneteenth celebration was seen as the second biggest event in the Remains. It was so unlike the biggest event and offered a respite and peaceful reminder of all that was possible in the Remains. Juneteenth highlighted the Remains strength and resilience. On display, that week, were a number of inventions, biographies, re-enactments, dramatic readings of the ancestors that had broken the chains of slavery to ensure a brighter future for all that lived in the Remains. Videos played everywhere in the Juneteenth celebration to make those that had forgotten all that had come before.

Juneteenth had the potential to be a somber event but thanks to the Juneteenth committee that was located in one of the offices in the Central Government buildings legislative arms, next to the Pandemonium Challenge building, the event was a Remains celebration. The event had been put on for nearly thirty years. The event culminated in the nightly dances that made some Remains famous.

Everyone focused on the celebration as a history lesson of the liberation from the bonds of slavery nearly eight centuries before. There were displays every year of the slow-motion retching process of a semblance of freedom in the nation that had shown moments of brilliance and instances of disregard of the 200 plus years of forced chattel slavery in the United States of America.

At Juneteenth, Harriet Tubman, Toussaint L'Overture, John Brown, Thurgood Marshall, Sojourner Truth, Martin Luther King, Malcolm X, Rosa Parks, Muhammad Ali, Jesse Owens, Joe Louis, Jackie Robinson, Shirley Chisholm, Richard Pryor, Biggie Smalls, Tupac, Barack Obama, Andre Washington, Bailey Coleman, Ruth Thompson, Ralphie Powell, Valerie Wright and so many others were displayed all over the gardens. Booker T. Washington and Frederick Douglass walked around the gardens of the Central Government for children to take pictures.

There were always men and women in costume. At every Juneteenth there were at least two or three Barack Obamas and Michelle Obamas walking around in costume. The six other black presidents, before the flash stood in costume for pictures as well.

Everyone in the Remains knew, before the flash, there had been half a dozen black Presidents that had been duly elected. Of the six, two had been assassinated. The first had been gunned down on the streets in front of a hotel where he had just delivered a speech about the threat of white supremacy. The second had been killed in a bomb blast at a college lecture on economic liberties. Two had been women; Issa Raye Hammond and Tiffany Dennis. Hammond had surprised many with her economic insights and begun the whole naming of black children after black icons. She had also been the first President to balance the budget in a decade and move the nation toward a sound infrastructure. Dennis had been popular and loud and threatening an international disaster with her xenophobic leanings.

In the Remains everyone knew the first black president and many in the Remains still carried his name, as a result. If there was a poll of the most popular it had to be Obama. It had taken a dozen years to see another black face as the leader of the nation. Thus, the first was the most influential as every other President was measured against him.

Before the challenge, there was the Juneteenth Celebration. Juneteenth, what most called the event, was five days of fireworks, dances, face painting, food festivals, contests and carnival rides, usually the second week in June, to celebrate the past victories and present achievements in the Remains. For the young, it was a time to participate in various food delicacies, fireworks, singing, dancing and all types of line creations. Juneteenth was held in the Central Government region, the walled city within a city, in the Central Government gardens. It was the biggest public event in the Remains. It drew, reportedly, 150,000 residents to the gardens each year. It was the biggest public event in the Remains, but nothing compared to the Pandemonium Challenge.

The same year of the Twenty-Third Pandemonium Challenge the Juneteenth celebration marked the handful of days before the challenge. Yet, two weeks before the Juneteenth celebration Zeke, Tee and Ralphie gathered at the front of the Foundry and prepared to separate for the last time as students that year in the Foundry. They had made it through their second to last year of education. They were fifteen. Mandated education ended at sixteen in the Remains.

Some, not all, opted out of education their sixteenth year and joined the enforcers. Enforcers were the rock stars of the Remains. It was every child's desire to be an enforcer. There were no superheroes more loved than the enforcers. They served. They protected. They were fearless.

"Ralphie, come down here," called Ralphie's father, Benjamin Reynolds, with a loud and booming voice. Ralphie, who was in his bedroom on the second floor of his house ran downstairs to answer his father's call. He did not think to tell his father he was busy. His father did not brook excuses.

Ralphie found his father in his study. In front of Benjamin Reynolds sat a glass desk and in front of that were two overstuffed leather chairs. Often, Ralphie had walked by the same study, when his father was home, and noticed that bankers, lawyers, politicians were talking with his father. Benjamin Reynolds was a man a significance in the Remains.

Standing in the doorway, his father looked up and waved his son into the room. Ralphie stepped in and looked around the study. Ralphie walked into his father's study and noted that his father was alone in the dimly lit room. The study was a dark corner of the house, now that the sun had set. The walls were dark wood. Behind his glass desk that had etched on it the rough sketch of the Remains was a wall of bookcases with hundreds of books that his father had retrieved from excavations. The books were first prints, mostly, of authors that had died centuries before. There were two windows that afforded a view of the street out front of the house and the other of the backyard. On the walls were framed pictures of maps of the Remains pre-flash and post-flash.

Benjamin Reynolds was a bull of a man. He was thickly built. He looked as if he could pull up tree stumps with his bare hands. His hands were big and vise like, in appearance. He was possessed of thick arms and neck and a square face. Dark wood brown and serious, Ralphie could not recall a time when his father was not calculating some important matter.

Yet, his father was two men, to Ralphie. At work, he was serious, deadly serious. As he sat behind the glass desk dressed in the Miller coveralls, a gun belt strapped to his waist and his trusty Colt M1911 sitting in the holster. Seeing his father still with his gun belt on, Ralphie knew that his father was still in work mode. In work mode, Benjamin Reynolds rarely cracked a smile. There was too much at stake, his father pointed out time and time again, when asked if he lightened up ever, at work. He was the CEO of Reynolds Construction.

The fifteen-year-old knew that his father was different when not in work-mode. In non-work mode he was this smiling, loving and welcoming individual that cherished his wife and children. He laughed and joked, just like anyone else would. He sat in front of his father in the overstuffed leather chair.

But that was not the Benjamin Reynolds who greeted Ralphie. His father raised a stubby finger and said: "Howard, that is what I pay you for," and tapped the device on his desk to end the call. Benjamin Reynolds looked at his son evenly.

"Dad, you wanted to see me?"

"Ralphie, your mom told me that you registered for the challenge today," Benjamin Reynolds breathed from behind his desk. He did not ask a question. He was merely stating facts. Ralphie sat and listened.

"She received the notification this afternoon and called me to ask if I knew anything about it," he continued. His dark eyes studied Ralphie. Benjamin Reynolds had told Ralphie that he was a human lie detector once. So, as he studied his son, Ralphie knew that he was trying to determine something. "I told her that you had not mentioned anything to me about the challenge." He paused. He steepled his thick fingers under his square chin and looked at Ralphie for a moment before continuing. "I told her that I was as surprised as she was at the news."

"Listen, dad," Ralphie began and stopped. His father had raised a thick hand in the air.

"You know that we raised you to make ... we cannot control your life. It is your life. We have tried to prepare you for the future. It is your life to do with what you may."

Ralphie began, slowly, not wanting to be disrespectful. "I know that, and I am grateful. I just figured that the challenge would give me a chance to be somebody...to be legendary," Ralphie stated.

Benjamin Reynolds stood up, from behind his desk. The giant of a man towered over his seated son. He stepped around the desk. The dark man took a few steps and placed a heavy hand on his son's shoulder.

"Let's go outside," his father said and Ralphie stood. The two Reynolds left the study and cut through the house to the kitchen. The house was still, his mother and sister were out somewhere. There were no lights on besides the kitchen and study. The pair of Reynolds walked out the sliding glass door to the backyard.

It was dim outside, as the sun had set nearly an hour ago. Ralphie stood on the patio as his father walked to the back wall of the house and tapped a few buttons and activated the lights under the awning that reached out fifty feet toward the grass and slight terraced hill that ended with a redwood fence that bordered their property. Under the awning were lounge chairs.

"Sit," the elder Reynolds gestured. Ralphie sat in one of the half a dozen lounge chairs on the patio. His father nodded at Ralphie and sat as well. He was an arm's reach away.

Ralphie watched his father adjust himself in the lounge chair. He was a big man. He did not look as if he would be comfortable in the lounge chair, as it seemed not built for him. The big man made a few adjustments and settled into the lounge chair. He exhaled and seemed to find peace with the lack of support of his bulk.

"You know that we have not been shy in helping you succeed," Benjamin Reynolds began, sitting in the backyard with his son. "Perhaps, it is the reason that you have decided to go to the challenge. We helped too much."

"No, it's not that," Ralphie tried to explain. "The challenge is... the challenge, anyone that survives becomes legendary."

Benjamin Reynolds nodded.

"Legendary," Benjamin Davis repeated. "Ralphie, there is no instant celebrity. There is no instant anything. Overnight success is a lie. That lie is just one of many lies that youth want to believe, even though it's not true. No one walks onto the field and dominates on the first day. That is not possible. Popularity, fame, riches are illusions. Being popular is short-lived. Fame is here today and gone tomorrow. Riches diminish. Being reliable, consistent, trustworthy those are things that people remember."

"You don't understand," Ralphie responded, suddenly annoyed.

"I don't understand," Benjamin Reynolds repeated. "I do not understand because I did not have the luxury of being a child during my childhood. I was a child, but I was a boy doing a man's job, working with my father and grandfather, in their business. I grew up quickly. I missed out on a lot of childish things. I don't regret missing out. I loved my father and what he was doing, focused on building our family's business. We began by finding and burying the dead from the flash. We built that up and turned our business into bricks. We cornered the market in the Remains in bricks. My dad is the person that saw all those bricks and began to stockpile 'em. We learned that if you are going to build you need bricks. So, we had the most bricks in the

Remains. When people wanted to build, they had to come to us," Benjamin Reynolds mused. "From the bricks we became a construction company. We sold bricks and bought equipment. That started the Reynolds Construction. You know that we, the Reynolds, have built one third of the Remains. That didn't happen by accident. None of it was instantaneous. We built one third of the eastern outer wall. We built nearly half of the eastern and southern inner wall and are doing construction in four of the seven compounds." Benjamin Reynolds stopped himself. He seemed to struggle, for a moment.

"But this is not about me or my struggles or our family's history. This is about you and your decision to participate in the challenge."

Ralphie listened. In the back of his mind he was thinking that his father was going to tell him that he could not participate in the Twenty-Third Pandemonium Challenge. Instead, his father said this.

"You know that when we had you, I doted on you for nearly a year. Nothing was good enough for you. Your mother was a wreck. I could not do enough for my baby boy." Benjamin Reynolds paused. He was looking off into the night.

"My grandfather didn't get to see you before he died. He died the week you were born. My father, your grandfather loved you. He also loved all those animal shows. He would sit in his room late at night and watch those programs that documented pre-flash lions and tigers and every type of animal possible. When I was born the flash and its effects were ending. There were no real animals anymore. The flash had destroyed so much. The world had changed. I can remember my father telling me that he had been a little child when the flash happened. He also told me that I didn't understand everything that had changed. And, I can admit now, that I did not. I figured that the world was this quiet and strange place. He told me that the world was not always the way that I grew up seeing. That idea surprised me.

"I can recall him telling me after the flash, there was this silence. There were no more birds. No animals. It was just silence for a long time. My grandfather, your great grandfather, told me that the first animal, wild animal, that he saw, when animals returned, was an eagle. Imagine that. An eagle. One of those big, majestic birds flying through the air. I thought that would have been an amazing thing to see," he paused and seemed lost in the thought.

"My grandfather told me that eagles make their nests up in these out of the way places, in the crags and crannies of cliffs or the top of trees where no one can get to their eggs. When the eaglets hatch, they are completely dependent on their parents for everything. They begin their lives so weak. These majestic creatures that have no animal predator begin as these fragile things perched in nests so high that if they fall, they die long before they strike the ground. Their parents feed them and protect them. Then one day, these weak things that have never flown before begin to jump from branch to branch in the nest. They are testing their abilities. Yet, the eaglets jump and jump from branch to branch and without coaxing from their parents they one day just jump out of the nest." Benjamin Reynolds stopped.

"Do they fly?"

"Some do. Some don't," the giant of a man answered. "Some are ready. Some are not," he paused again, thoughtfully. "They have to figure out if they are eagles or not, I suppose." Benjamin Reynolds stopped again and Ralphie watched him out of the corner of his eye. The man that seemed carved from obsidian, faltered. Benjamin Reynolds pressed his lips together as if he was fighting the words trying to come out of his mouth.

Ralphie's father climbed to his feet in the dim light of the backyard and stood for a moment. He walked the short distance to Ralphie and stopped just within arm's reach of his son. Ralphie looked up from his seat as his father placed a heavy hand on his shoulder. Ralphie looked up and was surprised to find sadness in his father's eyes.

"I know that you are worried about disappointing me and your mom," Benjamin Reynolds stated. "Don't worry."

Ralphie opened his mouth to speak only to close it. Ralphie smiled at his father's surprisingly gentle touch. Ralphie reveled in that moment. The silent moment extended, with the elder and junior Reynolds for a beat.

Then, without word, his father took a deep breath and turned on his heels. The giant of a man walked back toward the house. He left his son in the dark.

The younger Reynold watched the bull of a man hesitate at the sliding door and pause. Ralphie wanted to imagine that his father wiped at his eyes just as he entered the quiet house. In the dark and quiet that his father had left Ralphie in the fifteen-year-old thought about what he had to face before the challenge.

Miller fame had been a tough pill to swallow but Ralphie had somehow swallowed it and felt that he had gotten used to all the Millers collectively losing their minds anytime they saw him outside of his house. It was a little overwhelming at first. Step outside and someone Ralphie did not even know would run up to him and take a picture. Everyone in the neighborhood seemed to know that he had registered. He had expected a tick of interest from the Foundry because it was the Foundry. Kids were always curious about those registering.

At the Leathern Apron, Zeke, Jax and Tee were Miller celebrities already. There were a couple of others in the Leathern Apron that had registered. Ralphie had seen the others but not really talked to them. Zeke, Jax and Tee laughed at Ralphie's late arrival.

"Well better late than never," snorted Zeke.

Ralphie chuckled.

"Things change once you register," Tee admitted making a duck face and throwing up a peace sign as if posing for an old-fashioned photo.

"Yesterday you nobody," Jax mused. "Today you everyone's hope and dream."

"Get prepared to smile a whole lot," Tee advised. "It would be good to practice. You got to have your standard, premium and supreme photo op."

"What," Ralphie said.

Before anyone could respond three girls in Polar Star ran up and hugged Ralphie and Tee. A fourth girl with a camera took a few natural pictures.

"Standard," Tee teased and winked. She placed her hands on the girls' shoulders and cocked her head just a little to the left. Tee looked at Ralphie who seemed incredibly uncomfortable.

The three girls laughed and posed and hugged Ralphie and Zeke and finally Jax.

One of the girls, with a ponytail of braids and apple cheeks, stepped forward to Ralphie. She studied him with her big dun brown eyes.

"You think that you are going to make it to the third day?"

Ralphie did not reply. He had not expected the question and did not have a ready answer. He struggled to find words. Instantly, he wanted to run away from the three little girls.

The three girls, that were powerless and meaningless a day before, suddenly had all this power to Ralphie. They stymied Ralphie. He stood dumbfounded. He did not know how to answer the question.

Jax stepped in.

"We all plan to go further than the third day. We are Millers. We have been close a few times in the last five years. This might—this will be our year," Jax brightened.

Ralphie listened.

The three girls cachinnated, giggled and drifted away satisfied with Jax's response. Zeke shook his head at Ralphie. Jax just sniggered.

"It gets easier," Jax concluded.

"No, it doesn't," Zeke contradicted.

Ralphie twisted his lips in response, not knowing which was true but knowing that each was partially correct.

Celebrity was supposed to be something everyone wanted. Yet, Ralphie dreaded it. It was nothing that Ralphie expected. Celebrity, in the Remains, meant anyone and everyone with a camera and an ounce of courage would and could take a picture with Ralphie. Pictures were one thing. The questions and posing was another thing. The bold asked questions. The audacious asked to take pictures with Ralphie.

Ralphie thought of himself as a private person. He did not take pictures. At least, he did not like to be on any of the accepted social media. He had a handful of friends and that was more than enough. In his mind, Ralphie had decided to just make it sixty days in relative anonymity, in the compound, with friends, not going far from home and waiting for the challenge.

The Miller boys stood and watched the others filing out of the Foundry for the final day of the school year knowing that they would not be returning to the Miller educational facility. There was no need. They were selected for the Pandemonium Challenge.

"Can I tell you that I am not going to miss this place," Zeke admitted.

Jax smiled mirthlessly.

Ralphie smiled awkwardly.

"I had thought that before going to the challenge that I might get to kiss Wendy or at least see or touch some girlie parts, you know," Jax confessed.

"Calm down, Jax," Zeke said. "We don't need everybody in the Foundry to know you are a horn dog."

"I'm not a horn dog," Jax defended loudly. "I'm just an opportunist who doesn't want to meet my maker never having kissed a girl."

"Yeah, says the boy that never kissed a girl," Ralphie laughed.

"Think you were talking about a little more than kissing," Zeke laughed.

"Always want a little more," Jax laughed.

Just then Tee walked up. She hugged Zeke. Jax shook his head. Ralphie chuckled.

"What up," Tee said.

Looking at the hair trigger Tee, Zeke and Jax, Ralphie could not help but think that the educational facility for the Millers had failed. Zeke hated learning. Zeke was a bully.

Zeke was this sullen and angry boy that never seemed to be in a good mood. He sulked most of the time Ralphie recalled. Zeke was this banana colored goon that said little and was always ready to mix it up with anyone. In the short time that Ralphie had known Jax and Zeke he had witnessed at least four fights a year for Zeke at the Leathern Apron. He was suspended pretty regularly as well.

Jax was this goofy troublemaker, always joking, always getting in trouble and seeing conspiracies in everything. At the Leathern Apron he was always on the verge of suspension for one thing or another. Jax was an unapologetic trickster and prankster. He always thought that things were funny, no matter what. His sense of humor was borderline psychotic. Yet, Jax was at times, rare times, funny. At least, that was how Ralphie saw Jax.

Zeke and Jax, were a perfect couple, in that they were the exact opposite sides of the same coin. They fed off of each other. They were friends long before Ralphie arrived in the compound. Ralphie thought that Zeke was too serious and a little slow, a deadly combination. Jax was funny and silly. In the Foundry they were always in trouble for one thing or another.

"When I turn sixteen, I'm going to the enforcers," Zeke had declared to anyone and everyone that asked him what his plan was, after the education facility or whatever he was going to do for work.

"What?"

"This whole education thing is not for me," Zeke admitted.

Ralphie liked Zeke for his loyalty. He was loyal to a fault. He protected Jax and Tee. He was slowly warming up to Ralphie. Ralphie did not know if Zeke saw him as a friend. He knew that Zeke did not consider him an enemy. The distinction was important.

His thoughts about Zeke were broken by Jax sticking his face in front of Ralphie and breathing on him to break his concentration.

"What is your problem," Ralphie fumed.

"I was saying that you are about to enter a whole new level of line fame."

"What?"

"I said that Juneteenth will be the first time that the Remains gets to see us," Jax noted.

"What," Ralphie said, stunned by the words.

"What? You had to know that being selected was going to change things, going forward," Jax smiled his best Cheshire cat smile.

"What's wrong, Ralphie? You, camera shy," grinned Tee, leaning on Zeke's broad shoulder.

Zeke looked on silently.

"I knew, I just supposed that it wouldn't matter that much here, in the compound," Ralphie tried.

"Welcome to the challenge, my friend," Jax said hooking an arm around Ralphie's shoulders and grinning from ear-to-ear.

"Yeah, if you thought that being Miller famous was insane," Tee grinned maliciously. "Wait until the ones that don't know you get a chance to see you." Tee gestured to her head and made her fingers expand like bomb bursts.

Ralphie Reynolds lowered his eyes. He had not expected being popular or well-known was going to be painful.

"Got to go," Zeke interrupted. "I'm supposed to do some work for my mum, today," the sulking giant announced more to Tee and Jax. He held Tee in his arms and gave her a gentle peck on the cheek. He released her and gave Jax a fist bump before walking away from the group, without acknowledging Ralphie.

"You know that Juneteenth wasn't always a family event," Jax noted one day while walking from the Foundry. No one bit, but Jax continued. "I read somewhere that before it started catering to the face painting, jump houses, singing and dancing, foodie crowd it was more about reminding the community of the struggles that the criminal white society, under the guise of government, created and continued against us as a people." Jax paused. He looked at Ralphie dramatically. "So, why did it change?"

"To about face painting and the latest food trends," Ralphie questioned.

"Jax, you ain't telling us groundbreaking news. We all know the history of Juneteenth," Tee steamed, looking at Jax like some bug that she needed to squash.

"You may know the history but if it is the biggest event in the Remains and most think it's just an excuse for five days of food, fun and face painting are they misinforming us on purpose?"

"What's wrong with face painting?"

"Nothing. It is just a symptom of another problem we have," Jax began.

"Could you give it a rest," Tee asked. She was a girl with a swimmer's physique, broad shoulders, thin hips and long arms and legs. Tee had a spidery look about her. To compliment her spidery look, her hair was usually braided in some intricate fashion that looked a little like black tendrils of braided webs on her egg-shaped head.

Ralphie did not speak. Jax looked at Ralphie and back at Tee. Tee poked out her lip as if she was about to say more.

"The truth is the truth."

Tee squeezed her lips together as if she was going to whistle or explode. She did neither. Tee instead twisted her lips on her syrup brown face and shook her head and stomped loudly away without another word to Jax and Ralphie. Jax and Ralphie watched as Tee stomped away.

The two looked at each other and shrugged simultaneously. Ralphie twisted his lips, thinking.

"You going to go … and, you know?"

Jax followed Ralphie's eyes toward the retreating Tee. Jax looked back at Ralphie with a wry smile. Jax laughed at Ralphie's suggestion.

"You know that you don't always have to be so," Ralphie trailed off.

"I'm me good and bad, normal and weird," Jax noted. He smirked. "You know, before the flash, before the mass exodus, before the white flight, people lived together in cities and in apartments and houses that were too big for them, poisoned the waters and the air and everything that they could," Jax said, continuing the conversation as if Tee had not tried to stop his chatter. "My question is what changed? They, the people that balled up the world, were just like us. Why aren't we cocking up what we have?"

Ralphie did not answer. He was suddenly annoyed at Jax. He did not like how Jax treated Tee. She was human. She deserved, at the least, a little respect and if he had hurt her feelings; an apology.

He looked at Jax who was suddenly walking with his hands outstretched so that he might touch the light poles spaced equally down the street.

Ralphie did not speak for a long time as he and Jax walked on, Tee maybe one hundred feet ahead. That silence was enough to keep Jax fishing and talking for the next few minutes looking for the right topic. Ralphie did not really have an opinion about what Jax was saying. He rarely did. He just listened.

"You going to the center tonight," Jax asked as he reached the top of W.E.B. DuBois Court. Standing at the corner Ralphie looked up at the sign that read: Lewis Latimer Drive. The two boys studied each other for a moment. Ralphie always felt weird when Jax got quiet. He never knew what was on the quirky boy's mind.

"Think so," Ralphie said.

There was a lull in the conversation.

"You know the design of the Gathering Center was supposed to be a corkscrew pyramid but somehow the plans got mixed up and they began digging instead of building."

"Jax, you know that is not true," Ralphie chuckled.

"I saw it on the Interweb," Jax recalled as if that was enough to answer all questions.

Ralphie twisted his lips as if fighting the urge to respond.

"I'll message you and we can meet up," Jax suggested.

"Okay," Ralphie said and Jax turned on his heels and began walking down W.E.B. DuBois Street toward his home. Ralphie stood and watched Jax walking away. He laughed absently. "You know that you cannot trust 50% of what is floating on the Interweb."

Jax gave Ralphie a thumbs up and walked on toward his house.

Ralphie turned and ran toward Tee and caught up. She looked at him oddly.

"You know that he didn't mean anything by what he said," Ralphie attempted.

"You don't have to do that," Tee replied.

"Do what?"

"Defend him," Tee noted. "He is wrong for how he treats me," Tee concluded.

Ralphie opened and closed his mouth without words.

Tee studied Ralphie. The pair continued walking down Lewis Latimer Avenue. Ralphie shook his head and kept walking. After a minute or so he looked up and found Tee looking at him. Tee smiled mischievously at Ralphie but did not say anything.

"How did you and Zeke get together?"

"I don't know," Tee smiled sheepishly. In that moment, there was a hint of the girl that Ralphie had met when he first arrived in the Miller compound. "I think that he was there when I was down. He is … constant. He is … consistent."

Ralphie played with the idea of trying to say something snarky to Tee. He thought better of the idea and walked on, Tee just a few steps in front.

As he walked, he watched as Tee entered the Sean Carter Estates and she seemed to exhale and relax. Ralphie did not say anything about her change. Instead, he studied the pristine streets that his father and his company had built. Ralphie smiled absently at the fact that his father and his company had constructed most of the Remains and much of the 31 square mile Miller compound.

As a result, his father was a Remains celebrity. His family, the Reynolds, were the main builders of the Remains. Ralphie did not think of himself or his family as powerful. They lived comfortably but not lavishly. Ralphie knew that his father was influential. He did not wield the power that an Innovator might, but his word and name was significant.

His father's business took Ralphie and his sister to four of the seven compounds. Benjamin O. Davis Reynolds had been able to work outside of the Miller compound for several years. Ralphie had returned to the Millers compound after a short stay in three other compounds and upon his return met up with Tee and Jax and Zeke, in that order.

Life, in the Miller compound, was unique compared to other lines. The Millers believed in hard work and family. They worked hard to ensure that their families were well cared for. They lived for their families and worked to secure whatever their families needed.

Other lines believed in family, but none made family the ultimate prize of work like the Millers. Others valued work, but none saw it as a means to an end of a happy family like the Millers. The Millers were unique onto themselves in that sense.

So, the Pandemonium Challenge, which offered family celebrity and line fame was embraced by the Millers. It, the challenge, was seen as the ultimate sacrifice for family in the Miller line. It was also seen as the conclusion of a process that would cement the intentions of those brave enough to register and participate in the challenge in the memories of the Miller line.

Yet, there were some that entered the challenge for selfish reasons. Some had lofty motives and aspirations. There were some that announced they were entering the challenge because they were uninterested in conforming to the strictures of the Remains and the rules and regulations imposed on all the residents by the enforcers. Those bad boys that thumbed their collective noses at the laws of the Remains never went far in the challenge.

Ralphie Reynolds thought all of this silently as he walked with Tee toward his home. He could not say that he had an agenda. At fifteen, Ralphie Reynolds just wanted to be famous, legendary, and a name in the Remains, like his father. He longed for celebrity, but at fifteen was not sure that he would ever gain the success or fame that he so desired.

Chapter Five.

Preparing for the inevitable.

The June before the Twenty-Third Pandemonium Challenge, Ralphie began to gain line fame. He never got comfortable with the attention, but he tolerated it. The biggest change of mind for Ralphie was that he wanted to go to the challenge with no regrets. He decided, in May, to invite and dance with Bailey Beaumont at Juneteenth. Like Jax, Ralphie had hopes before he went to the challenge. In his mind, if he was to go to the challenge, he was going having danced with the most beautiful girl in the Remains.

It was his reason for going to the Gathering Center a few weeks before the Juneteenth. He planned to run into Bailey at the Gathering Center and invite her to one of the Juneteenth nightly dances. It seemed an easy task.

The easy task had many parts to accomplish. Ralphie had to figure out a reason to ditch Jax and Zeke, who he always went with to Juneteenth. He would say that he was busy. Everyone always used that excuse. Everyone was always busy. Ralphie figured that missing one day of the five would not be a big deal to his friends. They would understand. He just had to time it so that they did not get too suspicious.

He had to lay the groundwork with Bailey. He knew her already. They had become friends when he lived in the First Gen compound with his mother and father. He had been there with his father working on a First Gen redevelopment. Bailey and Ralphie had sort of hit it off after a bumpy start with the line toughs Emmett, Wild Bill and Mouse.

Bailey had saved Ralphie when Emmett and his crew had locked him in a dumpster just to be mean. Bailey was always around after that incident. She was Ralphie's friend. So, a week before Juneteenth, he messaged Bailey and quite casually asked: "Are you going to the center tonight? Me and a few friends will be there. Message me, if you are."

Bailey Beaumont finally responded nearly sixty minutes later. Ralphie beamed. She said: "I will be there, around eight. Message me if you get there earlier."

A few hours later, Ralphie met up with Jax and Zeke and headed to the Gathering Center to people watch and for Ralphie to secretly, accidentally, to make a date with Bailey Beaumont, the First Gen. Ralphie, always taciturn, did not tell anyone his plans, despite Jax and Zeke being his closest friends. They went to the Gathering Center on a Saturday evening much like they did every Saturday and noticed that there were a lot of boys and girls walking around the five story Gathering Center.

"What gives," complained Zeke, never one to enjoy crowds.

Jax looked around curiously. His dark eyes scanned the interior of the always busy Gathering Center. On each floor there were Trads, Poppies, First Gens and Second Gens dressed in their distinctive line colors and in small packs of boys and girls. The Trads were dressed in their black and white signature colors. The Poppies were dressed in the paint splattered bright colors of yellow, green, red and blue. The Gens were dressed in black and blue. The First Gens were defined by their Goddess Minerva running through their clothing. The Second Gens wore for their bear dominated designed hoodies. There were, here and there, the occasional Boomer dressed in blue and green camo. The Millers, Ralphie, Jax and Zeke were dressed in their distinctive black hoodies that had Millers stenciled and stitched on their sleeves. On the back of the hoodies were the Miller claw hammer and chainsaw with the Latin terms: *Tempora mutantur, nos et mutamur in illis.*

"Suppose that it has to do with Juneteenth or the challenge," Jax asked.

Zeke furrowed his brow.

"What? Why?"

"Juneteenth," Jax decided.

"You going," Zeke asked no one in particular.

Ralphie lowered his eyes.

Jax teased.

"What's that mean," Zeke asked. They were walking around the top floor of the Gathering Center. There were dozens of boys and girls mulling around the Gathering Center.

"Of course," Jax smirked.

Ralphie remained silent.

"What about you, Ralphie," Jax asked Ralphie.

Ralphie seemed shocked to hear his name. He looked up as if he had been woken unexpectedly. Ralphie pursed his lips.

"You going?"

"Not sure," Ralphie lied. Ralphie thought as he pushed through the crowd of pre-teens gathered at the entrance to one of the stores in the Gathering Center. Jax and Zeke were all smiles and shaking their heads.

"How you not sure? We always go to Juneteenth. Everyone goes to Juneteenth."

Ralphie was going to make up something when they walked up to a knot of kids craning to see something that held their attention.

"What's going on?"

"Two pin heads decided to get bully, and numbers are kicking them out," someone near Ralphie blurted.

"Numbers" was slang for enforcers. The enforcers were the Remains law enforcement presence. They were everywhere that people gathered. The enforcers were incredibly trained men and women that protected the Remains from within and without. Within the Remains the enforcers patrolled compounds and quelled any violent situation.

The enforcers were given a broad discretion to shoot or leak anyone they deemed dangerous. They rarely discharged their weapons, preferring to engage most violent individuals in hand-to-hand combat. Enforcers rarely discharged their weapons in the Remains. That was just something that never happened. What was more frequent was seeing an enforcer using hand-to-hand combat. No one in the Miller challenge group had seen an enforcer lose against an opponent using hand-to-hand combat. They were expert grapplers and never backed down from a fight. Enforcers losing was like seeing a hippogriff or unicorn on the same day. Their training made them masters of handholds, arm bars, finger locks and the like. Few that faced an enforcer got the best of them.

Two of the boys were dressed in the bright yellow of the Second Gens. The other two boys were dressed in the white and black of the Trads. All four boys had their wrists zip tied. Around them, foaming at the mouth, and growling were nearly twenty plus kids, not more than fourteen arguing, screaming and complaining.

"You know that there is no physical violence in the Gathering Center. No charges are being levied toward either of you, this time. Your names and pictures have been recorded and if any other hijinks occur then you will be banned from the Gathering Center for two weeks and your parents will be notified," one of the numbers was saying, but Ralphie could not see the number though they all pretty much looked alike. They were all dressed in matte black uniforms with a name plate over their heart that instead of a name had a number. They wore combat boots, military fatigues, web belts, gun belts, a sidearm and in some cases, in the streets of the Remains, carried assault weapons.

Ralphie pushed his way in and came face-to-face with one of the two enforcers bracing the four boys that had thought they could bend the rules. The enforcer was a little taller than Ralphie and that made that enforcer short comparatively. Ralphie was only five foot five inches tall. Most enforcers were six feet tall, at a minimum, Ralphie noted. The small stature of the enforcer suggested that she was a woman. The woman enforcer glared at Ralphie and he, instinctually, stepped back. She turned her attention back to the four boys.

"You are prohibited from coming to the Gathering Center for seven days," the taller enforcer declared turning on his heels and heading back into the Gathering Center.

"They were playing," someone in the small group of kids complained.

"Yeah, and I am the king of Siam," the smaller enforcer had a sharp chin and replied as she pushed through the crowd that had gathered, the boys in tow.

The crowd followed. Ralphie and Jax followed too, pulled along with the crowd. The taller enforcer pushed through the crowd as if the teens were not there. He had a bit of a scraggly salt and pepper beard.

"Have a good night," the smaller enforcer said snipping off the zip ties of the two boys she controlled. The boys rubbed at their wrists and stared at the smaller enforcer as her partner unzipped the other two boys.

"Adios muchachos," the taller enforcer rubbed at his cheek as he announced to the two boys he had released. The boys walked away sullenly. Their friends mulled around as the crowd slowly returned to the Gathering Center. The enforcers returned to the Gathering Center as well.

Ralphie and Jax were near the two enforcers as they turned and returned to the Gathering Center. Jax pointed to the two enforcers and made a few hand signals. Zeke looked left and right and nodded. Jax reached out and pulled Ralphie along with him and Zeke. Jax, Zeke and Ralphie walked near the enforcers and overheard their conversation.

"I hate this time of year," the taller enforcer noted.

"Yeah, they need to start the challenge," the shorter enforcer added.

"Don't I know it," the taller enforcer agreed.

"Of course, the problem is that Juneteenth hasn't happened yet," the smaller enforcer breathed.

"Diggity, diggity, dee zam," the taller of the two spat.

"Hey, watch your potty mouth. The impressionable are near," the shorter enforcer chortled and laughed. The two enforcers shared a laugh.

"All I'm saying is, the sooner the better," the taller enforcer croaked as he pushed through the crowd of onlookers and into the center proper. The pair walked east and were headed toward the ramp that led to the second floor.

On the ramp, with Ralphie and Jax in tow, the two enforcers stopped briefly in front of a boy who was dressed in a paint splattered sweatshirt. Zeke and Jax made faces at each other and behind the backs of the enforcers. Ralphie just walked with his friends knowing that they were playing a dangerous game with two dangerous enforcers.

The Poppy had short nappy hair and a carved design in his head that resembled a lightning bolt in his temple fade. He could not have been more than twelve or thirteen. On his shoulder was a clock design patch.

"You Poppies do not usually come to the center," the enforcer noted.

"Looking for inspiration," the dark brown Poppy explained.

Jax stepped forward and abreast with the smaller enforcer. He smiled a little uneasily at the enforcer. The enforcer slowed a step to take in Jax.

"Hey, you guys know where all the bodies are buried. Right? You should be able to tell us one or two secrets," Jax mentioned out of nowhere.

The smaller enforcer stopped and did not speak. On her web belt were the seemingly endless zip ties. There was a flashlight on the belt as well. On the enforcer's right thigh was a handgun holster and handgun.

The taller of the two enforcers turned and studied the three boys near them. Jax was dressed in a Miller hooded sweatshirt, jeans and combat boots. He stepped forward to the shorter of the enforcers.

"What you want, Miller?"

"Want to know if there are werewolves in the Remains," Jax announced as if that was a normal question.

The enforcer looked at Jax and grinned. The second, taller, enforcer, looked at Jax as if he had grown another head. He shook his head and laughed at the question. The taller enforcer walked to the railing and looked over as the other enforcer dealt with Jax.

"There is a video floating on the Interweb of a werewolf sighting in one of the lines, but no one is confirming or denying it," Jax noted. He quickly added, "There are rumors that they have been spotted up north."

"We are enforcers, kid," the woman enforcer explained calmly. "We are not werewolf hunters. If there were werewolves in the Remains, it would be our responsibility to get rid of them or to make everyone aware of it because they would present a concern for the general public."

"I'm not hearing a yes or a no," Jax noted.

"Kid, there are no werewolves in the Remains. There are no hair sprouting, human transforming wolf boys or girls in the Remains," the enforcer with the narrow chin stated emphatically.

"What about the video?"

Zeke nudged Ralphie and Ralphie and he broke away from Jax and his interrogation of the enforcers. Zeke shook his head. He and Ralphie walked on, bored by the werewolf conversation.

"That's your friend," Ralphie announced, looking back and seeing Jax notice that he and Zeke had left him.

"He's your friend," Zeke laughed.

Jax ran and shouldered into the two boys that had abandoned him.

"How you two going to desert me?"

"We figured that you had some hard-hitting questions you needed answered and wanted to give you your privacy," Ralphie attempted.

"You suppose to have my back," Jax scolded to Zeke and Ralphie.

"We did," Zeke chuckled.

"Far back," Ralphie chuckled.

Jax smirked at the two comedians before him.

They were suddenly on the second floor and near the railing. Jax and Zeke giggled and pointed at a group of boys. Ralphie looked up and around to see that he was in front of a retail store that sold trendy girl clothes. There were several mannequins in the store window portraying a scene that resembled dancing. Ralphie was going to mention the display to Jax and Zeke but they were near the ramp heading to the next floor.

He pushed away from the storefront window and looked left and right, scanning for Bailey. Ralphie figured he would message her when they went to the food court. At the food court he could sneak away and message Bailey without causing too much concern.

On the second-floor kids gathered and started to joke about lines. It was one of the easiest ways to start a fight.

"Keep moving," another enforcer, a tall coffee brown man with a beard, growled from behind his face guard to the pre-teens, between teens and teens that had gathered on the second floor and were making faces at one another.

"I don't have time for this," a square jawed enforcer growled as he appeared next to the first enforcer. The impatient enforcer stepped forward and into the midst of the crowd. The pre-teens were the first to scatter. The between teens moved away from the enforcer as if he had a contagious disease. The teens, full of angst and self-righteousness, were the last to move. The teens shot the enforcers their most indignant looks as they moved from the spot where the enforcer had situated himself.

"Enforcer brutality," someone dared and in response there was a smattering of giggles as the teens moved as if they were land turtles.

Ralphie could only shake his head at the pack of pre-teens who scattered and regrouped at another section of the Gathering Center. The between teens and teens just moved fast enough to stay ahead of the enforcers. It was a Gathering Center game that the pre-teens, between teens and teens played with the enforcers.

"Hey, gear heads shove off," called 1293, one of the enforcers. The enforcers talked into their microphones and immediately an enforcer on the third level was in motion.

"Let's go see what old-time movie is playing downstairs," Zeke advised.

Jax shrugged his shoulders in response. Ralphie looked from the smaller groups of between teens and teens and turned and followed Jax and Zeke. The boys quick walked away from the scene, ahead of the curious enforcer. The enforcer paused at the small crowd and tried to ascertain what had happened. The three boys jumped on the stairway that led down to the third and lowest level of the gathering place.

The bottom of the Gathering Center was spacious despite the corkscrew design. It, the center, was a cavernous and spacious property. There was a multiplex theater, a virtual gaming center, trampoline park and food court on the bottom of the Gathering Center. The food court was always busy and there were always plenty of people eating.

To the right of the food court was a virtual game stadium that allowed pre-teens, between teens and teens to compete against each other on the most popular games individually or in scheduled tournaments. To the right of the virtual game stadium was a smaller virtual reality arena to explore what remained of the post-flash world. To the right of the virtual reality arena was the three old fashioned movie theaters that allowed one hundred to sit in comfortable chairs and watch things that had not been seen in nearly a century. To the right of the three theaters there was a wall climb monitored by two enforcers.

Zeke and Jax headed directly to the movie theaters and stood and looked at the old-fashioned marquee that announced the movies available that night. There were six movies that had been big nearly one hundred years ago.

"Have you seen any of these movies?"

Jax studied the marquee. He scoffed at the selection.

"Shaft Returns Again Part Two is one of those black detective films that had been remade at least twenty times. This is the one about Shaft discovering that his sister is alive and in danger."

"Black Dynamite is a movie about this one-time cowboy outlaw who is pushed and pushed by a corrupt sheriff, once he returns home, and finds he has to fight enemies threatening some townspeople."

Ralphie shook his head. Ralphie had seen that movie with his father. He could not disagree with Jax's synopsis. What he remembered about the movie was that the man, did not want to fight but he had been forced to fight a corrupt crime boss for the safety of his family.

"Of them all, which one is good?"

"Probably, Hit Brother."

"What is that about?"

"It's about this kid who isn't afraid of nothing. He is an incredible fighter. He doesn't know much about his life. He is all alone and has amnesia," Jax recalled and shook his head. "It is really good."

"You want to see that again," Zeke asked.

Jax smiled ecstatically.

"Okay, if we are here when it plays, we should go check it out."

The next movie showing was thirty minutes away. So, Ralphie looked around and people watched.

"We can't just hang down here like some lowlife n'ar do wells," Zeke decided.

"What the H-E double hockey sticks is a n'ar do well," Jax asked.

"A criminal. An evil doer. A bad guy."

"Where do you get these words?"

Ralphie shook his head.

"The dictionary."

Ralphie could only smile at Zeke's response.

"I got to go shake hands with the mayor," Ralphie announced and separated from Jax and Zeke without another word. He headed toward the toilet. Before entering the toilet, he messaged Bailey.

Being on the lowest level of the Gathering Center and with all the activities, there were always groups of pre-teens, between teens and teens from all the other factions mingling. Ralphie watched the passing lines and recalled that he had gone to most of the compounds with his father as a child. He had been to the Poppies compound when he was four or five, at five he had been a part of the First Gens compound until he was nine, at six he had been to the Second Gen compound, for half a year he had been in the Trads compound which surprised him the most for its austere design and starkness and the Millers compound, where he had been since he was nine-years-old.

"Let's go back up to the second floor until the movie is about to start," Zeke suggested.

With no objections the three trekked back to the second floor of the Gathering Center. On the second floor of the Gathering Center Zeke and Jax positioned themselves on the balcony of the three-story inverted social entertainment area. They liked the vantage point of the second balcony for it afforded them the view of the girls' activity center. Zeke and Jax could not see much but they did not need to see much to giggle and elbow each other knowingly. They belly laughed and pointed at the girls' activity center where they could see groups of girls entering a curtained entrance.

The girls' activity center was hidden behind a high curtain that only allowed anyone to see who was entering. For Zeke and Jax that was enough. They leaned on the railing and made faces like maniacs and joked to themselves about the girls entering the center.

Ralphie bored of the winks, faces and things that Zeke and Jax rained down on the unsuspecting girls, people watched. Ralphie liked the Gathering Center for just the diversity of faces assembled. At any time, there might be a First Gen walking near a Trad or a Poppy creating some art piece for the center with a bunch of lines watching. The Gathering Center was friendly and dedicated to everyone in the Remains under the age of eighteen.

Looking at Jax and Zeke ogling the girls one floor below Ralphie had to make some decisions. He did not want to be associated with Jax and Zeke's shenanigans, but he did not want to be that far removed from them, just in case they went to see Hit Brother. So, Ralphie looked for a bench to sit on and people watch and wait for Zeke and Jax to become bored with their antics. Ralphie knew that he did not possess a higher level of maturity. He just did not find ogling girls, that he did not know, exciting in anyway.

He sat on the nearby bench and started to fish out his phone when Bailey Beaumont appeared by his side. She was all honeysuckles, freckles, big eyes, wide smile next to him. In a flash, Ralphie felt uncomfortable and thought to move away but fought his immediate response. He liked Bailey up close and so near to him. It was a strange feeling but one that he could get used to, he imagined.

"You been waiting long?"

"Waiting," Ralphie asked, being coy.

"Yeah, don't play with me Ralphie," Bailey smiled coquettishly, and her big deer eyes sparkled like the sun on the water before sunset.

"No. We got here a few minutes ago. The numbers are not taking any lip," Ralphie admitted.

"What happened?"

"They tossed out a couple of Trads and Second Gens," Ralphie noted.

"What happened?"

"Don't know really. We walked up and they were getting tossed out," Ralphie admitted.

Bailey nodded. "Well, I'm here with some friends, but wanted to see you, since you were here," Bailey smiled coyly, leaning on Ralphie just a little.

Ralphie liked Bailey's touch. She was this brilliant girl dressed in black motorcycle boots, black jeans, blue and gold hooded sweatshirt. On her earlobes were two golden 1G earrings. Bailey seemed so put together but without a made-up feeling.

There was a natural pause and Ralphie found himself just looking at Bailey. He studied her and could not see any flaws in this beauty. Her braided hair was pulled back into a tight ponytail of braids with two braids loose on either side of her heart-shaped face.

"Well, I suppose that I'll--" Bailey began, uncertain what to do.

"Wait," Ralphie said, suddenly panicky. It was now or never he decided. Bailey was standing and Ralphie was climbing to his feet to talk. He had a whole speech he had composed in his head but now all those words were gone. The words he had planned to say deserted him in the presence of Bailey Beaumont.

Bailey Beaumont looked at Ralphie and Ralphie knew that he had to say something, anything. Bailey Beaumont smiled awkwardly. She was so patient, Ralphie noted.

"I was wondering," he began, a little timidly. "I was wondering if you are going to Juneteenth?" He plodded on unsure of what he was going to say. "If you are going, maybe we can go together."

Bailey narrowed her eyes, studying Ralphie. Ralphie continued on, despite his fear that she might say: no.

"If you and me are going together, maybe we can go to the dance one night," Ralphie said and suddenly his hands were clammy. He swallowed hard. He was so close to finishing saying all the words that made sense and he wanted to finish strong. He took a deep breath to finish. "I would love to dance with you," Ralphie admitted. He had laid all his cards on the table. It was suddenly up to Bailey.

Ralphie found that he could not look at the girl that he joked with moments before. He looked up from the tile flooring and stopped at Bailey's knees. He took another breath and saw her delicate fingers intertwined in front of her. Ralphie tried to look at Bailey but could not. Instead he discovered that he was only able to look at the hooded zip front sweatshirt that had the goddess Minerva across the left side of the fabric. Ralphie could not lift his eyes from the round shoulders of the girl that he had just invited to Juneteenth. He looked down to the ground and toed the tile.

"Why aren't you looking at me?"

Ralphie looked up. Bailey was smiling. She tilted her head the way that allowed her big eyes to seem even bigger.

"I'm looking."

"I'll see you the second night and maybe we can dance a little," Bailey smiled timidly and turned on her heels. She walked away slowed and looked easily over her shoulder ever so briefly. She waved and turned back and continued on without looking back.

Ralphie watched Bailey walk away and felt his face warm. He had not been turned down. He had made a date with the prettiest girl in the Remains and she had not turned him down. It was his lucky day, Ralphie told himself.

Bailey ran to her girlfriends and turned a corner on the second floor and disappeared. Ralphie stood, smiling, thinking about all that had transpired. He was replaying the conversation when he heard the sound of someone raising their voice. Ralphie turned slowly and found that there was a group of people loosely grouped in the area where Ralphie had left Jax and Zeke.

"Hey, pervs, I'm going to get an enforcer to beat the breath out of you," one of the girls wearing a Second Gen light blue Apple Mac hooded sweatshirt with computer chips spelling out Second Gen along the arm announced. "For being pervs."

Jax was the first to react.

"Fish ain't supposed to talk," Jax barked.

"What did you say to me?"

"Again, it ain't natural for a fish to talk." Jax chided to the handful of boys and girls near. He never looked at the girl who was talking to him. "Maybe, you one of those robot fish?"

The girl with a black and white braided bun and dark eyes poked out her lip. She stared death and destruction at Jax, Zeke and Ralphie.

"Are you going to go all Super Sayan him, Tina," one of the girls that were close to the black and white braided girl said. Ralphie noted that there were two girls flanking the more talkative girl. One of the girls, the second to talk, the rounder of the two, was the color of white sand with glasses and midnight black braided hair, pulled back in a scrunchie, held seventy or eighty plus finger thin braids in a ponytail. She was wearing combat boots, jeans and her Eureka! Apple Mac orange hoody.

The other girl was taller than the other two and had thick arched eyebrows and a slightly piggish nose. Her hair was a fall of loose curls that framed her pie shaped face. She was dressed in the original Eureka! Apple Mac yellow hoody that had Second Gen written down the side of the right arm in embroidered computer circuitry. The girl in the braided bun put her hand on her hip and poked out her lower lip.

"Are you upset that we ain't looking at you?" Jax growled at the idea. Jax was a bit of a loudmouth. He was always talking about what he was going to do. His mouth always got him in trouble.

"Pervy weirdos," the girl with the braided bun challenged.

Jax, never one to back down to people that he imagined weaker than him, barked back.

"Fish you better swim back to your circuit board before you get beaten down by a Miller hammer," Jax growled.

"What you saying, handsaw?"

"I'm saying fish need to be in the water or they start to stink," Jax shot back.

The girl, Jax was directing his venom toward, rolled her eyes. A small crowd of pre-teens and tweens had gathered, all at once interested in the free entertainment.

The stick thin girl with the braided bun balled her fists and took a step toward Jax. Jax showed his teeth and stepped back.

"You know my mama taught me not to fight girls," Jax lied looking for an exit.

"What about me?"

Granville Summer, the Second Gen bad boy, pushed through the crowd and reached out to grab a handful of Jax. Granville Summer was a well-built caramel skinned boy with dark eyes and a crown of black twists on his blockhead. Jax reacted, a little shocked it seemed, shooting two misguided punches toward Granville Summer's outstretched arm. Summer brushed the two feeble punches away, like gnats, and closed the distance like a boy used to fighting.

Granville Summer dressed in a Eureka! Apple Mac blue hoody gritted his teeth and drove Jax toward the railing before he launched one rocket of a punch into Jax's face. The punch sent Jax sprawling into the appreciative and watching crowd bleeding. The one punch had Jax leaking from his wide and flat nose.

The screams of appreciation from the bored teens were loud and sudden. The crowd seemed to be waiting for something to happen that night. Jax getting clocked by Granville Summer was just the release that the pre-teens, tweens and teens seemed to desire. Ralphie had not been alive during the Roman gladiator times but he imagined this was how the crowds had to be back then.

Zeke jumped in and in front of Granville Summer and broke Ralphie's thoughts of the Roman empire. Zeke was the Millers labeled "bad boy" and was a muscular tween, just months from turning sixteen. Zeke fashioned himself as a backyard brawler and liked to show off his well-honed skills whenever he could. Zeke and Granville Summer circled one another. Bad boy versus bad boy.

The crowd of pre-teens, tweens and teens let out a collective scream of delight at the possibility of two bad boys duking it out. It was one of those chance encounters that everyone wanted to see happen but never happened because of outside factors. The potential to view disaster was electric.

"End him, chainsaw," screamed one of the dozens of onlookers in the crowd in the Gathering Center.

"Shut that tool boy down," another voice directed at one of the bad boys.

"Millers murk all," called one of the dark girls in the crowd.

"Deuces über alles," sounded out of the crowd.

That was when Emmett Carson, the First Gen tough, leaped out of the crowd and threw a punch at Ralphie, and by instinct alone Ralphie blocked the knockout punch, spinning away from the attacker. Ralphie crouched as if he might jump into the air like Bruce Lee and kick Emmett Carson in the face.

Emmett Carson frowned at his failed attempt to knock Ralphie out. Behind Emmett stepped Wild Bill Fordham, another First Gen bad boy. Wild Bill Fordham was a well-built an oval faced red boned boy with curly russet brown hair. He had dark eyes and cuts in his eyebrows as if he had been clawed by an animal.

"Black Superman," screamed someone from the crowd as Emmett balled his fists ready to attack anyone crazy enough to approach him.

The immediate brouhaha that followed was chaotic. The gathered three groups; Millers, Second and First Gen growled, and punches were thrown, lips busted, curses heard and unexpectedly there were three or four fights. It was instantaneous and explosive and the crowd that had initially gathered backed away to give the fighters room to maneuver.

Zeke was circling Granville Summers. Ralphie was measuring Emmett Carson. Harris Porter, a Trad, who had shown up out of nowhere, was squaring off with Wild Bill Fordham. These three fights kept the crowd of pre-teens, tweens and teens roaring for blood.

"You know drill bit, ever since I've seen your stupid face, I've wanted to punch the breath out of you." Emmett Carson grunted. "Your stupid face is… stupid," Emmett Carson added.

Ralphie showed his teeth at Emmett Carson and shook his head.

"You keep making bad decisions, pooper scooper."

"That's rude, One," Ralphie hissed at the well-built boy dressed in a First Gen hooded sweatshirt and faded blue jeans.

Emmett Carson's eyes became slits. Ralphie recoiled at the First Gen's reaction.

"What I do, One?"

"Looking at me with those stupid eyes," Emmett Carson smirked and stepped forward with his fast hands, big arms and big chest and launched into a fighting clinic. Emmett was a cool eyed character. He was a compact fighter who had boxing training. He was one of the Remains better fighters and never shy to show off his pugilistic skills.

Elbows in. One fist up by his ear and the other just in front of his face Emmett Carson marched forward, fearless. Right-left-right were the first combinations that Ralphie tried to fend off as Emmett began his barrage of fists and fists only.

Ralphie was no boxer but he knew how to fight. He blocked two of the three punches, but it was the one that he did not block that grazed his ear and drove him back into the anxious crowd of onlookers. The crowd threw Ralphie back at Emmett laughing and calling for blood.

"Knock his head off," screamed someone as Ralphie was thrown back at Emmett Carson who was crouched and ready for war. Emmett Carson smirked at Ralphie and prepared to tear into him when Ralphie received a reprieve.

The enforcers showed up and stopped Emmett Carson from beating Ralphie to a pulp. One enforcer put hands on Emmett Carson and for half a moment it appeared as if the teen was stronger than the enforcer. That moment ended with Emmett zip tied to a railing. Ralphie backpedaled. He thought that his eyes had deceived him. Not too many could best an enforcer. Before Ralphie could say anything, the enforcer had zip tied him to another railing, a safe distance from Emmett Carson.

"Tool boy, you got me in trouble," Emmett Carson fumed. Ralphie ignored the muscular boy's ranting.

In populated areas in the Remains the enforcers always broke up fights before they the really got started, to the disappointment of the bloodthirsty crowd. Four enforcers made nearly forty pre-teens, between tweens and teens scatter leaving the six bad boys zip tied against the Gathering railing.

"You know this ain't over screwdriver," Emmett Carson growled zip tied to the railing with the other boys. Zeke and Porter, the Trad, were between Ralphie and Emmett.

"You blind *and* stupid," Ralphie asked. "It is over and we're all in trouble and you keep bumping your gums and you'll be in more trouble." Ralphie shook his head at Emmett Carson. He had a history with the First Gen. Ralphie found that he could not help antagonizing the First Gen tough boy.

Ralphie tried to ignore the threats. They were meaningless. They were just nonsense.

"I'm going to break your arms and beat you with them," Emmett Carson steamed through clinched teeth.

"If you break my arms you won't be able to beat me with them. They will still be on my body, idiot," Ralphie pointed out.

Emmett Carson growled a deep guttural sound that was more beast than human. Ralphie was sure that Emmett was going to growl and howl, like a dog. He was so worked up.

"That guy might need to be tranquilized," Jax admitted to Ralphie from the railing. He was zip tied as well. Jax lifted his chin toward Emmett Carson and shook his head. He was zip tied but sitting on the Gathering Center floor recovering from Wild Bill Fordham's punch.

"I think that he might need to be tested for brain damage, really," Ralphie said to Jax and Zeke.

"He probably ate lead paint as a baby," Jax laughed.

"Brain damage," Zeke laughed.

Jax chuckled at that.

"Ate? He probably still eating lead paint," Ralphie laughed.

"Okay, Fight Club," enforcer 5309 smirked, cuffing the three Millers together and walking them toward the exit of the Gathering Center. "You know the drill."

Enforcer 3871 had the others zip tied together. The three others looked dejected. Heads down and embarrassed.

At the exit the two enforcers, and that was all that it took to corral and control the six boys that had fought on the second floor of the Gathering Center, took their names and photos. Granville Woods Summer, Wild Bill Fordham and Emmett Carson were under the supervision of the taller and wider enforcer 3871. Zeke, Jax, and Ralphie were under the supervision of the shorter enforcer 5309.

The two enforcers took all the boys' information and made sure that it was correct. Each line had different forms of identification. The Millers had dog tags. The First Gens had wearable technology that was used as identification. For the boys and girls, they wore finger rings. For all Second Gens their identification was the shiny badges that harkened back to pre-flash police, given to them in their educational facility. In the Trads, they all possessed Lady Justice pins. Poppies had wearable tech, similar to the First Gens. For the Poppies they wore a shoulder located, clock face patch, designed by one of the Poppies. In the Boomers, Ralphie had noticed, they too had rings. The Boomer rings though were silver, and Redwood focused with wolf designs on them. Ralphie had no idea what the Makers used for identification since they did not come to the Gathering Center, ever.

"You know that all your shenanigans are being uploaded to the cloud. Your parents are receiving a copy of your activities tonight. We are banning you for a week, seven days, to cool off. If you return to the property, for any reason, we will have you detained," 5309 explained from behind his face guard.

"Damn. There goes my chance for a Christmas present," snarled Jax.

Ralphie thought absently that he should have swung on an enforcer. Swinging on an enforcer never ended well for the person that swung. The enforcers were trained super soldiers, Ralphie mused. The fights with enforcers went one of two ways. The first way was that the enforcer dodged the punch and then proceeded to stomp the aggressor into submission. After that they would put the aggressor in jail. The second way was worse. The enforcer would react and dodge the punch or not but for some reason the enforcer lost their mind and did not just stomp the aggressor but dismantled the aggressor. In the Remains, kids called that "chopping down trees," and the enforcers were no joke when they decided to "chop down trees."

Ralphie preferred being stomped and put in jail to what awaited him at home. It was just another level of torture to Ralphie before going to the challenge. His mother and father would be waiting for him to read him the riot act. Ralphie all of a sudden wanted to never go home.

At the exit the enforcers stood watching, not judging.

"You know that the Gens started this," Ralphie complained before he could stop himself.

Emmett Carson cut his eyes at Ralphie.

"The sawdust boys began all this with their pervy ways," Granville Summer countered. "They called my sister a fish."

"If the fish fits," Jax whispered to Zeke and Ralphie and the two boys snorted despite the seriousness of the situation.

"We don't care who started this. It don't matter. All we care about is that you were being unruly," the smaller enforcer expressed with the badge that read: 2963.

The enforcers read the spiel that everyone that fought in the Gathering Center heard. There were just two enforcers controlling the six boys that had decided to disrupt the peace of the youth center. Ralphie stared at Emmett Carson, Wild Bill and Grantville Summers. The others divided their attention between Ralphie, Zeke and Jax.

"You are prohibited from coming to the Gathering Center for seven days," 2963 explained turning on his heels and heading back into the Gathering Center.

At the entrance to the Gathering Center the six boys stared at each other for a long moment. Granville Summers was the first to move. He headed toward the north and his compound without a word.

That left Emmett and Wild Bill staring down Jax, Zeke and Ralphie. Jax was the first to antagonize the First Gen boys by sticking out his tongue.

"Trowel boy, you just made my list," Emmett Carson exploded in a near scream. Wild Bill held him back.

"Can you get me a brand-new shiny bike," Jax giggled and slipped behind Zeke and Ralphie, smiling all the while.

"Think that I'm going to tear off your head and piss down your neck," Emmett Carson snapped.

"Calm down, One," Ralphie advised as Zeke stepped forward. Ralphie was not surprised by the move. Zeke did not back down from a fight. He had big arms and a big chest and a perpetual smirk on his face.

"Let's go, man," Wild Bill advised. "The enforcers are not going to let anything happen, anyway."

"You get a break tonight, wrench monkeys," Emmett Carson grumbled pushing Wild Bill away from him effortlessly.

"Oh, we get a break," Jax mocked, poking out his lower lip.

"This ain't over," Emmett fumed pointing back at Jax and the others. Emmett and Wild Bill reluctantly turned and started to walk away from the Millers and the Gathering Center.

Emmett Carson and Wild Bill Fordham walked east toward the Gen compound, finally. Jax and Zeke slowly turned and began their walk back to the Foundry. The two groups of boys were headed in different directions. At a distance from each other Jax turned and screamed the following:

"Ones open mouth kiss giant skunk rats!"

Emmett and Wild Bill turned around and stared daggers at Jax. Jax made faces and ran to catch up with Zeke and Ralphie. The two bigger boys just shook their heads at Jax.

"You know that in a couple of weeks they will be gunning for you?"

"Doubt it," chuckled Jax as he waved back at Emmett and Wild Bill who decided to keep walking the opposite direction of the three Millers. "They will be worrying about all sorts of other problems and not thinking about me calling them out about trying to make babies with giant cat rats."

"Insults have a way of coming back on you," Ralphie admitted.

Zeke nodded.

"Well, if they come for me or not it doesn't matter. We will be in the challenge and Remains famous." Jax concluded.

Ralphie smirked. He could not do anything else.

"You have a strange way of looking at things," Zeke laughed.

"What? We all have expiration dates. If I stirred up something or not, who cares?" Jax peered into the dark, in the direction where Emmett Carson and Wild Bill Russell Fordham had walked. "Maybe we have an enemy," Jax noted.

"*We* don't have an enemy," Zeke began. "As far as I can tell *you* made an enemy and Ralphie just renewed a fight that has been a long time coming," Zeke croaked.

Ralphie nodded.

"We are all going to the challenge and we can settle it there," Jax pointed out.

"Yeah, but you suddenly have a target on your back," Zeke pointed out.

"It's the challenge, Zeke. Everyone's going to have a target on their back until somebody wins," Ralphie pointed out.

"Yeah, you right," Zeke agreed.

Jax hooked his arms around Ralphie and Zeke's shoulders. "If those robo-heads want us, they have to get in line. Everyone will be gunning for us."

"Us," Zeke questioned unhooking Jax's arm. He looked at Jax. "You the one that insulted them."

"Aw, okay. You think that if I apologize, then they will be my friends," Jax asked with a wry smile, adding quickly, "They look like they are the types that would accept a hardy apology."

Ralphie and Zeke shook their heads and shoved Jax ahead of them.

That same night, as the trio walked back to the Miller compound, they received this notification.

"Pandemonium Challenge release first fifteen videos of 23rd Annual challengers. Included in the first batch of videos are the highly anticipated Innovator, three Artists, one Trad, two Millers, three Boomers, three First Gens and two Second Gens."

Ralphie read the notification.

"Two Millers," Jax noted. Ralphie's heart fell into the pit of his stomach at Jax's words. He looked at Jax who was smiling like a jack-o-lantern. Zeke had scrunched up his dark face with the notification. Ralphie did not say anything.

"I hope that it's me and you Zeke," Jax confessed. "They need to know what they are about to face. Brains and brawn. Or might and fight. Or something."

Zeke smirked and looked back again toward the First Gens and the Gathering Center. Ralphie shook his head and tried to smile, knowing what he was heading toward. He should have punched an enforcer. At least, hitting an enforcer was a dead certainty: beatdown and then imprisonment.

The electronic notice, that had been sent by the enforcers not 45 minutes earlier, waited for Ralphie in the hand of his unsympathetic mother. She was dressed in a yellow onesie of a cartoon character with an orange belly and matching furry house slippers. The outfit made his mother look like she might be in her twenties. But the look on his mother's face was not smiling. Ralphie scanned his mother's face for telltale signs that she was angry. If her toasted brown eyes were thinned it meant that she was not in a joking mood. If she was biting at her lower lip it meant, nine times out of ten that she was trying to figure out things. If his mother's nose flared, Ralphie knew, it was a signal that she was at the end of her rope and likely to scream or shout.

"Ralphie, I know that you are about to go to the challenge, but we did not raise and sacrifice for you and your sister to have you become a hooligan and hang out with criminals," Ralphie's mother said, her cinnamon brown eyes thin and nearly imperceptible. Bad sign. "You are fifteen and nothing is promised to you," she said as her brown eyes narrowed. "We know that we cannot watch over you 24/7," she admitted without biting her lower lip. Ralphie knew that the outcome, whatever it was, had already been decided.

"We have to trust that you can make good choices." Mae Reynolds paused and took a deep breath. Ralphie studied his mother's face and noted that her bay brown nose was not flared. At least he had that going for him, Ralphie concluded. "If tonight is any indication of your decision making, I am disappointed in your choices." There was no joking with his mother, Ralphie knew. "Go to your room, Ralphie. It's late. We will discuss this further in the morning."

Ralphie looked around and did not see anyone else in the front room but did not argue. He knew that his mother was not going to include him in the decision of his formal punishment. The "we" she was referring to was her and Ralphie's father. In the end, all things being equal, Ralphie knew there was no point in arguing with his mother. She would not listen to argument. She was all business and that did not bode well for Ralphie, Ralphie knew. If he had any chance of reprieve it would come from his father.

He left his mother and climbed the stairs toward his bedroom and noted the six framed pictures on the wall of the stairway. At the bottom, or closest to the bottom, was a picture of Benjamin and Mae Reynolds on their wedding day. His father, who looked like he was carved from wood, was dressed in a white dinner jacket, dark blue bow tie, white tuxedo shirt and golden floral boutonnière. His father was smiling and holding his bride. Ralphie's mother was this model with a gravity defying hairdo of raven black braids and curls and a string of diamond crystals pinned in a spiral atop her head. She was all big sepia brown, laughing eyes, a loving smile, long neck and a white bridal dress that seemed to go on forever. On her finger was a giant diamond ring. The next picture, just a few steps from the first, was a picture of Ralphie and his mother and father all dressed in the dark blue Miller coveralls, goggles, gloves and giggles. The picture was distinctive for the Reynolds Construction sign over the gigantic pit and the beginnings of a construction site in the background with half a dozen cranes frozen in action. At least thirty men were busy behind them. Ralphie recalled that photograph had been taken in the First Gen compound when he had been, maybe, eight or nine.

The third picture on the stairwell was of Macy and Ralphie and their parents, again all dressed in the dark blue Miller coveralls, goggles, gloves and giggles. In that picture their father was holding his 21st Century Colt M1911 in hand. In the background there was forest and another Reynolds Construction sign near an excavation pit.

The fourth picture was a picture of his parents with Ralphie as a baby. The picture had to be while his mother was still in recovery. He could not be sure of the timing of the photograph but based on his father's smile and his mother's glow it had to be in the first few days of his birth.

The fifth picture was similar to the fourth but with his parents and Macy as a baby. There seemed to be a theme to the pictures, Ralphie noted. His picture had to be days after his birth and Macy's picture was probably around the same timeframe. Whoever the photographer they had an uncanny sense of timing and symmetry.

The last picture on the stairwell to the second floor of their home was of his father, his sister and Ralphie dressed again in Miller coveralls, goggles, gloves and laughing about something in his father's construction site office. In the background was a window that looked out and over another construction site. That picture was of when they lived in the First Gen compound when Ralphie was only nine. Macy was then only five, Ralphie recalled.

He walked past Macy's bedroom with the stenciled picture of the art of Banksy on her door and smiled. His bedroom was at the end of the hall, at the opposite end of the hall from his parent's bedroom. At the door he turned and looked back into the dark and silence.

Once in his bedroom, Ralphie quickly dressed for bed. He turned off the lights in the smallish room and before climbing into bed turned on his computer monitor. It was late and he did not feel like chatting with anyone. Besides Jax and Zeke were probably grounded. They would not be good company to talk with, that night. They would be stinging from their punishment levied on them by the numbers and their parents.

"Everything sleep mode," Ralphie breathed. "Wait, open challenge website."

The screen darkened except for a single, solitary window.

"Send sound to earbud. Send video to foot of bed. Also, expand Pandemonium Challenge," Ralphie intoned.

The computer monitor blinked and switched from the monitor hanging from the wall to the projected screen at the foot of Ralphie's bed. The sound crackled in Ralphie's right ear. The symphonic music on the website oozed out of the earbud. The computer simultaneously expanded the Pandemonium Challenge website on the projected screen.

"Show me the latest challenger videos," Ralphie ordered.

At once, the screen blinked, and the gallery of contesters' videos popped up. There were fifteen battler videos available. Ralphie noted that there were nearly forty adversary videos that were blacked out and in silhouette.

The fifteen-year-old knew that the Pandemonium Challenge committee was ingenious in their release of the videos. There had never been more than eight videos released each day. This year the website had unexpectedly released fifteen contestant videos in one day.

It was a real production. For a week the videos rolled out. Every release was scrutinized and compared to the other hopefuls. The odds makers studied the videos for any secret details that might indicate a strength of weakness.

The video cued up and began with this oval faced boy who Ralphie immediately forgot. He had blue highlights in his curly black hair. Ralphie did not know the boy but right away assumed he was a Poppy. Poppies were attention getters. They dressed differently. They wore their hair differently. They were artists. Ralphie despised Poppies. They spent too much time trying to be creative and important. There was always this feeling when around them that they were on the verge of discovering something that everyone had overlooked. It had been viewed 4,534 times already.

The second video and the second rival of the Pandemonium Challenge that Ralphie might face appeared on screen. He was a bug-eyed boy, the color of copper, with a crooked smile. Ralphie studied the boy and felt like he should know him. Was he a Boomer? Was he a First Gen? The boy was a round headed character with round cheeks which made him look like he was twelve. He had on a blue and green hoody that labeled him a Boomer, but the boy seemed shy. In his short history of meeting Boomers at the Gathering Center few Boomers were shy. Yet, at the end of the video, Ralphie thought that the boy's name was Marcus or Marvin. But Ralphie could not be 100% sure. The interview seemed so uninteresting. The video had been viewed by just 1,257 people.

The third video that Ralphie watched was the most viewed challenge video on the site, already. The video had nearly 100,000 views. It was a featured video. There was a lot of buzz about the video. Ralphie had to watch. Everyone had to watch. A Maker in the challenge was news.

Ella Fitzgerald Buchanan's name was superimposed on a black screen. The screen faded in on the almond brown girl with the diamond shaped face and the enormous eyes looking into the screen. She was dressed in a buttery colored jacket that had a bear's head peaking over her shoulder. Ella Fitzgerald Buchanan had thin arched eyebrows and a straight but wide nose. Around her neck, in the video, was a golden chain that ended in a bear charm. Though she was being interviewed for the Pandemonium Challenge, Ella Fitzgerald Buchanan seemed very comfortable.

"My name is Ella Buchanan," the Maker began and Ralphie could not believe that this rich girl from the richest line in the Remains had volunteered for the challenge. "I'm the daughter of Gordon Buchanan," Ella Buchanan smiled self-consciously a perfect set of pearly whites. "That Gordon Buchanan."

Gordon Buchanan was this incredibly influential individual who had come into his vast wealth by replacing and rewiring lighting in the Remains. He and his company had single-handedly brought light to the Remains. The thing that insured his family's wealth was that he had contracted with the Central Government for the twenty-five-year rights to maintenance and repair of all the lights installed on the streets and avenues. It literally locked the Central Government into a deal with Gordon Buchanan and his company for the next quarter century.

"Don't think I want typical superpowers." Ella Buchanan crinkled her almond brown nose. "I think that I want to have the power to influence, to be a rabble rouser."

Ella Buchanan tilted her diamond shaped head to the right and looked amused.

"If I was a superhero, I would be Lunella Lafayette. She is the Moon Girl from Moon Girl and Devil Dinosaur. I like that her superpowers are her intelligence. Lunella Lafayette, at nine, is incredibly smart and resourceful. She is supposed to be the smartest person in the world."

"Favorite color is red, black and green. Of course."

Ralphie grinned. Everyone in the Remains had to smile at Ella Buchanan's response despite the prominence of Blue and Gold throughout the California based Remains. Most of the teens silently fought for the nationalist colors mentioned by Ella.

"I would love to have met Oprah Winfrey and asked her how she persevered despite all the naysayers once she was wealthy."

Ralphie knew Ella Buchanan was the daughter of an influential who decided how many streetlights were in the Remains. As a result, Ella Buchanan and her family were filthy rich. She had no real cares or concerns. Did she even know what a naysayer was?

"Favorite thing to do is to video chat and hang out with friends."

The fifteen-year-old had wanted to put her in a gilded cage of privilege and excess but she seemed down-to-earth and a little bit of a badass. Ralphie sort of found himself not despising Ella Buchanan for some reason.

"I don't really think that I am a fighter in the sense that you are talking about. I am a rabble rouser. I stir stuff up. But, from my research, you don't have to be a fighter to win the challenge. I know a few winners that were not the biggest, toughest or meanest and walked away with the crown. So, don't count me out."

Ralphie found himself smiling, despite the wealth of Ella Buchanan and the Makers.

"I registered for the challenge on a dare, really. I wanted to figure out if the challenge really mattered in the Remains. I mean, there have only been two Makers to participate in the challenge in all this time. The two were not the best or brightest of the line. They embarrassed the line, actually. So, I decided to participate to show my family and line that for all the hand wringing and protests that the Makers can participate if they want and compete if they want and to simultaneously point out that the challenge is unfair and unnecessary to the future of the Remains. This whole thing is playing on the ignorance of those that participate every year." She paused. "I know that my participation will make the challenge and everyone in it legendary."

Ella Buchanan paused and looked directly into the camera with those cool hazel brown eyes of hers and concluded: "I hope that this challenge wakes everyone up and makes everyone think about those that participate. Sometimes, there has to be a sacrifice. This is my sacrifice."

Ralphie could not help but smile at the Maker's interview. She was bright. She was friendly. She was warm and approachable.

After watching the Maker video Ralphie could not imagine that the Makers were going to allow Ella Buchanan to be a part of the challenge. He had watched the video and not believed his own eyes. Makers were the most powerful line in the Remains, and they did not jeopardize their power, even with their insolent children.

The Maker video rubbed Ralphie the wrong way. It had to be a stunt. The Pandemonium Challenge was not above a publicity stunt. It would be despicable, Ralphie knew, to make the Remains believe that a Maker was going to be in the challenge and in the eleventh hour, for some inexplicable reason, remove the Maker. But Ralphie did not put it pass the Pandemonium Challenge committee.

He knew that he should believe that there was a Maker participating but Ralphie could not wrap his head around the idea of a Maker in the Twenty-Third Pandemonium Challenge. It was unimaginable.

Ralphie recalled there had only been two Makers ever to participate in the challenge and none had made it passed the second day. Ralphie stopped the video and rewound it again. Ralphie knew the two before. Michael Jordan Lewis was the first. Dianna Ross Stapleton was the second.

Could Ella Buchanan really participate in the challenge? Would she participate in the challenge? More importantly, would the powers that be in the Makers allow her to participate?

Ralphie shook his head after watching Ella Fitzgerald Buchanan's video. It was unbelievable. He had been surprised and shocked to find that Ella Buchanan had doubts. Makers doubted? He rubbed his temple, thinking about what he had just watched.

The whole Maker thing would blow over. It was a publicity stunt, Ralphie figured. The Pandemonium Challenge was all about publicity. Getting a Maker to participate had to be a big deal. Ralphie knew that the challenge was a contest but simultaneously one of the biggest money-making events in the Remains.

The next video that Ralphie watched was Bailey Beaumont. He knew that the Makers video was a big deal but when the challenge began the celebrity of the Maker would quickly disappear. In the challenge everyone was exactly the same. They were adversaries fighting to win the championship. No one cared what line anyone was from in the challenge. The only thing that mattered was who was last and who won.

Bailey Beaumont's name appeared on a black screen. The screen faded in on the maple brown skinned girl with the heart shaped face and the enormous eyes looking into the screen. Even though she was being filmed Bailey Beaumont, dressed in her First Gen hoody with the goddess on it and owl and her hair in two braided buns, looked like she should have been a child video star instead of being interviewed for the Pandemonium Challenge.

"My name is Bailey Beaumont," Bailey began and Ralphie could not believe that she had volunteered for the challenge.

"I volunteered for the challenge this year for three reasons: I wanted my family and line to be proud of me; I wanted to challenge myself and see what my limits are; and lastly, I wanted to see if I was smarter, tougher and meaner than everyone else in the challenge this year." She paused. "I also want legendary status."

Legendary status, in the Remains, was similar to having your face carved on Mount Rushmore, when there had been a Mount Rushmore. Everyone in the Remains knew the names of the Pandemonium Challenge winners. Everyone wanted to be a Pandemonium Challenge winner.

"If I was a superhero, I would be Bumble Bee. I like that she doesn't have any superpowers. She is just incredibly smart and resourceful. She created her Bumble Bee suit and the suit gave her all her abilities."

"Don't think that I want superpowers."

"Favorite color is yellow and black, like Bumble Bee."

"I would love to have met Patricia Bath and ask her how she persevered despite all the naysayers."

"Favorite thing to do is to go to the Gathering Center, video chat and hang out with friends."

"I don't really think that I am a fighter. But, don't have to be a fighter to win the challenge. I know a few winners that were underdogs. So, don't count me out."

Ralphie could not help but smile, at Bailey's interview. She was bright. She was friendly. She was warm and approachable. Bailey Beaumont was everything that Ralphie was not. Her video had been seen by nearly 15,000 viewers. Impressive.

The next video was his arch enemy.

"My name is Emmett Till Carson," Emmett announced and smirked showing off his mouthful of braces. Ralphie stopped himself from fast forwarding to the next video. He needed to watch the video. He needed to know what he was going to face when Emmett Carson decided to beat the snot out of Jax and him and no one was around to stop him.

"I volunteered for the challenge this year because I figure that it's time. I'm about to turn sixteen and if I survive, I will be the first First Gen to win in nearly a decade. Just signing up makes me legendary already."

Ralphie liked that Emmett Carson was vulnerable to popularity. He seemed so confident and invulnerable at the Gathering Center. Ralphie noted that Emmett cared what others thought about him.

"If I was a superhero, I wouldn't want to be someone normal. I would want to be Bizarro. I like that he doesn't think that he is bad. He is this broken toy that wants to be loved like Superman but has this fatal flaw that he is not Superman. He has all this strength and power and super abilities but all he wants is acceptance."

"I want all the superpowers that matter. I want flight, speed, laser vision, cold breath and the whole package."

"Favorite color is red and black, of course."

"I would love to meet Frank Miller if I could meet anyone and ask him how he figured out how to reinvent the Dark Knight. Many tried and failed. He succeeded. That is interesting."

"Favorite thing to do is go to the Gathering Center and hang out with friends."

"I am not a fighter. I know that people will say that I like to fight. I don't. I like to protect my friends. The challenge is unique in that you don't have to be good at anything and you can still win."

Emmett Carson's video had been seen nearly 8,500 views.

The videos allowed everyone in the Remains to see who was participating in the upcoming challenge. Most watched the videos and decided by the video alone who would win the challenge. Many watched the contender videos and tried to determine the best battlers to bet on. The challenge was one of the most lucrative events in the Remains. There was 24-hour wagering on the challenge from the time that videos were aired.

For the next two hours he watched the first fifteen videos released for the upcoming challenge. No one had more than two or three thousand views except for EFB, Bailey and the jerk weasel Emmett Carson. Ralphie tried to think what that meant.

When the challenge began, Ralphie told himself, he would be gunning for Emmett Carson. He hoped that Wild Bill Fordham was also in the challenge to exact revenge on the First Gen bullies that had tried to break him when he lived in their compound.

The next morning, before breakfast Ralphie's news feed was dominated by Ella Fitzgerald Buchanan's unprecedented participation in the Twenty-Third Pandemonium Challenge. Every news source, news feed, sports channel, entertainment source had Ella Fitzgerald Buchanan as the top story. Ralphie was shocked. He had heard that a Maker was considering participation in the challenge, but he never believed that it would happen. Makers did not do the challenge.

"Ralphie, come down here and eat," barked Benjamin Reynolds, his father.

Ralphie quickly dressed and before leaving his room messaged Jax and Bailey. He did not expect a response. So, he headed downstairs to breakfast.

At breakfast, his father restated that Ralphie was grounded.

"What's grounded," Macy asked.

"It means that Ralphie will go to school and after school come home and nothing else," Mae Reynolds said to her nine-year-old daughter.

"Isn't Ralphie always grounded?"

"No," his mother chuckled.

"But, dad," Ralphie attempted.

His father said no words. He simply looked at him with his steady, unblinking look. Ralphie nodded. His father finished eating silently.

"You know that today and until the challenge you will be under the microscope," Benjamin Reynolds explained. "You are a representative of this family every time you walk out the door. From now until the challenge your mother and I need to know where you are."

"But, dad," Ralphie began only to stop. His father was systematically separating his eggs from his hash browns when he looked up and eyed his son.

Ralphie nodded. He knew his father was right. He had no argument that would sway his father. So, Ralphie dropped the issue. He had other things on his mind.

In a few hours or days his video would be aired, and things would change then and there. The fifteen-year-old tried to prepare himself for line celebrity. It was not Remains celebrity, per se, but it was more attention than most were accustomed to receiving.

In the middle of the week, after school, Ralphie and everyone in the Remains received a notification. The next fifteen videos were released. In that release Ralphie saw his video appear to be viewed. Seeing his name and a thumbnail picture of Ralphie and a short biography made his stomach drop. He thought he might be ill.

In that batch of videos Ralphie noted that three others, Tee, Jax and Dame were also released. That same day two Boomer videos were released. There were three videos for the First Gens. There were four challenge videos of the newest Second Gens. Three Artist entrant videos were available to be seen. The Trads had three new videos available to see.

He tried not to give into the desire to see his video, but he was only human.

Ralphie was not immune to the fascination with the release of contender videos. He was suddenly a celebrity in the Remains. Complete strangers came up to him and asked for photographs. Initially, Ralphie avoided the celebrity. It was just too intrusive. Then he ran into Jax and Zeke.

They were at the Leathern Apron and everyone that was in the Foundry seemed to be near them. Ralphie felt as if the walls were closing in. His hands were clammy. He was short of breath. Instinctually, Ralphie began to look for a logical exit. Then Jax laughed and snorted and embraced a kid that went to the Leathern Apron that everyone knew. Cellphones came out and suddenly, for the next five or ten minutes, Jax, Zeke and Ralphie were Miller famous.

Jax grinned from ear to ear and mugged for the gathered that the day before had looked at him and the others in passing as nobody important. Jax arched his eyebrows and looked delighted broadly for the handful of boys and girls trying to get a picture with him. Zeke seemed a little uncomfortable but not as much at Ralphie. Of the three, Ralphie looked the most uncomfortable. It looked as if he wanted to be invisible, all of a sudden.

Ralphie looked left and right as if someone were about to come and slit his throat rather than take his picture. The fifteen-year-old who looked like he would have been anywhere but there, at the moment, tried to put on a brave face. The group of students dispersed and left Jax, Zeke and Ralphie in their wake.

"Jax, how do you do it?"

Jax hooked arms around Zeke and Ralphie's shoulders and displayed his biggest smile ever.

"It's all about style, man. It's all about style," Jax smiled conceitedly. At the moment he was explaining a pair of girls dressed in Miller hoodies and pig tails walked up. Zeke and Ralphie looked at each other, awkwardly. Jax gave his friendly smile and spread his arms for the girls.

"You want to take a picture with the future champion of the Pandemonium Challenge," Jax grinned. "Well, who am I to say: No?"

The girls giggled dressed in dark blue hooded sweatshirts, jeans and sneakers. One was wearing braids, pulled back in a ponytail. The other was wearing braids that hung loosely in finger braids to her shoulders. She had one braid pulled back and tightly around the crown of her head. They both fished out their camera phones.

Ralphie liked that Jax was there to take the brunt of the attention from him and Zeke. Jax was definitely different from Zeke and Ralphie. He loved the attention. Zeke loved... well, Ralphie did not know what Zeke loved. He loved beating up people. He loved showing off his physical toughness. At least, that was something.

Of the three, Ralphie was the most skittish of the Alphabet Crew, what they called themselves. Ralphie did not like all of the attention. He did not seek undue attention. He was not a fighter like Zeke. Ralphie was suddenly, for no real reason, was thrust into the limelight because he was going to be a part of the challenge. Thankfully, the challenge was only four weeks away when the videos were released.

The first seven days were the hardest. In seven days, the Remains was introduced to twenty-seven of the fifty-four contenders. So, grounded and unable to do anything but go to the Leathern Apron and home Ralphie sat in his bedroom and poured over the videos that had been released.

"I am going to try and prove that the Millers are not just a bunch of grunts," Ralphie had been caught saying. That clip was run and rerun over and over on the Interweb. His video was viewed before the release of that statement 7,498 times. After the release of that statement his video views doubled.

Everyone in the Leathern Apron loved Ralphie for his comment. Before the challenge began Ralphie had seen a banner hanging from a stairway with hand painted sign of his words.

"You Ralphie, right," a boy not yet ten asked, dressed in a blue and gold hoody of the Miller line. He had a broad nose, small ears, high cheekbones and big umber brown eyes.

Ralphie had been startled by the sudden appearance of the boy beside him. Ralphie was at the Foundry and preparing to head home. The rush of students leaving the Foundry had slowed to just a drip when the boy walked up. Ralphie had grinned painfully in answer.

"Are you scared?"

Ralphie grinned again at the audacious nature of the little boy standing in front of him. Ralphie did not answer. He instead, thought about the question.

"I think that being in the challenge is brave and stupid at the same time," the boy with the broad nose opined.

"I can see that," Ralphie admitted.

"You don't look stupid," the little boy stated.

"Thanks, I guess," Ralphie laughed. "I don't think that I'm brave either. So, where does that put me?"

The little boy shrugged.

"You got a plan?"

"It doesn't matter. All that will figure itself out when things get going," Ralphie stated.

"We'll see," the nameless little boy admitted.

Ralphie grinned at the little boy and his boldness. He wished that he had half the boldness of the little boy. Ralphie was more a thinker than speaker. He spoke but only when necessary.

"Good luck, Ralphie," rung in his ears as he left the educational facility for the last time. People clapped him on his back. There were smiles that greeted Ralphie in the halls as he and the seven others prepared for the biggest test in their teen's lives.

He tapped his wrist and the phone messages appeared. There was a message from his mother.: I have Macy with me. We are at CG for E&A meeting. Food in the fridge. Dad should be home soon. Sent at: 1630 hours.

His father was supposed to be home, but he wasn't. Ralphie looked around and wondered where his father was? He walked to his father's study and poked his head in the cavernous office where influentials from the Remains came to talk to his father about projects and business. Ralphie recalled the last time that he had found his father in his study he was talking with one of the six families of the Second Gens about possibly remodeling one of their McMansions. The study that night was quiet and dark. His father was not there. Ralphie spun on his heels and went to the kitchen in search of something to eat.

After eating, Ralphie headed upstairs to his bedroom instead of checking to see if his father was home or not. Ralphie walked into his room and dropped his newly acquired backpack by the door. He knew that he was to take that backpack everywhere with him. He only removed it to sleep.

He was greeted by the comic book posters that he had searched all over the Remains to possess. There was a smattering of Golden Age, Silver Age and contemporary comic book artwork. His prized possession though had to be the rare find of a Speed Racer still that was framed and over his desk.

On his desk were six or seven statuettes. There were Batman and Robin and Superman. On the far side of the desk was Black Panther and Storm and Speed Racer and his Mach 5. In between the statuettes sat his latest collection of comics, stacked neatly beside his computer monitor. There was a statuette of Miles Morales, Robin, Joker and Harley Quinn and Black Manta as well on the desk but nothing more.

Ralphie's bedroom was oddly sparse for a fifteen-year-old boy. He had his bed. He had a five-drawer dresser that rested near the closet. On top of the dresser was a $1/10^{th}$ scale model of the Doctor Who Tardis. Beside the Tardis stood a statuette of a Cyberman and a Dalek. Beside the dresser was a small closet where all of his clothes were either hung or folded, neatly.

Ralphie sat in his ergonomic rolling chair and slid under his architecture desk and prepared to chat with Jax. He tapped the wireless keyboard and his monitor's eye blinked to life. On the desktop screen was yet another comic book character. This time the character was that of the impossible to find Batman: Damned screenshot of Batman crouched on a building and dozens of wires stretching across the city night.

Ralphie tapped a chat window and waited for Jax to appear. While he waited, he checked his dozen or so messages. He had quickly read the filtered messages of encouragement from friends and family that knew Ralphie was about to participate in the Pandemonium Challenge. In his inbox there were hundreds of messages from people that Ralphie did not know. He hesitated to read those messages.

"What up," Ralphie asked.

"Sugar-Honey-Ice-Tea." Jax grinned absently appearing on the small chat window. Ralphie enlarged the window and magically Jax was half of the screen. Jax was eating some type of candy. He was always eating candy. He had a sweet tooth. "What's up with you? You going to the sendoff tonight?" Jax shook his head up and down as an answer. "You trying to see your Boo before the challenge?"

"What? No," Ralphie scoffed. "I'm grounded remember? Once in, I'm in." Ralphie added: "I ain't looking forward to the sendoff." Ralphie attempted.

"Why?"

"It's just so over the top."

Jax smiled mischievously on the screen. "Think if there were no cameras or livestreaming you would be cool with it?" Jax paused. "Knowing you, you wouldn't want anything except a warm handshake and good luck for your send off."

"Just hate all the attention," Ralphie admitted.

"You are such a weirdo, Ralphie," Jax noted. "We are all trying to be legendary. You want to be legendary too. You may act like you don't want that attention but secretly, you know you do."

Ralphie opened and closed his mouth.

"There ain't nobody in the challenge that don't want to be legendary without a lot of attention."

"I'm not saying--," Ralphie began.

"Yeah, you may not like the build-up but if you win all the effort is going to be worth it."

There was a natural lull in the conversation. Ralphie did not know what to say. Jax, the talker of the two smiled smugly, thinking. He seemed caught up in his thoughts for some reason.

"Did I tell you that my pops wasn't happy about the whole challenge thing," Ralphie asked. "He didn't want me to do the challenge." He lied.

"Why not?"

"I don't know. Maybe he expected me to take over the business?"

"I doubt that," Jax joked. "Think Macy got that position sewed up now that you going to the challenge."

Another chat window blinked on, halving the chat window with Jax in it.

Ralphie looked and saw that it was Bailey.

"Be right back," Ralphie rang off and enlarged the chat window with Bailey.

"Tell your girl--," Jax began only to be cut off.

"Hey," Ralphie smiled broadly.

The big eyed, caramel brown girl with a heart shaped face brightened. Her hair was in a crisscross of small raven wing braids with six thicker braids as the main focus of the hairstyle. Ralphie loved Bailey's style. That night, she was wearing a yellow puff coat and underneath the coat was a First Gen top that showed off her delicate neck.

"Are you prepared?"

"I think so," Ralphie noted. He always found himself smiling at Bailey. He added, "How about you?"

"We'll see," Bailey joked. She paused and looked into the screen with her big hazel brown eyes. "Are you nervous?"

"A little," Ralphie admitted.

"Yeah, I think that's to be expected."

Ralphie nodded.

"Well, just wanted to check in, since I won't be at the Gathering Center this weekend," Bailey announced.

Ralphie nodded.

Bailey hesitated.

"Hey, do you read any of the messages you get from complete randos?"

Bailey twisted her lips on her honey brown face, considering Ralphie's question.

"My mom said that she would read them for me, to keep me focused."

Ralphie nodded.

"What about you?"

"No," Ralphie admitted. "I just rather not know what they have to say. I mean, I appreciate them and all, but you never know what freakazoid might slip by and threaten to chop off your head if you don't win."

Bailey joked.

"When do you think that they will begin?"

"Soon. They have to begin scooping up people soon," Ralphie nodded.

Bailey nodded. Her big sorrel brown eyes seemed to grow even bigger on the monitor all of a sudden.

Ralphie found himself falling toward the monitor.

"Good luck, Ralphie," Bailey grinned delicately.

Ralphie smiled awkwardly.

"Good luck to you, too," Ralphie managed and Bailey blinked off the screen.

Ralphie opened the chat window with Jax. Jax chat window was empty. On the screen was a message: BRBRB. *Be Right Back Rat Breeder.* Ralphie snorted at the message. Jax returned a minute later.

"See my message," Jax brightened. Ralphie nodded. Jax cocked his head to the left. "No response?"

Ralphie shook his head; no.

"You through trying to be Casanova?"

"It wasn't like that," Ralphie protested.

"What was *it* like?"

Ralphie opened and closed his mouth but no words came out. Jax jeered. Jax shook his head.

"It's okay to like someone," Jax confided.

"I know that," Ralphie stated.

"How long you know Bailey?"

"Five or six years," Ralphie smiled goofily, unexpectedly flustered by the question.

"You've known her one-fifth of your life. It makes sense that you like her."

"I don't like her like that," Ralphie protested.

"You can say that you don't like her like that, but your actions don't line up with your words, my friend," Jax grinned.

Ralphie fell silent.

"Don't get all sensitive because you all of a sudden got feelings," Jax noted.

"I'm not *all* sensitive," Ralphie lied.

"It's expected. You are a boy. She's a girl. Things happen."

Ralphie did not respond.

Jax smiled foolishly on the screen.

"Can we change the subject?"

"Sure," Jax jested, enjoying Ralphie's discomfort. "All I'm saying is that there's a lock for every key. 'Nuf said. Okay, we are at the beginning of the month. We are figuring that we'll get picked up at the end of the week and the challenge will begin either Friday or Saturday."

Ralphie listened, still smarting from the lock and key statement before talking about the challenge. Ralphie liked Bailey. She was nice. She was smart. She was kind. He didn't like Bailey like Jax was trying to say. She was just a friend.

"Earth to Ralphie. Earth to Ralphie," Jax was saying from the chat window. He shook his angular head back and forth in the window. "You distracted."

"I ain't distracted."

"What were you thinking about so hard?"

Ralphie did not want to say.

"Can't distract you," Jax riffed. "Remember that the girls in the challenge are more like praying mantis than sweethearts," he stated.

Ralphie shook his head.

"I'm serious. The more I watch these old editions of the challenge the more I worry about the girls. They are boy kryptonite."

"Not for me," Ralphie stated.

"Boy kryptonite," Jax repeated.

Ralphie shook his head, disagreeing.

"Not too sure," Jax scowled. "I might have believed that before you started getting feelings. Now, don't know."

"I told you—. "

"I know you don't have feelings, but if anyone mentions your girl's name you lose your grip and we have to try and reel you back in."

"It ain't like that," Ralphie tried.

"Whatever gets you through the next couple of days." Jax paused and brushed his crown of hair back from his face. "Zeke thinks that they start scooping up folks this week. The challenge is close. It usually starts the second week of this month." Jax rolled his eyes and looked into the screen at Ralphie on the other end. "Make sure that you have your backpack on anytime you leave the house."

Chapter Six.

Juneteenth

The memories of Juneteenth were vague for Ralphie. There was just so many things that happened in those five days in the second week of June. So many things that led up to those five days dominated the memories of Juneteenth for Ralphie.

Juneteenth had happened and almost immediately Zeke and Jax went into overdrive for the challenge. Everything was about the challenge after Juneteenth. What they ate. How many hours they slept every night? Training and not training were studied. Everything mattered no matter how big or small before the challenge.

The three friends walked down Lewis Latimer Avenue on their way toward the biggest housing complex in the compound; the Estates. The Estates were built and developed by Ralphie's father and his company; Reynolds Construction. The homes were throwbacks to a time when there were McMansions that were considered small if they were only two thousand square feet homes and only had a three-car garage. The Estates was a highly coveted area in the Miller's compound despite its proximity to the wasteland on the other side of the development.

"What you like about Zeke," asked Jax. "I mean, other than the muscles, the confidence, the power and his whole strong and silent thing?"

Tee shook her head and smirked. Ralphie shook his head at Jax's question. Jax was likely to ask anything once he opened his mouth.

"Do you ever think before you speak?"

"Think about what," Jax asked.

Tee opened and closed her mouth.

"The whole strong and silent thing is real old," Jax concluded, half-kidding. "I think that most young ladies prefer a lighthearted jokester that doesn't know when to be serious, more than the typical, stereotypical brooding bad boy."

Ralphie scowled at Jax. He was always joking, the fifteen-year-old thought, silently. Maybe, he was not always being funny, Ralphie thought.

"Jax, you even like girls," Tee asked pointedly, breaking Ralphie's thoughts.

Ralphie winced at Tee's sharply worded question.

"Of course, I like girls. Why wouldn't I like girls?"

"Just saying," Tee said, twisting her lips under her walnut brown nose and rolling her dark eyes.

They were at the top of W.E.B. DuBois Street, all of a sudden.

"Make sure to have your backpack with you at all times," Tee advised.

Jax smirked and pointed to the backpack on his back and turned and walked down W.E.B. DuBois Street where he lived with his mother, sister and baby brother. His father was missing in action. Jax had not seen him in two years.

Tee and Ralphie headed toward their homes on Lewis Howard Latimer Avenue. His home was three blocks from Jax's and in the housing development that his father's company had developed. Tee Bennett's house at the top of the cul de sac.

Tee walked and noticed that Ralphie was looking at her strangely. Tee cut her eyes and pouted, directly annoyed.

"What you looking at?"

"You, "Ralphie smiled stupidly.

Tee glared at Ralphie.

"You remember that weird lizard," Ralphie asked, noting Tee walking a few steps to his left. He slowed. She came shoulder-to-shoulder with Ralphie. Tee was not as tall as Ralphie but athletically built.

"Yeah," Tee answered, not really paying attention to Ralphie.

"What do you think it was?"

Tee did not answer immediately. She and Ralphie walked another block before she responded. Ralphie thought to ask the moody girl the question again. Then, he thought that Tee would never answer.

"Think it was a dream," Tee responded.

Her answer made him think. It surprised Ralphie. He could not respond immediately. Ralphie noted that Tee was suddenly looking at him through glaring eyes.

"What? Why? I mean, why do you think it was a dream?"

"It appeared. I saw it. You saw it. Then it disappeared. I looked for that lizard all summer. Never saw it again."

"A dream?"

"Yeah," Tee replied and stopped herself from saying more.

The two walked onto their block and instantly, Ralphie felt that he was back in a different time. The Estates harkened back to a time when things were kinder and simpler. It looked like something that should have been in another time and place.

The houses were all made in the same format. Every house was two-stories tall. There were garages for non-existent solar and electric cars. Those spaces were used as extra room or space. The homes were gigantic and gorgeous.

"Hey, why did you ask about that lizard?"

"I just wondered what happened -- between then and now," Ralphie explained.

Tee Bennett nodded. She twisted her lips beneath her wide nose, thinking. "Life, I suppose," Tee breathed.

Ralphie nodded. He stopped. He looked for a second and thought to say something. Instead, he walked on thinking about what Tee had said.

Tee had been nice and friendly back then, four years ago, and nothing like the crazy and violent girl she had become. Tee, four years ago, was a bit of a tomboy, Ralphie recalled. She liked baseball, soccer and exploring the Remains.

Ralphie had heard from someone last year Tee's father had died. Her mother had begun dating. Tee was known throughout the Leathern Apron as an easy target. Ralphie heard the rumors. Tee had a bit of a reputation. In the whirlwind of rumors and finger pointing, Tee ran to Zeke.

Tee paused on the sidewalk and stared at the boy in front of her for a moment before she walked away from Ralphie without a word. As always,

Tee broke off and did not say goodbye or anything. Ralphie watched the girl that lived on the same block but seemed a million miles away from him climb the stairs of her porch, pause to unlock the front door and enter without looking back.

"Bye Ralphie," Ralphie joked under his breath to himself. "Thanks for walking with me. Thanks for remembering that time we found that lizard. You are so different than all the other boys that have used me and abused me," Ralphie said as he walked to his own home.

Ralphie thought all this as he walked into his home and threw his backpack down and immediately picked it back up off the ground and slipped it back on his back. He did not want to wear the backpack 24/7 but he had made a pact to wear the backpack whenever he was out of doors or going out of doors. Thinking of what he promised he threw his backpack back down near the stairs to the second floor and walked into the kitchen looking for something to eat.

Cold chicken, macaroni and cheese and what was left of the blueberry cobbler from the night before were Ralphie's makeshift dinner. He warmed the small meal in the microwave and while it warmed searched for something to drink. In the refrigerator Ralphie fished out some apple concentrate. He poured himself a glass of the yellowish liquid and retrieved his warmed food.

He ate alone. Ralphie had expected his mother to be home and realized that it was a Thursday and she would be out late. On Thursdays, his mother would be at the Central Government with two dozen other individuals discussing the progress of education and academics in the Remains. Ralphie's mother had been an instructor long ago. When she retired from instruction the Central Government recruited her for the Educational and Academic Board. The board was a powerful branch of the Remains central government.

His father, usually in Miller coveralls, would be either at the construction site in the Foundry supervising work or at the Central Government brokering deals for Reynolds Construction. That day, that eventful day, Benjamin Reynolds had been dressed in a business suit and finagling a deal with one of the compounds. His mother and father had hit it off and exchanged numbers.

It had been a hot and sweltering few days leading up to Juneteenth and though Ralphie usually went to each night, but he did not plan to go to the first night.

"How come you ain't coming to the first night of Juneteenth," Jax asked from the computer monitor.

"I have things to do," Ralphie attempted, in front of his computer screen.

"You ain't got nothing to do," Jax returned, looking at Ralphie skeptically. The boy with the big ears tilted his peanut shaped head and poked out his lower lip. "Come on. The first night is always the best," Jax tried. He shrugged. He twisted his lips on the screen. "It's going to be a good time."

"I'll see you tomorrow. I'm busy tonight," Ralphie said

"Whatever," Jax simmered with a shrug and rung off.

In the aftermath of Jax's anger Ralphie sat and looked at the monitor that hung from his wall and watched him. Ralphie rubbed the side of his face and tried to think of his next move. He could have tried to explain to Jax that he was going to meet up with Bailey Beaumont on the second night and that he was going to treat her to whatever she wanted. He could have told Jax that dancing with Bailey Beaumont was one of those moments in life that you dream about and hope for but seldom see realized. He did not have unlimited money and had to conserve. One night out with Bailey Beaumont at Juneteenth was worth a hundred nights with everyone else. But Ralphie did not say any of that. Jax would not understand.

No one understood. Instead of understanding Jax would be calling Zeke and Zeke would call Tee and they, the three-headed beast, would be talking about Ralphie not going to Juneteenth on the first night. Jax would be saying that Ralphie was full of himself. It was his criticism for most. Zeke would grunt and laugh and say that Ralphie was soft. Tee would cut the deepest saying that Ralphie was not loyal or someone to trust.

Ralphie lowered his head and tried not to imagine the back and forth that would go on between Jax, Zeke and Tee about him, in his absence. The fifteen-year-old sat in his chair and threw his head back and wanted to scream. Just because of a girl Ralphie was going to have to suffer the inevitable fiery darts and gruesome barbs of Jax and Zeke and Tee. Was it worth it? Ralphie did not know for sure.

It was just a meet up and a dance with a girl that he had wanted to dance with for a while. Yet, in deciding not to go to the first night of Juneteenth he would be ridiculed and laughed at by three of the most heartless Millers that he was also going to the challenge with.

Ralphie waved a hand in front of his monitor and found himself at the Pandemonium Challenge website.

The first night while everyone in the Remains celebrated the beginning of Juneteenth Ralphie sat in his bedroom and watched videos of dance moves. He watched so many dance videos that he did not know which signature move he was going to do at Juneteenth. All he knew was that he was going to wow everyone with his dance moves.

Juneteenth was a big deal and despite his attempt at trying to downplay the importance of the celebration and the dance and the night Ralphie knew that his social coming out was a big deal. In the Remains there were all of these rituals for boys and girls. Some of the rituals were public and spectacular. Other rituals and traditions were private and personal. Juneteenth was one such event that was public and televised across all of the Remains.

Ralphie thought all this the day that he was scheduled to meet Bailey Beaumont. He had begun his day like any other and when his parents left; his father to work and his mother to take his baby sister to camp, Ralphie had eaten breakfast. He had lounged around his house in his Black Batman pajamas. His mother had returned home and Ralphie had closed himself in his bedroom, listening to music and watching challenge videos. Late that afternoon Ralphie had made himself a lunch and maybe said a dozen words to his mother before she left to do errands.

A little before sundown his father returned from work and showered and shaved and prepared to go to Juneteenth. His sister was back and dressed like a nine-year-old in a summer dress and pigtails. Ralphie had checked in with his friends and for nearly an hour straight they had berated him.

"You coming tonight, pretty boy," Tee crowed.

"He might have other plans," Zeke spat.

"Yeah, maybe the Queen Bee has come back from the dead and asked him to meet him in the dead zone?"

"Maybe, it was The Thriller, and he wants him to wait for him to come over and play with his rotting corpse," laughed Jax.

"Come on," Ralphie pleaded.

They were on a tear and Ralphie knew that the tongue lashing would not end because he wanted it to, but when they felt that they had gotten his betrayal of them out of their system. Along the way they would also be launching fiery barbs at Ralphie that he could not defend.

"You know that I once had a three-legged blind dog," Jax began.

"He was more loyal than you," Zeke laughed, pointing at Ralphie.

"Damn," Tee laughed.

"You know I once saw a broke legged, snaggled toothed giant rat," Jax joked.

"And he wasn't as ugly as you," Zeke crowed.

Jax and Tee laughed. Zeke laughed as well.

Jax, Zeke and Tee messaged him throughout the first night of Juneteenth. They had lots of comments about everything that they saw. They were mean and snarky in their comments. There was few that avoided their venom.

Ralphie sat at home and reviewed the challenge videos. While Jax and Zeke sent pictures of people and comments about them he scanned the website and noted that there were going to be fifty-two contenders in the Twenty-Third Pandemonium Challenge.

The most viewed video was still EFB. She had nearly 445,987 views. The next closest was 223, 925 for Brooklyn Starling. The third most viewed video was Emmett Carson.

After sundown, Ralphie bored and unsure what to do returned to his bedroom and computer monitor. Ralphie went downstairs and watched an old movie. The movie was an old video of the son of a fighter trying to prove that he was as good as his father. Ralphie had seen the movie before. It was one of his favorite movies. He did not really watch the movie but had the movie watch him as he struggled with his own desire to go back upstairs and surf the Interweb.

After the movie, Ralphie checked the time and headed to his bedroom, trying to avoid his family's return and debrief about the first night of Juneteenth. He closed his bedroom door as his parents and baby sister came home. For the next thirty minutes Ralphie's parents talked and Macy headed to her bedroom.

Ralphie waited for the eventual knock at his door and his baby sister's pie-face to peer in before he answered. He sat in front of his computer monitor and waited. The knock came and before he could speak Macy appeared. She was dressed in basketball shoes, knee high socks, a skort and long-sleeved white blouse. In her hand was a crumpled dark blue jacket with the crest of Polar Star.

"Man, Ralphie, you missed it tonight. It was so fun. They had funnel cakes, cotton candy, those big turkey legs. You know what I'm talking about," Macy Gray Reynolds fired in a rapid-fire pace. She was all of nine-years-old.

Ralphie snickered.

"You going tomorrow?"

"I'll be there," Ralphie nodded.

"Okay, did I mention the fireworks? They said that they were the biggest tonight, ever. Tomorrow, they will be even bigger. We'll have fun. We're going again tomorrow," Macy said, tilting her head to the left, thinking. She had a plastic necklace on that read: Juneteenth.

"What was your favorite thing tonight?"

"The cotton candy," Macy Reynolds mused. "It was so good."

"Okay, I'll have to try it tomorrow."

Macy yawned and stretched like a big, lazy cat.

"You tired?"

Macy nodded and slowly closed the door.

Ralphie smiled broadly at his nine-year-old sister.

He thought absently of checking in with Jax but knew that was not a smart plan. He was sure to be still a little hurt because Ralphie had not gone the first night of Juneteenth. So, instead of poking at someone that was not going to be understanding, he waited them out.

The next day Ralphie prepared for his big day at Juneteenth. His parents and little sister had gone ahead of Ralphie. He had decided to walk and meet up with his friends later at the park. When he finally arrived, Ralphie stood dressed in his best blue jeans, Miller hoody and dark blue basketball sneakers.

All around him people chatted and moved toward the tented areas of the Central Government park. He knew that people were pointing and taking pictures and laughing but all that faded as the fifteen-year-old stood and tried to take in the sprawl of the Juneteenth Celebration. It was as if the Remains had been shrunken down into two acres of land and seven connected tents that night, as the Remains fireflies buzzed the night skies. With all the activity going on around him Ralphie found himself smiling at the harmless but loud fireflies. They had four-inch wings and were two inches long. They shouldn't be able to fly, Ralphie had heard people explain, but they flew awkwardly and crackled with energy that sounded like an old-fashioned popcorn popper. The hundreds of fireflies, that night, were a natural light show as they attempted to climb higher into the air blinking on and off in the summer night.

There were seven pavilions set up across the grand park. In the center was the largest pavilion. The six other pavilions circled the main pavilion. Each smaller pavilion had a flag sticking out of the top that denotated the line represented. Ralphie walked toward the Miller pavilion by habit. To the left he noted the walk of Remains leaders. Halfway to the pavilion Ralphie stopped and turned to the Ferris wheel that was slowly turning and lifting couples into the air to view the Central Government walled city and the lines beyond.

Along the pathway to the Ferris wheel Ralphie noticed the fairway where there were old school games of chance. There were basketball games, baseball games, ping pong ball games, ring toss games as well as water balloon games Ralphie noted as he walked toward the Ferris wheel. The fairway was crowded with hundreds of people.

Ralphie's nose was greeted by the smell of popcorn, kettle corn, hotdogs, butter, cheese and cotton candy. Girls dressed in tight jeans and knee-high boots walked past Ralphie with garish makeup. Boys, dressed in oversized T-shirts, baggy jeans and sneakers pushed through the crowds looking for trouble. The enforcers, stoic and unmoving, stood near many of the games their assault rifles at the ready.

"Can I take a picture with you," someone said from behind and a square faced girl with bug eyes and dull look on her face reached out and hugged

Ralphie as one of her friends, a tall girl with thin eyebrows and a wide nose, took a picture. Ralphie smiled awkwardly trying to recover as the bug-eyed girl released him and her friend exchanged places. The tall girl with thin eyebrows put her arm around Ralphie's shoulder. Another picture. Another awkward smile.

Ralphie walked stunned and confused through the park looking for familiar faces. He took a dozen pictures before he ran into someone he recognized from the Foundry. The person smiled easily and closed the distance to Ralphie, much to the relief of Ralphie.

"What up, Ralphie," said Marshall with a smile. He was a taller than Ralphie and with long curly hair that he combed into a mushroom of curls on his round head.

"What up, Marshall," Ralphie said politely as he and Marshall walked through the park. "How long you been here?"

"I got here early. My mom is a vendor. She's selling her art here," Marshall explained, showing off his braces. Marshall was the son of Dianna Ross Nelson, one of the Millers small art collective. Dianna was unique in the Miller compound. She was a Miller that made art out of the wood and wire that other Millers threw away after their work.

"Are you here the whole week?"

"Yeah, think so," Marshall said without enthusiasm. "My mom wants me to help her."

Ralphie and Marshall walked deeper into the park and on either side, there were games and carnival rides suddenly in sight. To the left of the pair was a teacup ride that slowly spun to the delight of kids nine-years-old and younger. On the far side of the path were the bigger kid rides. There was a pirate boat that moved in a systematic, pendulum motion. There was next to the pirate boat an octopus ride that was more tilt-a-whirl than octopus. Behind the octopus was a baby rollercoaster.

Several times, as Ralphie and Marshall walked, people ran up and asked to take pictures. Ralphie acquiesced. He had little choice.

"How's celebrity?"

Ralphie scowled.

"That great, huh?"

"I know I shouldn't complain but I have to admit I didn't think all the attention would be on me. I mean," Ralphie paused. "I just figured I'd sign up and do a video and go to the challenge. I didn't think anyone would want to have my autograph or picture. I always thought there were other people to focus on."

Marshall giggled and nodded.

"Well, for tonight, you're just a kid trying to fit in and enjoy yourself before the challenge," Marshall concluded.

A teen the color of burnt wood in blue jeans and sneakers chuckled. Ralphie knew the look. He had a notebook in his hand.

"Are you?"

Ralphie looked at the nameless teen curiously.

"Can I get your autograph?"

Marshall giggled and pointed toward the fifteen-foot banner with Ralphie on it and the other seven Miller competitors circling the Miller pavilion. Now that he was closer, he noted that banners were around each pavilion and featured the contestants in the Twenty-Third Pandemonium Challenge.

Ralphie could only shake his head.

"So much for just a down low, under the radar night, champ," Marshall snickered.

"Yeah, forgot about those," Ralphie chuckled.

Ralphie separated from Marshall and headed to the main pavilion where the dancing was going to take place. It was nearly nine o'clock when he finally entered the tent that could have housed a jet plane. There was bleacher seating on two sides of the pavilion. In the center was a 40x40 foot parquet floor. At the end of each set of seats there were two more sets of speakers. In the rear on a small stage was a disc jockey and two stacks of stereo speakers.

The disc jockey looked like one of those rap or battle disc jockeys with headphones on and one headphone of his ear as he meddled with the turntables and the music on them. He had on a gray hooded sweatshirt that read: I'M WITH THE BAND. He couldn't be more than twenty and the color of copper. He had thick eyebrows and a hint of a moustache.

The noise coming from the speaker was just barely audible. Ralphie listened and tried to place the music but it eluded him. Ralphie crossed from the still empty seats and toward the disc jockey and stage. He listened and as he got closer the music seemed familiar.

"Welcome to the Twentieth Annual Juneteenth Celebration of the Remains, hosted by the Central Government of the Remains. I am DJ Jazzy Jeff the Mixer and I am here from now until midnight tonight. This week we have the distinction of having four Remain favorite DJs that will coax everyone onto the dance floor. Last night, there was DJ Marvin the Martian. Tomorrow, we feature DJ Mixmaster Brandon. Thursday will feature DJ Herbie the Luv Bug. The last night of the Juneteenth Celebration will feature DJ Spinderella Gidget and special guests." DJ Jazzy Jeff the Mixer pushed the microphone from in front of his face and suddenly the music spilled out of the speakers and filled the pavilion from floor to pitched ceiling.

Ralphie drifted to the edge of the pavilion. He did not sit. He just hovered. He watched as the crowd grew and people slowly began to dance in groups of two or four.

Ralphie scanned the crowd. He was looking for one person. After twenty minutes in the pavilion Ralphie walked out and ran into Zeke and Tee.

"What up, Ralphie?"

Tee smirked. Zeke shook his head and pushed past Ralphie with Tee in tow.

Outside the pavilion the music was audible but muted, Ralphie looked up and took in the half moon overhead. Jax jumped on Ralphie's shoulders and laughed like a crazy person after scaring his friend.

Ralphie spun around, startled.

"Jax," Ralphie breathed.

"Ralphie, you boogie oogie ooging, tonight," snickered Jax. He had clipped his hair close to his box-like head and looked as if he was guilty of something, for some reason. Jax was wearing combat boots, black jeans and a blue and gold Miller hoody with Miller embroidered down the right arm.

"Not too sure," Ralphie admitted. He studied Jax. "I didn't think you were a dancer?"

"I'm not. I mean, I can put my left foot in and take my left foot out with the best of 'em," Jax answered, looking left and right as if expecting someone to appear suddenly. "But I ain't no shake it 'til you break it kind of guy."

"Yeah, me either," Ralphie admitted.

"Well, if nothing else, they have good food and games here," Jax added.

At that moment Ralphie saw Bailey. She had come around a corner and magically the crowd in front of her parted and she strode toward Jax and Ralphie. Bailey had her hair braided and pulled up into a loose ponytail of braids held together by a blue and gold ribbon. On either ear was the blue and gold earrings of the First Gens. Bailey was wearing blue jeans, sneakers and a First Gen zip front sweater. On her wrist was the computer watch that her line had created.

"Ralphie," Jax grinned, but his words were lost on Ralphie suddenly.

Ralphie blinked and found Jax in front of him.

"Man, you got it bad," Jax confessed. "She's going to be the end of you."

"What are you talking about?"

"Just be careful," Jax warned.

Ralphie smirked and walked toward Bailey.

"Hey," Ralphie grinned awkwardly. Bailey smiled coyly.

"Hey," Jax sneered and stepped in between Ralphie and Bailey. "I'm Jax, Ralphie's best friend ever. You are?" Jax extended a hand.

"Bailey," Bailey smiled awkwardly. She reached out and took Jax's hand. The pair shook hands.

"Ralphie asked me to come and check you out. You can never be too careful," Jax continued. He released Bailey's hand.

Ralphie shook his head. Bailey looked amused. Jax grin broadened. Ralphie shook his head. He opened his mouth and closed it, silently. Bailey smiled awkwardly.

Ralphie stepped between Bailey and Jax and gently pushed the loud and obnoxious Jax away. Jax feigned shock. Bailey smiled even more.

"Want to take a walk before we go inside?" Ralphie looked at Bailey. He did not wait for her reply. Instead, Ralphie turned and stared daggers at Jax. "Not talking to you, Jax."

Jax grabbed at his chest as if he were having a heart attack. Ralphie turned back to Bailey. Bailey snickered.

Ralphie and Bailey walked from the grand pavilion and toward the area where there were rides.

"You like all the people in costumes?"

"Don't hate 'em," Bailey smiled easily.

A pair of girls, not older than Ralphie stopped and pointed at Bailey and Ralphie. One reached into her fanny pack. As the one searched the fanny pack the other stepped forward.

"Can I take a picture of you?"

Ralphie stepped back as the pair of girls posed with Bailey. Bailey smiled broadly and seemed genuinely engaged with the young fans. Ralphie thought that Bailey should have been a celebrity.

The pair walked and Ralphie found himself smiling despite being stopped from time to time by Bailey's fans.

"You are pretty popular," Ralphie remarked after the third or fourth fan stopped Bailey. Bailey only smiled, in response. Ralphie could not be angry at Bailey's fans. He understood. They wanted what Ralphie wanted. Well, they wanted to spend time with Bailey but were satisfied with taking a picture with the photogenic First Gen.

Bailey walked on Ralphie's right and he found himself smiling as he walked past people, games, food and attractions with the attractive First Gen. Bailey seemed just so carefree as she moved beside Ralphie. She was everything he was not, Ralphie thought as he stole a glance at the First Gen that night framed by the string lights that announced the rides and attractions.

"What's your favorite thing about Juneteenth?"

"Don't know," Ralphie answered, sheepishly. He looked at Bailey and found her big ecru brown eyes smiling at him. He smiled, reflectively.

"It ain't that hard to figure out," Bailey said, twisting her lips into a slight smirk.

"Macy said that the cotton candy was really good. We should get some," Ralphie said, trying to change the subject. He asked, after a second, "You like scary rides or thrill rides?"

Bailey paused and looked at Ralphie curiously. She smiled haltingly after a second of thought.

"What's so funny?"

Bailey did not answer Ralphie's second question. Instead, she answered his first question.

"I don't really like the drop rides. They make me feel like I am about to be sick," Bailey admitted.

Ralphie smiled mischievously and stopped in front of the black and gold painted Condor ride. The Condor was four loops that held fifteen two-seaters that rose nearly one hundred feet into the air and spun around for a minute or two.

"Why'd we stop?"

Ralphie pointed to the carnival ride.

"You game?" Ralphie asked.

Bailey looked at the ride skeptically. Ralphie grinned at her hesitance.

"Not a drop ride," Ralphie pointed out.

"I'm ready," Bailey admitted.

The pair walked toward the black and gold ride. Ralphie ushered the First Gen to the line.

"This looks good," Ralphie smiled confidentially. He leaned in closer to Bailey. "It's just a look see ride. Nothing scary."

"Okay, good."

The line was not incredibly long. The pair stood for about five minutes before the ticket taker took the tickets from Ralphie and allowed them to find a seat on the Condor. The ride looked sturdily made. Ralphie had seen videos of carnivals pre-flash and knew that carnivals traveled across the nation and were seen as an underground secondary national criminal enterprise.

The Condor ride began and the organ music that pumped out of the dozen speakers on the frames of the ride got louder and louder. The music was familiar. It sounded like a penny arcade. The ride slowly began to spin. Ralphie grinned as the sound of giggling and chatter gave way to the sound of the growing organ music of the Condor.

The ride rose into the air. The Condor inched into the air. In seconds, the Condor was ten feet in the air. The second jump put the Condor at twenty feet off the ground. In less than a minute the Condor had risen to thirty feet from the ground. At thirty feet the Condor tilted to the left and a few screams were heard.

The tilt was the moment that Bailey reached out and grabbed Ralphie's arm for stability. Ralphie could not help but look down at the smaller hand on his arm and then up at Bailey. She was directly close to him. Ralphie relished the moment.

The Condor continued its rotations and eventually began to straighten out. The Condor descended, slowed and slowly came to a stop. The whole ride lasted less than three minutes. Bailey unexpectedly burst out in a throaty laugh. Bailey released Ralphie's arm as the ride came to an end and the ride attendant unlocked the safety bar for all the riders.

"You okay?"

"Yeah, I'm fine. The ride was fun," Bailey admitted.

Ralphie and Bailey walked away from the Condor and Bailey again reached out and grabbed Ralphie's arm again. Ralphie beamed. The pair walked past several other rides.

Ralphie reached out and placed a hand on Bailey's shoulder as they walked. He guided her through the crowd. That night they laughed and walked together. They also rode two other carnival rides; The Scrambler and The Wipeout, before heading back to the pavilion for their first dance together.

As Ralphie saw the pavilion rise in front of him his hands began to sweat. He rubbed his hands on his jeans as Bailey fell silent. For an instant, she looked more fearful than when she was on the Condor.

Ralphie studied the unexpectedly unsure Bailey Beaumont for a long moment and took a deep breath.

"We don't have to go in, right now," Ralphie admitted.

Bailey looked at Ralphie curiously. She did not speak immediately.

"We can take a walk around the park once again and then see what happens."

"Are you sure?"

"Sure," Ralphie said. "We don't even have to dance if you don't want to," Ralphie added.

Bailey studied Ralphie silently. Ralphie found himself looking at the heart shaped face and cocoa brown eyes of Bailey Beaumont framed against the whirling sounds and dazzling lights of Juneteenth. Bailey Beaumont seemed to be considering something. She paused and for a moment crinkled her nose and twisted her lips as if she were about to sneeze.

"We're here," Bailey concluded. "We might as well dance."

"You sure," Ralphie asked, uncertain all of a sudden. The girl in front of him seemed so unsure just a moment before. Now, Bailey Beaumont, she seemed resolved to see the proposal through.

"Hey, before we go in, I have a question," Ralphie said, stumbling over the words.

Bailey turned and looked up at Ralphie.

"Well, my question is: Why didn't you want to meet up yesterday?"

Bailey grinned in answer.

"Seriously," Ralphie pressed.

"I had to go with my family. My mom and dad, sister and brother, you know, a big ol' Beaumont event," Bailey said drained from the memory. "I usually go to the first night with them and then go to a few nights with my friends."

Ralphie nodded.

"Enough questions," Bailey declared.

Ralphie was giddy and Bailey Beaumont reached out and took his hand. Ralphie beamed at the physical contact between him and Bailey. It was as if Bailey touching his hand was a natural electrical charge that began with her fingers wrapping around his hand and was activated when her thumb closed on his palm. Ralphie there and then chortled despite himself.

Her touch made Ralphie walk taller, straighter and with more confidence.

"This doesn't have to be weird," Bailey confided.

Ralphie wanted to reply but suddenly they were in the pavilion and the music made conversation impossible. Ralphie was not much of a screamer. So, he chose not to respond.

He followed Bailey as she weaved through the crowd that had gathered in the pavilion since Ralphie's departure. There were easily three or four hundred people milling about the floor of the pavilion. Some slow danced. Some jerked and twisted. Others, boys mostly, moved around the strobe light and disco ball lit pavilion, in groups of threes or fours laughing and joking. Girls, in groups of twos and threes watched and talked to one another.

"Hey, Bailey," a boy said and Ralphie directly stepped up to find that the boy that had called was Emmett Carson, the First Gen bully.

"What gives?"

Emmett Carson was this muscle-bound creep with a square head and thick eyebrows who looked like a rust brown bullfrog. He was dressed in the distinctive owl and goddess light blue and gold First Gen hoody. Ralphie leaned in and almost simultaneously Bailey moved and Ralphie steered Bailey away from the confused and grimacing Emmett Carson. Beside him were his faithful cronies; Wild Bill Fordham and Mouse Clark. Ralphie watched the three until a group of dancers closed the space between him and the First Gens.

Ralphie, led by Bailey, moved through the crowd. On the other side of the space filled by the crowd Ralphie pulled Bailey back and stopped her progress. Bailey spun around and she seemed on the verge of tears.

"What was that," Ralphie asked Bailey.

She shook her head.

"It's okay," Ralphie said not sure if his words made sense.

Bailey shook her head and looked down, uncertain.

Ralphie took a step closer to Bailey.

"Bailey?"

"The challenge is close," Bailey stated.

"Yeah," Ralphie responded.

"Well, I'm just worried what's going to happen when we all get there," Bailey admitted.

Ralphie nodded. "I have watched a lot of challenges. There is nothing planned or expected about the challenge."

Bailey nodded. Then, she shook her head.

"Emmett said that he's going to drop everyone that's not a First Gen," Bailey Beaumont whispered and Ralphie strained to hear over the music that was playing. The Miller teen studied Bailey Beaumont evenly, thinking what to say. The First Gen seemed genuinely concerned.

"Emmett is a blowhard, everyone knows that," Ralphie dismissed. "The challenge will take care of itself."

"You know Emmett is a challenge favorite," Bailey confided.

"Yeah," Ralphie said with a smile. "You worried that he's gonna drop me?"

Bailey smiled, awkwardly.

"I'm not that same Ralphie from six years ago Bailey. I'm a little bigger. I'm a little meaner," Ralphie admitted.

"A little meaner?" Bailey repeated. "Should I be worried?"

"Worried? About me dropping you?"

Bailey giggled.

"You don't have to worry," Ralphie noted. "I won't drop you until the last day, if at all."

"You won't drop me," Bailey chuckled. "Well, if you won't drop me," Bailey laughed and shook her head. "I suppose I won't drop you either."

"Sounds fair," Ralphie laughed.

"Sounds fair," Bailey snickered.

Ralphie did not know what to do. He had more questions than answers and the questions muted his tongue and nailed his feet to the ground.

"Dance with me," Bailey sang as she reached out to Ralphie.

"Bailey," Ralphie began but suddenly the music changed, and the crowd was laughing and swaying to the slow beat of the drums. Ralphie stepped into the sea of dancers and made his way toward Bailey. Bailey Beaumont was transformed. She shed the heaviness that had threatened to make her cry an instant ago. All the tension was gone. Any semblance of anger or uncertainty or whatever had pained Bailey and made her march away from Emmett Carson was magically gone as the caramel skinned sprite spun and twirled and gyrated to the music played by the DJ. In its place was a bright and brilliant girl dancing. Ralphie watched as the petite beauty twisted and turned before his eyes. She seemed someone else in the rush and rapture of the music.

He smiled. He smiled because Bailey made him happy. Ralphie did not know before that moment that the First Gen girl had such an effect on him. He felt the smile etched on his face as he looked at the beauty in front of him. Ralphie could not stop smiling. He smiled because he would not scream. So, he swayed back and forth with Bailey Beaumont. They did not hold hands. They did not do any coordinated spins or turns. It was a freestyle dance that kept the pair close and distinctly intimate, or as intimate as the pair could be surrounded by six hundred eyes gyrating around them and the nine hundred or thousand other eyes that sat and watched from the bleachers of the pavilion.

Chapter Seven.

To the Waiting Room

It was just weeks after Ralphie had danced with Bailey and days before the beginning of the challenge, when it finally dawned on him, like a punch in the gut, that he, Ralph Ellison Reynolds, had danced with Bailey Beaumont at Juneteenth. He had danced with the most beautiful girl in the Remains and everyone had watched and videoed and talked about it. But more importantly, more immediately, he was one of fifty-three that were going to be fighting for the line privilege and honor of the Pandemonium Challenge.

Those magical moments on the parquet floor with Bailey should have been the most cherished moments in Ralphie's life, but with the challenge just days away Ralphie could not afford to split his focus. He could not afford to be unfocused. In some ways, that is what he told himself as he and his friends prepared for the toughest battle of his young life. The Pandemonium Challenge, Ralphie thought expectantly, would push him and everyone in the challenge to their limits.

In the shadow of EFB there was the subsequent release of the other competitors' videos. Unlike EFB's video the release of the combatants' videos opened the doors to the endless hours of wagering on every aspect of challenge and the warriors. There were bets on the first to be removed from the challenge, the first boy to be removed from the challenge as well as the first girl to be removed from the challenge. The betting was usually on who would win the Twenty-Third Pandemonium Challenge. Yet, there were side bets on who would still be in the challenge day-to-day. There were always bets on lines. There was a belief that the Boomers and Millers and First Gens would be still in the challenge by the second day. The biggest longshot, prior to the start of the Twenty-Third Pandemonium Challenge was: A poppy would make it to the fifth or sixth day of the challenge.

The Miller quartet, also known as the Alphabet Crew, scheduled a meeting by the man-made lake, near the center of the Forge in Maya Angelou park. The park was one of six carved out of the Miller compound to keep connected to the slowly reviving planet. Each park was unique in its design. Jax and Ralphie were the first to arrive.

"You figure that they come together?"

"Don't care," Ralphie smirked.

"Come on, everyone has levels of curiosity," Jax explained.

"Not me," Ralphie stated. "At least, not where they come in my mind."

"I just was thinking that couples in the challenge create all sorts of problems for those not in a relation," Jax pointed out.

"How," Ralphie asked, confused.

"Well, if you are a couple then you are more likely to protect your partner than someone else. Just saying," Jax concluded.

"That is just some made up Jax craziness," Ralphie smirked.

"We'll see, I suppose," Jax declared. "You watch the same videos I watch. You know that the last four challenges had couples in it and they deaded all sorts of line toughs threatening their Boo things."

Ralphie could not argue. He knew that Jax was always spouting off about one thing or another. Yet, there were times that his craziness made sense. More importantly, sometimes his ideas were correct.

In the lull in conversation the pair screwed around. Ralphie picked up a handful of rocks and walked to the edge of the lake and started throwing them into the dark water. Jax found a bench to lounge on while waiting for Zeke and Tee to arrive. Ralphie, after throwing his rocks, sat on the grass and watched dark water for fish.

Zeke walked up. Jax and Zeke exchanged an intricate handshake. Ralphie climbed to his feet and offered Zeke a fist bump. Zeke after the welcome, sat on the bench, suddenly serious.

"Tee has a surprise for us," Zeke said. "She's on her way."

Ralphie frowned. Jax scoffed. Zeke seemed surprised by the reaction.

"Come on Zeke, tell your girl to stop trying to hook me up with those bug-eyed, black lipped H-fiends she calls friends," Jax barked, with a laugh. He added: "I'm trying to prepare for the challenge. I need to stay focused."

Ralphie was the first to laugh. Jax raucous laugh followed. Zeke frowned at the unexpected response. At the laugh a few people close to the three stopped and turned to see what was so funny.

"What is wrong with you?"

"Don't play dumb, you know that Tee is always trying to hook me up with Heckle and Jeckle and I ain't interested."

Ralphie snickered at Jax's attempt at comedy. Zeke, not the funniest person in the Remains, frowned, confused. Ralphie shook his head at Zeke's confusion. Zeke was the biggest and leader of the group. He had an iron will and determination that made things happen.

Zeke stood up big, strong and looked like one of those baby's that watches his parent take their nose for the first time, mystified and a bit boggled. Ralphie could not help but smile.

"She ain't coming to hook you up," Zeke finally remarked.

Ralphie and Jax giggled at Zeke's slow response. Jax gestured to his temple and Zeke watched him intensely.

Tee appeared, dressed in gym shoes, tights and a hooded sweatshirt. Tee had an oversized duffel bag over her shoulder. She deposited the duffel in front of the boys.

Ralphie knew, as did Jax, that Tee was responsible for getting the survival kits for the crew. Ralphie and Jax had been skeptical. Once in their hands, they unzipped the backpack and looked inside. What they found inside was surprising. Inside the duffel were three solar powered backpacks. Inside of each backpack was everything and anything needed to survive a zombie apocalypse.

With all the survival backpacks distributed Tee sat next to Zeke and, for an instant, became the doe eyed Tee from the past, for a moment.

"All the backpacks have hydration packs as well. Load it with water and you don't have to stop for a drink. We all have to stay hydrated."

Zeke shook his head.

"Hydration," Jax repeated, curious.

"I'm sort of impressed." Then he turned to Zeke and back to Tee and made a face. "I still don't want none of August or Venus."

"What?"

"Don't pretend. You know that August is Jax obsessed," Jax laughed.

"They don't want you anyway," Tee noted.

Jax was about to say something when Tee continued. "We got other things to worry about." Tee said. "The challenge is going to be intense. We have to think about things that most forget to consider," the dark girl confessed.

The four had all slipped their survival backpacks on.

"You look mighty spiffy in your new gear," Jax joked.

"You look mighty nerdy, as well," Ralphie joked.

Ralphie nodded. He looked at Jax who looked like he had something to say. Ralphie just waited.

"You can say what you want but you know your train wreck girlfriends love them some Jax even if I am not feeling them," Jax kidded. After saying the words Jax shook his head at Tee. Zeke looked up from his backpack and noted that Tee and Jax were staring daggers at each other.

"What," Zeke asked, at that moment confused.

Ralphie shook his head at the stare off. He looked Inside of the solar powered backpack. Inside of his was the following: a water filter; a dozen fish hooks; box of 100 stormproof matches; a survival knife; tactical flashlight; utility cord; moleskin/first aid kit; hand crank radio; signal mirror; and camp cooking kit as well as a deck of cards. Also, everyone had been given a mini LED torch, fire steel a leather man super tool, a bandana, and a dozen fish hooks.

"You two cool it," Zeke advised and Jax sat next to Ralphie, in a huff. He looked in his backpack as well. Tee stood and crossed her arms in front of her and watched the boys looking through their new backpacks.

"Let's start thinking of ways to win the challenge. We have to have the winner mentality. We have to outsmart, outthink, outlast and outperform everyone else to win," Tee stated. She paused and added, "Booby traps, improvised explosives, anything that we can think of that will give us an advantage to win."

"All right, remember, that we are all wearing these backpacks whenever we go outside. When we are scooped up, we get to take what we have with us, but nothing else," Zeke noted. "We have to be ready to be scooped up at any time when we are outside. They will take us when we are the most vulnerable. They know we have to go to outside. So, they will probably take us on the streets."

Jax scratched his head and quieted. Ralphie noted the quietness of the jokester. He turned to Zeke and Tee and watched as the pair moved to the lakeside. He watched them for a moment.

Zeke and Tee sat on the bank of the man-made lake and stared at each other, as they sometimes did. Zeke and Tee were dressed in combat boots, black jeans and zip front hooded Miller sweatshirts. Zeke had a cartoon T-shirt on beneath his zip front hooded sweatshirt. Tee was wearing a concert T-shirt of some long dead rapper. Tee leaned close to Zeke. Zeke put his arm around Tee's shoulder.

Jax, at that moment, uncomfortable or bored stood up and walked to one of the half dozen benches on the walkway overlooking the lake. He looked to sit but instead bent down and pulled up an orange headed flower that grew in bunches near the lake.

"You think that this Maker is a trick," Jax asked no one in particular.

"What?"

"They might be putting her in the challenge to test us. I mean, the Makers don't really believe in the challenge or the reasons for the challenge."

"That doesn't make sense," Ralphie scoffed. "The challenge makes a butt load of money for the Remains. Everyone benefits. Even the Makers benefit."

"Yeah, but what if the Makers are in cahoots with the committee and using the challenge for another reason," Jax attempted.

"What other reason?"

"I don't know," Jax admitted.

Tee laughed at Jax. "Just because you see conspiracies and don't trust people don't mean that everyone you know is crazy and believes in your craziness," Tee noted.

"Just because I don't know doesn't mean I'm wrong," Jax noted.

"It don't mean you ain't either," Tee smirked.

The two stared at each other as if locked in a staring contest. Neither blinked. Zeke looked up and noticed that Jax and Tee were staring each other down again. The leader of the Alphabet Crew shook his head.

"We only have a few days before they scoop us up. We need to focus. We ain't got time to be worrying about things that we have no control over," Zeke interrupted. "Make sure to put your personals in your backpack today."

Tee looked to Zeke. "Agreed," Tee said. Ralphie nodded. Jax smirked, having won the unofficial staring contest.

"What happens if there is a red herring in the challenge," Jax continued, looking at Tee. "I mean, we could be putting our energy in the wrong place and be worrying about something or nothing that decides the challenge. I mean, I think that we need to try to understand the reason a Maker is in the challenge."

"We can't control that, Jax," Zeke attempted. "We have to have a plan for when we are in the challenge."

"Yeah, I think there are bigger issues to think about," Tee scowled.

Ralphie did not argue. There was nothing to argue about. Of course, Tee and Jax argued. Ralphie thought that the pair liked to argue with each other more than anything. It was kind of strange.

"So, the way I see it everyone is against us," Zeke said uncharacteristically commanding. "We got four others that won't gut us immediately. So, we got to trust them that first night," Zeke explained. The plan, as Zeke and Tee saw it was simple. It involved relying on the four other Millers to navigate the first day and then to create fast friends as the challenge got underway. They had to make it through the first day.

Ralphie did not offer any opinion. Jax was vocal. He had his own opinion about everything offered by Zeke and Tee. The meeting that could have been over after ten minutes took an hour.

Tee climbed to her feet and so did Zeke. Ralphie noticed the movement. He walked toward Zeke and Tee.

"Thanks," Ralphie said to Tee at the end of their impromptu meeting.

"Yeah, thanks, Tee," Jax said, real big.

"You're welcome Ralphie," Tee announced and stared at Jax.

"I said thank you, too," Jax pointed out.

"I know," Tee replied.

"You are such a road rash," Jax spat.

"Ew," Tee gagged.

Ralphie shook his head at the inevitable fracas between Jax and Tee. Ralphie did not want to stay and watch the fireworks between Jax and Tee. Ralphie spun on his heels and made his way toward the foot trail that would lead back to the Forge. A few minutes later Jax caught up with Ralphie.

"You know that you don't always have to start things--," Ralphie began.

"She started it," Jax cut Ralphie off. "I ain't going to be disrespected by nobody."

Ralphie did not want to defend Tee or Jax. So, he stopped talking. The two, Jax and Ralphie, walked in silence.

Ralphie and Jax made their way from the far side of the Foundry to the seven buildings that made up the main campus and labyrinth of the Foundry. They walked through the star shaped structures that all connected and were interconnected with one another. There was a building dedicated to the administration. There was a building just for the lower, younger, Millers. Two buildings were dedicated to the middle grades where Jax and Ralphie found themselves. Two buildings, closest to the rear of the Foundry, was the home of the older Millers and an unofficial college of sorts. In the Remains, Ralphie noted, there were no more colleges or universities. Colleges and universities were seen as the incubators of dissension. After the flash, colleges and universities had been banished.

On the steps Jax and Ralphie stopped and took in the cityscape of the compound that Millers had created. The buildings were not extremely tall or grandly built. They were glass and steel creations that stood as testament to the industry of the Millers. To the left of the Foundry stood the three tallest buildings in the Miller compound; the Renaissance buildings. They had been built to house the very rich and influential but had been relatively empty after the flash and decimation of the population. The Miller government had opened the Renaissance and all of the homes to anyone that occupied the structures for thirty days uncontested.

"Have you ever been there," Jax asked, idly, pointing to the Renaissance.

"No, why," Ralphie replied.

"Just curious," Jax replied.

"I heard they are mostly empty," Ralphie noted. "I don't think that I would want to live in an empty building. It seems like a horror movie about to happen."

"There ain't no more horror movies, Ralphie," Jax pointed out. "We are living in our own 24-hour, 365 horror show, you ask me," Jax concluded.

The pair walked down the steps of the Foundry and headed to their home. They watched as people rode bicycles, scooters, mopeds, motorcycles and mostly two wheeled vehicles back and forth in the streets of the Miller compound. Occasionally, rarely, there was a four wheeled vehicle that appeared and like a whale in a lake or a moose in a stairway the appearance was jarring and unexpected.

The pair crossed the street and fell in line with the flow of the early evening crowd. Jax weaved through the crowd. Ralphie, a little bigger than Jax, walked and watched as men older than his father seemed to move toward him only to stop inches from Ralphie, at the last moment, and avoid bumping into him.

At the Forge Tee was waiting.

"How did you get here so fast?"

"Magic," Tee joked.

"Don't say anything," Ralphie begged.

Jax closed his mouth, silently.

Tee smirked. Jax tightened his lips. Ralphie snorted.

The trio walked down the busy street. They walked the bicyclists riding on the streets. Every once and awhile there were the odd bus or car, but the streets were mostly populated with bicycles and mopeds and scooters.

At the corner of Martin Luther King and Oprah Winfrey Boulevard Ralphie looked up and took in one of the digital ads displays that was replaying news from the Remains. On the display was the PC23 logo. The logo faded and was replaced with the official names of the lines participating. For each line there were thumbnail photos of the challengers.

Ralphie pointed to the display.

"Did you see the Boomers send-off?"

"What send-off?"

The trio turned off Martin Luther King Boulevard and onto W.E.B. DuBois Avenue. The three walked toward the estates.

Jax, Tee and Ralphie walked down Lewis Latimer Avenue, headed for the Estates.

"You know, Jax, you can be a bit of an implant," Tee breathed one block from W.E.B. DuBois Street, where Jax lived.

"You know, Tee, you can be a bit of a drama queen baby when things don't go your way," Jax jabbed with a slight smile on his peanut brown pie face.

Tee pinched her lips as if the words behind her lips were poison. Ralphie waited. He knew that this was the normal back and forth between Tee and Jax. They both had these big personalities and voices and there was the inescapable clash between them.

Every day they fought. Every day they called each other names. Every day they swore they were done talking to each other.

"Stop talking to me, Jax," Tee demanded.

"You stop talking to me," Jax volleyed.

"I mean it, Jax," Tee said, her voice ratcheting up a notch toward anger.

"I mean it, Tee," Jax repeated, smiling at the anguish he was causing Tee.

They were suddenly at the top of Henrietta Lacks Court. Tee continued walking.

"Bye," Jax jabbed again, looking at Tee but instantly turning to Ralphie.

Tee continued walking. Ralphie caught up with Tee and the pair continued walking down Lewis Latimer Avenue in silence. Ralphie was not the talkative type. He preferred silence. So, he walked beside Tee, ahead of Tee and sometimes behind Tee as they walked to the Sean Carter Estates and Henrietta Lacks Street, where their families lived.

Tee peeled off without a word and headed to her house at the top of the street. Ralphie just exhaled and walked on. He waved to Tee as she climbed her front porch steps and entered her house without looking back at Ralphie.

Ralphie walked to the bottom of Henrietta Lacks Street and to the two-story Tudor house at the end of the cul de sac. Ralphie walked up the steps to his wraparound porch and unlocked the front door and entered. As usual, at that time of day, his mother was out and picking up his sister or taking her to soccer practice. His father would be at work until after dark. As a result, Ralphie had the house to himself.

An hour after Ralphie arrived home he got his first notification from his mother to shower and be ready to leave at seven.

Ralphie snacked and headed up to the second floor and his bedroom. He opened his computer and monitor. The monitor sat on the wall, an all-seeing eye, in the fifteen-year-old's bedroom.

With a few hand gestures the computer monitor blinked on. On the gigantic screen were several websites. Ralphie skimmed them and found himself at the Pandemonium Challenge website trying to figure out when the first pick-ups were going to take place. The website held most answers if you only looked, Ralphie knew.

What dominated the home page of the Pandemonium Challenge was the video footage of Boomer compound and their strangely cryptic send-off of their contestants. As Ralphie was trying to find information on the pick-up when Jax appeared. On screen there was as avatar of Jax winking and pointing toward Ralphie that signaled that Jax wanted to speak. Ralphie tapped the avatar and Jax's chat window opened up.

"Do you think that the Shakers are going to do a send-off?"

"They should," Jax sneered on Ralphie's computer screen.

"I don't see them really participating this year," Ralphie admitted.

"Yeah, they probably won't but EFB deserves to feel special."

Ralphie nodded.

The challenge, on its surface, was an opportunity for rivals to grab their five minutes of fame in the Remains. There was only one winner and that winner was heralded as the greatest fighter that year in the Remains until the next challenge.

A chat window notification appeared on the screen. It was a message from Jax. Ralphie opened the chat window.

"Are you going tonight?"

"Of course," Jax smiled awkwardly.

"Zeke and Tee will be there," Ralphie asked, casually.

"Of course," Jax said, confused. "This is the pre-challenge send-off party. Everyone in the Foundry will be there."

"Yeah," Ralphie nodded.

"We all have to go," Jax mentioned. "I mean, it is kind of a big deal."

"Yeah, I know," Ralphie admitted. "I'll see you there."

Ralphie sat in his room and watched the Interweb activity on his computer screen. The send-off party was the talk of the Interweb as it had been anytime there was a party. Add to the interest the live streaming of the send-off party and it was an instant Interweb sensation across the Remains.

Bailey's notice came up. Ralphie without thought tapped her window.

"Be right back," Ralphie announced and minimized Jax's window and opened another window.

Bailey was suddenly on screen.

"Hey," Bailey breathed, her voice buttery and warm in Ralphie's ears. She was dressed in blue T-shirt with a graphic of an old English Police Box on the front. Above the Police Box were the words: Who you gonna call? Her hair was braided up and in a sweep on her head.

"Hey," Ralphie replied.

"Aren't you supposed to be going to your sending off?"

"Yeah, I got time. It doesn't start until eight," Ralphie admitted, watching Bailey from his computer monitor. He added, "We are going to walk."

"You don't seem excited," Bailey concluded, her face suddenly serious.

"I'm excited," Ralphie tried. "I'm excited. Seriously," he added, trying to sound excited.

"What's wrong?"

Ralphie pursed his lips. He twisted his lips on his dark chocolate brown face trying to screw up the courage to ask a question.

"Ralphie, what's wrong?"

"I just don't like...," Ralphie hesitated.

"The attention?"

"I mean, I don't mind the challenge. I get the challenge and all, but the extra stuff is a little much," he breathed.

"I get you," Bailey acknowledged. "We had our send-off party a couple of nights ago. I was a little nervous, but my mom pointed out that what I was doing was giving our line something to be proud of. She pointed out that the challenge is the hardest thing in the Remains."

Ralphie was going to tell Bailey that he had watched her send-off. He had not known that her official name was Pearl Bailey Beaumont. That had surprised him. He had done a little research and found out that Bailey was named after a singer. In his mind, that made sense. She was entertaining. He recalled that she seemed at ease on stage. He enjoyed seeing her dressed in her blue and gold summer dress and matching Doc Marten boots. Her hair had been pulled back into a loose turkey tail of shiny finger thick braids for her send off. Ralphie had wanted to tell Bailey that he couldn't tell that she was nervous but chose to listen.

"It is volunteer. No one makes us do it. It is so different from everything in the Remains. People look at us differently for volunteering to be a part of the challenge. So, we owe it to them to be seen and smile and shake hands," Bailey stated.

Ralphie listened and understood the words that Bailey was saying but he was not an entertainer. He was a battler. He was a worker. He didn't start fights. He was taught to end fights. Because he was unafraid of fighting Ralphie was willing to be a part of the challenge but the other parts ahead of the challenge were hard for him.

Bailey seemed to read his thoughts. "Tonight, think when you are there that you are doing this for your line, your family, your friends. After they announce you and everyone loses their minds because you are going to the challenge understand that only eight of your line are going to the challenge."

"I get it," Ralphie stated. "I just hope that I don't do anything stupid."

"Too late for that, now," Bailey smiled innocently.

Ralphie chuckled.

"I'll stream you, tonight," Bailey admitted. "I'll point out all the stupid stuff you guys say and do."

"Wait, are they expecting us to say something?"

"Duh," Bailey chided.

"Like what?"

"Go challenge? Go Millers? Build stuff. Construct something. Thanks for your support? I don't know," Bailey joked. "Nothing too substantial."

"I think I can do that."

"I'll try not to laugh, too much," Bailey giggled.

"That's encouraging," Ralphie smirked with a shake of his head.

"I'll be paying attention to your hands and feet" Bailey joked. "They are dead giveaways of if you are nervous."

A few hours later Ralphie was backstage at the Forge, the central mall of the Millers. There was a stage in front of the eternal fire that burned in the Forge. His parents, his mother and father were seated in the front of the thousand seats that had been arranged to allow Millers to witness the eight going to the challenge. Seated next to his mother was his baby sister; Macy.

"What up, Ralphie," Jax grinned. "Nice outfit," he added pointing at Ralphie's shoes.

Ralphie had been dressed by his father. He had bought him a cutting-edge Miller blue suit from some designer that Ralphie had heard of but never imagined owning. His shoes were cockroach exterminators, pointy and long.

"You are going on stage," the pock faced handler declared backstage.

The eight Millers going to the challenge were lined up and given two handlers. Ralphie had a boy on his left side and a girl on his right. The boy had a curly head of hair and a broad nose. He was the color of wet brown paper. He had a sash over his shoulder that read: Build, Construct and Design. The girl on the right side had her hair braided in two French braids that wrapped around her round blonde curly headed head. She grinned and looked up at Ralphie as if he was a celebrity.

"You are so brave," the nameless girl beamed. She looked away embarrassed.

Ralphie smiled back, suddenly feeling odd, holding the little girl's hand.

"Remember, when your name is called to walk to the red dot and number on stage. Stop there and after the clapping dies down they will announce your name again and step up to the red ex and then wait for the clapping to end before you return to your spot," the stage manager, a thin black woman dressed all in black with bug eyes and wearing an old-fashioned over the head microphone reminded. On her thin hips was an old-fashioned black rectangular walkie talkie.

"We are moving," someone shouted.

Everyone lined up. Jax joked and gave a thumbs up sign to Ralphie. Ralphie smiled awkwardly despite wanting to run home and lock the door. The announcements began.

Damian Lillard Walsh, Tina Turner Bennett, Jackie Robinson Taylor, Elijah McCoy Tyner and Madison Washington names were called. Each proceeded to the stage and were greeted with the sound of thunderous applause. Ralphie felt his stomach drop, knowing that his name was about to be announced.

"Ralph Ellison Reynolds," boomed on the public announcement and across the Foundry. Ralphie felt the tug of the little girl, his escort, and fell in line as she led him onstage. Ralphie walked to the red "X" on the stage. Ralphie stood and listened to the applause. He squinted and shaded his eyes against the lights and looked for his family. There in the glare he made out his mother and sister and father standing and clapping.

When he arrived on stage there were only five others in front of the crowd. Dame, Zeke, Tee, Jax, Madison stood and waved and gave thumbs ups to the cheering crowd. The last three to take the stage were Regina King Bryant, "Gina", and Isaac Hayes Washington, "Isaac" and Ralphie.

The eight stood and smiled for the crowd. Ralphie watched as Dame, dressed in a blue suit, and Isaac, wearing a sports coat and jeans, exchanged fist bumps while Zeke and Jax made faces at one another. Tee, Gina and Madison were dressed in summer dresses and looked completely different and incredibly frilly. Ralphie waved at the girls not dressed in jeans or hoodies.

Tee was wearing a dress the color of fire; orange, yellow and white. Her hair braided and shining was piled on her round head. In her ears were gold hoop earrings. Gina was wearing a green, brown and red speckled dress that seemed to cling to her skin. She was a pie faced girl with sharp features. Her curly hair was shoulder length and held out of her face by hair bands. Madison, the prettiest of the three, the color of smooth peanut butter, wore a golden dress with black and red and green highlights. Her big fawn eyes seemed to have no end as she tilted her milky brown crème head and pouted. She was the wannabe model of the group, Ralphie imagined. Madison stuck out her lower lip, annoyed and adorable, a living banana creme kewpie doll.

"They love us," screamed Jax, pointing out toward the crowd.

Ralphie did not want to concentrate on the crowd gathered, but the noise of the cheering made him. The lights allowed Ralphie to see to the edge of the seats as the darkness was replaced by the glare of lights. The crowd was standing on its feet. They were clapping and cheering. Ralphie was surprised at how many people had come out to send him and the others off to the challenge. It was inspiring. Ralphie could see more people standing and seating on the grass beyond the chairs. Overhead, floating in the air, were dozens of drones recording and transmitting the event to the Interweb.

A cheerleading team came on stage. The cheerleaders danced and exited the stage. The send-off was not very long.

While on stage, Ralphie could not stop thinking about his hands. He tried not to look nervous, though he was. Ralphie looked straight ahead and tried not to look as if he was petrified, knowing that Bailey was watching. Thankfully, he was not asked to speak. That would have been a disaster.

On stage appeared the line leaders; Maya Angelou Higgins and Walter Payton Fields. Maya Higgins was a portly woman with a pie face and intense stare. She was not more than 65 inches tall and had a slight limp in her left leg, Ralphie noted. Higgins was dressed in her signature pants suit. Beside her stood Walter Payton Fields. He was a dark man with beard and moustache. Fields looked like a pre-flash football player. He was a stocky man with a low center of gravity. Dressed in a suit and tie the nearly bald man looked healthy and strong.

Maya Higgins delivered a speech.

"We come here tonight to appreciate these eight brave residents of the Miller compound. We thank you, firstly. We thank your families, as well. We thank the Millers, collectively, for all that you have done to mold these eight for the challenge ahead. As it has been said, long ago, "It takes a village to raise a child." We are that village. We are Millers. We are completely behind you and your upcoming challenges. Know that when you struggle, question or worry, we are behind you. You are not alone. Go into the Twenty-Third Pandemonium Challenge with the knowledge that you have twenty-eight thousand Miller faithful, behind you. Do us proud."

Walter Fields followed up Higgins speech and concluded the night with these words.

"Too often, we try to say too much, when the moment is bigger than ourselves. Tonight, we send-off our greatest chances of challenge success. The eight brave and daring souls before you have the power to change the course of our line in seven days. We can never express our gratitude and admiration for your participation. Your effort and courage inspire us all. Do us proud," Walter Fields concluded.

Afterwards, the daring souls were whisked from the stage to another stand where residents could get up close and personal. Ralphie stayed at the second event just long enough to fulfill the needs of the Pandemonium Challenge Committee before heading home.

"That was bananas," Macy Reynolds giggled. She was carrying a cut-out head the size of her of Ralphie. On her head was the signature hat for the Twenty-Third Pandemonium Challenge. On the cap were four figures: PC23. On Macy's nose were the PC23 sunglasses.

"You think that you have half a chance to make it to Day Three?"

"Macy," Ralphie's mother scolded.

"What? Everyone is trying to decide who can make it to Day Three. If you can make it to Day Three, then you are more likely to make it to Day Five. There's no guarantee that you will make it to Day Seven," Macy explained matter-of-factedly.

Her mother shook her head.

"We are going to not talk about the challenge for a while," her mother advised. "Your brother needs some time to think."

The distance from the Forge to the Reynolds' home was ten blocks and though, usually, it was a great distance that night the distance seemed cut in two.

"You did good tonight," Benjamin Reynolds said placing a hand on his son's shoulder. Ralphie did not speak. He did not have words. He knew what he was facing. He knew that when he was taken to the challenge it might be the last time that he would ever see his family again. He did not speak. He did not want to spoil the moment with words. Instead he tried to appreciate the looks and words that his family offered as they returned home. Ralphie seemed deep in thought.

"Is Ralphie okay?"

"Sure, why would you say that?"

"He's awfully quiet," Macy Reynolds noted.

"He has a lot on his mind."

"If he has a lot on his mind or not, he should still be able to talk," Macy concluded.

Chapter Eight.

To the Island.

The computer monitor sat in front of Ralphie an all-seeing eye, as the fifteen-year-old thought about checking some websites. He looked at his messages and counted the unread messages. He had 781 messages he had chosen not to read. The day before he had received nearly 1,200 messages. He had skimmed some and seen that the topics were mostly regarding the challenge. In the two weeks that his name and the other contestants' names became public knowledge he had received conservatively 25,000 messages about the challenge.

Initially, Ralphie had read the first few. They were encouraging. They were inspiring. They suggested a number of ways to approach the challenge. Then, he read a message from RockyB that suggested that Ralphie stop breathing and save the Millers the trouble of pretending to know him if he was not going to win the challenge. RockyB said that he would hunt down Ralphie's family and kill them all if he did not win the Twenty Third annual challenge. The message rattled Ralphie.

So, Ralphie turned away from the monitor. He looked at Harley Quinn with her red, white and black Harlequin outfit in tatters and holding her two pet hyenas, who were slathering on either side of her.

"I wish that my life was as simple as yours," Ralphie whispered. "All you have to do is create mayhem and let someone else clean up the mess after you." The fifteen-year-old thought about what he said and quieted. "The first sign of insanity is talking to yourself," Ralphie jested. "Perhaps, I am closer to you than I like to admit."

He rested his head on the desktop and thought of calling Jax. He, for a fleeting moment, thought of calling Bailey. What was the point? If he called Jax he knew how the conversation would go. Jax would be normal for a few minutes and then drop some conspiracy theory. There was no point in that so close to the challenge. If he called Bailey, it would only remind Ralphie of what he had to lose. He did not like to admit it but Jax was right. Bailey was a distraction. For that matter, Jax and everyone not going to the challenge was a distraction. He needed to focus.

He opened his backpack and for the tenth time made sure he had everything he needed for the challenge. He had seven pair of socks, underwear and a toiletry kit with a tin of Altoids, toothpaste, deodorant and toenail clippers and a sewing kit. Everything was in the backpack. All that he planned on taking to the challenge was in his backpack.

Ralphie thought about changing his shoes. He was supposed to be wearing combat boots. Jax and Zeke had told Tee and Ralphie to wear their hoodies, jeans, a long sleeve t-shirt and have a back-up T-shirt, just in case. Everyone was supposed to be wearing combat boots because there was a lot of broken glass, pipes and nails on the island.

Looking down, Ralphie noticed that he was wearing his blue Chuck Taylor Converse sneakers. They were comfortable. They were worn in. His combat boots were in his closet, stiff, uncomfortable and shiny like a wet seal. Ralphie thought about changing his shoes, but at that moment, he opted out of getting up from his ergonomic chair and searching his closet for his combat boots.

Instead, he tapped on the wireless keyboard and found himself on the Interweb. He sat dressed in his blue and gold Miller hoody with the logo on the back circling the hammer and chainsaw, loose fitting blue jeans and cartoon t-shirt from one of the comic book companies no longer around.

With a few clicks on his keyboard Ralphie found himself at a comic book website that he liked to visit. Ralphie studied the artwork on the splash page and found himself examining the seventy plus comic book characters all caught in action. The cast of characters were dark and foreboding. There were several in the air. A few were running. One was swinging on a rope. Ralphie tapped the site entry and proceeded into the website. Somehow, he found himself on a page with a handful of comic book artists that were now in charge of most comic books in the Remains.

The artists were prolific and incredibly talented. They had recreated the comic books that had been and infused a brighter future to the dark future that those that remained saw every day. The comics were hopeful. The comic characters were saviors. The stories were uplifting.

From the comic book website Ralphie clicked aimlessly only to find himself at the Pandemonium Challenge website. He liked seeing the newest information, especially before the launch of the year's challenge. This year, Ralphie mused, he had a vested interest in several contestants participating.

He had listened to the interviews of nearly all of the contestants. There were still three contestants that were in silhouette and had no interviews posted at such a late date. Ralphie found that curious.

Ralphie clicked on the three silhouettes and there was nothing. No video. No information. Was it a blunder? Ralphie made a mental note to point the three silhouettes out to Jax and Zeke. Zeke knew everything about the challenge. Jax was the resident expert of the challenge. He loved to point out the winners of all twenty-two challenges. If anyone knew if there had been an oversight of contestants in the challenge it would be Zeke or Jax.

Ralphie explored the Pandemonium Challenge website and found himself watching the story of the flamboyant commentator that had become synonymous with the challenge; Dean Fletcher. Fletcher had only seen three challenges before his death. The challenge was forever thankful for Dean Fletcher and all that he had done to make the Pandemonium Challenge one of the most popular events in the Remains.

After watching the Dean Fletcher story Ralphie left his bedroom, and before leaving turned around and grabbed his solar backpack. He walked downstairs to the main floor of his home. He checked the time. It was nearly nine o'clock and Ralphie was surprised that his mother and father were not home. For a moment, he wondered if Macy was home. She would not be home if his mother was not home, he decided.

Ralphie was about to call his mother when he heard a faint tapping against the window in the kitchen. Ralphie imagined that his mother or father or both were in the backyard. It was dark out but sometimes his father liked to sit in the dark and look up at the stars. So, Ralphie headed to the kitchen and the sliding glass door.

He opened the sliding glass door and stepped out and headed toward the light switch when he saw the black matte uniform of an enforcer. The sight of the menacing man wearing all black was jarring. The giant enforcer stepped toward Ralphie silent as death. Ralphie stepped back and felt a hand grab his right wrist and elbow. Ralphie turned to find that another enforcer to his left. The man that had grabbed Ralphie moved quickly and twisted his right arm behind his back before Ralphie could react. Another enforcer slipped an opaque hood over his head.

That was the last time that Ralphie was home.

Ralphie's memories of being scooped up were jumbled. He went from seeing enforcers to seeing nothing. He was zip tied and ushered to a transport. The enforcers did not rough Ralphie up. They were gentle and firm.

Once inside the transport there was muffled conversation but Ralphie could not distinguish the voices. His head was whirling. He had too much to consider. The voices were low priority. All that Ralphie could recall of that hectic few minutes was that he was being scooped up and taken to the challenge. He was not fearful. He was just receiving all the various sounds, smells and tastes in the transport.

The transport turned left and right and then left again. It could have gone a mile or twenty miles for all that Ralphie could determine. His mind was reeling.

Though the hood that was over his head was opaque Ralphie still tried to see through it. The effort was fruitless. The hood's fabric was a weave of some sort and let in little light. He looked down and hoped to see the floor of the transport, but the hood blacked out the downward view. So, Ralphie simply waited for the ride to end and for his next step in the challenge.

The enforcer led Ralphie into a building where Ralphie could hear there were a number of people inside. Once inside the building the hood was removed. Ralphie blinked and tried to distinguish shapes and colors in the flood of light.

"Relax, kid, you are about to head to the waiting room," one of the enforcers, closest to Ralphie announced. Ralphie continued to blink as his eyesight returned little by little. The first thing that Ralphie could make out was a woman with curly black hair, long eyelashes, broad cheekbones and a broad smile looking at him. She was dressed as an enforcer but that uniform behind a desk was an anathema to Ralphie. Never had he seen an enforcer seated.

"Okay, Harold, what we got, here," the woman enforcer asked with a smile. On either side of the woman were enforcers. Two enforcers stood with automatic rifles strapped across their backs. On their hips were side arms. They scowled at Ralphie and the two other enforcers.

"Ralph Ellison Reynolds, Miller, entering the waiting room," the shorter enforcer nearest Ralphie announced.

"Ralph Ellison Reynolds, Miller, entering the waiting room," repeated the woman holding a notebook computer and studying the screen next to the gigantic enforcer.

The second enforcer at the door lifted a gloved hand and stopped Ralphie from entering.

"There is no violence in the waiting room. You have made it this far in one piece. We want you to make it to the challenge unbent as well, but we are not afraid to bend you up, a little, if we need. Capisce?"

"Capisce," Ralphie repeated.

The enforcer nodded and the enforcer standing guard of the ornate wooden door gestured for Ralphie to follow him. The lean enforcer at the door waved a hand in front of the door and the lock opened. He opened the door and gently bowed.

The fifteen-year-old walked up a short flight of stairs and into a spacious room that could have been a gymnasium long ago. The room was huge and along the walls were eight enforcers. In the interior of the gigantic space and the vaulted roof the sheer space of the room made the dozen other contestants gathered seem incredibly small.

Ralphie scanned the dozen faces as he entered and recognized no one. There were Second Gens in the room, Ralphie noted based on their signature bear design on their clothes. There were a couple of Poppies in the spacious room that might have been a gymnasium or theater at some point, long ago. The Poppies wore multi-colored clothes with the California flag somehow visible. Ralphie liked the Poppies creativity. They were the first group that he had seen spray paint their shoes. There was a First Gen in the room, the techno-geek was fiddling with a small ball that rocked back and forth with the boy's hand movements. Ralphie seemed impressed at the ingenuity of the First Gens and as Ralphie moved on the outskirts of the small groups of tweens and teens he noted, leaning against the wall was one of the First Gens terrible trio; Wild Bill Fordham.

At once, Ralphie tensed. He had a score to settle with Wild Bill. He had a score to settle with all the First Gen bullies. Instantly, Ralphie was seething. All the bad things that the First Gens had done to him years before flashed before his eyes. Wild Bill had tripped him and made him fall in a mud puddle. Mouse, the bully, had punched him anytime he was in arm's reach. Emmett Carson had run him off the dirt trail on his bike. The terrible trio made his life, while living in the First Gen compound, a nightmare. But it had been Wild Bill who had pushed Ralphie over the railing near the First Gen skate park that had left a scar on his left wrist.

Ralphie instinctually balled his fists and stepped forward. He unexpectedly wanted to dash across the room and beat the smugness off Wild Bill for terrorizing him when he was a six-year-old. The always smiling Wild Bill, the evil Emmett Carson and the giant that had the name Mouse had made it their life's goal to make Ralphie's life a living hell, while he lived in their compound.

It was Bailey who had made Ralphie want to join the challenge when she quite by accident said that Wild Bill and Emmett were going to the year's challenge. Ralphie had thought that he wanted to go to the challenge before but suddenly having the opportunity to settle an old score made PC23 more appealing.

In May, just days after school let out, Ralphie got a chance to even the score with Mouse outside of the Gathering Center. Ralphie had walked up to Mouse and stood and waited for the giant First Gen to react. Mouse threw a slow right cross. Ralphie had brushed the punch aside and countered with a left-right-left combination that caught the cocky and malicious Mouse off guard. Ralphie punched the bigger and dull bully of a boy in the midsection and dropped him like a bag of nickels.

Mouse was no pushover. He was big and brawny and capable of taking punishment. But Ralphie had put him on his knees. He was trying to catch his breath and while Mouse seemed legitimately hurt, he did not seem so tough. Ralphie did not think about that. He knew if the situations were reversed Mouse would not show him mercy. Mouse was a sadist. To beat a bully, Ralphie's father had told him long ago, you had to make the bully understand that bullying came at a cost. So, Ralphie reared back and fired a shot that caught Mouse across his jaw and the fight that he had built up in his head for months on end, ended.

Jax had been there. Zeke too. They had ushered him away before the enforcers could put hands on him. They blended into the crowd of teens in the center. Afterwards, they laughed at Ralphie's fearlessness.

"When did you get hands?"

"Need to rename you Iron Mike after you tipped that big boy," Jax kidded.

Ralphie did not respond. He did not smile. He wanted to smile. He wanted to react but chose against it all. Those thoughts flashed in his head.

As he stood in the waiting room Ralphie thought of his short and decisive fight with Mouse. He was no longer the six-year-old that was afraid of Emmett or Wild Bill. Ralphie also thought of crossing the space between him and Wild Bill and knocking his head off. Yet, there were at least a dozen enforcers watching the room and at the ready.

Ralphie took a step forward and Wild Bill for the first time noticed him and looked away. Ralphie prepared for battle but Wild Bill did not seem to recognize Ralphie. Ralphie's dark eyes studied his torturer and instead of attacking he decided to wait for the challenge to sort things out. In the challenge, he could pay back the last two of the terrible three without punishment or reprisal.

More of the competitors arrived. The numbers increased by twos and threes. The hopefuls all wore the endless bracelets that Ralphie sported. It seemed as if he had seen all the people in the anteroom before at the Gathering Center at one point or another during the year.

In an hour there were twice as many people in the room. In that same hour Tee arrived and she was angry and ready for war. Almost immediately

Tee was fuming and looking for a fight. An enforcer, 2413, was shadowing Tee as a result.

"I don't need no damn babysitter," Tee squealed to 2413. 2413 did not flinch. 2413 just stayed within arm's reach of Tee.

"Tee," Ralphie attempted.

"You better tell this Robocop to give me twenty feet or I'm going to lose my mind."

2413 smirked.

"What is going on," Ralphie asked and almost immediately regretted feigning concern for the mercurial Tee.

"Tell that little moon pie girl to stop looking at me," Tee fumed. She was wearing her standard blue and yellow Millers hooded sweatshirt. She wore a mini skirt, knee high white socks and combat boots.

Ralphie looked in the direction that Tee was looking and there was a moon-faced black girl with her hair pulled back and away from her flat face. She had a short forehead, thick eyebrows, a straight nose, high cheekbones and thin lips. Hanging from her ears were golden hoops. In Ralphie's memory, the girl had an Ethiopian or Egyptian look to her.

2413 watched, silently. Ralphie watched 2413 and Tee and the Ethiopian girl. He did not know what was more entertaining. 2413 was tasked, it seemed, to make sure that Tee did not start a fight. Tee had come in hot and was just heating up. The Ethiopian girl had done nothing that Ralphie could tell and he put his attention on 2413.

Ralphie did not offer any advice. She wouldn't listen, he figured. He didn't think that anything he offered would have helped the situation anyway.

A few other people arrived, and Tee settled down, a bit. She was still angry and vitriolic but instead of focusing all that vitriol on one person she spread it to others in the hall.

"I don't like her," Tee seethed, looking at a pear-shaped girl with long chunky black braids that fell to her shoulder blades. The girl was dressed in a black and white hooded sweatshirt and black jeans. She was a Trad.

Ralphie studied the girl. She was pretty. She was the color of chocolate and caramel. She had hooded almond eyes. Ralphie noted that she was wearing the black and white of the Trads. She was also wearing black and white checked combat boots with pink laces. For a Trad that was absolutely crazy and by definition completely different and downright rebellious.

"What don't you like about her," Ralphie asked forgetting the last exchange. He braced himself for the acidic vomit that was inside of Tee and waiting to be spewed out on anyone willing to listen. Ralphie wished that he could have taken back his words, but it was too late.

"That straight nosed fish thinks she's better than me because she lighter than me. You can see it in her bug Cleopatra eyes. She has a stupid face. She thinks she's better than everyone. You can tell. She stuck up. Someone needs to go over there and beat the stuck up out of her. You a double stank stuck up witch," Tee barked to the girl in the crowd she was aiming her venom. Several people in groups of twos and threes turned at her words. "That stank witch didn't even turn when I talked to her. She's just made my list. She's a stuck up snaggle toothed witch."

Ralphie tried to step in between and block or distract Tee but blocking Tee's view only made her angrier. Ralphie looked at the girl that he had only seen as the cause of Tee's anger.

Ralphie felt like someone trying to hold back the sea. He stood and tried to think if he should try to do anything. Any effort suddenly felt futile.

"See how that fish walks and looks down at people," Tee barked, craning her neck around Ralphie. Ralphie looked back trying to single out the girl that Tee had lost her mind over. There were easily twenty people in the auditorium. Ralphie could not determine who Tee was talking about. More importantly, Ralphie did not want to figure out who had gotten on Tee's nerves. She was volatile at best and all sorts of crazy at her worst.

"She ain't better than nobody. Don't let her come over her," Tee whistled as if someone had stepped on her puppy.

Ralphie shook his head at his own foolishness. He looked again for the girl that Tee was so angry at, but she was lost in the crowd of faces. Ralphie blinked and thought about Tee. He was smarter than that, he thought. He had known that he shouldn't have poked at the crazy girl that he had thought he knew once, a lifetime ago.

While Tee looked for someone to be mad at Ralphie tried to remember Tee before she became this Tee. He watched the animated black girl sit down against a wall and unzip her backpack and pull out a black and white marbled composition book. She had a marker in her hand. Ralphie watched Tee shaking her head and pointing at people and making faces as if she had tasted something distasteful and remembered that he had been eight when he first met Tee.

Seven years ago, Ralphie had returned to the Miller compound with his family. His father's job had ended, and they were back in the Estates in the house that his father's company had built. Tee had been the first person in the compound to welcome Ralphie back to the compound. For sixty minutes, Ralphie watched Wild Bill Fordham and the enforcers and the various competitors mulling about in what looked like a wooden gymnasium.

By the third hour of Ralphie's capture Tee had decided that no one in the room was worthy to breathe air. Tee sat in the corner of the room with a notebook and hate shimmering from her. Tee was this puzzle, Ralphie thought. She was angry one moment and then sitting in a corner the next and doodling in her notebook.

Ralphie tore himself away from trying to understand the cause for all the piss and vinegar in Tee and watched as the numbers increased again in the chamber Ralphie noted some familiar faces in the holding area. There were supposed to be eight Boomers, eight Millers, eight Second Gens, eight Poppies, eight First Gens, and eight Trads. There were supposed to be eight Innovators as well, but they never participated in the challenge.

When Zeke arrived, Ralphie made his way to the unofficial leader of the Alphabet Crew. Jax had come up with the name of the rag tag group of Zeke, Jax, Tee and Ralphie. Ralphie did not usually have much to say to Zeke and the same was true for Zeke.

"What up," Ralphie announced, awkwardly.

"What up," Zeke responded.

Thankfully, Tee appeared, and for the next ninety minutes she relayed all that had happened from the moment that she had been scooped up in front of her house until she was disrespected by the Trad fish. Ralphie listened initially because Tee told Zeke things that she had not told Ralphie. Ralphie listened and learned that Tee had been heading to school when she was captured.

Tee began her tirade of arriving at the processing center and Ralphie found himself uninterested. He drifted off.

A few hours later Jax arrived.

Jax entered with a big pie eating smile on his face. It was as if things before Jax were in 2D and afterward everything was in 4D. Things were crisper, clearer, cleaner, directly.

"What up, Ralphie," Jax asked.

"What up, Jax," Ralphie repeated half-heartedly.

"Where did they get you?"

"Leaving the Apron," Jax recalled with a smile. "I saw them and began running. I knew who they were, but I always run from strangers." Jax was kidding. Running from the enforcers was a no-win situation. Most of the enforcers were trained to run in short bursts faster than most residents in the Remains. It was one of the reasons that the enforcers were so efficient in emergency response. The crime in the Remains was nearly negligible as a result.

"Did you outrun them?"

"Naw, man, think I got one of those track star enforcers on me," Jax explained with a smile.

"So, what happened?"

"Well, I see them and begin to run. I cut through an alley and start to jump a fence and I'm scooped up. Pretty simple, really."

"Pretty simple," Ralphie joked.

"How 'bout you?"

Ralphie told Jax how he had been caught.

"Typical," Jax sneered and shook his head. "You didn't even put up a fight?"

Jax and Ralphie took a lap around the auditorium. They saw many people that Ralphie knew from the Gathering Center. There were eight combatants from each line in the challenge this year. There were eight First Gens too, Ralphie knew. He was hoping against hope to see Bailey Beaumont before the challenge began. When the challenge began there were going to be little time to talk, Ralphie figured.

"Hey, what happened to the others?"

"What others?"

"You know, the others. The rest of the world? There used to be about ten billion Chinese people on earth, pre-flash," Jax explained.

Ralphie shook his head.

"You know that I'm right," Jax proclaimed.

"No," Ralphie stated. "We all know what happened." He paused. "The flash."

"No, I mean, I know that everyone said that the flash took away all those people, but why just the white people?"

"The flash didn't care. It termed everybody. They said it had something to do with the flash being biological." Ralphie shook his head again. "Hell, Jax, you sat in the same classes as me. You know all this already."

"Yeah, I know." Jax deflected. "I mean, yeah, I know. But what I don't get is what happened to the other races?"

Ralphie twisted his lips on his chocolate face. "I think they had a recessive gene or something. I know that one of our instructors said something about that, but I can't remember all the science."

"No, I know all that. The flash was biological and genetic and all that. I know that it was supposed to cannibalize specific genes and somehow destroyed all those people. I know that. But what I'm asking is: after the flash, why didn't whites come back? I mean, two blacks can make a brown baby. Two blacks can make a caramel baby. Two blacks can make a white baby. But, why aren't there white people now, in the Remains?"

"What?"

"Well, I mean that we all know that there are all these shades of black, right?"

Ralphie listened.

"How come we don't have white people now?"

"Jax, you think of the weirdest things," Ralphie admitted.

Jax and Ralphie didn't finish their discussion because at that moment Maddy Washington was in front of them.

Maddy Washington, the big-eyed beauty with this childish cuteness all rolled up in a body of a girl already beginning to develop faster than most, was sitting next to Zeke. Her hair, brushed up and into two Afro puffs, sat on her head in two perfectly round Minnie Mouse buns. She extended the Minnie Mouse image with two red polka ribbons wrapped around her buns.

"What up Jax," Maddy said not looking at Jax but with her arm around Zeke. Tee was leaning against Zeke as well.

"When did you get here?"

"Just got in."

Ralphie noticed that Isaac was there as well.

Isaac was a short dark brown boy with a chipped front tooth. Isaac had a pointy chin and squinty eyes. What distinguished Isaac from everyone else was that he was shorter and thinner compared to Ralphie. Isaac was Dame's closest friend. He was dressed in the blue and gold of the Millers line. He had on blue jeans and combat boots with yellow laces.

"Your girlfriend is here," Jax mentioned. He pointed over Ralphie's shoulder. Ralphie turned slowly and took in Bailey walking in dressed in her hooded sweatshirt, dark blue jeans and combat boots. Her sweatshirt sleeve had a dozen tiny robots embroidered on the sleeve to spell out: First Gen.

Behind her sauntered Emmett Carson. He was a well-built curly headed boy with dark eyes and an evil smile. He had his zip front hooded sweatshirt open and showing off his cartoon T-shirt that was an image of a bygone character that Ralphie thought he knew.

The others looked in the direction Jax was pointing.

"You like that black Barbie," Maddy smirked.

"Isn't she too hot for you," Isaac asked.

Ralphie shook his head and pretended not to pay any attention to Maddy or Isaac. He watched Bailey walking in the sea of faces. At that time, for Ralphie, all the other faces around Bailey fell away. The faces that dared walk in front of her were quickly compared and finding no comparison faded into the distance. Bailey had her hair combed up into a group of fist sized balls of curly hair that made a curly Mohawk. Bailey was a refreshing, uninhibited spirit that shined brighter than all those around her.

The Miller boy smiled self-consciously and thought for a moment to wave to Bailey. There were too many people for Bailey to see him, Ralphie realized. So, maybe, Ralphie thought, he could take a walk and "bump" into Bailey.

Jax was smiling as Ralphie turned and saw the others looking at him. Ralphie felt anxious. He wondered if he had done something or forgot to do something. Ralphie was about to speak but one of the enforcers took the microphone on the stage.

"We will move to the launch site in the morning. We have a few more stragglers to bring in before the morning. So, eat and rest and as soon as we have everyone we will be on the move."

"On the move," someone near the Millers asked.

"Yeah, stupid, we aren't going to magically be on Pandemonium Island after they scoop us up," someone said.

"This is about to get good," Tee said.

"It's about to go down," Zeke laughed.

Jax opened his mouth. Whatever Jax was about to say was at that time swallowed up by the latest drama just a few feet from the trio.

"Hey, what the hell is this," growled Gina standing up with one of those old-fashioned black and white speckled composition books in hand.

The eight Millers had been seated in a small circle, eating chicken strips when Gina barked and jumped to her feet. Directly, Tee was on her feet and clawing at Gina and her outstretched arm and composition book.

Ralphie stared at Gina and Tee and the other Millers backing away from the two as if they were spilled scalding water. Zeke and Dame, the unofficial leaders of the Millers, recovered and went into action. Zeke was the first to push through the small group and disappear. Next was Jax, one the heels of Zeke, who was pressing in, trying to get a view of what Gina had taken away from Tee Bennett.

Zeke and Dame stepped in and broke up the momentary dust up. Ralphie looked back at the enforcers that were vigilant and watching the seven pre-teens at once animated. It seemed that the enforcers were more concerned about line versus line friction and not much else. No enforcers moved.

"Give it back," Tee screamed as Dame somehow mystically had hold of the black and gray marbled composition book that Ralphie had seen Tee writing in.

"Calm down," Dame announced sticking out his thick hand and looking from Tee to Gina to Zeke.

"What the hell, Tee?"

"Yeah, tell him what the hell you have been up to, Tee," Gina bawled. Gina cut her dark eyes and twisted her lips into a snarl.

In response, Tee let the hate in her eyes simmer and boil in the direction of Gina. The two Miller girls fenced. No one spoke or did anything for a long moment.

"What is this," Dame asked, calmly.

"Give her back her book," Zeke said. HIs voice was even and with no anger in it.

Hearing Zeke speak Ralphie's ears perked up. He immediately paid attention to what was now going on in the circle of Millers. Dame looked at Zeke and Zeke studied Dame. Jax and Isaac watched as the two bulls seemed to silently determine something.

Dame smirked. He seemed to be trying to figure something out. Isaac was to his right. Gina on his left. There was Maddy, cute and pouting for some reason. Next to Maddy was Tee, the center of attention. Zeke and Jax were next to Tee. Ralphie stood with Jax on one side and Gina on the other.

For a tense moment Dame just studied Zeke. In that moment anything could have happened, Ralphie figured. Thankfully, nothing did. Dame stretched out his hand and Tee retrieved her notebook.

"Happy?"

"I'm not sad," Zeke replied.

"Great," Gina said, frustrated. "Now that she has it back, tell everyone what you have been doodling inside," Gina spat.

"I ain't been doodling. I been making a sap list."

"A what?"

"A sap list," Tee admitted. "Figured that someone was going to make one. I just happened to make one first."

Dame and Isaac looked at Tee through thin eyes, as if squinting would make what she said make sense. Maddy folded her arms in front of her and pouted.

"Damn."

"How? Why," Isaac began, shaking his head.

"The week the videos were released I started looking at them, like everyone else. Then I watched them again. I decided to take some notes. I watched the videos and thought about some things. I looked at the bad boys and bad girls first. Then I looked at the weakest of the weak. All those notes led to a sap list," Tee admitted like she was explaining why the President and the dictator had a pissing contest nearly a century ago and caused the flash. She had a new hairstyle for the challenge. Usually Tee had her hair in thin braids. For the challenge she had her thin braids in snake braids.

"Who's on it," Maddy asked, making her eyes big and poking out her lower lip.

"Everyone, really," Tee admitted. She quickly added: "I also included strengths and weaknesses. I think that makes the most sense. Everyone has strengths and weaknesses. Now, I ain't leading but if you ask me the smartest thing is to get rid of the strongest first." Tee stated as a matter of fact and for a moment she reminded Ralphie of the tomboy that played in the dirt. "If we can knock the strongest off, then everyone becomes easier."

Zeke raised his hand.

"Zeke, we aren't in school," Isaac noted.

"I know, but I wanted to make sure that--," he shook his head. "Why you think that we should go after the strongest?"

Tee opened her mouth, but Dame interrupted.

"Wait a minute," growled Dame, narrowing his dark eyes. "I don't have no list or nothing, but I know that the smartest thing is not to go after the strongest or the weakest, for that matter. The smartest thing is to sketch out a plan after the game is underway." Dame twisted his lips as if he were eating something sour. "Going after the strongest is a bad move. We all know about the challenge. The strongest that get targeted are always waiting and ready for the attacks. There has never been a challenge where the strongest survive. No matter what. What we need to do is make a plan to get somewhere safe that first night and then base everything on that moment forward."

"Yeah, we need to wait until we are in the game and then make plans," Isaac agreed.

Tee frowned.

"Why you frowning?"

"I just figured that knowing the strongest would be an advantage," Tee concluded.

"Knowing the strengths and weaknesses of anyone is an advantage," Zeke noted.

"Let's see this list," Maddy attempted.

"Yeah," added Jax.

Tee rolled her eyes at Jax's comment.

Gina wrinkled her nose as if she smelled something awful. Maddy cut her green eyes at Jax as if he had dropped his pants in front of her. Zeke twisted his lips as if he wanted to say something and thought better of it.

"I mean, can I see the list," said Jax, correcting himself.

"Sure."

Tee looked at the composition notebook that Dame had returned to her and she opened it for all to see. There were tons of notes scribbled by hand by Tee in the pages. There were doodles here and there. There were drawings of each entrant and strength and weaknesses. It was an extensive list.

"All the stuff before this page is just me trying to get to this page. I had to figure out a whole bunch of things."

Tee flipped to the middle of the composition book and grinned. On those last few pages were the complete list of contenders that she determined were the greatest danger to everyone. Ralphie had seen the videos and noted the heavy hitters were at the beginning of Tee's sap list. There was Brooklyn Starling, the tough from the Trads. He was the number one contender. Second to Brooklyn Starling was Emmett Carson, the First Gen bad boy. Zeke was on the list as well. Ralphie considered the names in the composition book and was not surprised that he did not see his own name on the first few pages. He imagined that Tee had him in the bottom half of the sap list.

"How did you figure all this out," Jax asked.

"How did you figure out the strengths and the weaknesses," Gina asked with a smirk.

"It was simple, really. The videos told everything. All you had to do was look and listen. Most people have strengths and weaknesses. Most try to focus on their strengths. That's the easy part. Say, someone keeps talking or joking. That might be seen as a strength. Right? Well, that could also be a weakness that they are hiding behind. They are filling the silence with noise to keep everyone from looking at them too closely."

"What, you think that you some sort of genius," Isaac Moore questioned.

"No, not a genius. Don't' have to be a genius. All the information is there. For example, maybe there's a contestant that ain't too smart and they get on camera. Now, they ain't going to tell everybody that they stupid. Instead when they are asked hard questions, they make jokes to throw people off or get super ridiculous, for no reason at all. They are trying to hide something."

"That sounds about right," Zeke nodded.

"Who made you educational facility counselor," asked Isaac.

"I have been with psychologists long enough to figure out some things."

"I don't buy it," Gina yelped.

"So," Tee responded a little too strong. She pulled back her claws a little. Tee added, "It's my opinion, my work and what I believe. You can gambol around the challenge and try and win or you can move with a clear purpose and hope to outlast and outplay and outsmart the other forty-five contestants before they figure us out."

"Hey, Jax, did you notice that there were three players that had no videos," Ralphie asked.

Jax thought a minute.

"Just because you said some big words and offered some ideas don't make it true," Gina growled. "Prove it. Let's see if you can figure out my strength or….how 'bout one of our groups weaknesses."

Tee cut her dark eyes at Dame.

Ralphie stepped in. Tee was a bit surprised.

"What's my weakness," Ralphie asked.

Tee did not answer immediately. She looked and then paused.

"Do you really want to know?"

Ralphie nodded, yes.

"I think your strength is that you are a thinker. You don't allow your emotions to drive your decisions. So, that would mean that your weakness is--"

Ralphie raised a hand. "You don't have to say," Ralphie surrendered. Ralphie knew his weakness. It seemed that Tee knew it as well.

Tee studied Ralphie and nodded.

"Okay, let me look at that list. I think that it would be helpful before we get to the island to have some priorities," Dame concluded.

The strongest, according to Tee, was Brooklyn Starling or Emmett Carson. The top ten were: Emmett, Brooklyn Starling, John Legend Olson, Brian McKnight Jenson, Ezekiel McCoy, Miles Davis Everett, Earl Campbell Leonard, Aretha Franklin Simpson, Eric Benet Middleton, and Esther Rolles Garrett. The bottom ten were: Ralphie, Joyce, Penny, Bailey, Izzy, Ava, Jax, Raven Mitchell, Dre, and Ella Fitzgerald, the Shaker.

"What do you think about that brat being in the challenge," Maddy asked.

There was suddenly a bunch of discussion. Ella Fitzgerald Buchanan was on everyone's mind.

"If I see her, once the challenge begins, I'm going after her," Tee stated.

"Why?"

"I protect her, and she gets back to the family and she remembers how I helped her," Tee imagined.

"You always thinking," Zeke chuckled.

"Doubt that will happen," joked Ant.

"Why?"

"She probably has bodyguards to protect her while she's in the challenge."

"They can do that?"

"They the Shakers, they have different rules. You know that," Jax noted.

Ralphie looked at and noted that Tee had put Bailey at the bottom of the sap list.

"Damn girl," Jax grinned after looking over the list.

Before Tee or Gina could speak or do anything in stepped four enforcers. The room was all of a sudden in motion as the enforcers holding stun batons rapped the bunk bed legs and drove the participants toward the exit.

Hours passed. The talk of the upcoming challenge came to a slow boil. Jax pointed out the obvious.

"We still have to get to Pandemonium Island. Figure that should be later tonight or no later than the morning."

The idea of being away from his family, without choice, chilled Ralphie. He had toyed with the idea of running away. Everyone did, Ralphie believed. Yet, realizing that he could not return to his house now, if he wanted to was different. He had no choice.

The day became night.

"Think I should ask one of the numbers about vampires," asked Jax.

"It's your beat down," replied Zeke.

Ralphie simply shook his head, no.

"They gotta know," Jax pointed out.

"Jax, don't poke that bear, right now," Ralphie urged. "Wait until we are in the challenge and they can't beat you for being…. You know … you," Ralphie joked.

The four enforcers staked out the bunk house.

"Sleep," a few of the enforcers commanded.

"We leave for the island in the AM," one of the numbers stated.

"Lights out in fifteen," a block of a man said near the middle of the barrack.

The aspirants prepared for sleep. They headed to their bunks. The bunk house quieted.

Lights went out fifteen minutes after the announcement.

"Try and get some rest if you can," one of the enforcers croaked. "You have a long walk ahead of you."

The words were supposed to be encouraging but they came out cold. Ralphie thought about what the enforcer was saying. He and the others were headed to Pandemonium Island and the Twenty-Third Pandemonium Challenge. There on the island they would be armed and allowed to remove any rival anyway they could to become champion of the Pandemonium Challenge all piped live to the Remains.

"Hey, any of you numbers ever see a vampire," Jax asked from the dark, making everyone laugh.

"Can that or I will come over and sing you a stun baton lullaby," growled an enforcer from the darkened bunk house. The bunk house quieted. Some slept. Some tossed and turned. Ralphie thought about the upcoming Pandemonium Challenge.

Chapter Nine.

Launch.

At 0600 hours the enforcers marched the blurry eyed pre-teens out of the bunk house and into the auditorium. In the auditorium they had a light continental breakfast of orange juice, bananas, oranges, grapes, boiled eggs, tea and toast. There was not too much talk that early and the enforcers gave the participants only twenty-five minutes to eat and then leave. From the auditorium they were led by three enforcers into the early morning day of a compound that Ralphie thought he knew but was not certain.

"Is this a Gen compound," Ralphie asked a boy dressed in a Eureka! Second Gen hoody. The sleepy-eyed boy with short-cropped hair, a long chin and big ears looked at Ralphie and rubbed at his hooded eyes.

"Think so, I don't know," he replied.

"How you not know? I mean, look at the street signs or buildings and there has to be some landmarks," Ralphie steamed at the nameless boy who stumbled along half asleep.

"Lighten up, Ralphie," Jax said, grabbing Ralphie's arm.

Ralphie looked down and shrugged off Jax's hand, noticing that his own hand was balled into a fist. He felt his breathing suddenly in his chest. Ralphie closed his eyes. He became quiet.

"You okay," Jax asked.

"I'm fine," Ralphie breathed, calming down and thinking that he suddenly understood how people in the challenge went from friendly to cutthroat in seconds.

They were suddenly on a winding road that had fencing that made it nearly impossible to tell where they were in the Remains.

It had taken them nearly two hours to move from the warehouse to the edge of the Remains. With nearly sixty contestants, the nameless enforcers were silent and brutal if any of the contesters stepped out of line.

"No one gets up this early," someone complained as he walked into the rear of someone in front of him.

"Why do we have to get up this early?"

"Nothing good happens this early," another line tough complained, rubbing at her eyes and moving like a zombie.

"Keep quiet," one of the numbers howled.

Jax appeared next to Ralphie. Jax was half asleep but excited that morning. Zeke and Tee were nowhere to be seen.

"You see this," he pointed to the mist. "This is the perfect time for vampires to be out and about."

Ralphie rubbed at his eyes, though he was used to waking up this early and working with his father. To see his father daily Ralphie got up early, usually before the sunrise, to spend a little time with his father before he left for work. Ralphie looked at Jax and laughed despite the conversation.

"Sun's about to come up," Ralphie giggled. "No bloodsucker going to be up this early."

"Maybe, you're right. But maybe, they are day walkers? Or they are up and getting ready to sleep." Jax paused. "I'm just saying," Jax pointed out. He looked around for someone to talk to that morning. The poor girl that Jax found was a sleepy girl from the Trads.

"Hey, you a Trad?"

"Yes," the girl responded.

"Me, I'm a Miller, just like my homeboy, Ralphie," Jax grinned and hooked a thumb toward Ralphie. Ralphie listened half-heartedly.

"My name is Jax, like 1-2 pick up sticks. You know ball and Jax?"

Ralphie moved behind the person in front of him. The morning was cool but not cold. It was the time of day right before the sunrise and there was a grayness that sat atop everything.

"What's your name?"

"Joyce," the Trad said. "Joyce Battle," she concluded.

"Joyce Battle, like?" Jax paused.

"Like Joyce Battle," the girl answered.

"Joyce Battle? Don't know no Joyce Battle. Know Joyce Bryant. The Black Marilyn Monroe? The Bronx Bombshell?"

"Okay, my full name is Joyce Bryant Battle, like the Black Marilyn Monroe," the girl said a little frustrated.

"Yeah, I'm named after Jackie Robinson," Jax admitted. The girl nodded and slowed down. Jax slowed down with Joyce Battle to her annoyance.

"You a Trad, right," Jax asked and did not wait for Joyce to respond. "You think that there are vampires in the Remains?"

"What?"

"Blood sucking vampires? In the Remains," Jax said. "There's a lot of evidence that points to there being at least one or two."

"It's too early for all this," Joyce Battle growled behind Ralphie.

"I'm serious. There are reports from all over the Remains of missing people. The Remains ain't that big. There's not a lot of places to go missing in, if you think about it," Jax pointed out.

"You need to dial this whole crazy conversation down," Joyce Battle finally steamed. "And, by the way, stop talking to me."

Ralphie could only smile. Jax was a lot to take early in the morning.

Weaving through the early mist that was not thick enough to be fog the enforcers remained silent and focused and that cut out half of the conversations that anxious morning.

Fifteen-year-old Ralphie recalled how crisp it was that dewy morning before sunrise, when no one was moving about the Remains. There was no sound of trucks, cars or bicycles wherever they had been sequestered. The large group moved in two divisions and the enforcers on the outside of the divisions.

"Where are we going," Jax asked and for his trouble he got a jab in the ribs by 3127, the enforcer. Ralphie did not ask questions. There were no good answers coming until they made it to the island. So, he moved and shook his head at the few that tried to talk to the enforcers. Numbers don't talk with non-numbers, Ralphie recalled Zeke pointing out long ago; the rule still held.

Arriving at the edge of the Remains was a journey in and of itself. The enforcer, 2153, was in charge. He was in the lead. 2153 walked up to the exit point of the Remains and exchanged salutes with the enforcer at the exit point. The exit point was guarded by half a dozen heavily armored enforcers carrying assault rifles. The exchange was quick and momentarily the divisions were moving forward.

"Why are all those numbers there," a paint spattered hoody pointed toward the northern end of the line.

Ralphie looked at where the Poppy was pointing. Everyone was looking longingly in the direction where the Poppy pointed. There, stood four enforcers around one person. Ralphie strained to see who the person was.

"Who's that?"

"Don't know," a girl with a curly purple tipped Mohawk and braids fumed. The russet brown girl had a longish face and a kind of slow look on her beige face. Ralphie imagined that she was a Trad.

Ralphie noticed that whoever the enforcers were guarding was not a boy. Therefore, it had to be a girl. Why would there be four enforcers around some unknown girl?

"Maybe it's the Shaker," Tee imagined.

"The Shaker is here," Maddy questioned.

"Anyone seen her or talked to her," another girl, close to Maddy asked.

"She all siddity," a girl the color of chocolate milk with a nose ring bayed. She was a black and white Trad wearing a black and white hooded sweat top, blue jeans and combat boots.

"They gonna let the Shaker participate," a boy with an apple head, buck teeth and brooding eyes said from behind Tee.

"The Shakers won't allow that," Jax admitted.

"If it's the Shaker, then you know she's under 24-hour guard," someone else said in the line of people walking.

"Bull," a boy with a flat nose croaked.

Ralphie had seen the video. He could not believe that the Shakers would allow their princess to participate in the challenge. Innovators did not participate in the challenge. There was a belief that the Innovators did not believe in the challenge.

So, even though there was an Innovator, Shaker, named in the Pandemonium Challenge no one, including Ralphie, expected her to start the challenge. The rich and powerful did not risk their wealth or their heirs on the challenge. It did not make sense.

All thoughts of Innovators and Shakers and heirs and how many challenges they had participated in evaporated when someone in the procession screamed and pointed to the archway and the blue and gold license plate signs that had been fashioned into a piece of art that read: Leaving the Remains.

On either side of the archway stood enforcers holding assault rifles.

"We're clear," someone announced.

There were shouts here and there. Ralphie looked up and saw the sign. He could only smile. The idea of leaving the Remains seemed impossible. It was like breathing without filling the lungs.

"Fuh-shiggity, man, we are out of the fuh-rigging Remains," shouted Raymond Porter, a Second Gen.

"This is epic," Jax announced, bouncing into view and disappearing almost as quickly as everyone picked up their pace.

"Crap, man, we are out of the Remains," Leah Michelle yelled.

"Holy hell, we are out of the Remains," a boy wearing glasses screamed.

"Stay quiet and keep moving," 4871 sang to his group. At that moment, the same message was being passed down the line by the numbered enforcers. The enforcer moved and Ralphie moved with him.

"Keep moving," the enforcer advised and the girl with the glasses moved along, holding the side of her face. The two enforcers nodded and continued to move the nearly sixty contestants up the broken bridge.

The enforcers that were escorting the line bad boys and girls were the only ones to speak. Numbers talking to numbers, Ralphie thought, mischievously as they passed through the reinforced gate that marked the exit of the Remains.

Two dozen enforcers tasked to get the battlers from the Remains to the challenge drove the group to the foot of what had been the six-lane wide Bay bridge. 90% of the Bay bridge was gone. What was left was a fifteen-foot-wide foot bridge. On the bridge's rail was what was once a pedestrian and bicycle pathway across the bridge to what had been Treasure Island.

Ralphie knew he was supposed to cross the footbridge as all of the other contestants had over the years. But they, all of the contestants, wholly, stopped and stared at the bridge way.

It looked less like a bridge than a single thick black thread suspended between the Remains and the fog covered clouds. Though Ralphie and the others knew that Pandemonium island sat in the middle of Acid Bay, that early, the fog covered any part of the island that might be visible, as if the single thick thread they were about to climb would lead to the clouds.

They moved mechanically up the incline. All the candidates could not help but look up and at the fog covered place they were headed. Ralphie moved not really caring if he saw Pandemonium Island from the bridge or not. They were going to the challenge and going to fight if they saw the island or not from this side of the Remains.

There was a small commotion ahead of Ralphie that caught his attention. A pinched face, dark chestnut girl with glasses and a pink backpack spat: "Don't touch me" and then, loudly, "Your breath smells like dog vomit," and in response the enforcer the girl was railing at punched the loudmouth hard in the face. The girl fell like mercury on a cold day. The next enforcer reached out and picked the stunned girl up and dragged her forward. Everyone around the girl fell silent.

"You ain't got no protection here, sweet cheeks. Our job is to get you to the island straight, bent or broken," the enforcer growled. Another enforcer stepped forward and watched with a thin smile.

The friends of the unconscious girl picked her up and dragged her along the walkway. Everyone around them bit their lips. It was the rule in the Remains not to taunt the numbers. Pushing the bounds with a number always ended up with someone unconscious, in the hospital or in detention.

"She thought she was going to show her ass once we got out of the Remains," Jax sneered.

"Shut up," one of the numbers barked. Jax cut his eyes and noticed how close the enforcer was and fell silent. He pointed to the enforcer and acted as if he would punch him. Ralphie grimaced.

"Keep moving," enforcer 5127 demanded, as Ralphie and the others came upon the broken and barely maintained, dangerous bridge that led to the challenge.

Ralphie hesitated. There was a bunch of grumbling. It was not unexpected, it seemed by the enforcers.

"Keep moving, if you make the first rest stop, we might be able to see the island," 4871 announced to the competitors. The divisions continued moving up the broken fifteen-foot-wide footbridge that had been along the side of the Bay Bridge long ago.

At the first rest stop most of the contestants pointed out the outline of the island that peeked out of the morning fog. Some looked back longingly to the Remains. They all took in the fact that they were unequivocally out of the Remains.

A girl broke down crying, for no apparent reason. She was comforted by a friend. The boy nearest her shook his head and gestured to his temple.

"She's homesick, all of a sudden," one of the girl hopefuls said to no one in particular.

"Homesick? Who can be homesick at a time like this?"

"There ain't more than five hundred people that been able to say that they been here and not lie," Tee pointed out.

"You feeling homesick, Ralphie," Jax asked.

Ralphie looked up and was about to answer when the enforcers appeared and ordered everyone up.

"Move," one of the enforcers barked and mechanically, stutteringly, the lines of contestants began to move again.

"One foot in front of the other," 4721 called, shoving one of the contestants forward and everyone was moving again.

The enforcers moved easily up the slight grade of the bridge and onto the flat section of the bridge way. The wind blew. The fog was just beneath the bridge and made the entire morning eerily peaceful and foreboding.

"Have any contestants fallen off the bridge," one of the boys asked the enforcers escorting the group.

2117, the enforcer closest to Ralphie, a beige thick shouldered brute with biceps the size of cantaloupes, shook his head in answer.

"Stay to the right," directed 4825 who was standing on the left side of the walkway where there was a gaping expanse of missing railing and walkway. 4825 was hooked to the bridge walkway and standing in front of the gap. He held his automatic weapon in his hands to push any curious contestants away from the dangerous gap.

Ralphie followed behind Jax and two others, as they snaked around the gap.

"What caused that?"

"Don't be stupid," Jax joked.

"Who you calling stupid? Stupid," the dull looking boy, wearing a blue and green camo hoody that signified his Boomer line, growled.

"Keep moving," the enforcer announced, shouldering the two boys forward.

Ralphie shook his head. There was more and more sniping suddenly going on as the motley group of boys and girls made their way across the ruined bridge. A fight seemed inevitable.

The two boys stared at each other with ill intentions. The enforcers watched for any sign of heightened rage or snipping. Ralphie, found himself aware of the tension in the group. The moment, the possibility of something physical happening, abated, and a semblance of normalcy returned to the group as they trekked across the broken bridge that went only to what had been Treasure Island.

"It's been nearly fifty years since the flash. Why hasn't someone fixed this?"

"No one comes this way except us," a boy wearing a Trad hoody pointed out.

"Low priority," a buck toothed boy near Jax and Ralphie reported.

Ralphie and Jax cut their eyes at the buck toothed boy but did not smile or give him any encouragement. They were about to begin the challenge. There were no friends to be made now that they were on the steps of the challenge.

The escort moved quickly and quietly across the span with the hopefuls in tow. It would take two hours to arrive at the island the enforcers told anyone that asked. The walk to the island would be quick and only broken up with two fifteen-minute breaks. The first break came where a dozen heavily armored enforcers waited with heavy machine guns.

"This line is outrageous," Jax fumed.

"We should be able to just whip it out and whiz off the side of the bridge," a boy who looked like he could have been a wrestler or bodybuilder said.

"You go whipping anything out and I have the right to tap a drum solo on that noggin of yours," the enforcer closest to the boy answered.

So, no boys whipped out anything. Instead, they stood in line for a chance to go to the fiberglass sheds that had the peeling labels Ho--- Buc--- on them. The line for the half dozen porta potties was long but manageable. The girl's line was long and Ralphie saw Bailey in line with Tee, Maddy and Gina. He looked away and pretended not to see Bailey in line.

All the combatants were given water and fruit to tide them over until the second rest stop. Fifteen minutes after they had stopped the fifty plus were on the move again. They seemed less cranky and mean as they climbed the steady ascent toward the entrance to the once functioning Bay Bridge.

At the top of the entrance to what was Treasure Island the group had their second rest stop. At the second rest stop there were another dozen heavily armed enforcers. Those enforcers checked to be sure that only the combatants registered for the Twenty-Third Pandemonium Challenge proceeded. Under the watchful eyes of the dozen enforcers stationed at the entrance to the launch point of the Twenty-Third Pandemonium Challenge the contestants passed.

At the last checkpoint Ralphie and Jax found their jaws unable to close at the sight of the two big canons that greeted them at the end of the path across what had been the Bay Bridge. The barrels of the canons were huge and Ralphie or Jax could have climbed inside the barrel easily. For the life of the pair, neither Ralphie nor Jax could imagine the size of the ammunition they used. The canons looked more like pre-flash military canons than anything else but there was an oversized pistol look to the mechanism that suggested that it could be loaded and reloaded easily. The two giant guns were aimed over the combatants' heads and back toward the Remains.

"You see this," Jax noted, pointing toward the canons. "This ain't normal. My question is: What are they aiming at? It ain't at the hills."

Ralphie shook his head in reproof, but he knew that Jax wasn't wrong.

The rest ended fifteen minutes after it had begun, and the group moved again. The last rest stop faded, and everyone prepared for their arrival on Pandemonium Island. Unlike the tensions that swept across the group earlier there was an anticipation that gripped everyone as they neared Pandemonium Island.

"Are we close," Halle Thomas asked.

The enforcer did not answer but instead pointed. Ralphie, who was near Halle Thomas, looked where the enforcer directed. In the gray of the day they could just make out a gate and the outline of men and guns.

"Is that it?"

The enforcer nodded.

The last mile was shorter, in time, than the first two as everyone in the group seemed to want to reach Pandemonium Island. The group barely slowed as the big guns came into view. Everyone noticed the dozen enforcers watching them enter the gate that few in the Remains had ever seen.

"We are here," Tee asked.

"Close," the enforcer smirked.

On the other side of the heavily fortified machine gun post was the entry point to the top of the hill that led to Pandemonium island where another twenty enforcers stood lining the way to the official launch site.

"Just about two minutes and you have made it," announced one of the enforcers on the road. He pointed to a little used one-story building that sat on the one road to the island below.

At the bottom of the road, Ralphie knew from viewing all the other Pandemonium Challenges, that there was a ten-foot-high iron wrought gate that would be opened right before the challenge began.

"It's 1013 hours. You all rest and at 2300 plus or minus hours you all will be released onto the island. You all have about fifteen hours to rest, recuperate and prepare," announced 3014.

"Remember there is no physical violence here at the launching point until you are released into the challenge. So, stay in your buildings until you are called. Any threat of violence will be summarily handled by our able-bodied enforcement team," announced 5301.

"The bunks are in the next two halls. Alpha and Beta. There are two sets of bunks. First Gens, Boomers and Poppies are in the first hall, Alpha hall. Follow enforcers Cobbs and Grace," 3014 noted.

The two enforcers lifted their arms and yellow beams brightened the air above their heads. The First Gens, Boomers and Poppies followed. Twenty-four contestants left the one-story building for rest and food.

"Innovators, Millers, Second Gens and Trads are in the second hall, Beta hall. Follow enforcers Solomon and Morton."

The two enforcers lifted their arms and yellow beams shined into the air above their heads.

"Okay, so eat and sleep and get ready for a little knuckle dusting," Jax joked with a smile once they were on the way to the bunk rooms.

"Hack and slay," Gina beamed. "Hack and slay."

"Yeah, this is going to be the real-life MMORPG," Isaac Moore laughed.

"If so, I'm going to be a high-level thief," Jax gleamed.

They marched from the one-story building and to the hall that had sixteen bunk beds arranged so that no one was too crowded. Two of the bunks were closest to each of the doors near the exit. There was a bunk bed near the bathroom. Solomon and Morton claimed the bunks at the western end of the hall. 4181 claimed the bunk closest to the bathroom. 1101 and 2604 dropped their weaponry at the eastern exit of the hall.

"How in the hell did I draw the short stick and end up with Fenner? That cat farts all night," 2604 complained.

"Can that," Solomon growled. "Watch the kiddies until we get them some food."

"Roger that," replied 1101.

Ralphie noted the four enforcers that would be dealing out justice and making sure that no one got too crazy before the challenge. There were three men: 4181, 2604 and 1101. Dressed in their uniforms, there was no real significant difference in the men. 2604 might have been the shortest of them all. 1101 might have been the tallest. The most muscled was 4181.

The lone woman on guard was 1101. She was a bigger dark brown woman with an oblong face and braids. 1101 looked like someone's grandmother on a bad day. 1101 looked perpetually angry and ready to pounce on someone.

"Might want to rest. The challenge is just a few hours away," Solomon announced in a Deep bass tone. Solomon was a light brown man with a black mustache and a downward turned expression. He had a habit of tapping his sidearm when he talked, Ralphie noted.

Morton was a milk chocolate woman in her late thirties or early forties, with a round nose and thin eyebrows. She had her hair shaved on the sides and kept her helmet on the entire time that the contestants were in the hall.

Ralphie sat on his bunk and would have remained there had not Jax and Tee appeared.

"Come on, Ralphie, we're going to rub elbows with the rich," Jax decided grabbing Ralphie by the arm.

"What?"

"Wipe that stupid look off your face," Tee insisted. "You know that it ain't often that a Miller gets to rub elbows with a Shaker. So, try and look smart."

"What you trying to say?"

"Hanging out with Jax has dulled your shine, just a bit," Tee pointed out.

"Should I be insulted by that," Jax questioned all of a sudden stung by the words.

Ralphie smirked.

"Should I," Jax asked again.

Sitting on a bunk dressed in black leather motorcycle boots with gold rivets on the sides, black jeans and a black leather motorcycle jacket was Ella Buchanan. Ralphie took in her tightly curled hair that was parted down the side of her round head. Beneath that mane of hair sat two gigantic eyes that seemed all at once to care and to see everything. Ella Buchanan's round nose sat perched above her full lips.

When Ralphie, Tee and Jax arrived there were several others sitting near her. Dame, Isaac, Gina, Zeke and Maddy sat listening to Ella Buchanan talking about something important. Ralphie noted that Granville Summer, the Second Gen that had gotten removed from the Gathering Center, was there as well. What struck Ralphie as odd was that there was an enforcer standing a discreet distance away from Ella Buchanan. Ralphie noted the number: 3967.

"Who's that," asked Jax.

"That's Ella's own personal enforcer," Gina beamed. "She has her own personal enforcer until she gets to the island."

"What the," Ralphie mouthed.

Just then someone in the tight group asked Ella Fitzgerald Buchanan a question and everyone fell silent.

"It is true that all Shakers have tutors," Ella Buchanan sang. Her voice was melodic. It was as if the words she said were lyrics to a song.

"I heard that every Shaker in the educational facility is given a top of the line First Gen authorized computer."

"I heard that Shakers cannot use their computers on certain days," Gina declared.

"Someone said that the Shakers are protected by robots," Jax mentioned.

"Shut up everybody, we got Ella here and she can tell us everything about the Shakers, because she's a Shaker," Isaac Moore reasoned.

"So, is it true?"

Ella Buchanan smiled effortlessly at the question. She had perfectly even white teeth. She was cocoa colored and easy to look at, Ralphie thought.

"Is what true?"

"About the computers?"

"Oh, yes, we all are given computers and access to the Interweb to complete our work assigned by our instructors."

"Given?"

"We had to buy our own. Jax and me," Ralphie protested, the words rushing out of his mouth before he could stop them.

"We went treasure hunting in the dead zone and found our latest and greatest system," Jax crowed.

"What's treasure hunting?"

Ralphie smirked at the question.

"What? Shakers don't treasure hunt," Jax laughed.

"That's what some of us do. We go into the dead zones and dig around for things. It's a crap shoot. Usually treasure hunters come up empty," Isaac Moore explained.

"Is it dangerous," Ella asked.

"It can be," Maddy said.

"Maddy don't know. It is. There are all sorts of things underground. There are treasures and traps. There are things underground that most don't see. People have died hunting for treasures," Jax admitted.

"But it's worth the risk if you find something valuable. You can be line rich," Tee explained.

"Line rich," Ella asked.

"It means, cashed, liquid, cred heavy," Isaac Moore attempted.

"Oh," Ella nodded.

"What about not using your computers?"

Ella Buchanan seemed to mull over the question for a long time before answering. "We aren't allowed to use the computers Tuesdays and Thursdays. It was agreed upon by the Shaker educational division that on those days not to give us homework, to make our line remember that life was not just a video game or computer screen."

Her answer was greeted by absolute silence.

"We are supposed to be outside doing something. No electronics on those days," Ella added.

"No homework on Tuesday and Thursday," Dame whispered.

"We need no homework on Tuesday and Thursday," Maddy agreed.

"Ella is it true there are vampires in the Remains," Jax asked.

Everyone who knew Jax rolled their eyes.

Just then, two enforcers, 2937 and 3281, rolled in trays of food for the participants to eat. The conversation was put on hold to fill empty stomachs. Everyone made their way to the trays of food.

The foodstuff was nutritious and plentiful. There was fruit, vegetables, chicken, pasta, boiled eggs, potatoes, salad and pizza. The drinks were limited comparably. There was only fruit juice, milk and water. There were mini cans of carbonated beverages. Every contestant could take no more than two mini cans of carbonated and caffeinated beverage. Most grabbed the carbonated drinks.

Ella ate with everyone else. 3967 stayed close. Isaac and Tee seemed the most protective of Ella. She was suddenly the sun, and everyone circled Ella Buchanan. It was as if being close to the most powerful might rub off,

Ralphie thought, and everyone wanted some of Ella Buchanan to rub off on them.

Ralphie, after getting his food, sat on his bunk, away from the others. Jax after getting his food, hesitated on going to sit with the others. He sat next to Ralphie.

"What gives, Ralphie," Jax questioned, sitting across from his friend.

Ralphie shook his head in displeasure.

"What? Man, this is the prime time to be up next to the Shaker," Jax smirked.

"You go," Ralphie attempted. "I can't. I just can't."

"Come on. She might be your golden ticket out of the Mills, man. You never know."

"I don't want to get out because she feels sorry for me," Ralphie tried.

"Pride, huh?" Jax was eating a piece of chicken and smiling. "I ain't got no pride no more. This world done beat it out of me."

"Shut up," Ralphie scoffed. "You go back over there and join the Maker fan club. I can't," Ralphie admitted.

"Come on, man, this all is just a big dog and pony show," Jax advised.

"What you mean?"

"I mean, none of this really matters. It's just fun and games."

"I ain't interested in that kind of game."

"I get that," Jax concluded. Jax looked to the group around Ella Buchanan and back at Ralphie. He leaned back and began to eat his food. Ralphie looked up and nodded at Jax.

"What? Everyone got to eat."

"Yeah, everyone got to eat."

After eating, most gravitated to their bunks. They talked, joked and rested. Tee had spent the majority of the time, after eating, pouring over her notebook.

While Ralphie waited, he tried to remember everything he had been told by Tee hours before. He had a good idea of the sap list having only seen it once. Ralphie was unimpressed with Dame. Ralphie was unimpressed with Isaac. He was unimpressed with Maddy the most. He understood Dame and his whole tough guy act.

Based on Tee's sap list Dame was strong, focused and like a locomotive on a train track. He did not handle spontaneity well. On the other hand, Zeke's strength was his hand-to-hand skills and his weakness was his temper. He was likely to fly off the handle and make a major lapse more often than not. Jax strength was his humor. His weakness was his paranoia about everything and unexplained need to be the center of attention. Then there was Tee. She was Zeke's girlfriend. Who had a girlfriend at fifteen? More importantly, Ralphie thought, who needed a girlfriend at fifteen? Ralphie shook his head in dissent.

At 2250 hours in walked four enforcers. Two enforcers, big beefy men, stood at the rear of the bunk house that everyone was in. Two enforcers, one a little soft around the middle and tall, and the other shorter and with short cropped hair on his square head, moved to the front of the bunk house and opened a doorway that led out and into the darkness. Ralphie noted that the shorter enforcer wore a badge number: 5013.

"Move," 5013 barked and all of a sudden, the bunk house was all in motion and chaos as every battler grabbed their backpacks and gear and headed toward the open doorway.

"Move. Move. Move," snapped all the enforcers as they banged on the bunk beds and drove everyone in the bunk house out of doors. Ralphie moved when the enforcer barked. He had grabbed his backpack and fallen in step with the others rushing out of the door and into the cold night and the darkness. Stumbling and confused and excited and frightened all at once as he realized that he was no longer in the Remains and that he was really in the Pandemonium Challenge. Everything that had happened before seemed a perfunctory, preamble and practice to this moment less than sixty minutes from the start of the Twenty-Third Pandemonium Challenge.

Once outside the enforcers shepherded the contestants toward a low-slung building where a door was open, and all the hopefuls entered. Once inside the scrappers found themselves in a bare room that might have been an auditorium at some point before the Pandemonium Challenge. But now, Ralphie thought, that he and the others were just yards from Pandemonium Island all the dreams, fantasy and thoughts of being in the challenge were gone. All the myth and pretend was no more.

A dozen enforcers stood at the ready as the contestants entered the space. Ralphie noted that his friends, the Millers, had moved to the right of the entrance of the auditorium. As Ralphie looked around, he noticed that there was a low stage in the rear of the room. Also, he noted that two enforcers were watching the Millers. 3829 and 3083 watched as Ralphie and the other contestants settled down in the sparsely furnished auditorium. The two enforcers stood and watched as the last contestant entered the building.

Once inside, the contestants were poked and prodded and finally quieted in the biggest room in the building. Ralphie did not remember if this was one of the buildings that he had seen in the numerous videos of the challenge. The room and building were not something that he recalled.

"Think that we are about to get the talk," Jax figured.

Ralphie nodded, thinking the same thing.

"We'll get the duffel bags here," Jax whispered as he watched the other contestants enter the room.

Ralphie thought about the duffel bags. Inside of each duffel bag would be fourteen protein snack bars, a canteen, water tablets, twenty-one matches, a battery powered flashlight, medical kit, Mylar blanket and various supplies. There was a paper map and a list of all the contestants. On the map were labeled each numbered building on Pandemonium Island. The map was an essential tool on Pandemonium Island.

Of course, the biggest question anyone in the challenge had was: What weapon was inside of the duffel bag? The weapons ranged from rim-fire guns to muskets and swords and everything in between. In one challenge every contestant received medieval weapons only.

In twenty-two Pandemonium Challenges there had been all sorts of weapons in the duffel bags. Anything from brass knuckles to hand grenades to a submachine gun might be in the army duffel bags. A weapon, the right weapon, could change the Pandemonium Challenge.

In the center of the auditorium was a makeshift stage where there were several microphones, the old pre-flash types, with stands and cords. On either side of the stage were two stacked monitors that looked as if they were floating instead of attached to the wall. Four enforcers, 3729, 5321, 7630 and 4511, marched onto stage and took their positions on the right and left side of the stage. There were two enforcers, 5670 and 6081 on the right side of the stage armed with side arms.

They snapped to attention as two more enforcers, 3676 and 2991 stepped onto stage. One of the enforcers, 2991 was a dark-haired woman wearing ski goggles that she lifted and rested on her forehead. The woman had several medals on her uniform.

The other enforcer, 3676, the man, was an olive skinned knock off Patton with an oval face and bushy eyebrows. Ralphie noted that the fake black Patton had a bandage on the back of his left hand. Fake black Patton placed his goggles on top of his helmet and scanned the crowd. He looked out across the gathered faces with open disdain.

Last to take the stage were the two enforcers that looked more like technicians than the usual brute enforcers. The two technician enforcers rolled out a cart with a video projector on it. One of the technicians touched some buttons and there in the auditorium was the Pandemonium Challenge peacock; Dean Fletcher, in his hologram splendor. Dressed in his gaudy fluorescent yellow suit, blue collared shirt, California grizzly bear tie Dean Fletcher appeared to be a 3-Dimensional figure. The hologram strode onto stage wearing pointy blue crocodile shoes with gold metal tips.

Upon seeing the hologram of Dean Fletcher there was a smattering of applause. He was a Remains celebrity, who had died nearly twenty years ago. Everyone knew his riveting blue eyes, big ears, long hooked nose, and jack-o-lantern like, always smiling face.

He was the man that everyone loved to hate in the Remains. He was a constant reminder, for students, to stay focused and do their very best in the education centers. Fletcher was the face that everyone dreaded because he was the constant voice of commentary at the Pandemonium Challenge.

Some would attempt to prove a point. They would die first. Then, the rest of us would begin to pick off the weak. It would be a one-sided battle initially.

The best and meanest and cruelest would distinguish themselves. It was going to be a bloodbath, and no one could stop it or more importantly, no one wanted to stop it. So, things would spiral slowly and predictably out of control.

It had been this way for twenty-two years. There was little that could stop it from happening this year.

"Once your name is called and you leave this building, everything you run into is a threat. Everyone can sleep you. Everything can be used against you. So, get ready. The challenge is about to get real, real quick" the familiar voice of Dean Fletcher announced from the two monitors in the auditorium. Everyone contestant in the auditorium was focused on hologram on stage despite the same image being on the monitors.

The enforcers stayed alert. None of the enforcers seemed concerned with the video. They watched the contestants making sure no one got jumpy or thought it was a quiet moment and opportunity to exact some revenge. With 50 contestants in one room anything could happen.

The auditorium listened. The contestants listened. The enforcers waited.

"One more thing. Once you leave this building you are required to stay in the western end of the fire trail until daybreak. We will post enforcers at the wrought iron gate and make sure no one is hiding in the bushes on the way down. There are numerous places to hide and stay safe. The enforcers will secure the launch site. The island headquarters are off limits. Any contestant foolish enough to attempt to enter the headquarters will be summarily executed by the enforcers, no exceptions." Fletcher smiled cartoonishly at everyone. The video faded to black. The hologram spun on the stage and did one of those patented Michael Jackson Thriller moves before fading away like the images on the monitor.

5321, oatmeal brown, square chinned and with a scowl on his face, looked at 3429. 3429 lifted a gloved hand. 3112 snapped to attention and swiftly marched to the edge of the auditorium and signaled to someone else.

Right away, eight enforcers wheeled in four industrial carts with blue and yellow canvas duffel bags on them and gigantic numbers hanging from the ends of them. The duffel bags were numbered one to fifty-six. Ralphie furrowed his brow upon seeing that there were three extra duffel bags. Was there a flub?

The enforcers in the auditorium prepared for the launch. They prepared, slinging their assault rifles and removing their stun batons. The auditorium was at once lined with enforcers. They stood in pairs by the closest doors forming a channel for an exit.

On the monitors Dean Fletcher reappeared. He was still dressed as he had been before. Fletcher smiled one of his mischievous smiles.

"Here comes your equipment. Everyone gets foodstuffs. Yum. Everyone gets a map. Everyone gets a medical kit. And, the most exciting gift from the challenge committee is a weapon. As most of you know, there are weapons scattered around the island too. Have fun."

Dean Fletcher blinked off the monitor. Every challenge began with the Dean Fletcher video, Ralphie recalled. This, video of Dean Fletcher, had been recorded by Fletcher before his death. He was quirky and conversational. He had the right amount of silliness and smarminess.

"Late Breaking News from the Pandemonium Challenge committee," a woman wearing horn rimmed glasses announced as she turned around from a monitor as if she was doing work. The woman dressed like a cross between a superhero and a pre-teen catholic girl in a catholic girl outfit. She had a rectangular face with big cheeks and toothy grin. Her hair was braided and piled on top of her head in a loose bun of braids. Beneath her flashed: Toni Braxton Nelson, Pandemonium Challenge News.

"The committee has added a wrinkle to this year's challenge. We have added three extra competitors. You may know them. They are two bad boys and one bad girl. So, be prepared. They do not play nicely with others." Toni Braxton Nelson winked, taking off her glasses in a dramatic flourish. She put her fingers casually through the frames as she spoke. "They are Eric Wellington, David Rogers and Brandy Johnston. Good luck."

Eric Wellington stood up and stepped out of the shadows of a corner of the auditorium where no group stood and smirked at the closest combatants looking at him. He was tall for a teenager, thin and dressed in black jeans, white collared shirt, and black jacket. He looked athletic and very confident. Eric Wellington was a Trad and Johnny Law. He had nearly been a contestant on the previous year's challenge only to be disqualified when his scores were re-evaluated, hours before the challenge. Eric Wellington was a cheat and an embarrassment because he had cheated trying to get into the challenge. The

Johnny Laws looked at Eric Wellington with open contempt. Trads did not cheat. They thought that bending the rules was the worst thing imaginable.

The second extra tough was David Rogers, who was wearing sunglasses and sitting in a chair when the Poppies and Second Gens closest to him realized that he was there. David Rogers was a Second Gen who most thought was suicidal. Rogers kicked his chair across the auditorium and the chair slammed into a Poppy, Walia Howard, who screamed in surprise, after careening off of some backpacks on the floor.

Wesley Howard fell to the floor and immediately jumped back to his feet as if nothing happened. His friends dressed in paint spattered hoodies and hand painted combat boots all went on alert. Robert Nesta, the smallest of the Poppies, had a cartoon T-shirt on beneath his paint spattered hoody. Scott looked as if he was ready to fight. David Rogers smiled mischievously at the smaller boy.

Ralphie seeing Robert Nesta bristle, braced for action and stopped the careening chair with his sneakered foot. Ralphie cut his eyes and made a fist and noted how close David Rogers was to him, all of a sudden. Ralphie didn't want to start a fight with David Rogers that he couldn't finish but the bad boy was all of a sudden within arm's reach.

David Rogers had been rejected on the Twenty-First challenge because he had some illness that threatened his life. No one wanted a contestant in the challenge that might die without a fight. That defeated the purpose of the challenge. Therefore, David had been rejected. Then he got better and petitioned to be re-evaluated. Voila. David Rogers, the sick and dying Poppy, was now on this latest challenge.

David Rogers grinned evilly at Ralphie's reaction. After the seven toughs closest to him were startled by his appearance. David jumped again and startled the line toughs again. He snickered at the second reaction more than the first.

Tee braced for a fight. Zeke and Jax crouched, ready for anything. Ralphie just watched.

Ralphie reminded himself of what the enforcers had announced over and over again. Even if David Rogers thought he was bad enough to fight someone the enforcers were there. There was no fighting between contestants before the challenge began. They were there to ensure that everyone made it to Pandemonium Island without laying a finger on each other.

"Pansies," David Rogers yowled. Looking at the four Millers he just sneered. "What they going to do now? They cannot punish me more than this."

Ralphie smirked at David Rogers' words. David Rogers looked at Ralphie for a moment. Ralphie and David Rogers stared each other down.

"He's right and crazy too." Jax straightened up and smiled affectedly. "Most of these challengers are soft."

Ralphie watched as Brandy, the third badass appeared from behind some enforcers near the far exit. She was dressed in some funky combat outfit with combat boots, camouflage jacket, in the blue and gold colors of the Remains. Her sister, Rose, had been the controversial winner of the twentieth challenge.

Rose Johnston, Brandy's older sister, was controversial because she had faked her death only to reappear as the final two faced off. Rose Johnston, a Second Gen, flatlined the winner of the ultimate last fight when the winner was hurt and tired. Rose Johnston won the challenge in an underhanded way. It was a sneaky and devious win but a win nonetheless, Ralphie recalled.

"That's all the video we have," 3429 stated.

Every contestant turned their attention back to the enforcers on the stage. Ralphie scanned the crowd for Bailey. He wondered if she was ready for the challenge.

3429 stepped forward and looked at the enforcers forming a path from the far wall to the stage.

"We are about to get this challenge underway." 3429 looked out on all the contestants. He looked back at the others assembled.

"Finally," a voice called.

There was a smattering of laughter from the crowd at the question. Ralphie searched the sea of faces for the wiseacre but only found Emmett Carson looking at him with evil in his eyes. Seeing Emmett in the auditorium made Ralphie wish that the challenge had begun and that he could beat the bad boy's brains out. Emmett Carson and his smugness made Ralphie's blood boil.

"All right, we have things to do. You have a challenge to participate in. So, let's get started," the enforcer smiled impatiently.

3429 and commander Mason stood beside the enforcers, 7630 and 4511. 3429 stuck the microphone he had in the face of 4251, the enforcer with the clipboard.

"Okay, when you hear your name, take everything with you. Once out of this room you cannot come back. Once out of the building you will be directed down the hill to the wrought iron gate. Once you cross the threshold of that gateway you are in the challenge. No violence until you are on the other side of the gate. Get ready," the enforcer spat into the microphone.

4268 was a bruiser of an enforcer. He looked like he was going to burst out of his uniform as he reached for the first duffel and flung it at Tavion Adams. Tavion Adams was a thinly built kid of fifteen or thirteen and when he jumped to his feet, after hearing his name called, he had run forward only to turn around and grab his backpack. Tavion Adams turned and received a duffel bag in the face. Tavion Adams caught the duffel and after a moment pounded out of the auditorium and onto Pandemonium Island.

Name after name was called. Challengers jumped to their feet and bang, pow they were slammed with a duffel bag either from 3586 or the hulking 4268. 3586 was tall and young and floated the duffel bag to the participant. There was no smack or exhale by the recipient when 3586 threw them their duffel bag. The boy or girl might be caught unaware or flat-footed but there was no risk of injury when 3586 doled out the duffel bags.

Tee received her duffel and disappeared like all the ones before her. Zeke and Jax looked at each other. They had rehearsed the departure a hundred times. They were to go one hundred yards straight or as straight as possible and wait for the rest of the Millers to gather. They were going to outsmart the other teams. Their goal was to outlast the other teams. Of course, Ralphie knew that the best laid plans were meaningless in the face of danger and uncertainty.

"Wait for us," Zeke reminded as he leaned over to Ralphie. Zeke had a squarish face and thick features for a thirteen-year-old. Ralphie looked at the boy that had thick shoulders, arms and chest and nodded; yes.

"Andre North," called an enforcer.

Andre North jumped to his feet. He grabbed his backpack. He walked forward and 4268 fired a duffel bag at the boy. Andre North caught the duffel and smirked at the oversized enforcer. He walked out of the auditorium.

"Remember the plan, keep going straight after the gate. We'll meet up one hundred yards from there," Jax reminded Ralphie.

"I know," declared Ralphie.

"Good luck," said Zeke.

Ralphie climbed to his feet and slipped on his solar powered backpack. He cinched the shoulder straps tightly so that the backpack did not come loose as he envisioned running through the hall and down the slight decline to Pandemonium Island. Leaving the auditorium and the launching was not the beginning of the challenge. The challenge only began once on the other side of the wrought iron fifteen-foot-high gate that would be secured once all ruffians were out of the auditorium and on the island.

Thus, Ralphie knew that once he got on the other side of the wrought iron gate the challenge would have begun and everyone was liable to do anything.

"Dre Prescott," was announced and Ralphie felt the gooseflesh rise on his arms. Ralphie knew that he could not be too far from hearing his name.

Another name was announced, and the first duffel flub happened. The contestant had scrambled to his feet and seemed scared and uncertain. The line tough was a round bellied boy with jowls and a gap-toothed smile, but at the moment, he looked like a scared black Santa Claus without white hair or beard. The enforcer had tossed the duffel bag to the scared black Santa and black Santa had reached out and completely missed the duffel bag. The duffel bag went spinning on the auditorium floor. Black Santa turned and turned too fast that he spun himself back down to the floor.

"Rayburn," the enforcer called. "Get out of my auditorium, on the quick."

Rayburn, the black teen Santa, climbed back to his feet and tried to smile about his clumsiness. Two enforcers from the back of the auditorium ran forward and escorted Rayburn to the hallway. The enforcers spun around and quickly returned to posts.

"Reynolds. Ralph Ellison Reynolds," someone shouted and as Ralphie climbed to his feet and looked, he was slammed with a duffel bag. He was caught off guard. He knew the duffel was coming but still the force of the unwieldy package threw him, just a little.

Instantaneously, he recovered and went running down the hallway. Enforcers were lined up every twenty feet or so holding high powered weapons. Ralphie wanted to walk. He slowed.

"Keep running," screamed one of the enforcers and Ralphie picked up the pace, adjusting the duffel in his hands as he did.

The fifteen-year-old ran to the end of the hallway and through a doorway. He was instantaneously outside and on the familiar front steps of the main staging building for The Pandemonium Challenge.

"Keep moving dweeb," one of the enforcers yelled, menacing Ralphie with his assault rifle.

He pounded down the stairs and onto the hardened dirt that would lead to the short path down to the wrought iron fence and entrance to the island. Ralphie ran forward toward the lighted road.

"Keep going until you get to the gate, dweeb," another enforcer yelled.

"Get your skinny ass down the hill and into the challenge," another voice barked.

"No one gets a free pass in the challenge," another wide shouldered enforcer standing by the others added.

Ralphie ran and looked back only once as he ran down the lighted path toward the wrought iron gate that waited at the bottom of the hill. Ralphie and everyone that had seen a challenge knew about the wrought iron gate. It was a feature of the challenge when it broke and fell in challenge nineteen.

The original wrought iron gate that had been at the bottom of the launching site had rusted and fallen into disrepair when the Pandemonium Challenge committee took over Pandemonium Island. They had hired one of the Poppies to make an ornate wrought iron gate that would say something significant. Ralphie knew all this because he had watched a video of the behind the scenes of the Pandemonium Challenge and the artist had been interviewed. He was picked because of his iconic sculptures in the central government mall. As Ralphie moved down the hill, his duffel bag over his shoulder he stopped trying to recall the name of the artist that had designed and created the ornate new wrought iron gate that welcomed every Pandemonium Challenge contestant onto the island.

As Ralphie ran down the hill and the paved road, he tried to dredge up the name of the artist that had created the new wrought iron gate that led to Pandemonium Island. Ralphie could not remember the name of the artist but could see his bearded long, triangular face and his dark eyes, that flitted left and right and rarely stopped scanning the terrain in front of him. He reminded Ralphie of a hawk because of his hooked nose and jumpy nature.

Ralphie shook the frustration of not remembering the artist's name to the immediate issues of several people, just off the path, digging through their duffel bags. Ralphie did not stop. He continued to descend the path but was surprised that there were several people hiding just to the left or right of the road.

Girls were huddled on the path that led toward the wrought iron gate to the left and right side of the road. Boys were huddled too. Ralphie did not stop.

The Alphabet Crew of Jax, Tee and Zeke, and the add on Millers, Dame, Isaac, Gina and Tee, had a plan. Zeke and Tee had told the other Millers the first night plan. Therefore, Ralphie imagined that when he found Tee, she might be there with the other Millers. But Ralphie had to get to the bottom of the hill and through the wrought iron gate first.

He reached the bottom of the hill and took a breath. Ralphie saw the outline of the wrought iron gate. Ralphie could not help but slow and take in the last bastion of safety. The gate was fifteen feet tall and twenty feet wide. It had taken nearly three months to finish after the art was signed off by the Pandemonium Challenge committee after the fifth challenge.

Standing there, in the dark, Ralphie could not help but place a hand on the ornate artistry of the gate maker. On one side, the interior of the gate, was what looked like a great and toothy mouth of some fantastic creature. Built into the iron above the great maw were the suggestions of eyes, but not one pair but dozens of eyes of various sizes all belonging to the fantastic creature. On the opposite side of the wrought iron gate was the image of the Remains beneath clouds. The eyes on the one side were transformed into clouds of various sizes and densities.

Ralphie paused. Once on the other side of the ornate wrought iron gate the challenge was real. All the safety and civility that had been imposed by the enforcers would be gone, Ralphie knew. On the one side there was safety. On the other side, just a few more steps and the challenge and danger were everywhere. Once, on the other side of the gate Ralphie knew he needed to be hyperaware because he was, all of a sudden, in the challenge. Stepping over the threshold to the challenge and away from the ornate gate and everything he had been told all his life was illegal and prohibited would be allowed and encouraged.

On the other side of the wrought iron gate Ralphie threatened everyone trying to win the Twenty-Third Pandemonium Challenge. He was a competitor for the Pandemonium Challenge. As a combatant he was a threat to everyone and everyone a threat to him.

Ralphie stepped through the iron gateway that delineated enforced safety from the lawlessness of the challenge. On the other side of the gate it did not feel different but Ralphie knew that the danger was all around him. He was a threat to everyone trying to win the challenge.

Once through the iron monster edifice Ralphie was greeted with three choices. In front of him was a dirt wall that led to a steep hill. At the base of the hill was a paved road that went north and south. Ralphie looked left and right and chose the lesser of the two options. Ralphie began to climb up the short but steep hill. He grabbed at the earth and low scrub brush to get a hand hold and foot hold as he climbed that early morning.

Chapter Ten.

Day One. 12:01-3:01AM.

"We got to get out of here and away from the lunatics as quickly as possible," Dame declared and before anyone could argue Gina, Isaac, Tee and Maddy were following. Zeke looked at Ralphie and Jax. Jax looked at Zeke. Ralphie watched as Zeke reluctantly followed. Jax followed behind Zeke. Ralphie followed Jax.

"Damn, Zeke, that is some hard cheese. Bad luck for you, looks like Tee and Maddy are suddenly bosom buddies," Jax said.

"What's that supposed to mean?"

"It's not supposed to mean anything. They just seem close, all of a sudden," Jax backpedaled.

"Shut up, Jax," Zeke squawked. "Keep up and shut up."

Jax looked back at Ralphie. Ralphie only smiled broadly in reply.

The eight Millers snaked their way through the twilight darkness and the various island booby traps and near-death encounters with the other forty-five contestants moving east to west. Led by Dame, the eight found themselves at a two-story building that, according to the map, was a long, long time ago a car storage building.

At the car storage building, the groups fell into comfortable lines of Dame and Zeke's friends. Isaac, Maddy and Gina gravitated toward Dame. Because of Maddy, Tee found herself trying to straddle a fence, that had never been a fence until that moment.

Jax, Ralphie and Zeke stood and studied the new group dynamics. Jax did not say a word. He did not have to. Everyone could see that Maddy and Tee were friendly.

"Okay," Jax declared, awkwardly. "Things have gone a little weird already."

"It's the first few hours," Gina began.

"Things change in the challenge," Ralphie offered.

"People are going to flip back and forth," Jax noted.

"Don't care about that," Zeke balked.

"Everyone makes decisions based on safety," Isaac noted, watching Tee and the others.

"Speaking of protection," Jax said empathetically. "We should check our weapons."

"We can check weapons after we figure out who is going to take the first watch," Dame corrected.

Zeke nodded. Jax smiled, awkwardly. Raphie only lowered his eyes and thought about how quickly things changed in the challenge once everyone was in the game.

"We're Millers. Not everyone is brave and strong. So, I suggest that four watch the first floor. I got me and Isaac, we'll take the first shift." Dame paused. "Who else?"

Jax, for some reason, volunteered and Gina, the thick girl, too, raised her hand for the first watch.

"I didn't volunteer for the first shift," Jax attempted. "I just wanted to know how long the first shift was going to last."

"Too late," Zeke giggled.

"Why me?"

"Why not you?"

Zeke laughed at Jax's protest. Tee shook her head. Maddy grinned.

"We will take the first watch from two to six o'clock," Dame began looking at his phone. Everyone checked their phones for the time. It was nearly two o'clock in the morning. "The second shift will be from six to ten o'clock, then we get out and get busy."

Zeke nodded. The group circled up on the first floor of the car storage building. Ralphie found himself near Jax.

"Okay, everyone, pull out your weapons and we'll figure out who gets what, for the good of the group," Dame declared. No one protested, Ralphie noted, tired but excited that first night. Everyone sat down and opened their duffel bags.

Jax pulled out a large bent knife that Ralphie remembered from history class as the kukri.

"What the hot steaming fudge bar is this?"

Isaac pulled out an ice pickaxe.

"This is a back scratcher on steroids," Isaac grinned hoisting the ice pickaxe into the air for all to see.

"Bingo," Tee laughed like a kid on Christmas day. Tee pulled out an old school ceramic Glock 21 with two extra magazines. She checked the .45 ACP burper like a soldier. At once, she had pulled back the gun slide and checked to see if there was a bullet in the firing chamber. Tee pressed the magazine release and checked if the magazine was loaded. The magazine held ten rounds. That meant that Tee had thirty rounds to play with.

Zeke pulled out a surgical tubing slingshot. Zeke lifted his newly acquired arm rocket and studied it. He was a big kid and with an arm rocket in his hand he all of a sudden looked mischievous. Zeke smiled broadly as he slipped the arm rocket over his forearm and pulled the slingshot pocket that would hold a rock back as far as he could. Everyone winced as they took in Zeke's new weapon.

Ralphie pulled out a croquet mallet. Ralphie did a double take. He let his dark eyes fall on the croquet mallet. He admired the 9-in x 2-3/8-in hardwood mallet. It had a hardwood shaft and hardwood mallet head. Used, in the right hands, this was a dangerous weapon, Ralphie mused.

Dame pulled out a military styled crossbow. The bow was a four-limb assembly. There were thirteen crossbow bolts.

Gina pulled out a trench knife. The imposing weapon seemed incredibly imposing in the hand of a girl that was still not five-foot-tall and weighed less than one hundred and fifty pounds. "Don't think that I will be using this too often," Gina giggled, nervously.

Madison pulled out the second burper in the group. In her honey colored hand, she turned over the Ruger Double-Action .22 Mag Revolver. In the duffel were two speed loading clips for the burper and twenty rounds of .22 ammo.

Straight away, after Madison pulled out her .22 Mag Revolver, there was a fifteen-minute trading war amongst the eight. Jax complained. He wanted Tee's Glock. Tee was not giving Jax her handgun.

"You know that I should have that burper," Jax reasoned.

"Why?"

"Because I should," Jax stated.

Tee sneered at Jax's reasoning.

"You ever shoot a gun?"

Jax stared at Tee with open disdain.

Ralphie could not help but laugh at the absurdity of it all. Everyone wanted the burpers. Only two in the group had ever pulled the trigger on a real burper, Ralphie thought. Maddy was not one of the two, the fifteen-year-old thought with a wry smile.

Dame took Jax's kukri.

Gina held onto her trench knife.

Madison kept the Ruger Revolver despite not ever shooting a gun in her life.

Isaac held onto his ice pickaxe.

Zeke ended up with the crossbow.

Tee kept her Glock 21.

Jax upgraded to Zeke's arm rocket slingshot.

Ralphie kept his croquet mallet. No one seemed to want the deadly backyard weapon used centuries ago to knock wooden balls through metal wickets, for no apparent reason. Ralphie did not really care. The weapons, he knew, were meaningless at the beginning of the challenge.

Everyone given a weapon was not proficient with that weapon, Ralphie knew. Of course, there were exceptions. A gun was the exception. Yet, someone shooting without accuracy was like having a machete and not any arm strength to fend off attacks.

So, Ralphie had just figured after the first 24-hours things would change. The ones that knew about combat would survive. The challenge was not about going on the offense all the time, at least, that was Ralphie's belief as the first day of the challenge got underway.

It was nearly two o'clock in the morning when Zeke, Maddy, Tee and Ralphie climbed to the second floor to rest for a few hours. Zeke, Tee and Maddy cozied up together near a wall and giggled and whispered about nothing. Ralphie walked to the closest window and hunkered down.

Two hours, Ralphie thought absently. It could not have taken two hours to go from the launching point to the first resting spot, but the time did not lie. Two hours to weave around the island and not be ambushed or killed by opposing groups trying to weave around the same island with all sort of lethal weapons. Ralphie calculated that once they landed at the warehouse, they had to look at the weapons and then trade the weapons and then divide the groups to watch over the others.

Ralphie was surprised that it had only been two hours to get to the warehouse and to prepare for the early morning rest before the real challenge began. Everyone was all nerves and adrenaline about the first tests of the challenge and secretly wondering if they could end someone ready to end them.

On the second floor, Zeke, Maddy, Tee and Ralphie found places to rest. Zeke and Maddy rested near each other. Maddy was in arm's reach of Zeke and Tee and not feeling like a third wheel at all. The threesome looked quite comfortable, Ralphie thought. Ralphie, on the other hand, felt like he was on the outside looking in at the three others.

He shrugged off his backpack and dropped his duffel bag on the floor and dumped out the duffel's contents. He was tired but he could not turn off his brain at that moment. He transferred his essentials to his backpack.

It was just a few minutes until three o'clock when Ralphie finally rolled his duffel bag into a pillow for the first time in the challenge. Next to Ralphie, were the things he decided he did not need. Beside him were four empty water bottles and his Mylar blanket.

Ralphie lifted the croquet mallet and let the shaft end slide into his upper thigh. The head of the croquet mallet tilted and in slow motion moved toward the corner of the wall closest to the window. Ralphie pulled on the croquet mallet and for an instant it froze in midair. Ralphie smiled as the mallet stopped its descent to the corner and reversed itself and headed back toward Ralphie.

"What the hell is that," Tee asked. Tee was looking at Ralphie through a jagged two-foot-high and long crack in the wall that separated her, Zeke and Maddy from Ralphie. Ralphie smiled broadly at the question. He had imagined that he was left all alone. He did not answer immediately, not sure that Tee was actually talking to him.

Ralphie lifted his newly acquired weapon again and allowed it to slowly descend. He caught the mallet in his right hand and lifted it a few inches from his chest. Ralphie looked again to the left and found that Tee was lying on her stomach atop the Mylar blanket looking at him with those pale brown eyes.

"I asked you a question Ralphie," Tee hissed.

Ralphie noted that Tee had her Glock 21 in her right hand and was suddenly not playful but serious. The Glock 21 slowly turned clockwise as Tee peered through the crack.

"Hope that thing has a safety on it," Ralphie joked, realizing how outrageous this conversation would have been had it only been a day ago. Now, in the challenge, Ralphie was going to have a conversation with someone armed and dangerous with a weapon that was built to blow holes in people.

"This ain't my first rodeo," Tee smirked. Ralphie closed his eyes and composed himself.

"The ancients used to use this to smash rats that were foolish enough to stick their heads out of their holes," Ralphie joked. "Like a real whack-a-mole game."

"Really?"

"Naw, I was kidding. This is from an old-fashioned backyard game called: croquet," Ralphie admitted with a devilish smile. "When people had backyards, they would invite people over and play croquet and whack a ball through wooden or metal wickets. I don't know how they won, but I think it was supposed to be fun."

"How you know all this?"

Ralphie lifted his digital map reader, which looked a little like an old-fashioned price scanner. On the screen was the information that Ralphie had just mentioned.

"You, stupid," Tee laughed and laughed. "I really thought you were coming off the dome with that info," Tee admitted. She was being playful, Ralphie noted.

Tee Bennett was rarely playful and Ralphie tried to hold onto that brief moment of the old Tee. It was as if she had dived into a pool and disappeared only to emerge as the kinder, gentler Tee that Ralphie longed to be around. The pale brown eyes of Tee took Ralphie in and held him there in that pool of sepia brown. Her small round nose crinkled with her smile just a little, as she pursed her lips, thinking.

Ralphie adjusted himself to get a better view of Tee. He took in the caramel colored fifteen-year-old that he had been friends with for nearly half a decade. Ralphie recalled that a year ago she had changed and become a different Tee. She was now this meaner Tee Bennett.

Ralphie did not like the meaner Tee Bennett. He looked at the girl with snake braids and tried to hold onto the Tee that he had first met long ago. She had been so friendly long ago.

Tee rested her head on her small fist and for a moment Ralphie figured she was going to say something that would make all the strangeness meaningless. Maybe, Ralphie hoped, she would tell him how her father dying created the mean and slutty Tee Bennett. Instead, Tee yawned and rubbed at her big eyes and folded her hands in front of her. She rested her head on her hands. "I'm tired," Tee admitted.

Ralphie looked up and into the corners of the ceiling, checking for anything unusual. In the dark of the ceiling Ralphie saw a red light that he knew was one of the hundreds of cameras on the island. There were cameras everywhere, Ralphie knew and instead of fixating on the continual recording, he listened.

The fifteen-year-old turned back over and onto his back with his croquet mallet. He thought for a moment that he should have tried to continue the conversation just to keep the conversation going. But there was no point. He checked the digital map reader and noted the time. It was late or early and he needed to rest. It was nearly three thirty in the morning and he was scheduled to guard the structure in less than three hours. So, Ralphie laid the croquet mallet on his chest and tried to fall asleep.

His eyelids became a little heavy and though tired, Ralphie could not shut off his brain as he laid near the open and ragged rectangle of space that had at one time held a window but was now just an opening to the street one floor below.

A few minutes later Ralphie opened his eyes to find himself in the dark. He sat up. Zeke, sleeping on the second floor popped up and studied Ralphie like he discovered a coiled rattlesnake in his sleeping bag.

"Why you up?"

"Got to go and whiz," Ralphie admitted.

"You can't hold it?"

"No, can't hold it for seven days, if that's what you mean?"

"All right be careful," Zeke advised.

"Don't have a choice," Ralphie smirked.

The digital map reader located the closest toilet. It was just a couple of blocks away. Ralphie descended the stairs and looked around for Dame, Isaac, Jax or Gina. They were nowhere to be seen. Ralphie did not think too much of it. He had more pressing needs.

He exited the structure and walked down the darkened street and to the overgrown field of grass and weeds. According to the digital map reader the porta potty was somewhere in the fenced in field. Ralphie cut his eyes in the dark and thought he saw the outline of two structures in the field. He climbed through the opening in the fence and moved to the far side of the field and the two porta potties.

Ralphie relieved himself in the light of his handy dandy lighted headlamp. He unlocked the porta potty door and as he was exiting looked down, for an instant, thinking he saw something. He stepped out of the porta potty and found himself dodging a boy with an old fashioned three headed flail. The three heads of the flail nearly smashed Ralphie but Ralphie stepped back and avoided the attack. He stepped forward and the headlamp on his head blinded the boy for a moment.

Seeing the boy throw his hands up to shield his eyes, Ralphie grabbed his croquet mallet and jabbed as hard as he could straight ahead at the boy but not registering how badly he punched him. Ralphie heard a comforting "humph" as the croquet mallet pushed into the dark and the boy and the boy fell out of the arc of light on Ralphie's head.

Ralphie looked left and then right and used the headlamp to guide him to the exit he had entered minutes before. He ran toward the hole in the chain link fencing. He did not think to bash in the boy's head or cheese him. Instead, he ran toward the hole in the fence. He wasn't sure if he hurt the boy or not. He did not care. All Ralphie wanted to do was get away from the boy.

Once through the fence and on the other side of the fence Ralphie looked back and noticed that he was not being followed. Ralphie clicked off the headlamp. He continued down the street in utter darkness.

Ralphie looked back and again there was no one on the sidewalk chasing him down to bash in his head. The attack was so unplanned and unexpected and just a bad memory. He slowed and checked behind him regularly until he started questioning if the attack had really happened. It was the challenge and when someone attacked, they usually did not stop until they had won the challenge. Yet, the boy with the flail had only attacked twice and stopped.

Looking back again and seeing no one Ralphie wondered had he imagined the whole thing. It seemed more likely that it was his mind playing tricks on him, Ralphie thought. This was the challenge. No one allowed threats to escape. He had an active imagination, at least that is what everyone thought.

So, when he reached the front of the two-story building where Dame, Isaac, Jax and Gina were guarding he hesitated. Ralphie looked back one final time and decided not to say anything to anyone about his near attack. He clicked off his headlamp and didn't have to say anything, as there was no one around as he entered. He made his way to the second floor. Ralphie sat down near his backpack and exhaled.

"You okay?"

"Yeah," Ralphie replied. He studied his body to see if he had any visible marks from the attack. He had no scratches or bruises from the encounter with the boy at the porta potty. Finding no damage Ralphie replayed the whole incident over in his head and figured that the whole incident had been a figment of his imagination. Who had a flail in the challenge?

He checked the digital map reader and noted the time. It was nearly half past two in the morning. It had taken him about fifteen minutes to walk to the porta potty and back. In fifteen minutes, Ralphie told himself, there had to be some kind of damage.

Returning to his spot Ralphie tried to sleep, thinking if he had actually had an encounter with the nameless boy with a flail or not. Ralphie dozed, never sleeping completely that first day of the challenge.

An hour before the first announcement of the challenge Ralphie was shaken awake by Zeke. Ralphie opened his eyes and there was Zeke pointing to Maddy's spot on the floor. Ralphie rubbed his eyes and looked in the direction that Zeke was pointing. Maddy was not in her spot.

"Where is she?"

Ralphie did not answer.

"Where is she," Zeke growled. Zeke was livid.

Ralphie pieced together what had happened. Zeke had fallen asleep. He had promised to protect Maddy.

Zeke woke up the heavy sleeping Tee.

"What's going on?"

Ralphie rubbed at his eyes trying to figure out why Zeke had woken her up.

"I didn't see her," Ralphie admitted. He had dozed off for a few minutes.

"What's going on," Tee questioned, waking to the continuous pacing of Zeke.

"Where's Maddy?"

Trying to focus on the madness that was Zeke in a panic, Ralphie rubbed at his eyes. It was a sight to see. He was wild-eyed. He looked as if he might spontaneously explode at any moment.

Tee and Ralphie watched as Zeke grabbed his divided bow and went to the stairs that led to the main floor.

The reaction was instantaneous. Jax, Gina, Isaac, and Dame tensed as Zeke came down the stairs wild-eyed, carrying his newly acquired weapon.

"What in the fresh French toasted hell is this," questioned Dame, a little louder than expected.

Suddenly, everyone was awake and ready for anything.

"Where in the bow-legged frog legs is Madison?"

"Put down the crossbow," Dame breathed through his braces angling toward Zeke. Dame had his kukri in hand. He held it like a baton, a deadly and dangerous sharp-edged baton.

Zeke seemed emotionally everywhere all at once. He looked left and right wildly. He was aggravated and seemed at times unable to communicate properly.

"Where is Maddy," Zeke growled. "Someone had to see her. You were all down here. Did she leave? Is she down here?" As he spoke, he continued to look in every direction at once and the bow swung back in forth in front of him tracking his head's motions. Jax and Ralphie followed closely.

Tee came down the stairs and rushed toward Zeke as Dame seemed prepared to hack off one of Zeke's limbs to protect everyone else in the deserted car storage. Tee seemed suddenly panicked yet determined. It was a distinct thing about Tee her ability to be two things at once. Tee stepped forward and Zeke, upon seeing Tee, lowered his divided bow, just a little.

"What the hell is going on," Tee asked, calmly.

"I took a nap. I wasn't sleep too long. Just wanted to rest my eyes for a few minutes. Then I woke up and Maddy was gone. She promised not to go too far without telling me."

"So?" Tee said. Ralph though the same but did not dare utter the word.

"So, she's *my* responsibility," Zeke shot back.

"She's probably making water somewhere or—," Jax decided with a shake of his head.

"Jax," Ralphie shook his head with a disapproving look.

"Scrap that," Tee cried, looking at Zeke curiously. "How's she *your* responsibility?"

"Ain't nobody nobody's responsibility once the challenge begins," Dame noted.

"This is the challenge and things are going to shake out the way they shake out, no matter what we try to do," Gina smirked, a hand on her hip and the trench knife in her opposite hand.

"Where the fig is Madison," Zeke demanded.

"I didn't see her," Jax, Gina, Isaac, and Dame all growled.

"How in the stupid Hello Kitty pink hair bow can she leave without any of you seeing her?'

Ralphie pressed his lips tightly together. He did not want to say that when he had left earlier and seen no one guarding the first floor.

"This is a big building. She could have slipped out through a window," Jax offered.

"What the hell is going on," Zeke exclaimed.

"What the hell Zeke," Isaac asked.

"You're not responsible for Madison," Tee pointed out.

"I know I'm not responsible, but I promised to watch over her," Zeke reminded Tee with wild eyes.

"Hell, Zeke, you can't promise that for any of us, let alone Madison," Jax chided with a shake of his head.

Zeke looked at Jax for the first time as if he were capable of hurting him. Ralphie was chilled by the look on Zeke's face. In that moment, Ralphie wondered if Zeke pounced what he would do. Would he intervene? Would he have to fight Zeke? Would the first punch lead to the end of a relation that was predicated on Jax's friendship.

"Sorry," Jax recoiled, lifting his hands in surrender. "But it's true."

Zeke did not attack. Jax and Zeke seemed at a stalemate. Ralphie breathed a sigh of relief.

"What in the ever-bugging trap house is going on," Zeke thundered. He shook off Tee and pushed past Jax and Dame. Isaac stepped out of Zeke's path.

The bull of a teen headed for the exit. Dame was the first to react. He spun on his heels and quickly found himself in front of Zeke.

"Where are you going?"

"Don't get in my way, Dame," Zeke warned. "I ain't got time for your Hands Across America team spirit horse hooey."

Dame did not move.

Zeke had slung his crossbow across his back and suddenly balled his fists and prepared for war.

Dame seeing Zeke ball his fist, smirked displaying his braces. He gripped and regripped the kukri, ready to chop off one of Zeke's arms if necessary.

Ralphie and Jax watched silently. They, Dame and Zeke, were the two biggest Millers in the challenge. If they fought it would be like two bulls fighting. The chaos and damage as a result would be substantial. The two seconds looked at each other silently.

Isaac and Jax, best friends of the big boys, stepped into the fray.

"Zeke, calm down," Jax begged. Zeke was staring daggers at Dame.

Zeke growled.

Isaac reached out and tried to calm Dame. Dame bristled with Isaac's gentle touch. Dame never took his eyes off Zeke, who was his immediate concern.

Isaac put a hand on Dame's massive bicep.

"Dame, we don't need this, right now," Isaac Moore advised. "We ain't fighting each other. We got everybody else to worry about."

Dame lowered his balled-up fists and stepped back.

Jax stepped forward and guided Zeke forward.

Zeke shouldered past Dame and Isaac.

Dame turned and cut his walnut brown eyes at the back of Jax and Zeke. Ralphie reluctantly followed.

"Remember, we in the challenge. Running off all crazy puts us all in danger. You get in trouble, don't bring it back to the house," Gina spoke to Zeke's broad back.

Zeke stepped out of the car storage building, Jax and Ralphie in tow. Tee hesitated and remained behind in the two-story structure, Ralphie noted.

"Stay close to the buildings," Jax whispered to Zeke.

Zeke cut his eyes at Jax again as if he wanted to rip his head off. Jax and Ralphie knew that Zeke was pissed off with everyone but more with himself for not being aware of where Madison had gone. But he had a short fuse and bad temper and the combination was dangerous.

Zeke and Jax walked down the sidewalk with their flashlights aimed at the ground. Ralphie followed in the dark of the pre-dawn, watching the roofs and second story windows. In his left hand was the mini flashlight. On his back he had slung his croquet mallet through the backpack straps.

A few minutes later, on the street Zeke slowed and stopped in a doorway. Jax stopped behind Zeke. Ralphie paused near Jax.

"Sorry," Zeke finally croaked a hundred yards from the building where everyone rested. "I just promised to watch out for Maddy."

Jax did not say anything. Ralphie looked up into the pre-dawn sky and saw the hint of light in the darkened night.

"The sun will be up in an hour or two," Ralphie offered. "If we are going to try and find her, we better get a move on before the early birds get to looking for us."

Jax nodded. Zeke did not seem to hear or care what Ralphie offered.

Ralphie looked back toward the warehouse they had come from and tried to calculate how many killers they might have passed that pre-dawn hour. All around him were brick front buildings that might have hidden any number of challenge contestants. He took a deep breath and resolved that at the first light they would go from hunters to the hunted in the challenge.

The trio headed north up Avenue E toward Eleventh Street. They only walked two blocks before they saw something that chilled them all. At the end of the street they came on one of Madison's shoes resting on the sidewalk. Zeke ran to the shoe, despite Jax and Ralphie trying to warn him that it might be a trap. Zeke knelt at the shoe.

"Don't touch me."

Zeke looked at the shoe and a wave of emotions swept across his face. Jax dared to place a gentle hand on Zeke's thick shoulder. He did not shrug it off. He just kneeled there on the sidewalk with the shoe in his hand.

He looked from the shoe, in the pre-dawn light, and found the hole in the chain-link fencing where Ralphie had entered and exited earlier. Ralphie did not offer any of his information as he looked around suddenly thinking about the unknown boy with the flail. He twisted and adjusted his croquet mallet in his hand, suddenly prepared for an attack.

"Don't go in, Zeke," Jax warned.

Zeke did not listen.

"Be careful," Ralphie cautioned. He recalled that on the other side of the fencing the toilet where he had been attacked earlier.

"She might be in that porta potty," Jax noted.

Zeke stepped through the hole in the chain-link fence. Reluctantly, Jax and Ralphie stepped through the hole in the chain-link, just a few feet behind Zeke. Just a few feet inside the chain-link all the boys saw a body laying prone in the foot-high grass. Madison's red highlighted hair was loose and covering her peanut butter hued face.

Jax and Ralphie stepped in front of Zeke. Jax attempted to restrain the bigger Zeke. Zeke pushed forward only to stop when he could see her plainly.

"You don't need to see this," Jax stated. "Step out, Zeke, and let's head back to the warehouse."

Zeke pushed forward and Jax, arms out against the bullish Zeke, just waited him out. Zeke stopped and was suddenly silent. He seemed to lose all power. He opened and closed his mouth silently, like a fish out of water trying to breathe. His muscular arms fell to his sides.

Jax gently turned the bigger Zeke around.

"Come on, man, you don't need to see this," Jax attempted gently. Jax gingerly turned Zeke back toward the exit. The two moved methodically, slowly toward the chain link fence exit.

Ralphie watched as Zeke and Jax walked back toward the chain link fence. He looked back where Madison lay and thought that he might find out if he could help Zeke by figuring out who had zapped Madison.

Ralphie hesitated. He clicked on his headlamp and swept the immediate area around the body, looking for clues.

"Ralphie, you coming?"

"Give me a few minutes," Ralphie mentioned. Under the headlamp light Ralphie studied the body and the ground around the body. He looked past the body of the girl and to the things that might tell him something of importance. Ralphie had seen dead bodies all of his short life, thanks to his father. Dead were not scary.

A corpse was just an inert thing that no longer housed a living being. He had learned to respect the dead. He never disrespected the dead but at the same time he did not fear the death that seemed close when around dead. Initially, Ralphie recalled, he had been confused about the dead, but his father had taught him the simple facts of death. "Everyone dies. It is the rare few that live," his father had said.

At fifteen, Ralphie thought, Maddy had not lived. She had been impulsive and rash and forgotten that she was in the challenge. Mental errors, Ralphie calculated, had been her end.

He stood up and walked slowly in a spiral fashion around the body and noted a few things before leaving. Ralphie had been in the field for less than five minutes. He jogged back to Jax and Zeke. They had not gone too far.

"What were you doing?"

"Looking at a few things," Ralphie announced as he and Jax walked Zeke back to the two-story warehouse.

"What did you find out?"

Ralphie did not answer Jax. He instead studied Zeke who moved in a lazy and unrushed fashion. It was as if finding Maddy had taken something out of the once vibrant Miller. He seemed to be in another world.

When the three returned to the abandoned car storage building Dame and Isaac were waiting. Dame watched silently as they entered. Isaac stepped out and scanned the lightening street for anyone.

Gina and Tee were uncertain what to do.

"Did you find her?"

Jax nodded. Zeke walked in as if in a trance. Ralphie studied Gina and Tee.

"Oh my God," Gina reacted putting her hand to her mouth.

Tee pushed past Isaac and Jax and to Zeke. Tee threw her arms around Zeke's neck. Zeke did not react when Tee approached. Tee embraced Zeke. Ralphie figured that he was shell shocked.

Tee and Jax guided Zeke to the far side of the first floor. The trio sat in one of the rooms that still had a semblance of privacy. Ralphie watched as they hunkered down and comforted Zeke.

Dame stepped in front of Ralphie.

Ralphie watched the muscular fifteen-year-old who was as old as Ralphie but seemed made of different material than Ralphie.

"You, Ralphie, right?"

Ralphie nodded.

"Your dad's Benjamin O. Davis Reynolds, right," Isaac asked.

"Yeah. So, what?"

"I heard that your dad did a lot of clean up in the Remains."

"Yeah, and," Ralphie replied, suddenly bored.

"Figure out of the three of you," Dame began with a friendly brace covered smile on his face. "You would pay attention." He added, nonchalantly, "You notice something?"

Ralphie liked the compliment. He thought to play dumb, but Dame already knew his father and what his father did. Ralphie was playing with the idea of saying nothing when Dame asked:

"What did you see?"

"What do you mean?"

"Don't play stupid," Dame declared, studying Ralphie. "You bagged and tagged people in the Remains if you do construction. You get to know things. You see things that most don't. That right?"

Ralphie did not like Dame, suddenly. He was smart and strong. He was observant, like Ralphie. He was someone that you had to watch. In the challenge someone like Dame might figure out your weakness and gut you before you knew he figured out your weakness.

"Madison looked like she been strangled. The way I see it, someone caught her, strangled her and zapped her," Ralphie told Dame.

"That it?"

"I think she was … misused."

"Misused?"

Ralphie nodded. "Her jeans were missing."

There was a pause.

"That don't mean noth—."

"I don't know nobody that takes off their jeans to poop."

Dame nodded. He looked at Ralphie questioningly. "Are you sure it was her?"

Ralphie nodded. He lifted his hand and let Madison's dog tag hang suspended in the air from the thin ball chain. Ralphie had taken Madison's dog tag when he did his cursory check earlier.

"How come you so calm about this?"

"You said it yourself, my dad did a lot of clean up in the Remains. I worked with him. Saw a lot of dead bodies when I grew up."

Dame studied Ralphie curiously.

"You are one odd kid," Dame concluded.

Ralphie smirked. He crinkled his eyes.

"Oh, yeah," Ralphie said absently. "Her gun was missing," Ralphie declared a little flustered. "Forgot to mention that."

Dame nodded at that. As if to punctuate that the second announcement was made over the various public speakers on the island.

"Welcome all to the Twenty-Third Annual Pandemonium Challenge. It is now 0600 hours, and this is the second official announcement of Day One. It is with deepest regret that we announce the loss of the following challengers: Tevin Campbell Adams, Desmond Tutu Felton, Michelle Obama Hyatt, Diana Ross Mitchell, Andre Young North, Raymond Usher Porter, Todd Shaw Rogers, Ben Folds Stevens and Madison Washington. Play on. It is not over until it is over in the Pandemonium Challenge."

That was the height of the challenge, Day One. Of course, the first day Ralphie and most of the Millers tried to regroup after the loss of Maddy. Everyone seemed to handle it differently. Zeke sulked. Jax seemed confused. He tried to cheer him up. Tee brooded.

Around nine or ten Dame and his crew meandered out of the warehouse and by lunch were back. They had stories to tell.

"It's wild outside, right about now," Isaac noted. "There are all these gunslingers shooting at their own shadows. It's like Chinese New Year's or something out there."

"Yeah, bullets are whizzing by like mosquitoes," Gina admitted.

"Think we might want to hole up and wait for things to calm down."

Jax nodded at the stories. Ralphie waited for Jax to go exploring. Zeke sulked.

Ralphie followed Jax to the far side of the building looking for a way to go onto the streets without being cut down by random gun fire. The pair came around a corner of the building and ran into Tee and Gina. Gina was braiding or unbraiding Tee's hair when Ralphie and Jax appeared.

"What you looking at?"

Ralphie looked left and then right as Jax backpedaled.

"This building is for everyone," Jax managed, turning and going the opposite direction he and Ralphie had come.

"What was that all about," Ralphie said as they created some distance between Tee and Gina.

"Man, you know that I don't' know," Jax declared.

Ralphie shook his head as the pair walked to the edge of the building and looked out and onto the street. Jax stopped at the outer wall of the building and hesitated. In the dark Ralphie could hear the continual sound of gunfire. It seemed as if the darkness was an inky gun range all of a sudden.

"Thinking that it might be good to just wait this madness out," Jax said.

Ralphie did not speak. He had other thoughts on his mind. Tee, the girl he knew a long time ago, was this nice tomboy who was friendly and welcoming. She had morphed into a piss and vinegar girl with a short fuse and willing to fight anyone that looked at her sideways. Then, there was the Tee that was this calculating malicious pre-meditated destroyer that had created a murk list. That same Tee was suddenly fast friends with Gina. She did not seem to be loyal to anyone, Ralphie thought.

Zeke was sulking as a result. Zeke had thought, like Jax and Ralphie, that Tee was his girl and that when the challenge began that she would be with him. Zeke had been blindsided literally when Tee glommed onto Gina. The challenge was a true litmus test of friendships and whatever was going on between those in something more than friendships. The concept was far above Ralphie.

"You know that the way I look at it is," Jax explained. "We only have one chance out of 52 to survive. If you expect everyone to be the same, then you have another think coming."

"That's supposed to cheer him up," Ralphie asked.

"Well, it's not going to make him feel worse," Jax admitted.

"Talking about us getting got is depressing," Ralphie advised.

"It's not that depressing," Jax noted. "I read somewhere that the thoughts of imminent death can be very enlightening."

Ralphie opened his mouth only to close it, silently.

"There is this part of your brain that makes you focus on only two things: fight or flight. If you are focused on fight of flight, then you aren't worrying about what your girl is doing with some other fish. Your mind is too busy thinking about fight or flight."

"You know that no matter what, I can always count on you to be Jax," Zeke mentioned. He rubbed at the side of his face. Zeke stretched his arms toward his friend and the conversation.

"You good?"

"I'll be all right," Zeke said and with that Jax felt that his work was done.

"All right," Jax said. He grabbed his backpack and gestured to Ralphie to follow. He and Ralphie walked out of the area where they had found Zeke.

"Are we going to get this challenge going?" Ralphie caught up with Jax.

Jax smiled mischievously, as an answer. Jax stopped and frowned.

"Think I should have told him that Tee ain't coming back to him no time soon?"

Ralphie scoffed.

The pair stepped out of the warehouse and what Jax had said was not an exaggeration. There was a steady sound of gunfire outside of the warehouse. On the street where they were Jax and Ralphie were relieved to find that there was no one walking or shooting. The gunfire was a few blocks over.

"Think that the party is just a couple of blocks over," Jax announced.

"So, let's go and crash that party," Ralphie suggested.

The pair made their way toward the sounds of gunfire. Jax with his arm rocket slingshot and Ralphie with his croquet mallet.

"You know that we'll probably die tonight," Jax noted.

Ralphie looked at Jax with his arm rocket slingshot and grinned. "We all got to die at some point."

"That's what I like about you Ralphie," Jax said with a grin. "You are such a glass half full kind of guy."

"Got to be somebody," Ralphie said.

Chapter Eleven.

Golden Child.

Ralphie opened his eyes to see the first streaks of sun cutting across the space where the Millers hid. He smiled big at the fact that he would see another day. He almost wanted to shout and scream at the fact that he and Jax were still alive on Day Two.

The night before he and Jax had walked around the island looking for trouble. At least, that was the plan. The walk had been a slow stroll and around the island had been just two blocks from the hiding spot that the Millers had found. Their luck had changed when they walked into a shootout.

"We came to a gunfight with a slingshot and a baseball bat," Jax hissed, backing into the shadows of a nearby building. Ralphie had bristled at the comment. He looked at his longtime sideways.

"It's the challenge, Jax, what did you expect?"

Jax had no words.

"We are not going to win with harsh words and mean looks," Ralphie continued, amused at the shock of the challenge on Jax.

"I know that," Jax smirked.

"Do you?"

"Yeah," Jax breathed.

The pair peered out of the shadows. At the top of the street there was this continuous buzzing of bullets and flashes of muzzles. Jax stopped. Ralphie stopped as well and looked at Jax curiously.

"The spot seems hot," Jax noted looking back and forth from the firefight and back toward the darkness from which the pair had come.

"What's your suggestion?"

"I say, that we get the hell out of here before we get zapped," Jax breathed.

Ralphie looked at Jax, with contempt.

"What?"

"The odds are always going to be against us, Jax," Ralphie chuckled. "It's up to us to make the odds and the situations better." Ralphie shook his head. "Hashtag Ben Reynolds." Ralphie smiled broadly at his quoting of his father's words.

"How so?"

Ralphie twisted his lips on his chocolate brown face, thinking. He surveyed the area. The gunfire was pretty steady just a block away. Ralphie looked up and down the block.

"Maybe, we go to the roof and get a better advantage?" Ralphie paused, thinking. "Maybe we sneak up on those triggered ninjas and beat the snot out of them because they are throwing lead every which a way possible but can't hit the ocean, because they can't shoot or fight."

Jax, cowed, lowered his eyes. "I get it," Jax said.

Ralphie pushed out of the shadows and he and Jax moved through a gutted building toward the gunfire.

"You sure about this," Jax asked, tremulously.

"No, can't be too sure of anything in the challenge," Ralphie grinned.

Jax nodded. Ralphie noted that Jax was wringing his hands. He would never admit it, but that was a tell, according to Bailey.

Jax and Ralphie appeared on the block where there was the sound of gunfire and just one hundred feet from them was a body riddled with bullets. The hooded figure was sprawled out prone in a spreading pool of blood with an outstretched hand and a machine pistol just out of reach. The thing that Ralphie focused in on was that the boy had only one shoe on. The barefoot did not have a sock on it, Ralphie noted. Not a Boomer. Not a Maker. Not a Trad.

Jax hissed and pointed to the left of the shoeless body. Ralphie followed Jax's finger a few feet from the ventilated corpse and the location of two more people lying dead. There was a girl with her hair in a braided bun, sitting on the street, leaning against what might have been a transport a long time ago. In her lap was an assault rifle. In an upward angle that ran from her hip to her shoulder were eight bullet holes that, Ralphie believed, had torn the life from the girl. Based on the Eureka! hoody, Ralphie recollected, she was a Second Gen. The boy was in arm's reach, and the only reason that Ralphie decided it was a boy was because he had thick shoulders. His head was missing. Three Second Gens flatlined, Ralphie noted.

Jax and Ralphie found themselves looking at each other unbelievingly. Ralphie lowered his eyes at the sight. He had never seen that level of brutality in the Remains. He looked up and back to Jax. Jax opened and closed his mouth but said nothing. He had his slingshot in hand, and he let the ceramic marble fall into his hand, harmlessly. Jax lowered his head to his chest and seemed drained of all energy and power.

"What did you expect," Ralphie asked.

"I know," Jax answered. "I know, but I didn't think that it would be that brutal, this soon," Jax, the prankster admitted.

Ralphie looked amused at Jax and peeked at the boy and tried to see what had decapitated him. Whatever weapon that had been used had left a jagged cut that looked as if whatever had done it had ripped the head off more than cleanly cut it off. In his left hand was one of the old-time revolver cowboy pistols that Ralphie had seen in cartoons on the Interweb.

Jax reached out and grabbed Ralphie. Before he could speak there was another burst of gunfire. Ralphie tried to figure out which direction the gunfire was coming from. Jax hid behind the shell of a transport for cover.

Jax again pointed into the darkness. Ralphie followed his outstretched arm and pointing finger in the direction up the street. Up the street, closer to the corner, there were two or three dark silhouettes shooting at someone or thing at the end of the block.

"I say we cut our losses before we get got," Jax said.

"You sure?"

"Hell, man, if we return with the assault rifle and machine pistol, we are better off than when we left," Jax grinned.

"We didn't come to the challenge to scavenge," Ralphie noted.

"Yeah, we came to win. Winning ain't got nothing to do with running out there and fighting everybody that looks at you sideways," Jax advised. "It's about making smart decisions and good decisions."

Ralphie hesitated.

"They also got a lot of firepower," Jax pointed out. "We would be Swiss cheese in seconds, you with your fake baseball bat and me with my marble hurler."

Ralphie hesitated. Jax was the first to retrieve the machine pistol. Ralphie reached out and scooped up the assault rifle. Jax grabbed him by the arm and pulled him back into the building that they had walked through to reach the street of blood and guts. Ralphie walked but reluctantly as Jax lead them back to the street where they had initially planned to kick butt and take names.

"I don't know, Jax," Ralphie said, looking back and through the building they had just exited.

"If anyone asks, we tell them that we just checked out the lay of the land or something pseudo-intelligent and then drop the whole subject."

Ralphie shook his head.

That had been his first night on Pandemonium island.

He and Jax had returned to the safe house and were greeted like returning warriors. Jax immediately laid claim on the machine pistol. Gina claimed the assault rifle. There were no real objections.

Ralphie figured that like him the others understood that a weapon did not win the challenge. Jax walked around like he was invincible. Ralphie could only shake his head.

"Don't you want to upgrade your fake Thor hammer?"

"I'm good," Ralphie shrugged.

Before midnight Ralphie laid down on the second floor of their hide out and had fallen asleep. The pair had been woken to do a shift watching the pre-dawn night for anyone that might sneak up on them. No one snuck up. No one threatened.

Two hours after his watch ended Ralphie was woken by this announcement:

"The Pandemonium Challenge has been suspended for two hours and two hours only. We repeat: The Pandemonium Challenge has been suspended for the next two hours. Anyone on the streets please find shelter. The enforcers will take the streets for the next two hours. They are under the supervision of the Pandemonium Challenge Committee and allowed to protect themselves from any and all aggression. Do not attack any enforcer. Any attack on an enforcer will be met with extreme prejudice. So, again the Pandemonium Challenge has been suspended for next two hours. Rest. Recover. Bandage the wounded. Attend to your own needs. But do not attack anyone for the next two hours. There will be an announcement again to resume the Pandemonium Challenge."

There was an eerie silence that followed the announcement in the Millers camp. Ralphie turned over and studied the three others resting in the safe spot they had decided on at the end of the first full day of the challenge. They were resting on the second story of a structure that had been some sort of restaurant. Despite its age, there was still a part of a counter and a sink behind the counter. To Ralphie, that suggested that the building had been a restaurant of some kind.

Jax was lying the closest to Ralphie, with his hooded sweatshirt pulled tightly closed that only his nose stuck out of the hole that usually showed his round head and big eyes. Jax was curled up in a fetal position and kicking at something in his dreams. Jax was a heavy sleeper.

Next to Jax was Zeke. Zeke was just lying on the floor with his backpack under his head and his eyes open. Zeke rolled over and looked at Jax, still sleeping and shook his head. Ralphie wanted to say something to Zeke but after the night before and loss of Maddy he knew that it was better not to mettle in things that were not things he did not care to fight over.

So, Ralphie watched as Zeke lay stone still, his hands folded across his thick chest, like a dead man. Ralphie cut his eyes and noted that Zeke, like Jax, was wearing his dark blue hooded sweatshirt which had Millers embroidered down the left sleeve. Like Jax, Zeke was wearing black jeans and combat boots.

Beside Zeke was Tee Bennett. Ralphie looked at Tee lying on the floor of the structure next to Zeke. Her box braids were pulled up and back from her diamond shaped face. She, as she tried to get back to sleep, had one loose braid that fell across her face like a black finger and that single braid reminded Ralphie of the girl that he had met so long ago on the dirt path dressed in a soccer jersey, shorts and gym shoes. Ralphie knew that it was only a trick of the light or lack of light and the early morning that made Tee seem gentle and innocent.

No one moved. Ralphie thought of climbing to his feet and seeing what was going on outside. He was curious. Instead, Ralphie pressed himself up on one elbow and looked at the people laying on the second floor. Zeke sat up on his elbow and watched Ralphie.

At 0615 hours the sounds of an armored transport could be heard rolling through the streets of the island.

Ralphie sat up.

Zeke watched but did not move.

Jax just adjusted himself in his blue and gold hoody sleeping bag. The others seemed unconcerned about the activity on the street below. So, Ralphie wiled away the time trying to find a way to watch the activities without Zeke noticing his curiosity.

Ralphie turned and twisted and finally leaned back to find a vantage point from the second floor down to the street. His vantage point came from a point where there had been a wall and flooring, that was now gone, that offered a limited view of the street below. Ralphie looked through the flooring and down onto the street to see half a dozen grown men and women, armed to the teeth, mulling about on the street with a mission. Some were wearing infrared goggles and carrying assault weapons.

In the quiet of the morning Ralphie listened to the gruff voices below.

"The target is supposed to be in Building 7 this morning," the bullish enforcer, wearing his goggles on his helmet shouted in the noise of the enforcers moving and looking for the Shaker.

"We just got a ping," the enforcer following the bullish enforcer and carrying a scanner announced.

"Donny, sniff Goldie out," the leader told an enforcer with a squinty-eyes and a big toothy smile. His goggles were on his helmet backwards. He had an assault rifle, but it was slung across his back. In his hand was a lighter sub-machine gun. On his hip was a black handled burper.

Donny went running at an easy lope up California Avenue and as quickly as he had begun disappeared.

Suddenly, Jax was awake and next to Ralphie. Ralphie grinned at the sudden appearance of Jax. He was either dead asleep or wide awake, Ralphie decided.

"Scout," Jax whispered from the second floor pointing at the running enforcer. Ralphie nodded. The enforcers were so disciplined and intense.

Most in the Remains wanted to become enforcers at an early age. They were the Remains superheroes. Everyone knew that they were fearless individuals against citizens of the Remains and rarely backed down, even if one of the citizens was hopped up on something or carrying a weapon.

Within each line there were men and women that patrolled the compounds in pairs. They walked the compounds and regularly quelled trouble. Enforcers policed the compound and made sure that Remains rules were adhered to by all residents.

Outside of the Remains, on the exterior wall, sat sixteen towers that protected the Remains from all dangers. All the towers were guarded by enforcers. In the exterior towers were no less than twenty enforcers under the command of the tower commander. The tales that were told of the Remains towers were unbelievable.

On the interior wall that was the second line of defense were eight towers that were tasked with insuring that no one or thing entered the Remains that the Remains did not want inside.

Ralphie laughed at the useless information that was in his head about the Remains and the enforcers. Despite his dismissal of the enforcers Ralphie admired the enforcers. They were fearless and dedicated. Few found fault in the enforcer's efforts. They were far from perfect, Ralphie thought, but most respected the enforcers presence wherever they were, even at the Pandemonium Challenge when everyone was armed and dangerous.

"Radio that in. We need to triangulate and shutdown the area around the Goldie."

"Location?"

"First Street and ….," the lead enforcer looked to the closest sign.

"We're in front of Building 11," an enforcer stated.

"First Street and Building 11. We are on the eastern shore side of the island."

"Roger that," barked an enforcer carrying a mobile radio system over his shoulder.

"Okay, need two men on California Avenue. No one coming in or out from B, F, I and M. Go."

Four enforcers took off in a trot to lockdown the side streets onto California.

"We'll wait until we have reinforcements. Then, we want to cover our retreat and exit."

"Roger that."

Jax and Ralphie watched and listened to the Remains elite fighting force as they went through their military plans. Men and women were moving in all directions. As an outsider, the chaotic nature of the directions might have seemed illogical. Yet, the Remains enforcers, seemed placed strategically based on the commander's instructions.

The lead enforcer looked into the rising sun and signaled for his remaining company to relax. The four enforcers lowered their weapons all of a sudden.

"Cap, command has us waiting for instructions."

"Roger that."

"Let's go ten and ten," the bullish leader grunted.

"Roger that," one of the enforcers replied and relayed the order to the others.

"Time?"

"It's 0630 hours. We don't have much time."

"We are just doing a retrieval. We should be out in plenty of time."

"Cap, Charlie company are coming up Fourth Street and should be coming down Avenue C in five," announced the radio operator.

"Roger that. Tell command that once Charlie company arrives, we will head to retrieve Goldie"

The radio operator spoke to command.

"Contact Charlie company and tell them to take our position and we will head to Building 11 when we get eyes on them."

The radio operator spoke to Charlie company.

"Think that the best exit is straight down California Avenue. Do we have any transport near Goldie?"

"Only three on island. One is on Twelfth Street, presently. There is one on Ninth Street. The last is on Avenue M and Eighth Street. That is the closest. It can be here in seven to ten."

"Roger that," came the response of the bullish enforcer.

"Hold for instruction."

"Charlie company to Zulu company," rang out on the radios of all enforcers.

"Charlie company, go 'head."

"We have Bravo company on their way in a quick. They are on Avenue J and estimate arrival in ten."

"Roger that," the leader of the enforcers replied with a hand gesture that brought his men to attention. Their once relaxed composure was gone. They had their assault rifles at the ready all of a sudden.

The sound of the transport proceeded the appearance of the armored transport. It was one of the older type transports that had been in use in the Twenty First Century and had one of the last combustion engines. It, the transport, moved on four oversized rubber wheels.

Ralphie watched as automotive history rolled by.

"Jax, the numbers have an APV," Ralphie gushed.

Jax did not move. Zeke turned over. For the first time on the island there was the sound of wheeled vehicles tearing through the broken streets of Pandemonium Island.

"Okay, take Alpha company to California Avenue. Lock down that street. No movement north or south. We will call Delta company and they will shut down Avenue F and H. Big Bertha will shut down Avenue I. We don't want any surprises. Thomas keep your eyes open and the engine running. When everyone is in place, we enter the structure and extricate Radiance."

"Roger that," repeated Thomas, the driver of the armored vehicle. He was a bearded peanut butter colored man with wavy black hair that was plastered to his round head. On top of his head were goggles. He had a slick looking burper strapped to his right thigh.

"What is going on," asked Gina half-sleep and yawning. She was a small framed dark cocoa beauty with round cheeks and bright eyes. She possessed a woman's body even though she was not yet fifteen. Her zip front blue and gold hoody was unzipped and showed off her Miller inspired T-shirt. The hammer and chainsaw emblem was proudly on display on Gina's chest.

Tee was dressed in a blue and gold hoody, jeans and unlaced combat boots and stumbling around that morning in a bit of a morning daze. She seemed attracted to the noise of Gina. Both girls walked around unconcerned about anyone in the area. Gina bumped into Tee and the two giggled.

Ralphie turned with the sound of Gina and admired the two Miller girls in the early morning. He smiled sheepishly at the girls and turned away before he smiled too much or thought too much about them. He shook the image of Gina and Tee from his head and concentrated his attention on the enforcers on the street below.

The noise attracted the attention of the others on the second floor. Ralphie tried to make a gesture to be quiet, as the noise also caught the attention of one of the enforcers on the street. The enforcer aimed his high-powered rifle up and toward the source of the noise.

"Shush," Ralphie advised.

Gina rolled her eyes as if she had been disrespected.

"The numbers are down on the street. If you keep being loud and curious you are going to get your head blown off," Ralphie cautioned.

"What time is it?"

There was a sound of men moving through the streets in armored vehicles. The men were armed and dressed in Kevlar. They, the dozen that were on the streets, moved systematically. For the first time on the island there was the sound of wheeled vehicles tearing through the broken streets of Pandemonium Island.

At the front of the dozen men were two men studying a tablet monitor. They were protected all the while by men with high-powered rifles.

Ralphie pulled out his digital map reader and tapped a number of buttons. The digital map reader had the ability to view broadcasts from other participants if their body cameras were on. Most competitors by default had their three body cameras set to broadcast.

Studying the digital map Ralphie tapped a few more buttons and watched the camp of someone somewhere to the east of his location. Ralphie had an earbud in his ear. He tapped the earbud and it synced with the digital map reader.

Ralphie smiled silently and watched the camera focus on a small room where two people were sitting. There was a boy wearing a hooded sweatshirt, jeans and combat boots. Well, the boy was playing with his combat boots, for some reason.

"What do you think is going on," asked a small framed brindled brown beauty with a piggish nose, dimples and bright eyes. Ralphie did not recognize her immediately. She was wearing a zip front hooded sweatshirt, zipped halfway up. The girl possessed a woman's form and her hair was in a loosely curled Afro. The girl was tying her combat boots.

"I suspect that the Innovators have decided to save their little angel" the second voice reported and suddenly the oval shaped head of a girl that looked strangely familiar to Ralphie appeared. Her smile was big and broad, and her natural curly hair was all over her head.

"They can do that?" The third girl sounded from somewhere in the small room. The cameraperson turned and there was the third girl with a head full of black curly hair divided down the middle of her round head. She was a desert brown girl wearing a Eureka! Second Gen hoody, jeans and blue and yellow combat boots. Underneath the dark blue and gold hoody was a bright yellow T-shirt.

"I didn't think that they would give her this long, honestly," responded the voice of someone that Ralphie knew. It was the solidly built Brian Jenson. Brian Jenson was the second boy in the small room.

"Cash rules everything around me," the small framed girl with a pug nose and freckles sang.

"Ain't that the truth," the tall and thin rosy brown athlete Ralphie knew as Campbell Henderson chimed in.

"They are Innovators for a reason," a bird-like girl concluded.

"Yeah, and dog farts stink," the short-haired boy noted. "We all knew that the little brat wasn't going to be with us the entire time."

"Yeah," Campbell agreed.

"Yeah, I suppose. It just doesn't seem right that the brat is saved because she has money and power."

"If you think about it," the short-haired boy reflected. "It *does* seem right. I mean, compared to everything else that makes sense. Save the best. Save the rich."

"What?"

"The Innovators are more important in the Remains than say… you or me." the short-haired boy rubbed at his brown cheek and continued. "Not everyone is as important as everyone else." He paused. "I know that we all want to pretend like we are all equal, but we aren't."

"What do you mean?"

"I mean that we are all born the same. We start off the same, but things change when we get older," the round-faced boy had to admit.

"What are you saying?"

"I'm saying that if it was your mother or Brandon White hanging from a cliff which would change your life if you saved them?"

"Can I save 'em both?"

"No," the boy replied.

"That ain't fair," Campbell Henderson noted.

"That's my point. Life ain't fair. We all know that. I mean, your mom is important to you. I get that. I ain't saying that we don't see that. All, I'm saying is that Brandon White, if you save him, could change your life forever. What is your mom going to do? Thank you? Bake you a cake? Give you a hug?"

"You ain't right."

"I ain't wrong either."

Chapter Twelve.

Day Two.

"When eight o'clock comes," Zeke beamed to Jax. "I think I'm out."

The announcement from Zeke was not a surprise. In the challenge there were only two options: go out or hide. Zeke did not seem like someone that hid.

"You want company," Jax asked.

Ralphie watched as Zeke sat up and frowned. Jax nodded but there was a weird silent exchange between the two friends. It was uncomfortable, jarring in the suddenly out of step nature of Jax to his close friend. Ralphie shrugged the silent exchange off to the second day of the challenge.

"You going all Rambo," Tee asked, concerned.

"Just need some time to clear my head."

Jax shrugged. Ralphie thought he understood. He, at least, wanted to give the impression that he understood. For some reason, that was beyond him, Zeke blamed himself for the loss of Madison. There was nothing that anyone could do to persuade him that he had not screwed up. Tee tried to make Zeke understand that even if he had been awake Madison would have probably done something else that would have gotten her removed.

Bored, Ralphie tapped another combination of buttons on his map reader. He watched as the map scrolled from the Second Gen camp to another nameless camp. Ralphie switched the digital map reader and found another open body camera.

"You know that this whole thing is an experiment in social dynamics?" a boy with bushy eyebrows announced, his bandana; blue and white wrapped around his wrist.

"Says who," asked the voice behind the camera.

"I read an article that said that the Pandemonium Challenge is all about working with those that you think are more powerful than yourself and taking advantage of that relation," bushy eyebrows pointed out.

"People write things that they believe," the girl the color of sienna said. "It isn't always true."

"Yeah, that's fiction," someone said off camera.

"Yeah, but I'm not talking about fiction. I'm talking about research that says that things like the challenge are doomed."

"How can the challenge be doomed? It's the best part of the Remains."

"Is it?"

The girl, that Ralphie had seen and tried to say hello to, Raven Mitchell, looked up and into the body camera and for an instant was captured there, like a picture. She was startling beautiful. Her dark eyes just seemed endless. Her nose had the slightest upturn. Her lips were glossy as she bit at her lower lip and fell silent.

"Say something," the third voice noted.

"You know that you are sometimes too smart for your own good," Raven Mitchell, the Boomer girl, whose hair was pulled up and into a loose bun of curls, asked.

"How can that be? Can you be too nice? Too happy? That just sounds like something that someone who is having a terrible life, by choice, would say."

Ralphie rolled his eyes at the girl's comments and adjusted the digital map reader. He knew that the reader would locate anyone's body camera, if it was on. Suddenly he saw several pictures on the reader. He looked at each thumbnail and counted out six that were active. Ralphie tapped a few and noted that most were still and on but not moving. The competitors had turned on their body cameras and forgot to turn them off. Then Ralphie came upon a body camera in motion and tried to figure out where they were hiding. They were in what looked like an apartment somewhere on the island.

"At 0900 hours here is the third report for Day Two of the Pandemonium Challenge: There are now only forty-two contestants that remain in the challenge. The Pandemonium Challenge wishes to announce the loss of the following contestants from the last three hours: Stephanie Mills Daniels, Jesse Owens Evans, Donald Byrd Fleming, Miles Davis Johnson, Charlie Parker Porter and Minnie Riperton Richardson."

Early birds, Ralphie smirked. The early birds had gotten out before everyone else and gotten zapped, the fifteen-year-old calculated. There was no benefit in leaving the safe houses and hideouts without a plan. In the challenge there was always danger lurking. If you wanted to find it then you only had to step outside.

Ralphie did not leave his hiding place. Instead, he watched as the reader showed him two girls walking down a street somewhere in the 567 acres of the island. The buildings they passed by looked like any other buildings on the island. Some of the buildings were painted. Some of them were weathered and with peeling paint. Most of the buildings were just mere shells of what they had been.

The girl leading, or in front of the camera, had long braided hair. She was a small thing, Ralphie noted. She couldn't have weighed more than one hundred pounds, if that. She had a purple monkey backpack on her back. The monkey looked as if it was holding onto the girl's shoulders, Ralphie registered. The oddest thing was that the girls were walking in the middle of the street. Ralphie did not give them long in the challenge.

"Who makes an announcement like that," Octavia Garrett sang to her two friends in her twangy tone. She was dressed like most of the others in the challenge: hooded sweatshirt, jeans, combats and carrying a Mac-10 submachine gun by the shoulder strap, like a purse. Round shouldered and still developing, Octavia had a pre-teen body and a little bit of a muffin top. She had thin braided hair that fell to the middle of her back. She was caramel colored and talking about nothing in particular.

"Octavia, relax," coaxed Simone Cooper, adjusting her glasses on her slightly upturned nose. Simone Cooper had a moon pie face and seemed in a perpetual state of curiosity. Her round cheeks only added to her moon pie look.

"Why you shaking your head, Leila?"

"All this talk about nothing is going to get us flatlined," the unseen camera person announced to the two girls.

"How is talking going to get us flatlined," Octavia asked and in response she got an arrow in the side of her neck. The arrow's head poked out of Octavia's neck by about a foot. On the other side were the feathers that had guided the arrow so accurately. Octavia crumpled to the ground.

The attack was so unexpected that Ralphie had jumped when Octavia was impaled. Ralphie blinked. He did a double take to be sure that he had seen what he had just seen.

Octavia fell to the ground in the middle of the street and as Ralphie watched the last minutes of the Second Gen girls lives in the challenge from Octavia's point of view.

Octavia could not speak, but she did not just flatline. She gurgled and complained. Her hand struggled to apply pressure to her mortal wound. Octavia turned and took in the madness and chaos the Second Gen girls found themselves in.

Simone Cooper, her hair in an asymmetric Afro that was bisected by two French braids scowled as she brought up her machine pistol and fired in the direction where the arrow had come from. She crouched and fired her first ten or fifteen shots. Surprisingly fierce and determined Simone Cooper took a defensive stance and seemed to know what she was doing with the machine pistol. Straight away, Simone Cooper was reaching for her next magazine as the machine pistol emptied.

"I told you that coming to this place was stupid," the toast brown Simone Cooper growled behind gritted teeth.

"Shut up Simone and end this Green Arrow wannabe," Leila barked.

The street and building that Simone shot at, from Octavia's perspective, was at least half a block long and mostly doorways and shadows used to cloak the attacker firing from inside one of the dark doorways or windows. The building where Simone concentrated her anger still featured some remnants of the original structure. There were windows and what looked like an archway that lead into the rear of the structure.

It was Leila, the one-time cameraperson, who seemed the weakest member of the trio of Second Gen girls. When Octavia fell Leila had shouldered her MP5 snapped off the safety and pulled the trigger and the blowback unleashed all sorts of death and destruction wherever the MP5 was aimed.

Leila took an arrow in the midsection. In response, Leila twisted and strafed Simone, flatlining her outright. Simone Cooper was riddled with bullets and spun and cut down Leila in her final effort. The two had fell to friendly fire.

"Two arrows, flatlined three people," Ralphie announced out loud and waited for the shooter to appear. He or she never showed up. Sometimes that was how the challenge went, Ralphie realized.

Ralphie found Zeke's camera feed but before he could determine where Zeke was Jax appeared. Ralphie tapped a button and the digital reader went dark.

"What's the plan?"

Ralphie shrugged his shoulders in response.

"Okay, think that we have to kick rocks. We need to go and find something to eat and maybe a new place to stay. Last night was bananas and I don't know if we are all going to be together after last night," Jax explained.

Ralphie nodded.

"So, what do you say?"

"What do I say about what?"

"Come on, Ralphie," Jax bristled. "You have to have an opinion."

Ralphie paused and thought about what Jax was saying. "Nope," Ralphie concluded.

"No opinion?"

"Not really."

"Fine," Jax said and jerked his head in the direction that he turned and headed. Ralphie followed.

"Where you want to go," Jax asked only to stop himself. "Oh, yeah, that's right. You don't have an opinion."

"Come on, Jax, I have an opinion about things," Ralphie corrected. "I just don't have an opinion about which direction to go."

"I say we head north to see what is what," Jax decided.

Ralphie shrugged.

"Okay," decided Jax. "Let's go west and toward the apartments. People are still just getting up and getting out. We might run into some unprepared knobs not ready for a fight," Jax grinned.

Ralphie acquiesced and followed Jax toward the western end of the island.

All the while knowing that Zeke was out and about and on the hunt.

The first twenty-four hours did not shake many. It was still too new. People were scrambling. They were running around and exploring and not really concerned about the challenge.

The fifty-three fighters had to try and digest the fact that they were out of the Remains first. Then they had to take in the idea of being in the Pandemonium Challenge. Add to that the fact that everyone that they ran into on Pandemonium Island was willing to end them and the paranoia in everyone was suddenly at eleven.

The way Ralphie saw it, and most watching the challenge, those that were smashed in those first few 24-hours were May flies anyway and not destined for long lives. They were destined for the grinder long before the challenge began. The first 24-hours shook out and usually took out the crazy, cocky, foolish, wild and weak.

The second day, the second 24-hour period, made the weak that had hidden visible. The weak, after the second day, became targets. It was as if everyone's weaknesses were suddenly visible. The cracks in people became apparent under the pressure of the challenge.

Ralphie thought about Tee's sap list. The list suddenly made a lot of sense. He tried to recall what Tee had believed were his strengths and weaknesses.

"Maddy was all sorts of spontaneous, good and bad," Jax was whispering to Ralphie. Ralphie listened but did not have anything to add or subtract from and said nothing.

"She was a leap-first-and-ask-questions-later type of girl," Jax continued.

That morning, after the resumption of the challenge, the only person to get up and leave the Miller safe house was Zeke. The rest, six others, sat or slept on the second floor of the partially covered gigantic building that protected them the night before. Ralphie was one of the few that watched as Zeke climbed to his feet and went to gather his things.

Zeke slipped out of the old building before anyone could say anything to him. It seemed like that was his plan, Ralphie thought. Ralphie, laying close to the window, watched as Zeke ran down Avenue M toward 13th Street. He turned south and disappeared.

Ralphie thought for a moment to alert Jax. There was no point. Jax had fallen back to sleep.

So, Ralphie waited and watched.

At 0830 hours Ralphie watched Jax turn over and one of his thin legs snaked out of the bottom of his blue and gold hoody. Ralphie closed his eyes and replayed the whole first night of the challenge back over in his head.

Ralphie had climbed the hill and nearly been flatlined twice before finding Tee. The others had found Ralphie and Tee. Ralphie was with Jax and the others and Dame and Isaac Moore were leading. They moved together and eventually found their first safe warehouse.

It was all so exciting, but it was late or early in the morning and everyone, though they had rested before the launch, were running on fumes. So, they allowed half of the team to sleep for a few hours. The other half was supposed to be on watch.

Ralphie recalled going to the porta potty and nearly being zapped by some random boy. The porta potty was also where Madison had eventually gone and been deaded. The fifteen-year-old marveled at the idea that all that had happened in less than nine hours after the launch.

At 0925 hours the second floor of the safe house began to stir. Ralphie could see and hear Dame moving. Tee stretched, fighting the grips of sleep, closest to Jax and Ralphie. Gina stumbled through the space, half asleep. Isaac woke and immediately started dancing like his feet were on hot coals. Ralphie smiled silently knowing the morning dance well. Isaac went stumbling toward the north end of the safe house. A few minutes later Isaac returned, his eyes half-open. He found his sleeping place and laid back down. In minutes he was sleeping again.

Jax tried to draw his leg back into the blue and gold hoody to no avail. Jax stuck his head out of his hoody like a sleepy turtle.

"Are you getting up," Ralphie asked Jax.

Jax did not speak. He seemed comatose. He was lying near Ralphie but non-responsive.

At 0940 hours Jax turned over and smiled his best Cheshire Cat smile. Ralphie hated that smile. It irked him to no end to see Jax pretending to be a mythical feline.

"Are you getting up, now," Ralphie asked, his back pressed against the wall that afforded him the best vantage point of the street below. Ralphie was still dressed in the clothes from the night before. He had toyed with taking off his gym shoes but chosen to keep them on, just in case.

"Look around," Jax breathed. "Everyone is still sleeping in. So, we sleep in. If everyone is up and knocking brains out, then we should be up and bashing heads in. It's that simple."

Ralphie listened. Ralphie tried to understand the words Jax had said. It came down to fitting in.

"Let's rest up and get ready for some madness," Jax yawned, stretching and suddenly having his blue and gold line hoody release his other leg. Jax balled a fist and stretched that one outstretched hand as far as possible before turning over on his side and adjusting his backpack and again drawing his knees closer to his chest.

Left alone and unsure what to do, Ralphie listened to the morning and waited for the others to rise. Isaac stumbled to the left and after a couple of minutes stumbled back into the room adjusting his jeans and shorts. Ralphie assumed that Isaac had gone and relieved himself near the building if not from the second floor of the building.

At five minutes after 1000 hours Jax sat up and looked left and then right and then left again. Ralphie watched, amused. He pointed in the direction that Isaac had stumbled earlier.

Jax returned to his comfortable spot and curled back up into a ball like a rollie polly. Ralphie thought of trying to see if Zeke had his body camera on. It was not on.

So, from the safe spot Ralphie activated the digital map reader. He tapped a few buttons and noted that several contestants had their body cameras on. He punched a few buttons and after the fourth try found the body camera of someone named: Kobe.

"Kobe, where we going," a boy said from off screen. Kobe stopped and turned to take in the angular boy wearing a camouflage colored hoody. He had a smile on his smooth brown face. The boy behind Kobe was carrying an old-fashioned double-barreled shotgun by the barrel. The handle and trigger was over his small shoulder. Behind the boy with the shotgun was another boy dragging a cricket bat.

"Crap, man, I don't know," Kobe said. The trio were walking down some street that looked like all the streets in the island. There were burned out buildings on either side of the street. The road was cracked, and weeds grew through the pavement. The center line was inconsistent.

"Okay, what do I know about the island? I know that all the numbers run east and west and all the names run north and south. The sky bridge is north. The steam pipes are east," the boy with the shotgun sounded.

From the body camera Ralphie watched as Kobe studied the map of the island near a building that had been a winery at one time.

Kobe stopped a few feet from a brick front building. He sat and ate a couple of bites of his energy bar and paused.

The camera turned and Kobe saw two hooded figures slip into a warehouse just a hundred feet from him. Kobe was carrying a divided crossbow similar to the one that Zeke had.

Kobe and the two others ran quickly across the street and toward the warehouse. The boy with the cricket bat led. Kobe was second and the boy with the shotgun trailed.

Kobe bounced past the boy with the cricket bat. Suddenly, the view changed. The warehouse was surprisingly big and mostly intact. It, the warehouse, was at least three-stories tall and took up half a block of space. There were no real doors or windows, just open space.

There was diffused lighting as the sun, still hiding behind clouds overhead, did not pierce the darkness completely in the shadowy warehouse. Kobe moved slowly and cautiously forward his crossbow at the ready through the dappled light.

"What you seeing," one of the boys said from behind Kobe.

Bored, Ralphie tapped a few buttons on his digital map reader and Ralphie found himself listening to some heavy breathing. Ralphie paused and looked on the screen only to find the screen black. A few seconds later the camera turned and there was a wall and a strange but familiar noise.

Ralphie checked the camera feed and noted that it was Zeke's camera he was watching. Zeke had been out and on the hunt for nearly two hours. Day Two found Zeke's first encounter was with two contestants was not what he expected. The two, who seemed more interested in hiding the pickle than protecting themselves from attack, were kissing and hugging and humping each other in a darkened corner of the warehouse, when Zeke appeared with his crossbow.

"This is the challenge and you have to always be ready to fight," he intoned and stepped into the office and fired his first crossbow bolt into the side of the caramel skinned girl with the well-developed form. She had her bright blue Eureka! hoody off and was wearing a cartoon T-shirt of an Anime character. Her blue jeans were balled up on the floor with her underwear.

The bolt tore through her side and the girl silently screamed as she reached feebly toward the bolt and crumpled to the ground, dead still atop the boy. The boy, without a shirt on and shocked, reacted immediately as the girl he was holding fell dead beside him.

The dark sandy brown boy grabbed his undone jeans and tried to dive for cover as Zeke reloaded and fired another bolt at the scrambling boy. The bolt pierced the scrambling boy in his shoulder flipping him like a bowling pin before he crashed into the wall and howling tumbled out of the space that had been a window or door.

Zeke reloaded his crossbow and took a few steps forward when the wounded boy appeared with a silver hand cannon and fired twice in Zeke's direction. The gun report sounded so loud in the echo chamber that was the warehouse that Zeke instinctively clamped his hands over his ears because of the two shots. Zeke backed out of the building, his ears ringing.

"Damn," was all that Ralphie could say.

"What," Jax asked stretching again. He was sitting up and looking at the others in the second story room. Ralphie had not intended to say anything out loud. He was surprised that he had.

"Jax, do you have one of these," Ralphie asked. He pressed a button and allowed the digital map reader to record Zeke's activities while Ralphie was not watching.

"No, I have a regular map reader. I don't have no old school, mini LED billboard, price gun, price checker, video game controller from I don't know when," Jax joked.

Ralphie rolled his eyes. He smirked. He wasn't going to waste the entire day waiting for someone to run in and end him, like that girl that Zeke had shot.

Ralphie stood up and suddenly felt hungry. He looked down and grabbed his backpack. He had transferred everything that he needed to the backpack. He decided all at once to just leave. Ralphie did not need to deal with the drama of the "cool" kids. He checked the time on the digital map reader. It was fifteen minutes to 1100 hours.

"What? You mad? You getting your feelings hurt?"

Ralphie shrugged on his backpack.

"Wait, don't be that way. I will come with you. You know that you cannot survive without me," Jax announced stretching again but now up and on his feet.

"You're a butt, Jax," Ralphie concluded.

Jax slipped on his jeans and combat boots. He adjusted his T-shirt and Miller hoody and grabbed his backpack. Jax tied one of his combat boots and then the other.

"Okay," Jax said. "Let's roll."

Ralphie shook his head. He walked to the stairs where hours before they had nearly come to blows with Dame and Isaac. Jax was well rested. Ralphie had slept and watched and was just raring to go.

On the main floor were the four watching out for those upstairs. Dame, Tee, Zeke and Gina were on guard. Zeke was not near the stairs when Ralphie and Jax appeared.

"Where you two going," Gina asked.

"Out," Jax said.

"Funny," Gina responded.

"I get that a lot," Jax said as he walked out of the warehouse.

"Well, funny man, we're trying to figure out our next safe spot, first. There a bunch of hotspots. We want to avoid them. We figure that it might be safest in the areas where most avoid," Dame cautioned.

"Hiding in plain sight," Ralphie noted.

"Right," Dame nodded.

"Well, our messages still work, I think, when you decide where you're going, message me," Jax stated. "Right now, I'm ready to get this day started and get my body count numbers up." Jax paused. "Bet by the end of the day I have a higher body count than all of you."

Dame smiled. Isaac, Gina and Tee scowled. Ralphie grinned and tried not to laugh as Jax left with a flourish.

Ralphie shrugged his shoulders and followed.

"Where we headed," asked Ralphie.

"Hell, man, this is the challenge," Jax smiled slightly. "We might head to the east. We might head to the west. We might head to the north or the south. All we know is that the challenge ain't in there. The challenge is all around us," Jax pointed to the streets they were on.

"What changed since last night?"

"I figure that we're here and that there is only one way off this rock. You got to win. Winning don't happen hiding in a building. It happens out and about," Jax admitted. "I figure that I want to see it coming. I didn't sign up to hide."

Ralphie nodded. He nodded because he did not know how to respond to Jax at the moment. He walked on with Jax.

"I just want to point out that, if all things were equal and we weren't in the challenge, quite possibly Madison wouldn't be dead," Jax explained to Ralphie. "But I want to stress to Zeke, that we are in the challenge. People are going to be ended. People who are ninja assassins and sharp shooters are going to be zapped like mosquitoes in a bug zapper. That is going to happen every day. It's a hard truth," Jax pointed out. "This is the challenge and screwing around gets you RIPed." Jax rubbed his head and pushed his mop of curly hair back out of his face and stared at Ralphie and smiled thinly. "By the way, you can be a butt too. So, what. This is the challenge and it is more likely that we get flatlined than survive. This is the challenge."

Ralphie could only shake his head at Jax and his comments. He did not want to argue. He couldn't argue. The challenge was cruel. The challenge was unfair. The challenge was everything that was great and wonderful about the Remains.

"At 2100 hours here is the seventh report for Day Two of the Pandemonium Challenge: There are only forty-two contestants that remain in the challenge. The Pandemonium Challenge wishes to announce the loss of the following contestants from the last three hours: Isaiah Bell, Simone Cooper, Octavia Butler Garrett, Money Green, Victoria Houseman, Leila Porter and Zion Williams."

The pair of boys listened to the announcement and Jax chuckled. Ralphie twisted his lips on his dark chocolate face, thinking. He tried to understand if he had been the cause of any of those competitors being removed from the challenge.

"Losers," Jax guffawed. "How did so many get ended so quickly?"

Ralphie did not respond.

"Losers get taken out early," Jax continued. "Easy pickings."

Ralphie opened his mouth to say something but chose to remain quiet.

"Bet they didn't even have a plan."

They continued down the street.

"Okay, need to figure out how to use this arm rocket," Jax declared once outside and on the streets.

"You don't know how to use a slingshot?"

"I mean, yeah, I know how to use a slingshot, but I don't know how to do the whole hit them right between the eyes thing," Jax admitted.

"Well, you probably ain't going to be able to William Tell anyone between the eyes with that but you should be able to bruise the hell out of them."

Jax nodded.

He and Ralphie walked down Avenue M toward 13th Street. Ralphie thought to tell Jax that Zeke had gone this way but that was hours ago. Ralphie had no idea where Zeke was at that moment.

Ralphie and Jax walked around the island for nearly four hours and in that time nearly were deaded six times. The first time Jax was still trying to figure out how to use the slingshot. He fired into a building, by accident and out of the door came two scallywags with red and green tipped crowns of nappy hair. One of the boys had a burper. The other boy had a baseball bat. They looked menacing.

"Run," screamed Jax and he and Ralphie ran away from the two bigger and meaner boys. The two boys chased, but they could not catch the faster and more frightened boys.

The second time that Jax and Ralphie were nearly flatlined happened on the heels of the first incident. Jax slowed and stopped only to sit down on the steps of what had been a church or theater. Ralphie was resting a little bit further from Jax, his hand against a wall.

The ender in the church used a bullwhip to strangle Jax. The ender was ingenious. He had snaked the bullwhip out of a latticework design and over Jax's head. Jax was caught entirely by surprise.

Jax's muffled screams caught Ralphie's attention and straight away Ralphie went into action. Without thought Ralphie rushed to Jax's aid. He jabbed at the unseen ender behind the latticework with his croquet mallet. He pounded the strangler until he released Jax enough to allow Jax to escape the bullwhip's deadly chokehold.

Jax, once freed, slid down and away from the reach of the unseen ender. Ralphie jabbed again and again until there was no resistance. Ralphie figured that the ender, or attempted ender, had enough and chose someone else to attack.

Turning from the church Ralphie found a tall, thin girl with her hair pulled back into a single thick Afro bun, standing, holding a weapon that Jax and Ralphie had only seen in ninja movies. The chestnut colored girl had a wide, evil smile and looked a bit deranged. The weapon the girl held looked like something used by farmers to cut down weeds. The thing that was frightening about the wooden handled weed whacker was that attached to the bottom of it was a length of chain with a metal weighted ball at the end.

"Hey, I need a minute," Jax breathed, rubbing at his throat. "You take her on."

Ralphie smirked. He looked at the girl and her weird clown smile and back at Jax. Jax continued to rub the back of his neck.

The girl attacked, swinging the weighted metal ball with incredible accuracy. Ralphie barely escaped the first attack. He did not have time to appreciate his near escape as the girl stepped forward and the weighted ball swished by Ralphie's head, barely missing him again.

The girl did not speak. The girl dressed in her line black and white dominated hoody, blue jeans and combat boots could not have been from any other line, Ralphie thought. She was a Trad. This girl was deadly. She knew how to use the archaic ninja weapon. That meant, to Ralphie, that she was trained. Training meant Trads. It also meant that if he disarmed her, Ralphie's thoughts went, she might be even more dangerous than with the awkward weapon.

So, Ralphie hatched a plan. He could not allow the girl to end him or worse to leak him and Jax. He would have to trust his talents despite what short-term pain was inflicted.

The girl sidestepped Ralphie and the weighted ball arced into the air and toward Ralphie once again. Ralphie dodged the deadly ball and instead of jumping away instinctually, he moved into the interior arc of the weed whacker and girl. He figured that in that suddenly indefensible area the training and skill of the girl would be on full display.

Ralphie only had his croquet mallet and his fists against this unknown girl. The girl, upon seeing Ralphie within her defenses smiled evilly that malevolent smile that suggested insanity. He had hoped that the girl would have shown fear or shock but that was a dream.

The weighted ball fell harmlessly behind Ralphie and in a flash, the girl went to work with the threshing tool. Ralphie defended against the blade with his croquet mallet. The thin girl pressed in and tried to slash and end Ralphie.

Ralphie felt the slash of the blade on his shoulder. He let the croquet mallet fall through his hands to the head and re-gripped his only weapon. The girl silent as death prepared to cut Ralphie when he drove the head of the mallet up, like an uppercut, into the girl's chin. The croquet mallet smashed the girl hard and there was the sound of her clicking teeth hard in her mouth. The sound of the croquet mallet against the girl's chin and the forcing of her teeth to snap together was chilling. The scythe scraped across Ralphie's neck leaving a welt and a trail of blood.

The girl flipped over like a flapjack, blood coming out of her mouth. Ralphie placed a foot on the girl's chest and swung his croquet mallet at the prone girl's head.

Jax climbed to his feet a little woozy.

"You didn't seem to need my help," Jax admitted rubbing at his neck.

Ralphie looked down and saw that there was a trickle of blood coming from the cut he had received from the girl. He tried to lift his arm. He was in pain. The pain in his arm would subside. The memory of him putting his foot on the girl's chest and swinging his croquet mallet to end the girl would be with him forever.

Jax grabbed at Ralphie and pulled him from the flatlined girl. Ralphie did not argue or resist. He followed a few steps. The further away he got from the skirmish the clearer his senses became. Maybe a block away, Ralphie stopped and looked at Jax.

"Where are we heading, Jax," Ralphie asked looking at his overacting friend who continued to rub his throat.

"West," Jax gestured looking at the unmoving girl on the sidewalk. Jax kicked at her and ran toward Ralphie. Ralphie hefted the croquet mallet onto his uninsured shoulder and headed west.

After the first three attacks Jax and Ralphie headed toward the western end of the island. While walking Jax received a message from Dame.

"Dame just messaged," Jax reported. "He has a new location for us to lay our heads."

Ralphie continued to lift and lower his leaking shoulder. He winced and grimaced from the pain.

"Hey, what do you think is going on with Tee?"

"What do you mean?"

"You know, the whole Zeke and Dame thing," Jax began.

Ralphie knitted his brows, confused.

"Come on man, that is some weird stuff right," Jax asked.

Ralphie thought about answering and paused. He lifted his chin in the direction that they were walking. Jax turned and stopped.

One girl stood in the middle of the street. Ralphie and Jax froze. Jax stepped forward and studied the girl holding a cane knife in her hands and smiling like a lunatic.

"Oh, I think I saw your sister earlier. You got a sister in the challenge this year," Jax asked.

"Be careful Jax," Ralphie warned. "This is a classic challenge trick," Ralphie noted.

Ralphie looked back and was not surprised to find that two boys were suddenly grinning as they blocked Jax and Ralphie's exit. The boys dressed in hooded sweatshirts were holding a machete and a mace. The taller boy was holding the mace. The smaller boy spun the machete like a machete expert.

"Gotta admit that I didn't want to take out a girl first," Jax noted. "Kind of wanted to take down a badass first."

"You about to meet a badass," the unknown girl sneered.

Jax loaded his arm rocket and prepared to fire on the girl with the cane knife.

The girl stepped forward. Jax fired a ceramic ball at the girl. She dodged the ceramic ball. Jax reloaded.

The girl continued toward Jax.

Ralphie turned and found himself preparing for the attack from two strangers.

"Jax, need your help here," Ralphie announced as the two boys ran forward preparing to bash in his head.

"Ralphie, you won't believe it," Jax laughed, suddenly beside Ralphie. "I hit her right between the eyes. Crazy huh?"

The boy with the mace nearly caved in Jax's head. Ralphie swung his croquet mallet as hard as he could and whacked the fast approaching boy in the thigh, making him miss Jax. The boy tumbled and did a headfirst slide across the sidewalk. The boy, grimacing, tried to stand only to fall to one knee.

The machete wielding boy stepped forward and Ralphie prepared for the attack. Jax pulled the slingshot back. He fired a couple of ceramic balls from his arm rocket at the injured boy. The boy tried to avoid the ceramic ball attack, to no avail. After the fourth ceramic ball smashed the nameless boy he collapsed. Jax smiled broadly at his accuracy.

Ralphie laughed at Jax's newfound courage. Before he could fully appreciate Jax's achievement he found himself dodging a machete slash from the second boy. Ralphie countered the missed attack with a brutal and powerful swing from his croquet mallet that drove the boy back and over a broken bus bench near the sidewalk.

The boy crashed hard on the street and dropped his machete. Ralphie paused and prepared to finish the boy with the machete. Jax stepped forward and shot more ceramic balls at the slightly stunned boy. The boy tried to get to his feet but directly found himself under attack by Jax and his slingshot. Four ceramic balls ripped through the air and forced the nameless boy to drop his mace trying to protect himself. The ceramic balls tore into the boy. The boy spun and twisted. With the third ceramic ball released the boy fell to the ground. With the fourth ceramic ball the boy stopped moving.

Ralphie watched as Jax stepped up to the unmoving boy and toed the unmoving boy's head and laughed like a kid who had gotten a star on a homework assignment.

"I don't know if this is the best day or worst day of my life," Jax noted. His arm was extended, and he was holding the sling pocket, filled with one of the ceramic balls that had disabled the boy at his feet. Jax looked at Ralphie and gave a comedic wink and released the sling pocket and the ceramic ball.

The sound of the ceramic ball against the boy's head was similar to the sound of popping a bag of chips, Ralphie thought. It, the sound, reverberated through the air. Ralphie tried to shake the image of Jax over the unmoving body of the boy that had tried to chop his friend in two with a machete from his head. He closed his eyes to Jax as he braced the boy for anything valuable.

"This is the challenge, baby. We in it to win? Or just in it 'til somebody decides to end us," Jax asked suddenly confident. In less than twenty minutes Jax had cheesed three competitors.

"In it to win it," Ralphie repeated, biting at his lower lip.

"Come on," Jax grinned slipping another ceramic ball in his slingshot and moving away from the destruction that he and Ralphie had caused.

The pair walked west. Ralphie had to admit that he was a little impressed with Jax and his arm rocket. He just smiled as a response.

By 1700 hours Jax and Ralphie had arrived in the western end of the island. Jax messaged Dame. Dame messaged back with the address where they were hiding.

"I'll message Zeke," Jax mentioned as they found the military housing that they were going to be hiding in for the night. They entered one of the apartments. Ralphie found a corner where he could watch the entrances.

Jax sat down across from Ralphie. He still had his arm rocket on his forearm. Jax was rolling three marbles in his free hand.

"Hey, might want to take off your sweatshirt," Jax decided. "Need to check your shoulder."

"I'm fine," stated Ralphie.

"Okay, suit yourself," joked Jax.

"Jax said that you got a boo-boo," Tee grinned coming into the room where Ralphie was seated against a wall trying to will his shoulder to stop throbbing.

"A boo-boo?"

Tee had her Glock 21 on her hip. She grinned and nodded. She raised her hand and in it was a white plastic box with a red cross on it.

Tee seemed to be in a good mood. She knelt down beside Ralphie. Ralphie stiffened as the sandalwood brown girl was suddenly in front of him.

"You qualified to use that?"

She looked up and without saying a word or changing her facial expression leaned over and punched Ralphie in his shoulder. He winced at the punch.

"Ow," Ralphie moaned through gritted teeth.

"Sorry, Jax didn't say where your boo-boo was," Tee apologized.

Ralphie held his shoulder gingerly.

"I didn't mean to… you can be such a jerk," Tee apologized suddenly flustered.

"That doesn't make me feel real confident about your medical skills," Ralphie admitted, holding his shoulder.

"Well, that makes two of us," Tee laughed. "At least, you will know that going in."

She crossed her legs, sitting next to Ralphie. Ralphie could not get over the transformation of Tee. Here Tee was, this little chestnut brown girl with braids, this extremely confident and mean girl that Ralphie knew was no longer the same Tee that used to wear soccer cleats and ride bikes and play baseball. The girl that sat next to Ralphie was this bad ass who was the girlfriend of Zeke and super dramatic about everything with a Glock 21 on her hip.

"Are you overthinking something," Tee asked from beneath her arched eyebrows.

Ralphie looked up and found Tee smirking. She had one of those I-just-read-your-last-message-that-you-didn't-want-anyone-to-see looks on her face. Her dark eyes twinkled just a little at the knowledge that she had seen into Ralphie's mind, if only for a moment.

"Okay, thinker, let's have a look at that owie," Tee grinned.

"I wasn't overthinking anything," Ralphie lied. He looked guilty all of a sudden.

Tee smiled big.

"Owie? Boo-boo? How old are you," Ralphie joked, attempting to change the subject.

"It's how my dad used to describe things," Tee explained as a matter of fact and at that point it was. Tee had changed because of her father's death. She rarely talked about how it made her feel. So, having her blurt out something about her personal life was gigantic. Ralphie braced for anything. Ralphie did not know what Tee would do. More importantly, he did not know what he should do.

Suddenly, Tee was vulnerable. She had opened up a wound that had never healed. Ralphie did not blink. He was not sure what to expect. Maybe, he hoped, nothing would happen. Maybe, he would have to comfort Tee. He waited the awkward moment out.

Tee took a deep breath and Ralphie watched. She seemed to be on the verge of breaking down and crying but held it together, barely. Tears rimmed her dark eyes suddenly and Ralphie looked away, allowing her that moment.

"You okay?"

Tee stared at Ralphie as if he had grown another head.

"Just concerned. Caring," Ralphie fumbled. Ralphie did not know what else to say.

Tee blinked. She stared at Ralphie, silently.

"Not everyone has the right words or does the right thing at the right moment all the time," Ralphie stated.

Tee twisted her lips on her chestnut brown face, studying Ralphie for a moment. A myriad of emotions washed across Tee's face. For an instance, it looked as if she was considering punching him again in the injured shoulder.

"Nobody's perfect. As long as we're alive we're going to make mistakes. That's what makes us human," Ralphie offered. "We stumble, we fall, we have to get back up."

"Ralphie, stop."

"What?" Ralphie suddenly felt embarrassed.

Tee wiped at her dark eyes.

"No one lives—"

Tee put up a hand. Ralphie stopped in mid speech.

"What about my shoulder?"

Tee grinned.

"You mean your owie?"

"No doctor I know says: Owie or Boo-boo."

Tee scratched her cheek, thinking.

"Need to take off your hoody," Tee declared.

Ralphie hesitated.

"Do you want help or not," Tee asked, staring at him, suddenly annoyed.

"I just--"

Tee smiled big.

"What are you afraid of that I won't be able to control myself when I see your naked chest?"

Ralphie opened his mouth and closed it wordlessly. He lowered his head and swallowed his unspoken words. He slowly pulled his sweatshirt off.

"Wow," Tee jested. "Ralphie you are hot. Man, I need a fan or towel. It's getting hot in here," Tee joked.

"Cut it out."

"Okay, let's get down to business," Tee announced. She turned Ralphie's head and examined his shoulder more closely.

"Is it bad?"

"No. That's not that bad," Tee grinned opening her med kit and finding some ointment and antiseptic.

Ralphie smirked at the comment.

"I've seen worse," Tee joked.

Ralphie grimaced and tried not to whimper as Tee cleaned up the cut and bandaged his shoulder. The process was painful but bearable for Ralphie.

"You are being a tough guy," Tee joked as she finished the bandaging.

"Quit it," Ralphie winced.

Tee examined her work.

"You can put your hoody back on."

"You done?"

"Yes, that should hold you until you decide to do something else... stupid," Tee joked.

Ralphie flexed his shoulder and though it was tender it did not hurt as much as it had before Tee's care.

Tee studied Ralphie as he slipped his hooded sweatshirt back on.

After Ralphie had pulled the hoody over his head he noted that Tee was looking at him curiously.

"What?" Ralphie asked, wiping his nose and mouth. "Do I have something on my face?"

"No," Tee stated with a smile. She looked away from Ralphie suddenly. "You know that the worse thing is to get an infection out here. Things go from bad to worse pretty quickly."

"Thanks," Ralphie nodded.

At that moment Jax stepped into the room with his arm rocket and ceramic marbles.

"Look at this black Romeo and Juliet thing going on back here," Jax joked. "How was our little black Florence Nightingale," Jax grinned. Tee upon seeing Jax smiled awkwardly and created a little more space between her and Ralphie.

"Did I interrupt something," Jax grinned like a madman. "Were you two having a moment?"

"Shut up, Jax," Ralphie replied. "We were not having a…anything."

Jax had one of those gigantic Cheshire Cat smiles on his face all of a sudden. He looked from Ralphie to Tee and back. In the silence there was all sort of innuendo.

"Jax, why did you come in here?"

"I just came up the stairs to tell you that Zeke is back, and he has zapped at least half a dozen people today. He is all chewed up. He said that he Swiss cheesed the boy that swatted Maddy. He is all amped up about it too."

Tee upon hearing Zeke had returned gathered her med kit and climbed to her feet. She looked from Ralphie to Jax and back and then headed downstairs. She pushed past Jax.

"Thanks, Tee," Ralphie managed as Tee exited.

Tee did not respond.

Ralphie smirked at the departure of Tee from the floor and wall where he had been resting.

Jax leaned in close and grabbed Ralphie by his unharmed shoulder. Ralphie and Jax were suddenly very close. Jax smiled and advised: "You can't be into Zeke's girl, man."

"I am not into Zeke's… Tee."

"Whatever," Jax began with a shake of his head. "I came upstairs to tell you that Zeke said that he wants to get out from under Dame and his crew as soon as possible. You in?"

Ralphie looked at Jax and nodded.

"Cool," Jax confided. "The plan is to pretend to go out for the night and find a new place to stay while we're out."

"Sounds good to me," Ralphie agreed, suddenly a little tired. "I'm going to crash for a couple of hours. Wake me when you are ready to go."

Jax stood up to leave and over his shoulder Ralphie saw one of the dozen black bodied robo-spiders that kept the island clear of contestants that had been retired from the challenge. The robo-spiders were eight feet by eight feet with a dozen mechanically enhanced eyes that circled its egg-shaped body. From the center of the incredibly sturdy body emanated the eight retractable metallic legs. The robo-spiders had four smaller arms that could grab, pull, grip and bag the retired competitors. In the body was a compartment that held a dozen body bags. The robo-spiders could carry four contestants with relative ease. Ralphie blinked as the robo-spider climbed up the side of the building and into a structure just a stone's throw away.

The last memory that Ralphie had of his conversation with Jax was of him climbing to his feet with the sun turning the sky purple and pink behind him and Jax leaving.

Ralphie woke up with Jax and Zeke standing over him smiling.

"Ralphie, heard you and Jax were being Billy Bad Asses?"

Ralphie did not respond.

"Hell, to the yay, we were," Jax joked. "Think my body count ins three or four, just from today."

Zeke laughed, impressed.

"Ralphie took out two today," Jax confessed. "Think my body count is higher."

"Think we are even," Ralphie corrected Jax.

"What did you do today Zeke?"

Zeke looked left and then right before he spoke.

Zeke pulled out the .22 caliber Ruger Revolver.

"So, why did it take you so long?"

"You got jokes," Zeke joked.

"The island ain't that big," Jax noted.

"The island may not be big but for one person to find one ass clown who purposely swatted Maddy in one day is like winning the lottery twice in the same day."

Tee and Gina appeared, and the subject changed.

"We have five days to survive," Gina pointed out. "We have to keep our squad tight."

"We have to keep our squad tight."

"So, we are going with the plan to go out two by two and do as much damage as possible. North, South, East and West," Gina advised.

"Who came up with that plan?"

"Dame," Gina smirked.

"Want to point out that the plan doesn't work two by two when we are only seven," Jax noted.

"Ass clowns," Zeke breathed.

"Well, we'll wait until Dame returns to figure out the best plan," Gina decided. "He and Isaac should be back soon. We also have to find a new safe spot."

Ralphie fell asleep. Maybe he passed out. All he knew was that one moment he saw Jax and the next he was looking at the darkening sky through the window.

"Time to rise and shine, sleepy head," Jax smiled sleepily.

Ralphie climbed to his feet. His shoulder hurt a little. It was nothing that he could not handle.

A few minutes before 1800 hours Gina and Tee arrived. Dame and Isaac Moore returned a few minutes after the 1800 hours' announcement.

"Okay," Dame announced in the military apartments that they had staked out. "We are going to rest and recover and as soon as it gets dark enough to cause some damage, we are going to get back outside and do damage." He paused. "I know that there have been questions on the plan. It is still in effect. Me and Isaac Moore are going north. Gina and Tee will go south. Jax and Ralphie can go east. Zeke, you go west. The goal is to end as many threats as we can. Whoever we come in contact with before the first announcement is an open target." Dame stopped, thinking. "One last thing as we leave this safe spot, we will be looking for a safe spot in the East. So, Jax and Ralphie will have double duty. They will locate a new safe spot for us."

Chapter Thirteen.

Control Room

Julius Erving McCarthy unfolded himself from his transport and stepped out and into the morning air. Julius McCarthy was a tall man, rail thin, the color of a copper penny with a broad forehead and thick eyebrows that made his face look pensive, most of the time. Dressed in a gray suit, white starched collared shirt with a gray striped print silk tie and matching pocket square, Julius McCarthy looked the part of the director of the Pandemonium Challenge.

He tapped his earbud and wirelessly connected with all his electronic devices. Music from the 21st Century oozed from the earbud and made Julius McCarthy remember why he had taken the difficult and demanding position of director of the Pandemonium Challenge.

"Social mode. Mute with conversation," Julius McCarthy announced into the air and the earbuds beeped twice acknowledging the request.

"Mister McCarthy," one of the dozen enforcers guarding the parking lot of the central government announced and the music in his ear was muted.

"Good morning," Julius McCarthy replied. He listened to his music restart as he walked through the archway that looked out and over the Central Government park. The park stretched for nearly one square mile end to end. A white painted three-foot high fence bordered around the park. There were manicured lawns, dozens of topiaries, four fountains, 24 benches, six gazebos, several ponds but the main attraction was the fourteen statues that overlooked the central walk that cut through the park.

The walk was a wide stone path that led to the Central Government grounds and offices and buildings. Throughout the entry to the grounds were pairs of enforcers situated strategically, armed and at the ready. Enforcers were given the daunting task of protecting the park from the thousands of visitors that daily walked through the park.

Featured on the walk were the fourteen statues that highlighted the founders of the seven lines, groups and the talents of the same seven distinct lines in the Remains. The walk sloped down to the main buildings and ended at the main governmental buildings that was surrounded by seven statues of the principals of the Remains. Twenty-one statues, in total, watched over the Central Government grounds.

The senate building was the largest building in the Remains central government. All laws and discussions of laws in the Remains happened in the senate building. The judicial building was the second largest and executed justice daily. The third building was the Remains Presidential offices. It was the smallest building of them all. The Presidents were expected to participate in justice or law and nothing else.

The Pandemonium Challenge Committee building, where Julius McCarthy was headed, was a three-story white Victorian home that had been transformed into an office building specifically for the committee. It was dwarfed by the judicial building, one hundred yards from the Remains governmental buildings where the Remains leaders worked to strengthen and keep the small remnant of society going.

As McCarthy walked and passed the first statue of the regal Innovators; on one side there was the stern looking Alvin LaFleur. He was captured in bronze holding a guitar that he had invented or been somehow involved in creating, Julius McCarthy was no longer sure. LaFleur had been a technological wizard and gamer and used his talents to create one of the most popular video game distractions of the time. Captured in a suit LaFleur did not look incredibly imposing but his business acumen was legendary. He was always thinking three or four steps ahead of everyone. After the flash, he had brushed himself off and looked around the wreckage and decided to establish the Innovators, a small group of forward thinkers, to guide and direct in the rebuilding of the cities, towns and states after the flash. On the plinth was written near the base: Risk Takers.

Innovators embodied LaFleur's gambler nature. In the past, it had been LaFleur who had reached out and found like-minded individuals and insured the livelihood and their dominance in the Remains by contracting, at first, and then buying up all the land that looked down upon what was once Berkeley, Oakland, Hayward and Castro Valley.

That purchase had cemented the Innovators as one of the most influential groups in the Remains. On the opposite side of LaFleur was Josephine Newman, arms crossed, looking over her half-moon glasses perched on her thin and slightly rounded nose. Newman had brokered the first deal between LaFleur and herself to expand the footprint of the Innovators in a deal that stretched the Innovators real estate holdings from what was once Hayward all the way down to the destroyed Fremont hills.

"Morning Vince," McCarthy declared to the statue of LaFleur. Vincent LaFleur stood there, dressed in a suit and tie and lizard scaled pointy shoes, looking out toward the horizon. On his lapel was a flower. Resting on his thin nose were a pair of round rimless nez pence. McCarthy shook his head at LaFleur. He always seemed a little aloof, McCarthy mused. "Still looking down on people I suppose," McCarthy continued with a smile. "You look like someone that would have gone out of your way to make people call you: Vincent. I know your type and all your money-grubbing flea tick wannabes. I could never see us just sitting on the porch and shooting the breeze."

Julius McCarthy stopped near the Innovator founder's counterpart; Josephine Newman. Unattractive, thin, and motherly, Greta Newman looked the exact opposite of the stodgy Vincent LaFleur.

"Good morning Jo," he crooned with a wave to the statue of Josephine Newman. The statue, in bronze, caught Newman with one foot forward and looking up and into the sky. Her hair was piled on top of her oval head showing off her long and slender neck. Josephine Newman was dressed in a knee length dress and combat boots. In her left hand was a book. On her back was a small backpack that looked oddly like a child's toy. McCarthy stopped and studied the statue of Josephine Newman. He liked this statue much more than the Alvin LaFleur statue.

"You know I think you and I would have gotten along swimmingly," McCarthy mentioned to the statue. He stepped toward the statue and stopped at the foot of Josephine Newman. He read the plaque at the foot of the statue that stood on a three-foot plinth.

"Money won't create success, the freedom to make it will." --Nelson Mandela

"You were one smart cookie," McCarthy confessed looking up at Josephine Newman's statue admiringly. McCarthy shook his head looking up at the statue of the woman that had expanded the control of the most influential in the Remains with two words to Vincent LaFleur. The nuptials had brought together the most powerful that had survived and without much warning the Remains was rebuilding with the vision of the remaining visionaries.

"Of course, you didn't plan on the challenge," Julius McCarthy admitted. "Or your line throwing a monkey wrench into the challenge this year."

McCarthy turned from Josephine Newman and continued on under the eyes of other bronze cast leaders of the Remains. Closest to the Innovators were the First Gens statues. There were the Four Geeks: Harold Jenkins, Samuel Leopold, Richard Cort, and Robert Jefferson, that had initially rewired the Remains. Jenkins and Leopold were on one plinth. Cort and Jefferson were on the other plinth. These four technological wizards had been the start of the First Gen line. In the First Gen compound there were statues of Richard Cort and Robert Jefferson everywhere since they had died in the effort. Harold Jenkins had a building named after him. Samuel Leopold, before his death, had created the First Gens multimedia center that had become the center of the First Gen community. On the plinth was the simple principle of the First Gens: Tinkers.

McCarthy nodded as he picked up his pace and looked pleased at the Second Gen statues of Barack White and Dianna Thomas. Though Barack White was seen as a controversial character in the Remains because he had brought to the attention of everyone what the Four Geeks had failed to achieve and instead of simply complaining figured out a solution. Barack White had diagnosed what the First Gens had miscalculated. Animosity was intense between the two Gen lines.

Dianna Thomas enlisted several of her tech experts and she and Barack White was a technological genius and with an algorithm brought the

Remains back online and reconnected most technology. White and Thomas were legends in the Remains for their technological accomplishments.

The two statues were the only two statues that had two enforcers situated near them. Both statues featured a live feed of the historic restarting of the Internet in the Remains. White was kneeling next to his monitor with goggles, heavy gloves, and work boots. Dianna Thomas had a ponytail, angular face, long neck, spidery arms and legs, short sleeve T-shirt, work belt and combat boots.

The feed was looped and synced to start when anyone was near the statues. So, as McCarthy walked past Barack White the monitors had sparked to life on the walk as they had all over the Remains, four decades ago. The grainy pictures of the world after the flash appeared and tore the hope from all that held out the slimmest hope that the destruction was not as far reaching as believed. Then the reports came back slowly.

"The world that we knew is gone, never to be seen again," one of the Internet reporters announced in his most dramatic and brassy tone. "All that we once knew and relied upon has been wiped from this earth. If you are receiving this announcement know that this once blue marble is a dark and dying ball. We that survived live in the shadow of what was." The reporter pressed a finger to his ear, receiving news. Behind the reporter flashed a graphic of the largest land mass on earth; China. "China now, is home to an estimated ten million residents. Every major capital has been obliterated. The hardest hit countries were the United States, Europe, Russia, the Middle East, India and China." The reporter had paused, and the monitor had shown the destruction of the various capitals, landmarks, and endless destruction in familiar and unfamiliar places. "Our information comes from the street reporters who have come from beneath the rubble to report and document the worse devastation ever recorded in our short history. If the numbers that we are hearing are even close, the world population has taken an unimaginable hit. Pre-flash there were nearly eight billion people on earth. Post-flash, based on our unscientific calculations, there are now less than one hundred million in China and our rough estimate clocks our planet's population at just below one billion people on earth."

"Sometimes, ignorance is bliss," Julius McCarthy noted.

He passed under the eyes of Charles Miller, the original Miller, Julius McCarthy had to be impressed with the giant of a man that had led the labor force to rebuild the Remains. Charles Miller was a bull of a man. He looked like he was chiseled out of bronze. He had this ancient physicality that suggested unimaginable strength and power at the tips of his fingers. Charles Miller looked as if he might be able to uproot a tree on his own. He was a throwback to times when muscles and brawn were valuable and essential.

The Millers believed in work. There was a calm that came from work for the Millers. They taught that work ethic to all that would listen. The Millers and those that followed in their efforts believed as well in the joy of work.

Cast in bronze Charles Miller was dressed in coveralls and holding a sledgehammer in his gloved hand. The sledgehammer rested on his thick shoulder. Around his bullish neck were a pair of welder's goggles. McCarthy paused and thought how Miller's life had changed thanks to Shirley Miller, Charles Miller's wife.

Shirley Miller was on the opposite side of her larger than life husband and cast in bronze as well. Shirley Miller stood just fifteen feet across the Remains walk from her husband dressed in a simple dress, curly hair, round cheeks, and no chin to talk of. At her feet were a dozen books. In her hand was a yardstick. Shirley Miller was a lifelong learner. She was also very disciplined. Shirley Miller believed in self betterment. She believed in education. Shirley Miller had two sons and one daughter in her life.

"Everyone wants to be famous. Everyone wants to be seen. The challenge allows the attention starved an opportunity to be seen and appreciated, if for only a moment," Shirley Miller had suggested at the Central Government legislative meeting.

Thus, Shirley Miller pointed out that work in ignorance was not peace or contentment, but mindless slavery. It was through the forward thinking of Shirley Miller and her insistence that Mills not only be laborers but educated and capable of taking any position presented in the Remains. Julius McCarthy and hundreds of Mills were able to break from the unstated Remains caste system and aspire for greater goals.

"Thank you for your guidance," Julius McCarthy whispered to the mother of the Mills. "Thank you for your trust."

Julius McCarthy walked on and nodded to the ornately designed bronze statues of Barry Michaels and Sunshine Thomas the legendary leaders of the Remains most bohemian group; the Poppies. He was cast looking up toward the sky with building blocks at his feet. Barry Michaels, thin, small, and wearing welder's goggles, shorts and combat boots, had done the first mural in the Remains entitled: The Revolution Was Televised. The image had been of a Nagasaki-like photo of people running but being disintegrated as a nuclear blast mushroomed behind them. In the crowd, were iconic images of a little child running with virtual glasses on, a mother and daughter dressed alike running in inappropriate jogging attire, a dreadlocked black man gripping his high heels and making the most comical sad face imaginable and others. The mural was done on the wall of a bombed-out church after the flash, in the forbidden area where things were extremely hot. Michaels was a painter and sculptor who tragically died a year after the all clear from exposure to radiation in the forbidden zones of the Remains. Before Barry Michaels died, he had created a number of pivotal pieces that were scattered throughout the Remains.

Some of his artwork was on a grand scale. "The Rise and Fall of Capitalism" was a gigantic piece of twisted steel that melded the image of the Statue of Liberty and the flash on the steps of what had been the home of one of the baseball teams in the East Bay. Some of Barry Michaels work was tiny. It was all art and focused on scale.

All of it was distinct and done to incite conversation. Michaels work was compared to some of the most controversial street artists before his time. There was a Michaels mural on what had been the Masonic Temple that McCarthy always simpered at for its beauty and sadness.

Sunshine Thomas had been the brains behind the creation of the Poppies. She was a painter. She created the artist collective that became the Poppies in the shadows of what had been an art school. Artists had gathered at the collective and the Poppies had begun. Thomas was famous for her moodiness. She created in her moodiness. Sunshine was famous for her fifteen-foot-high panels that seemed just splotches of paint but when placed together created a complete picture and message.

Sunshine Thomas had extreme mood swings. She was loving. She was vindictive. She was empathetic. Sunshine was a victim of her moods, but those very same moods allowed her to create hundreds of panels. As she drew close to death there was a revival of interest in her art. Close friends capsulized her art into four phases in her artistic lifetime: blue, green, yellow, and red. Blue was her sad and moodiest phases of art. They were dynamic and filled with dark images. Sunshine's green phase was the hopeful and vibrant stage of her art. These were distinct in that they usually revolved around nature and the hope of a better time. The yellow phase of Sunshine Thomas' art was driven by the fears that plagued her and everyone in the Remains after the flash. There were frightening images of monsters, aliens, death, destruction and the constant reminder of the flash; the dead bodies. Perhaps her most controversial phase was the red phase for Sunshine Thomas. In the red phase there were images of war, armies, enforcers, blood and incredible power. Few saw the blue or red paintings because there were so few available.

Julius McCarthy loved that the Poppies had allowed Sunshine Thomas's statue to be painted in the four distinct colors of her phases. It was the only statue in the Remains walk that was not the naked bronze that the sculptors had intended.

The second to last pair of bronze statues that Julius McCarthy passed that morning were of Jean-Michel Goodman and Emma Watters, the Boomers. They were the youngest of the Remains founders. They had been named: Boomers because they believed in many of the Baby Boomers philosophies, theories and concepts. They, unlike the others, modeled their line on a generation that had invented the cellphone, computer and Internet. Jean-Michel Goodman, not more than sixteen or seventeen, was orphaned after the flash. He had single handedly banded together hundreds upon hundreds of orphans and begun the Boomers facility in what had been a school campus on a hill that overlooked all the destruction below. Goodman was a pimply faced teenager with a vision that other orphaned teens seemed to understand. Like the statues before them Jean-Michel Goodman was captured in bronze dressed in his signature baseball cap, T-shirt, blue jeans, gym shoes and backpack.

Emma Watters, not yet twenty, was street tough. She was a sassy and unblinking girl that had seen her family die in front of her. Emma Watters had found the Boomers campus and been enthusiastic about the idea of being a part of something significant after the flash. Watters had created the first organized musical expression in the Remains. The Boomers were noted for their musical abilities. She stood looking out and toward the Acid Bay with her mutt lap dog, that had survived the flash somehow, at her heels. Emma Watters's braided hair was piled on her head to accentuate her round shoulders and pear-shaped figure. She was cast in combat boots, blue jeans, T-shirt and backpack.

At the end of the walk, just another twenty feet, stood the Trads, the traditionalists or what most called them in the Remains; the Johnny Laws. McCarthy turned before reaching the pair of statues. He did not have to go the Trads statues to see them. He knew the statues well. The two Trads, the final pair of bronze statues before the Central governmental building, stood like guardians, arms akimbo, rigid, ever watchful, and dressed like modern day warriors.

Julius McCarthy always shook his head upon seeing the two traditionalists. The Trads, traditionalists, focused on rules and regulations and used those rules and regulations against their opponents like weapons in every situation. Thus, their Remains nickname: Johnny Laws.

Marco Wyss and Amber Porter were dressed in army fatigues, combat boots, helmets and carrying assault rifles. The pair stood stiffly on their plinths that read: Principled. Both Wyss and Porter stood unblinking and fierce before the Remains central government buildings. At their feet were papers and books. Marco Wyss' statue went so far as to have the broad-shouldered pot-bellied leader standing, with one foot on a pile of books.

"Marco and Amber, you two were a pair, for sure," Julius McCarthy mused. They had created the Traditionalist campus from what had been one of the many college campuses abandoned after the flash and in a year the campus had been transformed to resemble the baby of a military complex and a creative technological complex.

The director mused aloud, "If you two were around today you might have created a better mousetrap or more efficient Interweb." He smirked at his thoughts. "The sky was definitely the limit for you two." Thanks to the Traditionalists the Remains had discovered and refurbished damaged helicopters that were salvageable at the one-time devastated international airport. The traditionalists helped outfit every citizen with a bicycle as fossil fuel was nearly non-existent.

"We owe so much to you and your quirky group."

Julius McCarthy turned off the path and there he was greeted by the hundreds of protesters that stood picketing the challenge. There were men, women, boys and girls holding picket signs and walking back and forth in front of the doors to the three-story Pandemonium Challenge Committee building.

Enforcers stood on the stairs to the entrance to allow anyone interested in walking in the front door entry. Julius McCarthy took a deep breath and walked toward the doors of the three-story building where the Pandemonium Challenge committee was situated. As McCarthy walked, he was suddenly greeted by two enforcers that walked him unmolested through the protesters.

The protest was sizeable but nothing that the enforcers could not handle, Julius McCarthy thought. The numbers never got much larger than the numbers he saw in the morning. The enforcers stood on either side of Julius McCarthy and walked him through the picketers and their signs. On the other side of the line of protesters Julius McCarthy was handed off to the next two enforcers that stood at the main entry. All of the enforcers were dressed in the dark blue fatigues of the Remains military. The enforcers had side arms holstered. In their hands they carried the sleek and futuristic assault rifles that all the enforcers carried.

"Good morning Mister McCarthy," the enforcer croaked. "Need to scan your badge this morning and a scan your belongings as well."

Julius McCarthy grinned at the familiar speech he heard every morning. He pulled out his identification badge. The enforcer who had spoken took his handheld device off his belt and scanned the badge. McCarthy smiled at the enforcers efficiency. Everyone that entered the Central Government buildings were subject to search.

He received a message that he glanced as he walked into the lobby. The message troubled him. The director of the Pandemonium Challenge walked up the main staircase that led to the second floor and to his office. On the second floor he was greeted by two more enforcers. He nodded at the enforcers.

Julius McCarthy walked down the hall toward his office. He pushed open the door and saw, as he saw every day, Michelle Sanderson, his personal assistant, at her desk. She was not five feet tall. Michelle Sanderson had her hair in a loose black Afro of three-inch high black hair, framing her oval face and almond eyes. She was an example of efficiency.

That morning, Michelle Sanderson was dressed in a simple blue dress, a yellow plastic necklace, a California bear brooch and matching pre-flash California state earrings. Her long loosely curled hair on her diamond-shaped head. Julius McCarthy grinned when he saw Michelle Sanderson studying the monitor in front of her desk, her hand playing with a single curl of her own hair as she always did when concentrating.

"Good morning," Michelle Sanderson smiled.

Julius McCarthy nodded extending his hand and his assistant handed him a stack of color-coded paper. There were easily twenty sheets of paper folded and paper clipped now in Julius McCarthy's hand. He knew that the top ten papers were the most urgent. Beneath that ten were in reverse order urgent to simple information.

Julius McCarthy smiled and nodded.

"The Maker is out of the competition," McCarthy acknowledged.

Michelle Sanderson nodded.

"Are there any new issues?"

Michelle Sanderson did not speak. Instead, she bit at her lip. Julius McCarthy studied his assistant.

"What?"

Michelle Sanderson did not speak. Instead, she handed him a red file folder. Inside of which was one sheet of paper. Julius McCarthy skimmed the paper. He looked up and at his assistant.

"What do you know about this serial killer thing?"

"This is the first time I am hearing about it."

Julius McCarthy nodded, thinking.

"Do you need me to do anything?"

"No, give me a few minutes to suss out the day," he paused. He corrected. "Give me twenty and then we are heading to the control room."

Julius McCarthy closed his door and the LED lights flickered on. The first thing that McCarthy concentrated on was the space of his office. There were two chairs in his office in front of his old world, pre-flash, wooden desk.

Along one side of his office was his private library that housed over 800 books that he had read that year. McCarthy had a bonsai placed strategically in his slightly square office. The Chinese Elm bonsai tree had been passed down for nearly four centuries. McCarthy stepped toward the nearly foot tall bonsai tree and paused.

The bonsai was his prized possession because it had survived the flash and somehow against all odds flourished. The Chinese Elm, when he had first received it, looked as if it was on the verge of death. It was a thin and weak looking specimen. It had no leaves if McCarthy memory served him correctly.

For three years, the bonsai was more stick than bonsai. By the fourth year it sprouted leaves on what had been dead limbs. Eight years in and the Chinese Elm was nearly a foot tall and thriving. Ten years, McCarthy thought, he had been caring for the Chinese Elm. A decade he had cared for and worried about this majestic miniature tree.

The Chinese Elm sat in a hand thrown glazed blue marbled vase. It had a thick trunk and full bloom of textured silky green leaves that McCarthy doted over. Of all the items in his office the bonsai tree was McCarthy's most valued.

Julius McCarthy walked a few steps from the bonsai and looked behind his desk and at the framed and now historic 2019 United States map on the wall. On the wall behind his desk was one of the last pictures of the Bay Area before the flash. In the Bay Area picture there were the three bridges that crossed the San Francisco Bay; the Bay Bridge, the San Mateo Bridge and the Dumbarton Bridge.

On the far right of McCarthy's desk was a bronze bust of one of the late Presidents. In the rear of the room, and in front of the floor to ceiling window, sat McCarthy's desk. The desk was an old-fashioned oaken hand carved piece of art masquerading as a desk. On the desk was a pre-flash desk lamp. There was a desk plate on his desk that read: Julius McCarthy, Director Pandemonium Challenge.

The director placed the papers that he had been handed by his assistant on the desk. He looked briefly at the few papers on his desk and turned from his work. He did not want to start his work.

Julius McCarthy walked to his office window and peered out the window and over the rose garden below and in the rear of the building. There was a manicured garden below McCarthy's window. Inside of the garden were ten rose bushes represented the ten principles of the Remains. The roses were in bloom. At present, as McCarthy looked out of the window there were seven of the ten rose bushes blooming. He appreciated the various colors of the roses beneath his window.

Looking out of the window McCarthy stood and took in the roses. They fascinated him. Even so early there were Tees flitting around the roses looking for pollen. McCarthy looked down amused at the gigantic mega bumble bees rising and landing on the rose petals seeking nectar. The big bees should not be able to fly but they defied physics. They leaped from the rose petals and with delicate and seemingly too small wings the bumble bees rose into the air and returned to wherever their beehive resided.

The bees and the roses were nearly extinct when Julius McCarthy took over the challenge. He insisted on the Remains sending a team of researchers to locate the seed bank beneath the old University of California, at Berkeley Botany building and liberate all the seeds. It was through the sheer will of Julius McCarthy that the Remains would recreate botanical life.

Both projects cost money. Julius McCarthy and the Pandemonium Challenge generated incredible amounts of money annually. Julius McCarthy negotiated a deal with the Central Government to unearth the seed bank and to find any and all living bumble bees to be regenerated in the Remains hives.

The project was ambitious and an unprecedented success. Julius McCarthy and the Pandemonium Challenge Committee insured that the Remains inhabitants had fresh and sustainable foodstuffs through the seeds and bumble bees. As he stood in the offices watching the bumble bees and roses, he knew that he had other issues to address.

Twenty minutes later Julius McCarthy stepped out of his office.

"Do you need me to come with," Michelle Sanderson asked from her desk.

"Yes but meet me there. I'm going to take a walk and clear my head before the meeting."

Julius McCarthy liked to see people. He was a hands-on manager. If there was a problem, he wanted to be involved. Julius McCarthy was not a micro-manager by any stretch of the imagination. Instead, he learned about problems and listened to the men and women in charge to understand their problem-solving skills.

In the hallway, from the weapons and supply area to the control room, there were framed pictures of the posters for the twenty-two Pandemonium Challenges. Julius McCarthy had been in charge of the Pandemonium Challenge since the Nineteenth edition.

Each poster that had been displayed throughout the Remains seemed to be better than the first. None were like the previous edition. Each had Roman numerals and the Roman numerals were the only thing in common.

Julius McCarthy turned the corner and was at the doors of the control room. At the control room stood two enforcers. They scanned Julius McCarthy's credentials. He entered the control room.

Michelle Sanderson was waiting. She held her notebook computer in her arms waiting for Julius McCarthy to give some needed directions.

"Alicia should be meeting with us. Need you to take notes," Julius McCarthy explained.

He placed a hand on the scanner that unlocked the control room conference room directly across from the true control room where at least thirty engineers monitored the four dozen screens that monitored the various activities on Pandemonium Island.

Alicia Charles, the head of Pandemonium Logistics, stood up as Julius McCarthy and Michelle Sanderson entered the conference room. The head of logistics sat at the head of the wooden table where at least half a dozen men and women sat dressed in collared shirts and suit jackets. Alicia Charles was a forty-something pie-faced woman the color of warm chestnuts. She was petite and with friendly personality. She was slightly attractive. Alicia Charles wore a pink striped blouse and black jeans.

Alicia Charles greeted Julius McCarthy with a slight smile and handshake.

"Thank you for coming by," Alicia Charles grinned an awkward tight-lipped expression. Alicia Charles looked to her team and with a terse gesture half of the team gathered their things and left the room.

Julius McCarthy and Michelle Sanderson sat as the three non-essential members of the team left. in the wake of the departure left Alicia Charles and three of her control room managers to sit with Julius McCarthy and his assistant. Mackenzie Meyer, Quincy Drummond and Mary Howard sat at the conference table listening.

Julius McCarthy cleared his throat. "So, what seems to be the biggest problem right now, Alicia," Julius McCarthy asked, in a matter of fact way.

Michelle Sanderson had her notebook out and ready for the answer.

"Keeping up with the obscene amounts of money that we were making having Ella Fitzgerald Buchanan in the challenge this year," Alicia Charles nodded. "The betting on that line was insane before her departure. No one expected her to last more than three days. Most bet on 48 hours. There were not many that picked 49:45. Of course, we will pay out for the closest time selected." Alicia Charles nodded.

As the people at the table spoke Michelle Sanderson documented everything being offered.

Mackenzie Meyer, Quincy Drummond and Mary Howard nodded and grinned at Alicia Charles statement. Mackenzie Meyer, a milk chocolate brown oval faced person, was dressed in a light blue collared shirt. Meyer was wearing Internet glasses and viewing the progress of several challengers on Pandemonium Island. Mackenzie Meyer had a short-trimmed haircut very similar to the mandated military crew cut given to enforcers. Quincy Drummond, big eyed, big nosed, mustached and with a thick head of black nappy hair, was wearing a starched white button-down shirt, and periodically looking at his notebook computer. The fourth woman in the conference before Michelle Sanderson entered was Mary Howard. Tucker was an angular woman wearing a black, blue and yellow print short sleeved top and slacks. She was easily forty.

Julius McCarthy smiled mirthlessly but did not laugh.

"Things are going along swimmingly, Julius," Alicia Charles continued. "Our numbers are up. We have a 65% share right now. We usually do not see those numbers this early. The online betting is through the roof. The top ten challengers are trending as usual. There are some outliers that are getting traction. The niche betting, the oddball betting, is up as well. So, generally, cannot say that there is any real concern."

Julius McCarthy listened silently. At the end of Alicia Charles' report Julius McCarthy's smile disappeared. He examined the control room supervisor silently. Julius McCarthy was a no-nonsense individual.

"Glad to hear the good news, Alicia. I am surprised that you did not mention the turd in the soup bowl." He paused. "According to notes, this morning, there were two girls that were ended without any coverage?" Julius McCarthy stated, looking at Alicia Charles and Quincy Drummond, the head of camera operations, curiously.

"Well, we weren't--," Alicia Charles began.

Quincy Drummond raised his hand and stood up. "Let me answer this one." Quincy Drummond was a camel brown man in his thirties with small eyes and a short-groomed haircut. He had a rectangular face and rugged look. Quincy Drummond had thick arms and chest. "We thought that the island was covered. We spent three months checking every camera. There weren't supposed to be any dead spots," Quincy Drummond stated.

"How many cameras are on the island," Julius McCarthy asked.

"We have 2,500 working cameras on the island," Quincy Drummond answered without thought.

Julius McCarthy knew the numbers already. That was his job. He knew all the ins and outs of Pandemonium Island.

There were cameras everywhere on Pandemonium Island. The committee had painstakingly combed the island and made sure that cameras were positioned strategically throughout the 5,520-foot-long island. There were an estimated 2,500 cameras trained on the streets and buildings as well as inside of the buildings and structures of Pandemonium Island. All that being stated there were times, rare times, that the cameras missed events.

"Where did we lose the feed?"

Quincy Drummond did not readily answer. He consulted his notes. After a minute Quincy Drummond answered, "We think that it was in section seven or nine. There are some dead spots."

"Dead spots," Julius McCarthy noted. "That is unacceptable in the Twenty-Third Pandemonium Challenge."

"It is unacceptable for us as well, Julius," Alicia Charles agreed.

"Are there any more dead spots or anomalies that I should be aware of," Julius McCarthy asked, pointedly. "I don't want to be blindsided by anything that I should know when the investors come in for their annual."

Alicia Charles shook her head; no.

"I don't want to leave and hear that we have another Odetta Packard situation."

"It's not going to get to that level Julius," Alicia Charles reassured as Julius McCarthy stood up. Michelle Sanderson continued typing.

"I hope not. This is the Twenty-Third edition, not the First edition of the challenge. We should be running smoothly with little or no glitches."

"I think that is a low priority," Mackenzie Meyer chirped. "I think that we might have a serial killer in the challenge this year."

"A what?"

Michelle Sanderson paused.

"That is not possible. We ran psychological tests on all the participants," Alicia Charles corrected.

Mackenzie Meyer shook her head and cautioned, "Those tests are meaningless. I told you that from the beginning. Those tests scan for the ultra-violence tendencies that are displayed often later in life."

"The concept of a pre-teen or teen serial killer is just science fiction," Alicia Charles growled, angry all of a sudden at Mackenzie Meyer.

"Should I worry," Julius McCarthy asked.

"No, you shouldn't worry," Alicia Charles began in a soothing voice. "The idea of a serial killer in the challenge is far-fetched, at best. In the end, in a contest that is ultra-violent we are going to be able to see some of the more disturbing elements of our youth. Still, simultaneously, the challenge offers us all a chance to see the creativity and resourcefulness of our youth when pressed and challenged to problem solve."

"Yeah, yeah, I know the one sheet. I helped write it," Julius McCarthy pointed out. He added, "So, when I leave here, I should be confident that there will be a psychological test on my desk in the next 24 hours to weed out pre-teen serial killers and that there will not be any dead spots in the next edition of the Pandemonium Challenge."

Alicia Charles and her team nodded, in agreement.

Julius McCarthy signaled Michelle Sanderson and she climbed to her feet. She followed Julius McCarthy out of the conference room. The pair walked down the hallway and at the foot of the stairs to the second floor stopped and stared at each other.

"They don't ooze confidence," Michele Sanderson admitted.

"To say the least," Julius McCarthy concluded.

Chapter Fourteen.

Night Three.

Day Three began as all the others in the challenge. Ralphie woke with the first announcement. He decided, no fought, not to jump up and get out early. Ralphie decided that morning to wait for the second or third announcement before getting up and going.

In that time, Ralphie lay in the silence of the hiding spot and thought of the first two full days of the challenge. Ralphie had his scrapes and five times had nearly died in those first two days. He wanted to just hide and hope for the hunters to overlook him but knew that was not to be in the Twenty-Third Pandemonium Challenge.

A flare gun and a croquet mallet were the only weapons that Ralphie had. He had been shot at several times but thankfully in the challenge having a gun did not mean marksmanship. The bullets whizzed by most harmlessly and living targets were dropped running into or running from the bullets. It was the way of the challenge. You could prepare and prepare for the challenge and be out of the challenge by some random act. Some living targets were out of the challenge being in the wrong place at the wrong time.

The sun had not risen when Ralphie yawned and reached out and found his digital map reader. He lifted the small handheld device from his side and studied it. The digital map reader looked like a notebook computer with a handle. The screen was gigantic and looked sleek and modern. The screen looked like one of those iPhones that were really popular in the Twenty First Century. He toyed with the idea of powering the digital map reader on and wasting time but chose to just lay and rest. Ralphie lay on the floor of the safe spot and heard the click-click-click-click of the robo-spiders moving through the island.

There had been fifty-three participants at the beginning of the challenge and by Day Three there were eleven rivals gone. According to the first two announcements there were two more adversaries had been removed. So, on Day Three Ralphie calculated that there were only forty bullies left to fight in the Pandemonium Challenge.

By the third announcement, and a report that no combatants had been lost in the last three hours, Ralphie sat up. He only sat up. He checked and refilled the bladder bag in his solar backpack and slipped the one piece of essential challenge wear that he could not live without. Ralphie, from his seated position, rubbed at his dark walnut hued eyes, watching Isaac Moore and Jax still lying on the floor of the safe house and fighting the tug of semi-consciousness.

By the fourth announcement Ralphie stretched and began to prepare for the day. He finally got up and was a little surprised to find that he was not the only one. Dame and Isaac Moore were sitting on the far side of the room where Ralphie, Jax and Zeke had all hunkered down. Isaac Moore was up and stretching as well as Jax. In the far room Ralphie could hear Tee and Gina stirring.

The Millers separately abandoned their Day Three hiding spot. That safe spot, a one-story building off of one of the numbered streets, had been cramped and one of the spots found by Jax the night before. Zeke, sulking and cranky slipped out, by himself, before Jax and Ralphie. Jax did not even protest. He just watched Zeke leave. Gina and Tee, newfound friends, left next. Dame and Isaac Moore left after Gina and Tee. Jax and Ralphie were the last to leave the safehouse.

"You okay," Ralphie asked.

"Yeah, man, why?"

"You know," Ralphie began, gesturing to where Zeke had been earlier.

"Scrap that fool. He's still all butt hurt about Maddy. He... He needs to remember that this is the challenge. We ain't playing no video game. This is real deal, 100% or welcome to a long dirt nap. You make a mistake and you're face down in the dirt."

Ralphie listened and did not respond. Jax seemed to be all over the place. Ralphie understood.

"No one got time to babysit nobody in the challenge, Ralphie" Jax continued.

Ralphie listened and refused to agree or disagree.

"There are just too many psychos running around to try and protect someone, when you need to protect yourself. You know?"

Ralphie walked along and hoped for Jax to lose steam and end the one-sided conversation.

"I mean, once we began the challenge all the gloves were off," Jax pointed out. "No one is safe. Everyone is a target. Everyone." Jax looked at Ralphie and Ralphie continued to walk on silently, carrying his croquet mallet.

Sometimes it was better to let things unravel on their own. He would listen but he wouldn't pick at that wound. It was too fresh.

So, the pair walked and stalked and hunted.

"What are you still mad that you got that lawn hammer?"

Ralphie winced at the jab but did not respond. Instead, he paused and listened to the crackle of the air. Jax paused and listened to the midday. There were sounds of gunfire now and then, but not the way it had been the day before.

"The real murkers got the gats, now," Jax declared. "Any fool that has a burper, now, better know how to use it or become target practice for someone that knows how to spit."

Ralphie smirked at Jax.

"Don't look at me like that," Jax said, sheepishly.

"You got to admit it's kind of funny that you were jonesing for a burper and got one and lost it before you could use it."

"How's that funny?"

Ralphie part his lips but could not smile at the memory of Jax acting all tougher than nails because he had that machine pistol. They had walked to the eastern most end of the island and stopped to admire the disused pier when Jax asked: "Do you think there are any fish alive in the Bay anymore?"

"Think that there might be something in there," Jax decreed. "I am thinking that it might be a Bay monster. It would make sense. I mean, isn't that how Godzilla was made?"

"Godzilla was made with a nuclear bomb, Jax," Ralphie pointed out.

"I think it was the atomic bomb, but it was some kind of bomb," Jax agreed.

"Yeah, atomic or nuclear I know that Godzilla was not created out of acid," Ralphie noted.

He was practicing his quick draws and the machine pistol clattered on the uneven boards that looked as if they were ready to collapse and the pistol fell through a gap in the boards and into the Acid Bay. The bloop of the pistol hitting the water sealed the comedy of the moment.

Jax fell silent. He poked out his lower lip and for the first time in Ralphie's memory looked like he was about to cry.

"Aw, man, that was one in a million," Ralphie said with a shake of his head.

Jax looked down through the boards and into the surface of the Acid Bay and back at Ralphie.

"Damn, damn, damn" Jax fumed.

Ralphie had just allowed his friend to vent. Jax spun around tried to punch something. Finding nothing to punch he looked for something to kick. He walked to the street where they had come from and saw a pile of trash near the pier. He kicked at the trash and stomped on the trash and growled and barked until his anger subsided.

"You cool?"

"No, I lost my flipping burper and never got a chance to even pull the trigger," Jax said, suddenly despondent.

"Think of it this way. You didn't have it at the beginning of the challenge, and you don't have it now. It's not like you lost something. It's more like you shed some weight, more than anything, really," Ralphie tried.

Jax chortled and nodded at Ralphie's logic. He looked pleased at Ralphie.

"You know most people think that you are a little stiff," Jax admitted. "Not me. Not me. You make me laugh."

Ralphie laughed at Jax's compliment.

Finding a safe spot to rest in the challenge was like finding buried treasure. Jax preferred structures in the middle of blocks.

"You just jealous because you gave your assault rifle to that girl and got nothing in return."

"I told you that the burpers don't decide the challenge," Ralphie laughed.

"They help," Jax countered.

"If you say so," Ralphie said.

The fifth and sixth announcements of the day were uneventful. They stopped on Avenue B and sat in the shade of a two-story structure that sat in between two other two-story structures in the middle of the block. Jax liked buildings in the middle of the block for resting points.

There was a slight noise in the partial rooftop of the building where they were resting, and the pair looked up and into the shadowy darkness overhead. In the rafters was one of the robo-spiders. Its dark body was nearly invisible.

"You seeing that," Ralphie asked.

"They are coffins with body bags inside," Jax pointed out.

Ralphie nodded. "I know," he finally stated.

"Whoever made them, was not trying to be subtle," Jax assured.

"Yeah," Ralphie agreed.

"We should leave," Jax decided.

Ralphie climbed to his feet.

"The sun will be setting soon," Jax announced, as a matter of fact.

Ralphie tried to think of a way to distract Jax and where his mind was heading.

"You know that we are lucky to be on the island," Jax stated.

"Don't start Jax," Ralphie begged.

"All I was going to say was that being on the island there is less chance to run into vampires."

Ralphie grimaced.

"They don't like crossing water, for some reason."

"Come on," Ralphie chided with a shake of his head.

"There is some historical stuff about vampires that continues down time, from the first reports of them to even now."

"Can we change the subject?"

"I was thinking the other day where would they be hiding if they were in the Remains? I mean, it's a good question."

Ralphie chose to be quiet. He had learned to just weather the storm that was Jax on a tear. So, Ralphie did not argue but remained quiet.

"Okay, say that they are in the Remains, where would they be? Now, we know that the outer walls are not possible. Too many numbers guarding that. The inner walls," Jax paused. "Now, I ain't saying that they are there but I ain't saying that they aren't there either. It makes sense. I mean, think about it. They get passed the outer wall and make it to the inner wall. Now, there are thousands of blood bags available but they ain't stupid. They don't want to give away their location. So, they wait it out. They got time. They live longer than we do. They strike during the day, at first. They get stronger. They slip into the Remains. They become a part of the Remains. They are a part of the Remains. They have seen the rise and fall of empires. This, this destruction is nothing to them."

Ralphie rolled his eyes. He refused to say anything.

"What? You don't have nothing to say?"

"Jax, though I love a good vampire conspiracy story just as much as anybody, we got more important things to worry about." Ralphie scoffed. "We got to keep our heads on a swivel," Ralphie advised, repeating what he had heard from the commentators of the challenge whenever they gave advice about surviving the challenge. The number one way to get taken out of the challenge is not to be aware of your surroundings, one of the commentators suggested.

"Maybe, maybe not," Jax cautioned. "All I am saying is if we come upon a night walker then nothing will stop it. There are too many theories on how to stop a night walker. I don't think that crosses work. Why would they? I don't see the whole religion side of vampires."

"Jax, don't you realize that we are in the challenge and that there are people gunning for us?"

The challenge was two types of fights, Ralphie thought. There were the long-range fights that usually involved choppers, burpers, spitters or whatnot. They were over pretty quickly. Long-range, in the right hands, could mow down three or four people at a clip. The other fight was up-close and personal. The up-close and personal was usually what people saw in the last few days and hours of the challenge. Not too many were comfortable with the up-close and personal fighting, let alone the idea of ending someone that way.

The preference by most in the challenge was long-range attacks. There was this distance in the fighting that gave much of the responsibility to the weapon and less to the person using the weapon. Ralphie could only shake his head at the idea of dispatching someone with his long-range weapon. He had a flare gun.

Jax was dangerous compared to Ralphie. Well, everyone was dangerous compared to Ralphie on the island. Jax had his arm rocket slingshot and thirty ceramic balls to fire at anyone stupid enough to come within one hundred yards of him. For up close and personal Jax had found and carried in a sheath, on his back, a jungle chopper machete.

Comparably, Ralphie, had his croquet mallet for up close attacks. For long range Ralphie had found a single shot signal flare gun and five flares, to keep the curious at bay from long-range. Of course, the problem was that Ralphie had horrible long and short-range weapons.

Ralphie did not take that moment to point that out to Jax. Jax did not care. Jax did not believe that he had the better weapon.

Jax raised a hand. He sniffed the air. He bent down and held the position for a moment.

"Jax," Ralphie grumbled.

"I like this one," Jax noted.

Ralphie studied the building that they were in front of suddenly. Ralphie paused. He studied the building.

"We can talk about it on the other side of this run. We going to flash through, just for fun," Jax explained and pointed to the building. Jax closed his eyes for a moment, preparing for the inevitable. He took a Deep breath. Jax twisted his head on his neck to loosen his muscles.

Ralphie closed his eyes too, knowing that Jax planned on running at breakneck speed from one end of the building to the other. Ralphie allowed his body a moment to prepare for what lay ahead.

"For those of us about to enter this battle I salute you," Jax murmured. Jax mused ten feet from the building and turning back to lift a single finger to his lips; very dramatic. "Keep the chatter down."

Ralphie nodded, silently. Ralphie tightened his backpack. He was holding his up close and personal ground billiard weapon.

As Jax leaped over a broken piece of what might have been a wooden chair long ago Ralphie gripped and regripped his croquet mallet. Jax and Ralphie ran toward the iron skeleton of a shopping cart sitting in the middle of the floor just one hundred feet from the entrance of the building. Even though Ralphie was faster than Jax, he did not run ahead of his friend. He allowed Jax to lead. Despite being next to Jax he still felt extremely exposed.

In his head, Ralphie had come to grips with being a part of the Twenty-Third Pandemonium Challenge. It was Ralphie versus the six other divisions in an attempt to prove the value of each line. Ralphie and all the Millers families would be rewarded for their efforts and the Millers would receive a million Remains credits for the winning member and his family. Being a part of the challenge was a high honor and being selected cemented his and every participant's immortality in the Remains, if only in their compound.

Of course, all the contestants dreamed of winning the challenge. Winning the Pandemonium Challenge was a hard ask. In the Twenty-Third Pandemonium Challenge there were fifty-one combatants and only one would walk away with the most coveted title of Pandemonium Champion.

When Ralphie tried to understand the twists and turns of the challenge, he always found himself baffled. The strongest did not always win. The craziest did not usually win. The smartest did not guarantee anything. All Ralphie knew was that in the challenge people lived and people died. The difference in either seemed random and unpredictable.

Those that prepared and were vigilant died just as those that were carefree and foolhardy. The Pandemonium Challenge was a seven-day slugfest from beginning to end and there were no guarantees offered. The only guarantees were that there were no guarantees in the Pandemonium Challenge, Ralphie decided.

Chapter Fifteen.

Day Four.

"The challenge changes people," Jax admitted.

"Yeah, but it shouldn't destroy things," Ralphie countered.

They continued down the street.

"I ain't said that things were destroyed. They are definitely broken," Jax admitted.

Ralphie thought about what Jax said and instead of arguing just continued walking. Jax pursed his lips and struggled with something as the pair walked on. Ralphie watched and figured that if it was important Jax would say something. Jax was not shy.

They were on Avenue H heading east toward the Remains when Ralphie looked up at the weathered signpost. Jax had his arm rocket slingshot on his left arm and ready to fire one of his one inch in diameter ceramic balls. They, Jax and Ralphie, were out and looking for "easy" targets on the northside of the island.

Jax paused and Ralphie paused as a result, just a few steps behind his friend. Jax cocked his head and slowly, methodically lifted his arm rocket to chest level. Ralphie slowly lifted his croquet mallet and looked straight ahead trying to see what had made Jax stop. He looked left and then right as Jax moved slowly to the right. Ralphie followed uncertain what had stopped Jax's progress. The pair slipped inside a crumbling brick front building. Ralphie noted that the building was small and squarish and had two bases for what might have been planters or electric boxes. In his mind Ralphie tried to think what the building he was walking had been before the flash.

Half a century ago, Ralphie mused silently, the building might have been a petrol station.

Once inside the building Jax pressed against the closest wall and peeked around the brick corner. Ralphie scanned the interior of the building and finding nothing looked at Jax, annoyed.

"What gives?"

"Think we might be walking into an ambush," Jax admitted, watching the street from the safety of the building.

"What did you see?"

Upon hearing Jax's words Ralphie re-scanned the exterior of the buildings they were near. He stepped close to Jax and looked over his shoulder, in the direction of the way they had been walking. At the end of the block were two big buildings that looked like the corner of industrial structures. One of the buildings had openings on the first floor, where there would have been windows and doors long ago.

"Thought I saw someone near the opening," Jax admitted.

Ralphie looked at the only building that could have offered any opportunity for ambush. He paused. He studied the streets and the building.

"What do you want to do?"

"Well, smartest move is to find another way around that corner."

Ralphie nodded.

"There's always the other option," Jax mentioned. "We could just keep going and see if I was mistaken."

Ralphie puckered his lips, as if he was about to whistle.

"I was just kidding, man," Jax joked.

Ralphie looked at the building on the corner and looked into the darkness for anything that suggested that Jax was correct. He did not see anyone. Maybe, Ralphie considered, Jax was just trying to get a rise out of Ralphie.

"You should have seen your face when I said that we should just keep going," Jax joked. "You look like I must have when I dropped that burper into the Bay."

Ralphie smiled despite Jax serious look.

"You need to stop playing," Ralphie suggested.

Jax smiled broadly at the suggestion. He looked around and pointed to the building that had not offered danger.

"We gonna rest, for a moment, regroup and then make some decisions," Jax stated. "That's option two."

Jax shrugged off his backpack and sat so that he could see the building on the corner as he sipped water from his backpack's bladder.

"So, we rest and after that? Ten minutes we move out," Ralphie smirked, slipping off his backpack and sitting on the threshold of dusty interior of the brick front building that was one leg of the two buildings that seemed to close off the street.

"Yeah, sometimes have to zig when people expect you to zag," Jax explained.

"What's that mean?"

Jax did not say. He simply sat and watched the street and the building at the end of the block. The quiet and cool of the interior of the structure made Ralphie's eyes heavy. He was seated on the opposite side of the entrance to the building watching the street in the direction of the way the pair had walked. He was on the lookout for anyone trying to catch them unaware.

Ralphie closed his eyes and for a brief moment was nearly asleep. He felt his head tilting toward his chest and opened his eyes only to find that he was not looking at the street but the top of his thighs and the croquet mallet in his hands. He snapped awake and looked across to see Jax smiling.

"Look," stated Jax, pointing toward the interior roof of the building they were in.

Ralphie looked and saw the dozen red lights ten feet above the ground that signified a robo-spider resting, recharging or doing whatever they did when they were not moving around the island collecting and bagging contestants.

"Those things are bad news," Jax declared with a shudder. Ralphie involuntarily shuddered. Few liked seeing robo-spiders. "When you see those red eyes, someone is about to take a dirt nap," Jax added.

"This is the challenge, Jax," Ralphie pointed out. "Someone is always about to take a dirt nap."

"Yeah, I know that, but you know what I mean," Jax corrected. "I mean, the spiders are bad juju."

"Bad juju? You believe in superstitions?"

"Superstitions are based on something that happened in history. I mean, people fear black cats because they believed that cats could transform into human form and were the spies of devils and demons," Jax declared suddenly serious. Jax noted. "Superstitions are based on something. They just aren't made up."

"Where do you get all this stuff?"

Jax pointed to his temple and winked.

"If you are so smart, then why you think that we can find an "easy" target on Day Four?"

"People are stupid, Ralphie," Jax pointed out. "They get lazy. They do stupid things. They aren't always trying to do stupid stuff, but they do stupid stuff because it is a part of their make-up."

"You know there are no "easy" targets on Day Four," Ralphie tried.

"People always think that they are better than other people because of their last name, or what their dad does, or whatever. They think that where they live matters."

"Jax, none of that matters, here," Ralphie said gesturing to the street they were on. Ralphie looked at the crumbling buildings. Ahead of them was more desolation. Pandemonium Island was frozen in a state of entropy. Nothing was new on the island. The Pandemonium Committee took painstaking efforts to keep the island looking as if it was about to fall down.

Jax shook his head. Jax was not hearing Ralphie's logic. He had other thoughts on his mind.

"I read somewhere that there was this powerful empire that conquered all these countries and enslaved all these people. They went to Africa and tried that on the Zulu nation and the Zulu nation sent for their top general and he destroyed this invincible army. He chased them back to the seat of their power and changed the nation forever," Jax grinned.

"Jax, we ain't in Rome and you ain't Hannibal," Ralphie pointed out.

"I know, but the point was that in that powerful empire the best people were only the best because of money. There were poor in that country that might have changed the empire but were never given a chance," Jax smirked. "Rome fell into ruin because they relied on those that did not care one whit about anyone that was not rich, when their real resources were in their own borders and under their own noses."

Ralphie opened and closed his mouth, wordlessly. He lowered his head in response. There was no reasoning with Jax, when he believed he was right.

Jax and Ralphie walked on. They stayed on the broken sidewalks and were hyper-alert when they walked past open doorways and windows of buildings. They did not move quickly or incredibly slowly. They listened to the streets they were on. The lack of noise alerted the pair to possible danger.

"You know that someone is always waiting around the corner," Jax insisted.

Ralphie dismissed Jax's paranoia.

A few hours before the fifth announcement, the pair had found a broken down, four-walled hovel that might have been a house at one time, and rested.

"Why we resting?"

"It's hot Ralphie," Jax said, entering the broken-down structure.

"It's only two," Ralphie pointed out.

"This is a marathon, Ralphie," Jax countered. "This is not a sprint."

"What does that have to do with anything?"

"I'm hungry and I don't think that there is a lot of sense being out under the hot blazing sun, when everyone else is resting and preparing for battle."

Jax shrugged off his backpack and searched for the perfect place to sit. Jax padded around the interior of the hovel like a cat trying to tamp down the grass to create a perfect mat to lay upon. Ralphie sat in the shade of the collapsed roof and watched as Jax found his place to rest.

"You ain't hungry," Jax asked, unzipping his backpack. He fished inside of the interior of the backpack and retrieved a protein bar.

Ralphie grudgingly shrugged off his backpack. He too unzipped his backpack and retrieved a protein bar from inside. The protein bar was chocolate dipped and the coating was the only thing that tasted good. The bar was a combination of pressed nutrients and essential vitamins. Ralphie imagined that in the making of the protein bar the manufacturers had pressed out the taste of the bar itself, leaving only nutrients and protein.

"How long you want to stay here?"

Jax chewed on the protein bar like he was biting an iron spike. The effort to chew looked painful.

"I don't know," Jax admitted. "Eat a couple of these untasty treats, replenish, refresh and hope that the sun is a little lower in the sky and then we get after it," Jax mused.

The pair sat in the ruins of what could have been a house or office or storage unit for all Ralphie knew and rested. Jax sat on one side of the structure, in the shade of the two joining walls. Ralphie sat beneath a beam that had snapped for some reason and left part of the roof in the interior of the building.

While Ralphie gnawed on his first protein bar he pulled out his digital map reader and searched for the video that Zeke had recorded on Day Two.

He tapped a few buttons and with a little effort found the Day Two video of Zeke that he had refused to talk about with Jax or Ralphie. So, in the quiet and mild heat of the midday Ralphie turned and watched as Jax leaned back and took a deep breath. Ralphie could only smile as he watched Jax close his eyes. In minutes he was napping.

Ralphie turned on his digital map reader and watched the day that Zeke chose to avoid talking about. The video began as Zeke left the resting spot and made his way toward one end of the island. The video was pretty mundane until about 110 minutes in when Zeke hid in a building; then there was a girl's voice heard.

"I mean, everyone seen the videos and watched the movies but I ain't never pulled no real trigger. I ain't no killer. I am too pretty to be a killer. I mean, I am no push over either. You step to me and you will get got, but I ain't no enforcer with a burper." There was a pause. "What about you Diamond?"

"I feel you, Momo. They should have given us those super claws so that we could have been like some badass ninja cat killers or something."

Zeke swung around the corner and took in Momo and Diamond. Momo was this itty-bitty caramel girl with big brown eyes and freckles on her round cheeks holding one of those gigantic handguns that have a triangular and more angular shape. It looked like a cannon in Momo's small caramel hands. Momo, upon seeing Zeke and his crossbow, tried to lift her gun and fire. Zeke fired first.

The bolt tore through the petite girl's chest. Momo winced as the crossbow bolt delivered a fatal wound. She fired her gun prematurely and the report was deafening. Zeke watched as Momo's gun bucked out of her hand and cartwheeled to the ground. Everyone near Momo and her gun closed their eyes to the controlled explosion of the hand cannon.

The ringing in the ears of everyone seemed to slow Zeke a millisecond. Zeke reloaded his crossbow. He seemed nonplussed by Diamond and her sword.

"Damn, Miller, that ain't right," Diamond mouthed, jumping back seeing Zeke and his crossbow. Diamond, who was all of five feet tall and dressed in combat boots with black and white laces and tight jeans and a black hoody closed and opened her eyes, her hands ready for a fight. Diamond, in an elegant movement, drew her sword from its sheath with her right hand. The movement seemed practiced. The sword was just a foot shorter than Diamond. Diamond waved the sword in front of her like she might be able to do something.

Zeke fired.

Diamond avoided the first bolt. She was quick. She was not going to run. "You dying for sleeping my girl," Diamond growled from behind clenched teeth. Tears welled in her dark eyes.

Zeke fired again, this time watching Diamond's hips. The bolt sat just above her waistline. Diamond grunted with the bolt's impact. She collapsed near a square patch of dirt that had at one time held grass.

"You...done...me," Diamond breathed. Her breathing was suddenly labored and hoarse.

Zeke reloaded. He walked to the small caramel toned girl with her hair combed into two Afro puffs, lying on her side, her head just inches from the curb. Zeke leaned down and looked at Diamond with a slight smile.

"I did," Zeke admitted and placed the crossbow on the side of Diamond's head and pulled the trigger.

Ralphie fast forwarded to the point where Zeke was somewhere on the island. The crossbow wielding teen was sitting and watching an apartment when out of nowhere a bespectacled boy wearing a baseball cap and dirty jeans appeared in the building just one hundred yards from his location.

The camera showed Zeke slip from his hiding place and made his way across a deserted courtyard to the building where the boy in dirty jeans was hiding. He climbed the stairs, his crossbow at the ready.

Zeke peered through the window and saw that the boy was sitting on the floor with his duffel bag against the wall. He was watching the door as if Santa Claus was on his way.

Zeke aimed the crossbow and fired through the window. The glass shattered and as the big shards of glass fell and crashed in.

The body camera showed a bolt pinned the boy to the wall. He was wailing and in intense pain but not dead. Zeke entered the quiet apartment and as the boy whimpered Zeke noted that the boy only had a stun gun. He fired again, this time in the boy's privates. The boy howled.

"Stop. Stop. Stop," the nameless boy begged, tears in his eyes, blood visible around the two crossbow bolts. Zeke pulled another crossbow bolt and notched it. He fired his crossbow again and the bolt went through the boy's temple, aerating him.

Zeke grabbed the boy's duffel bag and found nothing. Searching the apartment Zeke found the boy's backpack and inside discovered what he had been looking for since Madison's death. He found Madison Washington's Ruger .22 Revolver.

Zeke ran. Zeke ran and made sure that no one followed him. He ran in a circuitous fashion to throw anyone off his trail. Zeke slowed.

He ran and found himself on Avenue H. He had not gone very far in his running, but he had made sure that he was not being followed.

"Damn," Ralphie concluded.

Jax woke suddenly alert and hyper aware.

"You okay," Ralphie said, looking at Jax.

Jax looked at Ralphie as if he had asked him for a kiss. Jax scowled. The fifteen-year-old rubbed at his eyes suddenly annoyed.

"How long I been... How long we been here?"

"Maybe, eight minutes. It's still Day Four, Jax," Ralphie joked, knowing that is not what Jax meant.

"How you not tired?"

"Power naps," Ralphie admitted. "You cannot sleep here. So, have to power nap. Ten minutes here. Twenty minutes there. It is not sustainable but, in the challenge, we only have to survive seven days," Ralphie noted.

Jax laughed at Ralphie.

"Okay, here's what I'm thinking," Jax conceded. "The numbers would be the ones that know if there are vampires or giants or werewolves or whatever. Right," Jax postulated.

Ralphie did not speak. He listened. He knew that Jax had peeled back another layer of the Remains conspiracy.

Jax stopped. Building 73 was, according the to the digital map-reader, an abandoned wooden chair factory. It was a gigantic building. Building 73 stretched across Fourth and Fifth Street.

"We going in there?"

"You scared?"

"Naw," Ralphie lied.

Jax beamed. He looked left and right. Jax and Ralphie stood outside of Building 73 for a long moment. Ralphie looked to the left and right and checked to see if anyone was targeting them as they stood on the sidewalk.

"You know that I wish that I had a burper," Jax admitted, lifting his left arm which held the arm rocket slingshot. "I mean, I don't mean to suggest that, if I had one that I would be some badass, like in those old crime vids, but man, no one would mess with me."

"Jax, you ain't even pulled a trigger."

Jax moved into Building 73. He had his arm rocket at the ready.

"I know that, but if I had one, no one would mess with me."

"We in the challenge, man, and everyone is messing with us," Ralphie hummed under his breath. Sometimes, Ralphie thought frustrated, Jax was only focused on the trees and not the forest.

Jax turned to say something and that is when things changed forever in the Pandemonium Challenge.

Five shots rang out. The air cracked and the noise followed as if there were thousands of Tees everywhere all of a sudden. To the left of Jax. To the right of Ralphie. In front of Jax. Near Ralphie. Then a boy, in the dark, was running toward them.

"I got this," Jax insisted, lifting his arm rocket slingshot and taking aim.

Ralphie held his croquet mallet as if that weapon was going to matter against someone with a gun.

Jax drew back the surgical tubing connected to his slingshot and when the tubing seemed almost to his ear, he released the ceramic marble into the dark. Jax placed another ceramic marble in the sling and stretched the surgical tubing back and fired.

Then things went terribly wrong. Ralphie peered into the dark at Jax, who turned and smirked cockily. He had that Cheshire Cat smile plastered on his face when all of a sudden Jax's facial expression changed. It was as someone had turned off his smile, like a light switch. Jax had been wounded.

Ralphie watched as Jax stood stunned by the idea of being hit by a bullet. He did not scream. Jax blinked and jerked and then spun. In less than a minute Jax was lying on the floor of the numbered building, unmoving.

Ralphie had no idea how many attackers he and Jax were facing. It seemed like there were at least four shooters. It did not matter, Ralphie realized.

All that mattered was that Jax had been zapped. Ralphie had barely escaped Building 73. Under fire Ralphie had crab-walked backwards with his croquet mallet as his only defense.

Somehow, some way Ralphie had escaped the deathtrap that had snatched all the air out of Jax and left him dead on the numbered building's floor. Ralphie had left Jax and his arm rocket and ceramic marbles.

He had blinked and found himself out of the building, face down and in the dirt, leaking, cut from glass and whatnot. None of the murkers in Building 73 had come out to finish the job, Ralphie thought. They were sloppy, the fifteen-year-old thought as he pushed himself up and saw a shard of glass in his left forearm and leg. He limped away from the quiet front of the building that Jax had entered and would never leave again. Ralphie stumbled as a handful of bullets dug themselves into the dirt near him.

The sleepers, Ralphie imagined, had decided to search for him and he had climbed to his feet and made himself a perfect target. Ralphie crouched and felt the various cuts and bruises claw at his left side. He awkwardly and as gingerly as possible crab walked away from the front of Building 73 and the short burst of gunfire.

Ralphie had dragged himself away from the charnel house and thought only of surviving. In the darkness and tenuous safety of another structure Ralphie stopped and examined his injuries. He could not go too far without bandaging the wounds. At the least he had to bandage the wounds to stop the trail of blood that most hunters would follow like hungry wolves on the trail of a wounded prey. Ralphie looked for a place to remove the glass shards and bandage his wounds.

If he survived then maybe, just maybe, he could avenge Jax, at least that was his thinking.

"At 2100 hours here is the seventh report for Day Four of the Pandemonium Challenge: There are only twenty-one contestants that remain in the challenge. The Pandemonium Challenge wishes to announce the loss of the following contestants from the last three hours: Quincy Bufford, Deandre Fleming, James Graham, Devin Johnson, Isabella Rodriguez, Zion Stewart and Jackie Robinson Taylor."

Ralphie dragged himself painfully into a small building just off the street and took a deep breath knowing what was ahead for him. He removed his shirt and pants and surveyed the damage. There were a dozen small chards of glass in his fingers, forearm and leg. Ralphie pulled the biggest shards out of his left hand and made small bandages for each finger. On his forearm there were four shards that were bandaged with one big bandage. The most painful were the cuts on his left leg. Somehow Ralphie had scraped his hip and cut his leg in three places below the knee. He pulled the final glass shards from his leg as he heard the last announcement of the day on Pandemonium Island.

Chapter Sixteen.

Day Five resumes.

The blue combat boot slammed into the mallet's shaft and a chestnut brown hand reached out and grabbed Ralphie by the neck. Ralphie was so startled by the two deft actions that he did not react for an instant. He blinked and, realizing that he was in the challenge, Ralphie tried to break the unyielding grip on his windpipe.

From the shadows appeared a chestnut colored boy with hooded eyes, wide nose, thin, evil smile and blue and black highlighted curly hair. The boy was bigger across the shoulders than Ralphie and powerfully built. The boy grinned one of those jack-o-lantern grins at Ralphie's feeble attempt to defend himself.

The stranger, with the knife thin smile, twisted the croquet mallet out of Ralphie's hand without any real effort. His hooded brown eyes took in Ralphie, coldly. The thin smile parted and out slipped a red tongue that flicked between his thin lips.

"When an artist gets his creative juices flowing things can move along rather quickly," the blue and black-haired boy stated as if he was talking to a classroom. He held Ralphie pressed against the wall with little effort, despite Ralphie's struggle.

Ralphie tried to free himself. The boy redoubled his efforts to hold Ralphie against the wall. He smirked, a slight upturn of his thin lips as he studied Ralphie like a botanist might an unknown plant. Tilting his head left and then right the muscular Poppy released Ralphie.

Ralphie backed up the stairs a few steps to gauge the boy who had disarmed him. He rubbed at his neck, recalling how easily the Poppy had restrained him. Ralphie studied the boy for a long moment. Unarmed and facing a stronger opponent Ralphie tried to determine what to do.

"What the hell, man? I didn't attack you? Figured that Poppies were non-violent or something," Ralphie breathed, massaging the back of his neck and looking at the bigger boy. "Who are you?" Ralphie asked looking past the boy at his weapon in the boy's hand. The boy spun the croquet mallet in his hand casually.

"Pablo, Pablo," the boy with a wide nose and thin smile grinned. "And you," he asked from behind hooded eyes.

"Ralphie," Ralphie coughed.

"You aren't a Poppy. So, why you here?"

Ralphie did not want to say that he came to snatch the breath out of Robert Nesta and avenge Jax for a fight that he had lost months before or that Ralphie was feeling guilty because Jax had been foolish in the challenge and been flatlined because of his foolhardiness. Ralphie hesitated. For an instant he thought about how Robert Nesta had disrespected the challenge. Then Ralphie thought of another tact.

"I came to hide out for a couple of hours. Need to close my eyes for a few and figured that I could come here, and no one would bother me."

The boy listened and nodded, poking out his thin lower lip. "Too bad you ran into me, little dude," he admitted, putting the croquet mallet in the alcove he had been hiding in. From behind his wide and muscular back the boy turned and pulled a red handled fire axe. "You walked into the spider's den. So, I gotta eat you. This is your last stop."

The boy lifted the axe over his head like a mad lumberjack and chopped. Ralphie jumped back and barely avoided being gashed by the fire axe. The axe slammed into the stone stairs and the loud metallic chunk sounded throughout the dim stairwell. An instant four-inch divot bloomed where Ralphie had been. Ralphie retreated.

He jumped up three stairs and looked up to notice that he was easily a dozen stairs from the next landing. Ralphie refused to turn his back on Pablo, Pablo. Pablo, Pablo swung, this time like one of those old-fashioned baseball players, swinging for the fences. The fire axe swung right to left, and in that moment, Ralphie learned that Pablo, Pablo was left-handed. The axe's head mixed Ralphie and glanced off the stairwell railing, chopping, biting and peeling a foot-long swath of blue paint off the rail.

Again, the boy swung the axe like an old-time baseball player. He swung left to right, barely missing Ralphie as he swung trying to cut Ralphie's head off. The momentum of the swing was so powerful that it spun the boy completely around. Ralphie tried to step forward but the boy recovered faster than Ralphie imagined and before Ralphie could act Pablo, Pablo swung the fire axe expertly again.

Sliding back Ralphie misjudged the next step and momentarily lost his balance just long enough to fall back on the stair. Ralphie climbed back to his feet and feigned as if he were moving forward. Pablo, Pablo, the artist, swung the axe as he had the previous times but this time Ralphie moved as the blade passed his face. Ralphie used the momentum of the boy's attack and timing to slip under the bigger boy's arm swing and through his legs to the alcove and retrieve his croquet mallet.

Upon retrieving the mallet Ralphie spun on the artist as Pablo, Pablo attacked with an overhead chop. The overhead attack missed the mark biting into the stairwell wall and caring out some stone, instead of Ralphie. But as the axe bounced off the wall, the fifteen-year-old countered with his trusty croquet mallet. He swung as hard as possible and connected with the back of Pablo, Pablo's head.

It was a lucky swing that drove Pablo, Pablo, the axe killer, over the stairwell railing and into the dark that was waiting on the other side of the railing. The boy and axe disappeared and Ralphie knew, based on gravity, the paint splattered boy plummeted unhindered to the ground two flights below.

Ralphie strained and listened to the darkness. He heard the chilling crunch of bones in the silence and had to admit that he had been startled by the finality of the sound, because he had expected something else, anything else. Maybe, he thought Pablo, Pablo would have landed catlike and come storming back up the stairs all hate and venom. At the very least, Ralphie imagined that after the fall, if Pablo, Pablo was hurt he would have screamed. But the axe-wielding artist did not come rushing up the stairs or scream or make a sound in the darkness.

There was no other sound in the stairwell, other than his own breathing. In the challenge, Ralphie knew, silence usually meant that someone had been ended. Most who were injured made noise. There were a few that were true stoics and when hurt or injured just kept going, in silence, but those were rare exceptions. Ralphie decided that silence was enough for him.

He was halfway to the third floor when he decided to go back down the stairs and check and make sure that Pablo, Pablo had the breath kicked out of him. In the challenge, it was always better to make sure that the job was done. He didn't want to be ambushed by someone that he thought he had ended. That would be the worse.

Ralphie took a deep breath and walked back down the Cosson Hall stairs and in the dimness of the stairway he could just make out Pablo, Pablo's lifeless form below. Ralphie closed his eyes to the broken body and tried to concentrate on the wall and the stairs and anything but what awaited him below. After only a handful of steps the fifteen-year-old reached out and needed to hold the railing. He noticed his hands were trembling. He felt the croquet mallet slip from his hands.

His legs gave out on him and Ralphie reached out and grabbed the railing. Holding onto the railing for stability he felt his body slow motion collapse to the steps. Ralphie sat and trembled.

He could hear his heart in his ears. The boom-boom-boom threatened to deafen him. Ralphie closed his eyes and tried to just breathe. He needed to stop everything that was happening to him and climb back to his feet, but he could not.

Ralphie was used to seeing dead bodies. He had become comfortable with the dead. His father had made him comfortable with the idea of cadavers. That is what his father called the dead bodies. The Remains sat on top of what had been the world pre-flash.

Cadavers were just things that the construction crews found and Ralphie and other newbies were asked to remove for collection in the Remains. Being asked to remove cadavers was just a low-level job. Ralphie learned quickly from the others that what made the cadavers interesting was how they died. There was betting every day on what caused the death (COD)of cadavers.

The construction workers bet on CODs every day. The workers chose unusual finds to bet on. Ralphie thought it was a sick and twisted game, at first but the more he worked with the men and women in the pits removing obstacles and cadavers, the more it seemed just a way to while away time and forget the back-breaking work.

Ralphie had never bet on CODs. If he had he might have made a pretty penny. He had a knack for deducing. He could puzzle out the cause of most of the cadavers untimely deaths. Flash causes were always avoided. Stabbing. Strangulation. Blunt force trauma were things that Ralphie saw when others did not. He was a savant but refused to bet. Asked how he figured out the CODs he simply explained that it was a guessing game based on evidence. "Knowing the outcome of the game made things easy to predict," Ralphie explained.

"Don't they creep you out?"

"People live. People die. They, we, everyone eventually became cadavers," was Ralphie's belief.

Yet, for all that experience Ralphie had not removed, tagged or numbered anyone that he knew. That distance, that fact, allowed him a certain business mentality of death.

Maddy, when they found her that first night, was a cadaver. He did not know her well. He knew her and looking at her lifeless, in the tall grass, only made her seem more cadaverous. It was just Ralphie examining a cadaver.

Jax, his friend, had been flatlined and that had been hard for Ralphie. It, the flatlining of Jax surprised Ralphie at how hard it felt for the fifteen-year-old. He knew that people lived. He knew that people died. It did not help that he cared about Jax.

Maybe, Ralphie rationalized, it was the residual emotions of Jax that attached to the Poppy. He didn't care about the Poppy. Did he?

The Poppy had tried to end him. Pablo, Pablo, the Poppy, was different than the other cadavers even compared to Maddy. Pablo had been alive just a few minutes before Ralphie had to send the artist over the railing. It didn't matter to Ralphie that Pablo had tried to chop Ralphie in two. Pablo, Pablo had also tried to cut off Ralphie's head. That had happened and there was nothing that could bring Pablo, Pablo back. Only Ralphie was breathing in the Cosson Hall stairway.

With that thought in mind, Ralphie, still trembling, climbed to his feet. He picked up his croquet mallet and a little shaky, noted that there was an eerie silence in the stairway. Ralphie looked down at the broken body of the paint spattered artist. Blood pooled at his head. Ralphie looked at and simultaneously tried not to look at the boy who looked as if he was trying to say something. He steeled himself to the task ahead. He took a step forward and concentrated on the paint spattered hoody. The fire axe lay a few feet from the boy's foot, useless and inert.

He reached out and groped for the boy's left shoulder and finding it pulled at the boy's clock patch. At the corpse's shoulder, on his hoody, he found the Poppy patch and tore it off after a little effort. Ralphie gripped the patch and turned at the fact that he had pilfered a trophy from the dead body that was only dead because of him.

Ralphie mounted the stairs. He stopped at the alcove where Pablo had hidden earlier. Ralphie took a moment to look through Pablo's supplies before proceeding upstairs. There was nothing of merit in the alcove. The fire axe was the only weapon. There were a dozen spray paint cans with the directional tops removed. Besides the spray paint cans there were stencils of a rat that Ralphie had seen around the island.

Ralphie shook the idea of Pablo, Pablo being the artist behind the stenciled rat from his head. He decided, then and there, that if he ran into another Poppy, before Robert Nesta, he would turn around and leave. Ending artists did not sit right with Ralphie all of a sudden. It was like cutting down and tree or not recycling or destroying a painting that someone had worked long and hard to create to win a game.

Ralphie moved to the second floor of the Cosson Hall but did not find anyone, thankfully. He walked around the painted floor marveling at the talent on display. It was as if the Poppies all had come here in the previous twenty-two challenges and left a memory on the walls of the Cosson Hall. Ralphie walked silently around the second floor and the only thing that he came upon that was close to a challenge or a reminder of the challenge was the discovery of a double-barreled shotgun in the middle of the floor.

Ralphie picked up the shotgun and felt the weight of the weapon. He admired the manufacture of the weapon. The handle was made of polished wood. The two barrels were polished blued steel. He studied the weapon for a long time before he figured out how to open it. Inside of the barrel were two spent shells. Ralphie looked around for more shells. Finding no extra shells Ralphie placed the shotgun in a doorway and continued his search for Robert Nesta.

Ralphie climbed the next flight of stairs. He opened the third-floor doorway and entered. Ralphie searched. Art was on display everywhere. There was no one on the third floor.

He continued to the fourth floor of Cosson Hall. Ralphie found that the artwork was on every floor, but unlike the first, second floor and third, on the fourth floor up there were fewer, but larger drawings and artwork.

It was on the higher floors that the artists made these massive drawings, paintings and artworks that made Ralphie stop and take them in, despite the challenge and the threat of flatline. The Cosson Hall was a true art gallery. The art was vibrant. The artwork brilliant. It was like nothing on the Remains.

As he approached the sixth floor Ralphie found himself looking at a piece of art that was of three black boys of various shades looking at one another curiously. The darker of the three was pouting and had a fist balled and ready to fly, it seemed. The caramel skinned boy with a grimace and sneer was studying the boy with the balled fist. The lightest caramel skinned boy with curly black hair was studying the two boys. All three had crown halos painted above their heads, despite the various looks. Underneath the three boys were the simple caption: "Blacks can't be racist. But they sure try."

Ralphie chuckled at the artwork and found the door to the next floor. He walked up the flight of stairs and opened the door. Ralphie knowing there were only a few floors left started to second-guess himself. Had he missed Robert Nesta? Could the artist have left without Ralphie seeing him? Was this all just a snark hunt?

Then he heard the sound of movement on the floor where he was searching. Ralphie prepared to protect himself from the artist. Ralphie slowed and moved cautiously and quietly toward the noise up ahead.

Robert Nesta was in the middle of finishing his piece when Ralphie appeared silently around the corner, carrying his croquet mallet. Ralphie smiled coquettishly at the artist. Robert Nesta, upon seeing Ralphie, threw his can of spray paint at Ralphie and ran as fast as he could for his duffel bag. Ralphie immediately reacted, ducking the can and moving to intercept the smaller paint spattered boy. Robert Nesta reached the duffel bag, but before he could grab it, Ralphie shoved him hard toward the wall just a few feet away.

Ralphie grinned as Robert Nesta bounced off him and toward the inner wall. He knew Robert Nesta. He knew that Robert Nesta knew him as well. He had to know Ralphie, Ralphie figured, if only as the boy that had watched him beat up Jax a few months ago in the food courts of the Remains Gathering Center.

Ralphie replayed the night that the Poppy had taught Jax a short and painful lesson. It was the typical thing, Jax had thought that he could talk to one of the Poppy girls anyway that he wanted and came face-to-face with Robert Nesta.

"Don't know how you talk to girls in your complex, but we don't call girls out their name," Robert Nesta barked.

Jax had smirked in response, in Ralphie's memory, months before the challenge. Jax had looked to Zeke and then to Ralphie before swinging hard at Robert Nesta. It was a classic Jax attack, Ralphie recalled.

The fight did not last long. Robert Nesta had hands. He nearly knocked Jax out before Ralphie and Zeke could step in and shut down the short conflict. Of course, with Ralphie and Zeke there Jax got loud and disrespectful.

The short fight was over but Jax swore that he would finish what he had begun. Ralphie grinned broadly at Jax's words. Jax was gone. Zeke was gone. It was Ralphie who would finish what Jax had begun.

Ralphie watched Robert Nesta nearly slam into the far wall. Robert Nesta reached out and prepared for an impact that did not happen. He spun around and in so doing fell on his butt.

Ralphie lifted a hand, stepping in front of the duffel bag and noticing the Uzi submachine gun inside. Robert Nesta climbed slowly to his feet.

"You even used that nasty looking burper?"

Robert Nesta did not speak.

"Well, it don't matter. There will be none of that," Ralphie pointed out to the smaller boy seething in the hallway in front of his artwork.

Ralphie did not move to remove the deadly weapon but stood, an immovable force, between Robert Nesta and what he wanted. Ralphie studied the artwork as he watched the boy standing and brushing himself off.

The artwork was detailed. It, the artwork, was the classic little fish being eaten by the bigger fish mural but instead of fish the teenage artist had used dogs seven times on the wall in orange and blue and white. The dogs were running across a broken cityscape and almost three dimensional with the shadowing and details Robert Nesta had added. Underneath the art was the simple statement: "Dog eat dog at the Pandemonium Challenge."

"You good," Ralphie pointed out.

"Thanks." Robert Nesta responded, examining his hand that he had landed on when Ralphie shoved him away from the duffel bag. He flexed his fingers.

Ralphie studied the boy in front of him and followed his eyes back to the duffel bag that he wanted to reach so badly.

"You know that getting to that bag is not going to happen? Unless you think you're some kind of badass," Ralphie grinned like a Cheshire cat.

"I don't," Robert Nesta answered. "I am an artist."

Ralphie grinned at Robert Nesta's words. "Yeah, yeah, I know, and I am a socially awkward misfit," Ralphie replied. "Everyone is a snowflake."

Robert Nesta cut his eyes at Ralphie's words and then back to the Uzi that was still visible in the duffel.

"You really want the burper?"

Robert Nesta twisted his lips on his sandy brown face. "This doesn't have to end with you flatlining me," Robert Nesta announced.

"What you mean? This is the Pandemonium Challenge. No one is getting off this island unless they off someone."

"You don't have to off me."

"No, think that I do. I just think that I don't have to off everyone, but I'm sure I'm going to have to flatline at least one or two to get off this rock."

"That's not true."

"What you mean?"

"You see the lion?"

"What lion?"

"The lion, in the mural?"

Ralphie looked up and noticed the outline of a lion a little further back from the dogs that were chasing and attempting to eat each other.

"How did I miss--"

"We don't have to dead each other. They want us to flatline each other. That's clear. But we don't have to dead each other. There will be those that zap each other. They are the dogs chasing each other. There will be those that chose to not flatline each other. There will be divisions." Robert Nesta continued, "The way I see it, we're the dogs chasing after each other and flatlining each other. The lion is everything else. The lion is all the people in the Remains watching. They're just as bad but they never gut anyone. They just watch."

"The dogs are deading each other?"

"Right," Robert Nesta nodded.

Ralphie twisted his lips on his chocolate face, thinking.

"We could not give the business to each other today and when we see each other again recognize that we were still human beings, despite this place," Robert Nesta reasoned.

Ralphie did not respond. He, instead, continued twisting his lips on his dark chocolate face, thinking.

"What are you thinking?"

Ralphie rubbed his round brown nose before answering. "How'd you come up with this? I mean, it's just so different." Ralphie paused. "Are you some kind of genius," Ralphie asked.

"I'm an artist. I don't conform. I don't want to do what they say. No Poppy comes to the challenge for the reasons everyone else does. We come to make a statement. None of us come to win."

Ralphie winced at Robert Nesta's words. Robert Nesta paused and studied Ralphie silently. He sneered and continued.

"We don't care about the challenge the way everyone else does."

"You crazy? Everyone comes to the challenge for the same reason. We all want to be legendary. We all want to become famous," Ralphie suggested.

"We aren't like you, Miller." The Poppy smiled contemptuously. "The challenge is our canvas. We come to leave art. We volunteer to come here to leave art that will transcend time and the challenge."

"Those are some big words," Ralphie noted.

Robert Nesta laughed at Ralphie's comment. For the first time he seemed to relax, a little. The boy looked at Ralphie and the croquet mallet and rubbed his nose. "So, are you a dog or a lion?"

Ralphie twisted his lips, thinking.

"That my only choice?"

"Yeah, think so, at least here and now."

Ralphie nodded, agreeing.

"So, we don't have to do nothing, right now. You can let me finish this work. You can stay and watch. You can do whatever you want but we don't have to do what they want us to do. We can be bigger than the game."

"Bigger than the game," Ralphie grinned and repeated. "I like that," Ralphie nodded to himself. He stepped on and kicked one of the spray cans from the ground, up and into the air. Ralphie caught the spray paint can out of the air and studied the paint spattered boy wearing paint spattered jeans and combat boots.

"Here," Ralphie smiled mirthlessly offering Robert Nesta Marley Scott the spray paint can.

"Thanks," Robert Nesta Marley Scott smiled taking the spray can.

"Go 'head and finish. You started it. You might as well finish," Ralphie stated. He looked around and sat on a bit of broken steps that led to nowhere. He sat between Robert Nesta Marley Scott and his duffel bag and Uzi.

Ralphie watched Robert Nesta restart his painting effort. He watched and after a while looked up and noticed that the building, they were in was crumbling around them. It would be a heap of stone by the end of the year. There was a chunk of the corner that had tumbled and been buried deep into the ground near the steps that led nowhere. That corner had been a part of the face of the building that Robert Nesta was now spray painting.

There was so much destruction and ruin on Pandemonium Island. Everywhere Ralphie looked there were broken buildings, shattered windows, and weeds and chain link fences throughout the expansive man-made island. Nothing was maintained, Ralphie noted. It seemed as if the challenge planned on using Pandemonium Island until it could not be used any longer.

Ralphie smirked as he let the croquet mallet rest on his shoulder. He watched Robert Nesta spraying orange and yellow on the wall that would become the body of the lion. The banana colored boy with a crown of twisted black hair was an artist, Ralphie thought absently.

Robert Nesta worked feverishly and suddenly the wall seemed to come alive with the dogs and the chasing lion. It was well done. It was clever. Ralphie admired Robert Nesta Marley Scott and his artwork. He held his croquet mallet in both hands and watched as the boy spattered in paint stopped and studied the wall.

Ralphie sneered and nodded at the finished artwork.

"That is really good," Ralphie admitted.

"Thanks," Robert Nesta Marley Scott smiled self-consciously.

"Is it finished?"

"Almost, just have to put on my signature," Robert Nesta said.

Ralphie nodded. He watched as Robert Nesta picked up a different can of spray paint from the dozen cans on the floor. The Poppy took a moment and walked to the left and bent down and scrawled his distinctive signature.

"Nice."

"Thanks," Robert Nesta replied.

"You know, you asked me if I was the dog or lion earlier," Ralphie reminded Robert Nesta.

The artist nodded. Ralphie was close, maybe six feet from Robert Nesta as he admired the artwork.

"Well, I been thinking about it. I think I'm the lion."

"Hmmm," Robert Nesta hummed. "How so?"

Ralphie smiled cruelly at the question. Out of nowhere and without warning Ralphie swung his croquet mallet as hard as he could to catch Robert Nesta across the side of his face. The impact drove Robert Nesta off his feet and five feet and to the left. Ralphie watched as the banana skinned boy with almond eyes seemed to take flight only to crash and roll, stunned and speechless across the stone flooring of Cosson Hall.

Ralphie advanced with the croquet mallet, parallel to the ground.

"Whut...are...you...doing?" Robert Nesta blinked, a trickle of red coming from his nose and mouth. He was holding his jaw. He spit out a broken tooth.

"What you mean?"

"I...thwat...we...ad...a...deal? I thwat...we...undastood...eaf...utha?" Robert Nesta mumbled holding the side of his suddenly swelling face. His ear and cheek were blood red suddenly.

Ralphie smiled maliciously at the boy's words.

"See, I been thinking about that mural. I decided to be the lion. Like the lion, I watch the dogs." He paused. "My dad liked those animal videos. That was his thing." Ralphie paused. Ralphie looked back at Robert Nesta. "You see your drawing is good but there is a big difference between dogs and lions. Dogs don't eat each other. They run and try and be stronger, faster, louder. But they aren't going to eat each other on purpose. But, now, if you look at the lion. The lion is a killer. A lion doesn't off just to off. It Rubs outs because it's in its blood. When the dogs get tired of running around being stupid, the lion eats the slowest dog. I eat each dog until I'm full." Ralphie shrugged. "That's life."

"Thawt's...wong. Da...li-yons...ar...da...Wa-mains," Robert Nesta spat, blood dribbling onto his chin. "Ya...not...a...li-yon," Robert Nesta garbled through a mouth of blood and broken teeth.

"We'll see," Ralphie intoned. Ralphie lifted the croquet mallet menacingly.

Robert Nesta lifted a hand, pleading. "Why?" Robert Nesta gestured to the mural.

"I suppose that drawing ... on the wall, not being finished," Ralphie declared. "That would've bugged me."

"It's...a...muw-El bub bliike," Robert Nesta spat, blood suddenly from his mouth, angry and narrowing his eyes at the boy with the croquet mallet. He placed a hand on the ground and himself to his knees. He spat out more blood. "I tink youf bwoke my yaw."

Ralphie paused and winced at the correction. "Doesn't matter," Ralphie concluded. He wanted to suddenly attack Robert Nesta. There was this sudden wave of animosity that gripped Ralphie. For an instant, Ralphie thought of pounding Robert Nesta for Jax and Jax not being there, now. Ralphie twisted his lips on his dark chocolate face.

"Whut...now, li-yon?"

Ralphie gave a smug look. He controlled his anger and watched Robert Nesta as if he was suddenly a broken toy. He reminded Ralphie of those old robot toys that moved with locked arms and legs and were easily tripped up. Once down, Ralphie noted, the robot toy usually could not find its feet again.

Robert Nesta tried to climb to his feet. Blood continued to drop out of his mouth. Robert Nesta held his jaw as if removing his hand would allow it to shatter. He cut his eyes at Ralphie.

Ralphie laughed at Robert Nesta. He was not going to go quietly, Ralphie noted. The artist put a hand down and pressed himself unsteadily to his knees just enough to force Ralphie to lift his croquet mallet and place the heavy head of the lawn game piece on Robert Nesta's shoulder.

"I like your pluck," Ralphie admitted.

The tween artist scrambled to his feet painfully knowing that his life suddenly depended on his reaching the duffel bag. He placed a hand on the olive-green duffel and as he did, he felt Ralphie launch into a relentless attack.

Ralphie did not see Robert Nesta anymore. All he saw was someone trying to end him. Ralphie' attack was aimed at first toward Robert Nesta's head and then his shoulders and back. Robert Nesta instinctively reacted to the attack. He had tried to reach the machine gun inside of the duffel bag but suddenly the machine gun was meaningless under the weltering attack of Ralphie.

Robert Nesta curled up, leaking from his head, nose and mouth. His entire body was suddenly one exposed nerve, open to the unrelenting brush of a million pains. Robert Nesta Marley Scott covered his head trying to stop the ringing in his ears. He was defensively in a fetal position. The Uzi suddenly seemed insignificant to the cowering artist.

Ralphie continued his attack until the boy he was attacking no longer moved or moaned. Blood covered the croquet mallet and there were specks of blood all over Ralphie shoes and pants.

Ralphie straightened up and looked at his handiwork. Robert Nesta lay unmoving a paint splattered conglomeration of blood and clothes and broken bones.

"I didn't have to let you finish," Ralphie stated in the still hallway, tears rimmed his dark eyes. "I let you finish because I wanted to be bigger than the game."

Defeating Robert Nesta and Pablo, Pablo in Cosson Hall by himself was a big deal. He had avenged Jax. He had beaten the challenge.

He was working his way back when his digital map reader dinged and alerted him of a video recorded and ready for review. Ralphie decided that, as he had done for the last few days, to find a safe spot and rest for a few hours and then, when night fell, to go out looking for more rivals.

Yet, the ding of the digital map reader drew his attention. He had figured out a way to be alerted to Miller's body cameras. He could not figure out how to get alerts on anyone else. So, Ralphie detoured and found a temporary resting spot to watch the video that was suddenly ready for review.

He sat in the quiet of a half collapsed building off Avenue J. Ralphie found that he had a video recording of Zeke. He had watched part of the crazy Zeke video when he went looking for the boy that murked Maddy, but he had no idea of what he might find until he viewed it.

"At 2100 hours, here is the seventh report for Day Five of the Pandemonium Challenge: There are only fourteen contestants that remain in the challenge. The Pandemonium Challenge wishes to remind all of the loss of the following contestants from the last three hours: Antoine Carter, Lucas Mason, Ezekiel Elliott Newman, Sunday Olson, Petey Pablo Picard and Robert Nesta Marley Scott."

The digital map reader was an unblinking eye that witnessed and recorded the most gruesome events and relayed them back to the Remains.

Ralphie wanted to condemn the Remains but he had watched the ultra-violence over and over and become numb to it as well. The violence was just another part of the challenge. It had to happen to separate the weak from the strong.

Perhaps, that was why he watched the video. He wanted to see the strong prevail. He wanted the weak to be put in their place. Ralphie did not know.

All Ralphie knew was he had flatlined two Poppies in Cosson Hall and now was in a safe spot, a half-collapsed building threatening to fully collapse if the wind blew, watching as Zeke snapped off the body cam and spoke to the camera.

"It's one hour after the sixth announcement on Day Five of the challenge and I am out and about to kick some ass and give out some bubble gum. The sad thing is that I am all out of bubble gum." Zeke grinned for the camera and made his eyes really big before replacing the body cam on his chest.

Zeke stalked through the island looking for someone to confront. He was walking down Avenue K when Zeke stopped and prepared himself for a possible attack.

"Okay, looks like it is go time," Zeke stated and adjusted the crossbow in his hand. "Someone is going to die. Say: Bye Bye, baby."

Zeke ran a little toward Avenue J before he ran into his first face-to-face challenge.

"I hope that it is Brooklyn or Emmett," Zeke breathed as he ran forward and found himself on the street alone. The boy that he had been after had disappeared.

"Damn," Zeke dictated.

"Were you looking for me?"

David Rogers, the wildcard of the challenge, stepped out of a doorway and grinned evilly. In his hand was a blue steel Walther PPK. Across his back was a katana sword. He was dressed unusually, for someone in the Remains. He was wearing a long black jacket, black collared shirt, black jeans and high-topped black combat boots.

"You see, I could have just ended you now," David Rogers announced stepping onto the sidewalk, the burper aimed at Zeke.

"Drop the crossbow, Robin Hood," David Rogers demanded.

Zeke gingerly laid the crossbow on the street.

David Rogers grinned again.

"Why are you smiling?"

"Because I am about to dismantle you, the old-fashioned way, in less than a minute, and you don't even realize that there is nothing you can do about it," David Rogers proclaimed releasing the magazine of the Walther PPK and depositing his gun, it's magazine and his sword on the sidewalk in front of Zeke.

Zeke looked from David Rogers' arsenal and back to his crossbow.

"You touch that crossbow and I may have to make you suffer," David Rogers grinned evilly.

Zeke hesitated.

"Okay, bad boy," David Rogers began stepping forward cautiously. "I'm going to give you the first attack then it's the best man wins. I won't make you suffer. I'm not heartless," David Rogers breathed casually glancing at his oversized wristwatch.

Zeke looked at his over-sized wristwatch and as he did David Rogers attacked without another word.

David Rogers was a street fighter. He was unafraid as he attacked. David Rogers was all fists and elbows at first and then knees and feet. Zeke tried to fend off the initial attack by David Rogers.

The second attack by David Rogers was blistering. Zeke was knocked back. He retreated but David Rogers seemed to be everywhere at once. Once or twice Zeke punched and kicked and knew that he had off David Rogers, but the two-time challenge contestant did not flinch. David Rogers had this eerie calm look on his face as he punched Jax and knocked him to the ground.

Zeke was a fighter but as he fought David Rogers there seemed to be real fear in the Miller puncher's eyes. David Rogers kicked Zeke and he hit the ground and somehow found himself near his crossbow.

"That ain't fair," David Rogers protested as Zeke swung the crossbow and fired from the ground and without much effort David Rogers expertly dodged the crossbow bolt. Zeke tried to get to his feet only to have David Rogers kick him several times in the side.

"You know this fight is already over, you just don't know it yet," David Rogers grinned as if his fight with Zeke was more a distraction than effort.

David Rogers dark eyes seemed so innocent. From out of the camera's frame appeared the katana sword. He allowed a slight grin to appear on his lips. Rogers took a moment to focus and then he raised the sword over his head and brought it down like he was chopping wood.

Zeke screamed. Ralphie turned off the video.

There was no point in watching the rest. He knew the end of the story. Zeke was done. Zeke had been bested by David Rogers and there was nothing that he or Zeke could do about it now.

Ralphie pushed the digital map reader away from him not wanting to be tempted to keep watching the video. In the half-collapsed building Ralphie sat, unmoving, silent and like the digital map reader, the holder of the last memories of Jax and now Zeke.

Looking at the digital map reader Ralphie rubbed at his dark eyes and tried to imagine if he was as unfeeling as the ingenious machine that no one seemed to care about and exhaled, exasperated.

Studying the bulky handheld device Ralphie found himself returning to the question that he had no real answer for: Was he a robot? Did he feel things?

He felt hunger. He felt pain. Yet, the pain was mostly physical. Perhaps, Ralphie thought idly, he was a maniac and his mania had been locked away until he arrived at the challenge.

Maniacs did not care for others. Maniacs were self-centered and only focused on themselves. Maniacs had no real friends or relationships, Ralphie had heard someone say in one of the videos he had watched criticizing the challenge.

Ralphie had a few friends. Well, he had Jax and Bailey and maybe Tee and Zeke. Ralphie searched his memories. He had relationships that were not focused solely on himself, he rationalized. He liked Jax, Zeke, Tee and Bailey. He even could go so far as to say that he liked Dame, Ant, Madison and Gina.

What about before the challenge? That thought crept into his head and Ralphie closed his eyes to the question. Was Ralphie a maniac? Was he an unfeeling monster?

He climbed to his feet and headed toward the broken exit. Ralphie made his way slowly and cautiously out of the half-collapsed building. Ralphie moved slowly down Avenue J as the sun sat overhead and drove heat spears down upon his head. He looked up, shielding his eyes from the heat, hoping to see clouds. There were no clouds in the sky.

Under the unrelenting sun Ralphie moved hoping to see another day.

Chapter Seventeen.

Night Five.

Climbing over the fence Ralphie listened for any noise. He knew that as the challenge drew down to less than 48 hours in the challenge vigilance was of the utmost importance. On the fence, he stopped a few feet from the top and let the fence stop rattling long enough to hear everything else around him. Ralphie climbed to the top of the fence and paused again, just to make sure that no one was approaching, before dropping onto the other side.

Once on the other side of the fencing, Ralphie padded across the dirt and gravel and searched for an open door or window. He knew that being in the open and without back up was the easiest way to end up dirt napping in the Pandemonium Challenge. Ralphie tried several doors on the first floor of the gigantic building before deciding to explore a little. The fenced in building Ralphie found himself in front of reminded him of one of the smaller machinery buildings in the Foundry. It was a three-story brick building that had to be a factory, Ralphie figured.

He was considering breaking a window but stopped himself, knowing that breaking the glass would draw attention to his secret hideout. In the challenge, to survive, Ralphie knew that most of the time no one wanted to be noticed. Being loud and dramatic were symptoms of a dead rival in Ralphie Reynold's mind. So, he continued looking for an entrance into the building that would not draw attention. He turned a corner of the building and found a window that was open just enough to give him entry.

Inside of the three-story building Ralphie for the moment felt safe. At least, no one from the outside could hurt him, the fifteen-year-old thought.

He was safe, for the moment, but then again, he had to make sure that no one was in Building 3.

Building 3, according to the digital map reader had been a bunch of things in its history on Pandemonium Island. It had been a warehouse and a military facility. Building 3 had been a maintenance facility at one point the digital map reader noted but the last thing, before the flash, it had been home of a startup company. Ralphie had read about the work ethic of the 21st Century and their startup companies and had to imagine that Building 3 had been one of those bright-eyed companies trying to grab the attention of the generationals.

Building 3 was this space that was more air than offices or rooms. It was a shell of whatever it had been. In the square three-story building Ralphie found one piece of furniture still in its Twenty First Century shape. The one piece of furniture was a steel frame of a counter near the biggest opening of the three doors in Building 3. There were broken and unusable built-in shelves on one wall. In the shelves were various lengths and thicknesses of metal. The ceiling was exposed, and several beams were visible above Ralphie's head. The second and third floor was an open and spotty above the first floor.

Near the rear of the building Ralphie dropped his backpack, and after a few minutes listening to the strange noises that he thought were strangers or hitters, Ralphie relaxed. He had bandaged his forearm again. He checked his leg and the leaking had finally stopped. That was a good thing.

There was a dimness in the space and Ralphie opted to create a little light in the building. He found a piece of flattened metal and pried off a wooden slat that was over one of the windows and right away that action let in a shaft of light in the previously dark space. With a single shaft of light lanced into Building 3, where Ralphie sat, was suddenly not as frightening or oppressive. Quite the opposite, the space, in Building 3, was uncluttered and relatively clean.

Ralphie checked his digital map reader and calculated how much time he had before the line toughs decided to begin hunting. It was nearly time for the fourth announcement when Ralphie finally felt that he was safe enough to let his guard down.

They, the others, would not move out, he figured, until the sun went down. In the past few days most activity occurred when the sun went down. So, that meant that Ralphie had at least seven hours to rest and recover and plan out his final assault against the fifteen hard liners still in the challenge.

In the dark of the Building 3 Ralphie took a deep breath and tried to turn his mind off for a few minutes. He looked at the digital map reader that he had received and lifted it to see the screen.

Four days into the challenge and Ralphie found that he had only delivered the fait compleat when under attack. That had made Ralphie uneasy. He lost sleep. He could close his eyes and try to relax but sleep did not come as it had before the challenge. Ralphie would close his eyes and suddenly be assaulted by every manner of thought and minute sound. Gone were the simple quieting of his mind and the embrace of sleep. Nothing on the island allowed Ralphie to close his eyes long enough to find the embrace of sleep.

Four days ago, Ralphie had been someone else. Four days ago, Jax was alive. Four days ago, he did not have so much blood on his hands. Now, Day Five, things had changed.

He tried to force himself to rest for a few hours. He tried to erase his actions and the actions of Zeke and the death of Zeke and Jax and what was ahead, but nothing removed those memories.

Occasionally, Ralphie found that he would close his eyes and for a few minutes drift off, but sleep eluded him. Ralphie opened his eyes and found himself lying in the dark in Building 3. Ralphie rubbed at his eyes and tried to understand what five days in the challenge had accomplished. Was it all a dream? Was this world just a dream he had just been woken from.

He looked into the darkness of the building and knew that he was in no dream. At his side was the digital map reader, and on the screen, a running clock noted that he had rested for nearly four hours. Ralphie tried to remember the last time that he had rested more than three hours in the challenge.

Blinking, Ralphie recalled that he was nearly six days gone from the Remains. This was the Pandemonium Challenge. He was one of nearly sixty hopefuls in the Twenty-Third Pandemonium Challenge that had begun with hopes of winning the challenge.

The truth of being in the challenge was frightening and grotesque. It was a slow-motion accident where everyone in the Remains watched vicariously the destruction of battlers vying for a trophy that only one could possess. It, the challenge, was everything good and bad about the Remains.

Of course, Ralphie did not see it that way. He could not. All he saw was that he was in the challenge. He had made it to Day Six and there was only 24 hours remaining. If he could survive until the end Ralphie knew that his life would forever change.

For 140+ hours Ralphie had tried to fly below the radar, to be invisible, to be a fighter but not an ender, but that had worked only for so long. The challenge had a way of eroding values. Flying under the radar only worked for so long and then the lions noticed. Being invisible was only possible when there were lots of other choices. Yet, with less than a two dozen hard liners left in the challenge things became dog-eat-dog. Fighting for defense gave way to being seen and pre-emptive attacks.

Ralphie had not wanted to be a hitter. The challenge did not care what Ralphie or anyone wanted. It, the challenge, only cared to strip away the artifice and reveal the ultra-violence just under the surface of anyone.

The fifteen-year-old closed his eyes and realized that being in the challenge had already changed him forever. Ralphie, in the quiet of Building 3 ticked off all the heinous things that he had ended up doing in the challenge despite his desire to outsmart, outplay and outlast everyone.

"Got damn it," Ralphie growled and checked himself immediately. "I'm still following," Ralphie admitted. "What is wrong with me?" He clamped a hand over his own mouth, listening to the words that came from his mouth.

Everyone in the challenge was dangerous. Everyone in the challenge had the potential to skewer and shish kabob someone. That was the very nature of the challenge.

He had mentioned the same thing to Jax the day before. Was it the day before? He looked up and noted that it was no longer Day Five. It was now night and soon Day Five would give way to Day Six.

"No one is a pushover in the challenge," Ralphie had reasoned nearly twenty-four hours ago.

"Yeah, I know that," Jax responded dismissing what Ralphie had said. "But there are some targets that are easier than the bad boys spoiling for a fight," Jax countered. Ralphie could only shake his head at his Miller friend in his memory.

Without warning, triggered by that germ of an idea, the day before came spilling over the locked doors, barred entrances and four-foot thick steel bank vault that Ralphie had tried to lock them behind. Those memories were supposed to be hidden and buried deep within Ralphie's subconscious. He had attempted to secure them for fear that they would unhinge his composure and threaten his untested steel will.

All the precautions and protections fell away with an unplanned thought. Ralphie froze. Without warning there was a knot in his stomach, and he felt as if he might throw up. He tried to breathe. Controlling one thing led to another. Unexpectedly, he was crying in the dark, remembering Jax. He pressed his hands to his face. Ralphie squeezed his eyes tightly.

The fifteen-year-old steeled himself against the memories of Jax and his foolishness and the memory of his final day in the challenge. The thought of the loss of his friend hurt. Jax always had a joke in the blackest and most miserable moments of the challenge.

Ralphie closed his eyes. Closing his eyes Ralphie hoped for nothing to appear. He did not want to imagine the last time he had seen Jax. He opened his eyes and was greeted by the night and Pandemonium island. The painful memories ebbed and seemed locked away again with his feelings, for the moment, and gave the fifteen-year-old time to think of more immediate issues.

He took a deep breath and the pain in his gut subsided. Another breath and Ralphie felt himself returning to a more even keel. The emotions and thoughts and memories of Jax had threatened to capsize him. Now, he had righted his self and was feeling as if he could survive the challenge, at least until Day Six.

Ralphie did not want to consider his chances. Someone in the Remains would be doing that. There were thousands that were betting on or against him now, Ralphie imagined. He was one of a handful of contenders that had made it to Day Five. That was an accomplishment in and of itself.

Yet, against logic Ralphie thought about the end goal: winning the challenge. He knew that he had a little more than 48 hours to outlast the other warriors and possibly win the Twenty-Third Pandemonium Challenge. 48 hours to beat as many people as he ran into on the island with his croquet mallet.

"Okay, Ralphie," Ralphie spoke to himself, stretching but remaining seated and against the wall he had found earlier to support his back. "There are only a dozen challengers left. I am going to figure this out. I am going to find a way to survive this madness, for me. I am going to survive this -- for me and Jax and my family and all the Millers."

Ralphie paused and looked around the darkening space he was in. There was no one on the spacious first floor of Building 3 with him. Ralphie laughed at his goofiness. "The first sign of insanity is talking to yourself," the fifteen-year-old noted. He paused and wrinkled his brow, thinking. "The first sign of insanity is talking back to the voices in your head," he corrected.

Ralphie climbed to his feet. "For the Millers," Ralphie growled, hefting his croquet mallet onto his shoulder. He took a few steps and paused.

"What happens if someone has a burper?"

Ralphie shook his head.

"If someone has a burper then I got to outwit them," Ralphie reasoned.

"Against a burper? Think that you better say your prayers," Ralphie conceded despite not wanting to say the words.

"If it's my time then it's my time," Ralphie confided to himself, scooping up his backpack.

"What about Emmett and Brooklyn and--" Ralphie thought out loud.

"No negative thinking," Ralphie told himself. "It's the challenge. Anything can happen. Better people have lost."

Ralphie walked to the window he had slipped through hours before and climbed out of it with little difficulty. Outside, the sky was still purple and blue as the last light fought the darkness. Ralphie walked quietly to the chain link fence and effortlessly climbed over. He dropped down on the other side. He was suddenly back in the challenge.

In the dark he could hear faint noises, to the north of his location. He did not move immediately. Instead, he listened. There was a faint noise of metal against metal just to the west of Building 3. He reminded himself that there were only fifteen ruffians left. There were fifteen Remain toughs trying to be the winner of the Pandemonium Challenge suddenly.

Ralphie moved cautiously away from Building 3, covering his tracks, and not stepping into the street immediately. Instead, he walked down the street where Building 3 sat hearing to the west a scattering of gun fire. He moved north. He figured that the big showdown would be at or near the sky bridge.

As Ralphie crossed California Avenue he was shocked to see a small figure step out of the shadows and into the street. Between him and the stranger was one streetlight to illuminate the entire street. Ralphie paused and immediately took his croquet mallet in hand, ready for war. At the distance of three car lengths he knew that if the smaller figure had a gun or bow and arrow Ralphie could do little except hope that they missed on their initial attack. He would have to hope to get away or hope against hope get close enough to use the croquet mallet.

"Ralphie? Is that you?"

He noticed that the smaller figure looked very familiar. Ralphie frowned. In the moon light Ralphie could see the reddish curls and big eyes of Bailey Beaumont. Ralphie relaxed just a little and then, right away increased his vigilance.

"Don't forget that girls are our kryptonite," Jax had coughed. "It happens the same way every challenge. The girl draws the boy in and guts him."

Bailey Beaumont was standing in the middle of the street dressed in a hoody, jeans and combat boots when Ralphie approached Avenue L. Ralphie turned and without word became very aware of his surroundings. He gripped his croquet mallet and thought that this moment was the moment that he either lived or died in the challenge. The end was nigh.

Bailey Beaumont grinned and raised her hands. Ralphie examined the innocent looking fifteen-year-old. He cuts his eyes to the left and then the right expecting an attack from Emmett Carson or someone he did not see. Ralphie took a step forward and wondered if he was walking into a trap.

"Ralphie, it's me," Bailey Beaumont beamed.

"I know," Ralphie responded. "But what I don't know is, what you are up to?"

"I'm not up to anything. I saw you and decided to talk to you. Is that a crime?"

Ralphie did not respond. He suddenly was unsure of what he should do. He looked back and made sure that no one was sneaking up on him unbeknownst to Ralphie. There was no one sneaking up behind. For the moment, there was just Bailey and Ralphie.

"What do you want to talk about?"

Bailey Beaumont, her hands still in the air, grinned broadly and tilted her round head to the left and the right. Ralphie could see the spray of freckles across her cheeks and the bridge of her round nose. Beneath that nose Ralphie watched as Bailey Beaumont showed off her perfectly white teeth.

He blinked and focused on Bailey. She was dressed in a hoody, T-shirt, jeans and combat boots. There was one of those bandoliers across her chest that revealed a samurai sword strapped to her back. Ralphie peered at Bailey in the darkness and noticed that she was wearing an oversized belt around her waist but there was nothing noticeable attached to the belt.

"Just want to make sure that you're okay," Bailey admitted, lowering her arms slowly. She paused. "Can I lower my arms?"

Ralphie nodded.

"How did you find me?"

Bailey took another step forward.

Ralphie lifted his croquet mallet defensively.

"Are you going to bash my brains in? Is that what you want to do," Bailey joked under the single light on the block and raised her eyebrows to emphasize the point.

Ralphie turned around and made sure that no one was behind him.

"You think that I am setting you up?"

Ralphie did not respond.

Bailey Beaumont looked genuinely hurt suddenly. She pulled absently at the drawstrings on her hoody.

"No, it's not that," Ralphie stammered. "This is *the* challenge," Ralphie tried as he lowered his croquet mallet in response.

"You think that I'm trying to term you? Me?"

Ralphie felt embarrassed suddenly.

"No, I don't think that you would term me," Ralphie said embarrassed. He added, "We are friends."

"Are we?"

Ralphie paused. Bailey was this apple cheeked beauty with a head full of red and brown curls that was now just a loose bunch of tendrils framing those big doe eyes of hers, Ralphie thought.

"Do you see a weapon in my hand?"

Ralphie studied Bailey for a long moment in the darkness. He was not sure what she had but she had to have a weapon. She was in the challenge. Everyone had a weapon of some kind. But she did not have a weapon in her hand at the moment. He lowered his croquet mallet.

In the distance, to the east, Ralphie heard gun fire. He tensed with the sound.

"Don't worry about that," Bailey Beaumont chirped. "Emmett says that all those with burpers are nearly out. They didn't get endless ammunition."

"Emmett?" Ralphie growled looking around for Emmett Carson, his sworn enemy.

"Yeah, he knows a lot about the challenge."

"Is he around?"

"No," Bailey chuckled. "He went west earlier. We are planning on meeting up near the sky bridge before the last announcement of the day."

Ralphie listened. He studied Bailey, suddenly curious.

"How did you find me?"

Bailey teased and tapped her body cam.

"Does it ping our locations?"

"No, but you can sort of determine where the closest person is to you," Bailey reasoned, tilting her head to the right. "I sort of have been watching you."

"Stalker," Ralphie giggled.

"Yeah, no," Bailey tittered. Ralphie listened to her light laugh and found himself mesmerized by this gentle and unpretentious girl.

"So, be careful, the last few hours are the most dangerous. Everyone gets a little careless as they get close to the end," Bailey sang. Ralphie and Bailey were within arm's reach.

"Thanks," Ralphie grinned.

"Be careful of Emmett," Bailey warned.

"Why you say that?"

"You know," Bailey joked. "He doesn't like you."

"Yeah, that guy is certifiable."

Bailey laughed.

"What's his weapon?"

"He has a few. Long range he has a gun. Short range he has one of those samurai swords," Bailey shook her head.

Ralphie nodded.

"Got to have a long and short-range weapon," Bailey added.

Ralphie had a flare gun for long range attacks. It was a horrible long-range weapon. His real weapon was the croquet mallet because most did not know what it was. It surprised everyone whenever he used it.

"You like some kind of challenge consultant?"

Bailey grinned and chortled a little. Her snort and light chuckle surprised Ralphie. It was just so unexpected.

Ralphie studied Bailey, who was smiling in the darkness. Ralphie found himself mesmerized by Bailey's expressive big, fawn eyes. It seemed, that moment, that Bailey was this carefree soul despite being on Pandemonium Island and in the challenge.

"What are you thinking about?"

"Just curious how you have survived this long without a weapon," Ralphie stated.

"Never said that I don't have a weapon," Bailey corrected. "I said that I didn't have a weapon in my hand." She paused and let that sink in. "I still don't."

"Do you have a weapon?"

"Of course," Bailey grinned mirthlessly. "It is *the* challenge."

"Have you--"

"Have I zapped people?"

Ralphie nodded.

"It is *the* challenge."

The pair fell silent. The night was bright as the moon shone down on the two teens. There were no clouds in the sky.

Bailey fished around in her hooded sweatshirt pocket front, nervously. Ralphie noted Bailey playing in her sweatshirt pocket front but thought little of it. If she had wanted to gut him, she had ample opportunity. Ralphie did not imagine that Bailey would try to gut him now with whatever was in her sweatshirt pocket front.

"So, how do you think this... ends," Ralphie asked. "I mean, between you and me."

"I don't know," Bailey admitted. "If it comes down to you and me then I won't be mean. I won't make you suffer," Bailey joked.

"You won't make me suffer," Ralphie chuckled. "You better not." He paused and laughed, mischievously. "Suppose, I won't make you suffer either if it comes down to that."

"Thanks," Bailey giggled.

"Hey, since you aren't going to make me suffer, we get another day?"

"Suppose,"

"I suppose tonight I give you a pass. Tomorrow we figure it out," Bailey decided.

"A pass," Ralphie agreed and nodded. "I like that."

"Okay," Bailey crooned. "Be safe. See you tomorrow."

Ralphie watched Bailey smile, her round cheeks rising as she turned around and walked back toward a building that sat open to the elements.

Bailey slipped back into the shadows and once in the darkness spoke again.

"I left something for you on the fire plug."

Bailey Beaumont had left Ralphie on Avenue C and Ninth Street.

Ralphie looked into the darkness and knew that Bailey was gone. She had appeared out of the dark. She had disappeared the same way.

He had walked slowly and methodically to the end of the street where the white fire hydrant was planted. Sitting on the fire hydrant was a handmade bracelet that had Ralphie's name weaved into the plastic weavings. He scooped up the bracelet and looked into the darkness.

"Thanks," Ralphie said into the darkness.

He peered into the night, not knowing if Bailey was there or not. He shrugged his shoulders and backed into the darkness and safety of the night. Ralphie looked left and right and headed north away from where Bailey had gone. He did not take the straightest route to the sky bridge. For some reason, he headed back south and away from the sky bridge that night. He found himself back on California Avenue. He had made a complete loop and returned to Building 3. He looked amused at the words of Jax in his head.

"You have to stay focused or get DOA," Jax warned.

Ralphie cut through the field beside Building 3 and found himself on the eastern most side of the island. The only thing further east was a retaining wall and the Acid Bay.

He walked north and behind another huge warehouse. Again, in the distance somewhere Ralphie heard the sound of gun fire. There was not a lot of gun fire like the first three days.

He knew that all he had to do was walk straight four blocks west, at the most, and he would be at the sky bridge. Yet, he hesitated.

He turned back and looked out and across the dark waters that made up the Acid Bay. He looked back at the Remains. There was nothing on the shoreline that appeared above the twenty-foot high wall.

Situated on the great wall were the smaller watch towers that overlooked the Acid Bay. There were three visible guard towers. Ralphie knew the three guard towers were all named after some famous enforcer. He did not recall the names of the three enforcers that had been named for the guard towers protecting the Acid Bay. They had to be minor enforcer heroes, Ralphie figured. All Ralphie knew was that there was a guard tower that faced the Acid Bay that was closest to the First Gen complex.

Ralphie scanned the horizon and thought that he had found one of the two smallest guard towers on the Remains grand wall. The wall was a massive an expansive thing that stretched as far as the eye could see that morning on the shores of what had once been prime land in the Bay Area. Ralphie disliked the thought. The Bay Area was gone. It had been erased from the maps nearly seventy years ago. In its place was the Remains. Wrapped around the Remains now were two walls; outer and inner, both twenty feet tall.

Protecting the outer walls were a dozen guard towers manned by hard men and women known as the enforcers. Ralphie grinned at his memory. He had listened and learned in the educational facility. He liked history. So, as he stood, that morning on Pandemonium Island, in the midst of the Pandemonium Challenge he could not help but remember what Jax had said when they were heading to the island and now noted, that on the wall, just a mile away from him, was the smaller of two gigantic stone battlements that protruded out and over the wall; facing the Acid Bay. Ralphie narrowed his dark brown eyes to the bay. He could just make out movement from the handful of enforcers, tasked to protect the Remains from any uninvited guests, on the outer walls.

The fifteen-year-old wondered what the enforcers were protecting the Remains from on the Acid Bay side of the Remains? There was nothing that could make it alive across the toxic mix of liquid that made up the Acid Bay. At that moment the question did not merit any further thought. Ralphie had other thoughts and priorities.

Ralphie had been trying to solve that problem when out of the dark someone screamed to his left and all he saw was the blur of a screaming face flash past him and nearly hacking off his face with a glinting machete blade. The figure, dressed in hooded sweatshirt, landed on the weed covered ground and spun around with not one but two machetes in his hands. The boy was spidery thin and had wild eyes and a wide crooked grin. Ralphie noted that the boy had thick eyebrows and a thick mane of hair and ears that stuck out from his round head.

"Die, stupid pop tart," the boy growled as he raised the pair of machetes and rushed forward.

Ralphie did not have time to respond. Instead, the croquet mallet flashed up in front of Ralphie as the boy rushed at him, all aggression and energy. Ralphie defended himself from the attacker as he passed in this first round of a ruthless duel.

The boy, a little shorter than Ralphie, skidded to a stop and without delay spun on his heels and launched a second attack. The boy was thin but muscular. Even beneath the hoody Ralphie could see that the boy was ropy. Ralphie had just enough time to lift his croquet mallet up and fend off the second attack.

The boy was all frenetic and aggressive and as Ralphie defended against the second attack the nameless boy kicked out with battered motorcycle boots and managed to nick Ralphie on the wrist with the boot or blade. It all happened simultaneously as Ralphie twisted the mallet and drove him hard toward the left and into the dark. In the dark the boy growled like some wounded animal and came sprinting at Ralphie all wild-eyed.

Leaking, Ralphie glared in the direction of the boy and prepared for the third attack. The boy, again rushed at Ralphie all aggression and anger and Ralphie noted that the third attack was like the second and first attack and took a step back, preparing for a counterattack. As the boy raised the machetes over his head Ralphie simultaneously stepped forward and drove the croquet mallet sideways, like a professional golfer of old, swinging the mallet up and towards the boy's chin. The mallet's head met the boy's chin and the meaty thunk sounded followed by the clicking of the boy's teeth together and directly the boy was gone. The impact of the hit rippled down the croquet mallet and through Ralphie's hands, wrists, arms and to his shoulders. Ralphie closed his eyes at the sound and kickback of the impact. In the dark the croquet mallet bounced back for an instant and then rose and finished the arc. Ralphie and the croquet mallet spun around as the machetes went flying.

The boy, who had been running full speed at Ralphie had gone pinwheeling to the right and backwards into the dark weed field. Ralphie looked down and saw one of the machete blades quivering in the weeds, somehow stabbing the ground. The other blade had disappeared. He flexed his hands as if he needed to push blood in them suddenly.

In the rear of Building 3 there was suddenly silence. Ralphie looked and made out the boy lying on his back, unmoving. He moved forward knowing without knowing that the fight was over.

Standing over the boy, Ralphie studied the hoody, the jeans and the motorcycle boots. He was a Boomer. Ralphie listened to his own breathing as he thought absently about the idea of bashing a Boomer.

Reaching down Ralphie took one of the boy's rings on his fingers. A token, he thought, to prove that he had flatlined the boy. Ralphie took the ring and examined it in the dark. The ring was silver and had a distinctive design on the crown; a wolf head.

Fifteen-year-old Ralphie looked pleased at the wolf head design on the ring and looked around to see if anyone else saw what he saw. He looked again at the design and shook his head. Ralphie looked at the boy that he had thrashed and wondered would he get back up. Could werewolves come back to life if they weren't cheesed with a silver bullet?

Ralphie snickered and in mid-snicker stopped himself. He shrugged off his backpack just enough to unzip the front pocket of his backpack and dropped the wolf headed ring inside.

Inside of the front pocket Ralphie knew were his mementos, keepsakes and trophies of his conquests. There was the Lady Justice pin of the psychotic girl; his first real bash. There was Pablo and Robert Nesta Marley's paint spattered clock patches. Now, he had added the nameless Boomer's wolf headed ring.

At 10:01PM Ralphie was leaving the rear of Building 3 and making his way toward the sky bridge. Going to the sky bridge was a death wish, Ralphie mused. Anyone that was suicidal went to the sky bridge. It was a death trap.

Ralphie walked around, hiding in the shadows and waiting to attack anyone foolish enough to come down the same street. In his head, Ralphie reasoned, he wasn't a hitter. Well, he wasn't a hunt down and dirt nap a body kind of cutthroat. At least, that is not how Ralphie saw it.

Ralphie had to admit that if he hunted down anyone it was Robert Nesta. In fact, Ralphie tried to rationalize, he had hunted down Robert Nesta for Jax since Jax was unable to pull the trigger on the only person in the challenge that he wanted to face mano-y-mano.

He had only really attacked one person in the whole challenge; Robert Nesta. He had termed Pablo, Pablo because the axe murderer had tried to split him in two like a piece of lumber. That wasn't an ending, per se, it was more defense. He had zapped the boy on the hill for the same reason. Everyone that had tried to sleep Ralphie had met with a terrible end because Ralphie did not want to be termed. Even the latest, the boy with the machetes, had attacked first. Ralphie had no choice.

As Ralphie walked, he found himself thinking that of the six fatals he had ended, he had never taken his opponents weapon. Ralphie thought about that especially after talking with Bailey. He did not have a real long-range weapon. He had a flare gun. What good was a flare gun against people with burpers? In five days, he hadn't faced anyone with a gun. The worse thing was that weird weapon the psychotic girl had.

Walking around that night, after bashing the boy with the machetes, Ralphie tried not to be all in his head. He walked and hoped to find someone, anyone to come across and prove that he was more than just an add-on.

Ralphie hoped his luck, or whatever, held out. He only had that to depend on. The next opponent that Ralphie faced, the fifteen-year-old calculated, was more likely to be carrying a gun than not. Ralphie hoped that the next tough he faced did not have a long-range weapon. If he had to face someone with a rifle the fight was over before it begun.

Suddenly, Ralphie was at the edge of the sky bridge. Ralphie paused. He checked his digital map reader. It was still early, relatively. It was ten minutes to the seventh announcement of Day Five. The moon was big and bright in the star filled sky above. There were just a few wisps of clouds in the sky but nothing to make the night inky black.

Bailey and Emmett would not be there, at the sky bridge, he knew. Bailey had said that they would show up at the last announcement of the day. Ralphie looked down and around the quiet location and tried to figure out if he would hang out around the sky bridge for the next three hours. He was not at the sky bridge. Ralphie had stopped near the sky bridge. He knew that fools went to the sky bridge. People died at the sky bridge.

So, Ralphie tried to figure out if he was going to wait out Emmett and Bailey in the shadows of the structure's blocks from the sky bridge with the hopes of seeing Bailey again. It was a fool's play. Ralphie would have better luck trying to figure out where the challenge would end than wait on Bailey. Someone was always looking for people focused on other things.

As far as Ralphie knew Emmett was walking around trying to break people in two like kindling wood. Bailey was… Ralphie paused. He had no idea how Bailey had made it as far as she had in the challenge. All he knew was that the First Gen was smart and athletic. They, he calculated, were off skulking around the island trying to be ninjas, Ralphie concluded.

Now, Ralphie knew that stepping on the sky bridge, during the challenge, was like tapping the head of a two-ton bull or swimming with sharks or running through the dead zone in the middle of the day. It was a painless death but death, nonetheless. Trying to go to the sky bridge before the line knobs thinned was something you did, and if you lived to tell about it, the story would, in and of itself, be legendary.

Few in the challenges braved the sky bridge for fear of death. The sky bridge was the place that most knobs were DOA'd. Snipers, assassins, hitters and shooters picked off every foolish naive knob that went to the sky bridge from Day One. The robo-spiders were always busy near the sky bridge.

For the thrill of it, Ralphie turned his attention to the sky bridge. The sky bridge was a block long expanse stretched across the Former Lakes of Nations that had become a toxic soup that threatened to eat anyone or thing stupid enough to fall into the black liquid. On the sky bridge sat the Pandemonium supply dump machine. The supply dump machine was a distinctly created machine that looked more like one of those Twenty First Century vending machines that dispensed almost anything. The supply dump machine was indestructible and on a daily timer. It opened every three hours usually five or ten minutes after each announcement.

So, with time to kill, Ralphie thought he might try and go and replenish his supplies that night. It was the end of Day Five and there were only a handful of toughs left. They could not be everywhere. The island was big. The chance for a line tough to be waiting Ralphie out was slim to none with the numbers of combatants down to a dozen.

At the foot of the sky bridge, Ralphie, armed with his croquet mallet, stepped onto the well-constructed foot bridge. He looked left and right and back before taking his second step onto the sky bridge. He figured that if there was anyone looking to face him now, they would want to do so up close and personal. At least, that was his thinking.

The snipers would be long gone by now, Ralphie assumed. So, Ralphie walked toward the middle of the sky bridge where the fabled vending machine he had seen so often on video sat. He took a few steps and looked back. No one was there. No one was coming to attack him.

Ralphie walked a few more steps, now maybe twenty yards from the machine, when he heard metal on metal behind him. Ralphie turned slowly and was not surprised when he saw a boy wearing a long black jacket that fell to his thighs and baggy black jeans. In his hand was a burper. He grinned a one-sided smile that looked like his left cheek was painfully pulled by an invisible fishhook. The boy had thin eyes and thick lips. Across his back was a katana sword.

"I could have just cheesed you, but I didn't," the boy that Ralphie knew as David Rogers said, his burper aimed at Ralphie from the foot of the sky bridge.

Ralphie looked at David Rogers, the Remains bad boy. He grinned. He grinned like someone with a secret. He grinned because he could not help but smile at David Rogers.

"Why you smiling like that, Miller? You insane or something?"

"I'm not insane. I'm smiling because it makes sense," Ralphie grinned, feeling the corners of his mouth broaden. He did not want to smile but he could not help it.

"Drop the whack-a-mole hammer, John Henry. There ain't going to be no steel driving tonight," David Rogers sneered holding the silver burper in his hand as if he was comfortable with the weapon.

Ralphie jested with his eyes on David Rogers' request and instead of complying moved toward the bad boy.

"Hey? Didn't you hear me?" David Rogers crinkled his forehead. He lifted his gun and waved it in the air in front of him. "Hey, stupid, I have the burper. You planning on dying?"

David Rogers leveled his burper, suddenly all business.

Ralphie raised his hands and the croquet mallet at the same time. He had closed to about ten feet of the boy and stopped. Ralphie looked at David Rogers only to smile again. He looked up and seeing the croquet mallet in his hands smiled coyly and lowered it to place it gently against the bridge railing.

"Are you deranged? What is wrong with you, whack-a-doodle?"

Ralphie did not respond.

David Rogers shook off Ralphie's actions.

"You know, I was going to be nice and end you quick. Now, I am about to dismantle you, the old-fashioned way and you don't even realize that there is nothing you can do about it," David Rogers proclaimed, releasing the magazine of the Walther PPK, placing his gun, it's magazine and his sword at the foot of the sky bridge.

Ralphie studied David Rogers. He could not help but smile. He looked from David Rogers toward the east and where the Remains sat.

"Okay, bad boy," David Rogers declared stepping forward cautiously. "I'm going to give you the first attack then it's the best man wins. I won't make you suffer. I'm not heartless," David Rogers declared.

"You ever watch videos? I mean, really watch videos?" Ralphie paused. "I do. I kind of love how you can watch something and dissect it, you know? I mean maybe 30 hours ago you said pretty much the same thing to one of my friends. You did your whole pscyho exer weirdness. But that made me aware of a few things."

"What are you talking about?"

"The thing that I don't understand is that you are a Poppy," Ralphie pointed out. "I just don't understand how you derailed."

David Rogers opened and closed his mouth. He studied the boy holding the croquet mallet. The termer hesitated. In that hesitation Ralphie attacked.

He lunged at David Rogers and closed the space between them almost instantly. David Rogers tried to take a step back and prepare but the speed and intensity of the attack took the challenge bad boy by surprise. Ralphie jumped on David Rogers and the two boys went to the ground. On the ground, Ralphie popped up punching. He drove a dozen punches into the face of David Rogers. The punches were pile driving punches that slammed into David Rogers face like bricks dropped from extreme heights. In less than 60 seconds the fight was over. David Rogers lay unconscious under the weight of Ralphie, leaking in half a dozen places, but mostly his mouth, nose and eyes.

Ralphie stopped himself and studied his bloody hands. He had cut his knuckles on David Rogers. Ralphie could not recall if David Rogers had struck him once in the entirety of the brief but intense fight. Ralphie breathing heavily pressed himself up and off the boy that had ended Zeke.

Standing Ralphie swayed just a little feeling the blood rushing from his head, for a second. He reached out and found the stability of the railing of the sky bridge.

"You want to destroy a bully? You have to meet him with undeniable force and fearlessness," Ralphie breathed the words that his father had told him time and time again, to the unconscious boy lying on the ground.

On the railing Ralphie looked at the burper that David Rogers had pointed at him earlier. Ralphie looked at the burper and the magazine. He smiled knowingly at the empty magazine. Ralphie then looked down the barrel and was not surprised to find that it was empty as well.

Ralphie took the katana and sheath and strapped it on his back. He was not a sword fighter or bad boy but having the katana on his back made Ralphie feel like he might be able to pull off the look.

David Rogers groaned from the darkness. The sound brought Ralphie back to the challenge. Ralphie grabbed his croquet mallet and walked back to the side of David Rogers who was coming to after the beating.

Ralphie placed the croquet mallet by David Rogers and leaned down to see how badly he had beaten the bad boy. David Rogers was bleeding from his mouth and nose and seemed disoriented. The bad boy reminded Ralphie of a turtle when flipped on its back. He lay there, still on the ground, on his back and trying unsuccessfully to sit up when Ralphie arrived.

"You bladed a friend of mine, the other day. The cold part is you pretty much said the same things to me." The Miller with the croquet mallet mentioned. "You did the same things. You reading from some script or something?" Ralphie smirked at David Rogers. "The challenge deserves better than you."

"Whud mud yud watt," David Rogers tried, but lips were cut and bleeding and quickly swelling and his cheeks cut and puffy, so nothing he uttered made sense.

Ralphie straightened from his crouching position and studied David Rogers, with contempt. He scowled at the broken and suddenly harmless boy. Ralphie lifted the croquet mallet onto his shoulder. He took a moment and spun around and let the mallet swing into the air and down toward the unsuspecting David Rogers. The weighted mallet's head moved in a tight arc and came down as hard as it could on the head of the bad boy. David Rogers howled. Ralphie lifted the mallet again and redoubled his actions and efforts.

The flatlining of David Rogers only took three or four swings of the mallet. Ralphie concentrated and aimed his attack to end the bad boy quickly. Though the exing was short Ralphie could not stop his thoughts of how hard he was breathing. His heartbeat was pounding in his ears and David Rogers became something else; a silent and unmoving thing at the foot of the sky bridge. He refocused and tried to control his labored breathing. When he had brought his breathing to a manageable level, he took a deep breath and shook off the excess adrenaline. He bent down and tore the paint spattered clock patch off David Rogers jacket's shoulder.

"Whack-a-mole," Ralphie intoned as he wiped the sweat and blood from his face and walked across the sky bridge unmolested.

After ending David Rogers, walking on the sky bridge, bashing the Boomer, Ralphie decided not to push his luck any further. He had done a lot at the end of Day Five. He would find a resting place and wait for the day to break. He was bone tired and not trying to be extremely clever.

So, cut and bruised Ralphie headed back to Building 3. He considered waiting and seeing Bailey again. By his calculations she and Emmett Carson were scheduled to meet in two hours at the sky bridge. Ralphie thought about the meeting, with Emmett Carson there, and chose to rest instead. Ralphie was not sure if he could defend himself from a friendly puppy suddenly let alone a determined Emmett Carson.

Ralphie climbed, tired, back over the fence and made his way into Building 3 and rested. Of all the places on the island Ralphie knew that Building 3 was safe. He had been there hours before and no one had come to slit his throat or bash in his brains.

So, Ralphie hunkered down and prepared to rest for a few hours and hope for sleep, if sleep is what you called the handful of hours of waking and closing your eyes and never feeling completely rested. It, those moments of not running around and being targeted or chasing someone was not refreshing. It only allowed Ralphie time to bandage himself and make sure that he was fueled and hydrated enough for the next bouts.

Sitting on the floor of Building 3 exhausted, Ralphie did a check of his body. He felt relatively good until he flexed his wrist and felt it aching. He flexed his wrist and felt the minor cut that the boy had managed.

Checking his wrist, Ralphie noted that he was leaking, just a little. It wasn't a deep cut but enough to cause some concern. So, Ralphie patched himself up as best he could in the shadows of Building 3.

"At 2400 hours here is the eighth and last report for Day Five of the Pandemonium Challenge: There are only fourteen contestants that remain in the challenge. The Pandemonium Challenge wishes to announce the loss of the following contestants from the last three hours: August Charles, Yvonne Holden, and David Rogers."

By the last announcement of Day Five Ralphie found himself physically and mentally exhausted. He lay in Building 3 and just closed his eyes. Immediately, he was not sleeping but doing something that looked like sleep to most but gave very little of the benefits.

Chapter Eighteen.

Day Six.

The next morning, Day Six, Ralphie was still tired and achy. He had rested but found little rest in his sitting and lying in Building 3. The first announcement was announced Ralphie thought he heard it, but it was distant and as if being broadcast from underwater. By the second announcement Ralphie stirred. He was sore all over but nothing too debilitating. Even though he was just sore it took him another announcement before he could manage to roll over and begin Day Six.

"At 0900 hours, here is the third report for Day Six of the Pandemonium Challenge: There are only eleven contestants that remain in the challenge. The Pandemonium Challenge wishes to remind all of the loss of the following contestants from the last three hours: Joyce Bryant Battle has been removed from the Twenty-Third Pandemonium Challenge."

By the third announcement for Day Six Ralphie was up and moving. He was slow and creaky and achy but moving. Ralphie figured that moving he would shake things out and hoped that he would be right as rain in a couple of hours.

He shrugged on his backpack and grabbed his croquet mallet and waved goodbye to Building 3. Ralphie gingerly climbed out of the window and the effort was more strenuous than he initially remembered. He rolled his shoulders and tried to loosen his neck muscles as he walked toward the fence that bordered Building 3. Ralphie resolved to climb the fence without complaint. As he climbed the fence and landed on the other side Ralphie could not help but look back and think how wrong Jax had been about numbered buildings. They did not all spell death. At least, not Building 3.

He walked and as he hoped, after an hour out in the open his body seemed to catch up with his mind. There was a dull pain in his side but nothing that Ralphie could not manage.

"At 1200 hours, here is the fourth report for Day Six of the Pandemonium Challenge: There are only nine contestants that remain in the challenge. The Pandemonium Challenge wishes to remind all of the loss of the following contestants last three hours: Brooks Starling and Brian Jenson have been removed from the Twenty-Third Pandemonium Challenge."

Day Six was a surprisingly solitary day. Ralphie walked, limped around on a sore ankle and tried to loosen the muscles in his back that had tightened during the night. He had bandaged all of his cuts and injuries and thanks to his hoody looked unharmed. His jeans had a big cut in the right knee. Though he was only fifteen Ralphie felt like an old man on Day Six.

"At 1500 hours, here is the fifth report for Day Six of the Pandemonium Challenge: There are only eight contestants that remain in the challenge. The Pandemonium Challenge wishes to remind all of the loss of the following contestants last three hours: Winter Ross has been removed from the Twenty-Third Pandemonium Challenge."

Tired and hungry Ralphie decided to find shelter. He was on the western side of the island. There was a building that looked like the roof had fallen in on itself. The roof made entry difficult but not impossible. Ralphie weaved his way into the front of the structure and knew that most would not dare enter that way. So, in the nearly impassable structure Ralphie hunkered down and rested in the rubble strewn interior. He was not planning on staying in the structure long. He just needed a temporary resting spot.

"At 1800 hours, here is the sixth report for Day Six of the Pandemonium Challenge: There are only six contestants that remain in the challenge. The Pandemonium Challenge wishes to remind all of the loss of the following contestants last three hours: Morgan Davidson and Penny Sullivan have been removed from the Twenty-Third Pandemonium Challenge."

Five minutes before the seventh report Ralphie heard the sound of his digital map reader's distinctive beeping chirping just three feet from his head. He reached for and turned off the alarm. He stretched and prepared to head into the night and into the challenge.

"At 2100 hours, here is the seventh report for Day Six of the Pandemonium Challenge: There are only six contestants that remain in the challenge. The Pandemonium Challenge wishes to remind all of the loss of the following contestants from the last three hours: Lauren Fullerton and Ali Washington."

Climbing out of his hiding place, feeling better but still aching, Ralphie moved westward. He was at the northern end of the island. Tired, Ralphie walked toward the west and saw a building in the distance that had a small fire burning inside. Of course, because it was the challenge, Ralphie thought he should avoid the building. It had to be a trap.

Ralphie slowed. Ralphie looked in every direction. He listened for any unusual noises that might give away the location of someone preparing for an attack. Ralphie moved as if he was in a minefield. Every step suddenly seemed important. Every noise significant.

One or two hundred yards from the building with the fire Ralphie found a building that he could cut through. Once inside Ralphie looked and listened for anything unusual. Finding nothing in the building and no activity at the building with the flickering fire Ralphie looked around the structure he was in. It was four walls, barely. Ralphie saw that the building opened out to the street behind. So, the fifteen-year-old beelined through the shell of a building as quietly and cautiously as possible, all the while watching the building with the small fire in it and the street and structures around it for any movement.

On the far side of the structure and on the opposite street Ralphie pressed himself up against the edge of a structure and watched the building for another few minutes. In his mind, Ralphie thought simply, anything unusual in the challenge had to be a trap. Ralphie walked slowly back and away from the building and down a dark wide street, all the while watching the flickering lights inside the building at the top of the street.

The two-story building that Ralphie decided to rest in that night was a shell of a building. The interior only had beams to support the walls and ceiling. Ralphie picked the building because he could watch the building with the fire in it from his location.

He searched the interior of the building for things that he might use for the inevitable fight that had to be coming between him and the final bullies. Ralphie searched the building and found three empty wine bottles. At a generator that was hidden along a wall Ralphie found that there was just enough gasoline to siphon out. Finding a disused plastic tubing Ralphie half-filled the three wine bottles and stuffed rags in them.

Ralphie situated the three improvised Molotov cocktails just out of reach, for use if need be. Why not, he thought. It was the last night on Pandemonium Island and there were only five contestants left.

If he was attacked, and the attacks were going to come now, Ralphie imagined then, he wanted to be prepared. Then he thought about the building just a couple of blocks away with the fire.

In six days, no one had a fire burning at night. He thought about going to see who was in the building. Ralphie also thought that the fire was a trap. It had to be a trap. It was the challenge. Everything was a trap. Everyone was a threat. Yet, with only a few hours left in the challenge taking out anyone made it more likely that Ralphie could be the winner of the Twenty-Third Pandemonium Challenge. So, he decided that he would do the smartest thing. He had taken out David Rogers. He had mopped the Boomer.

So, Ralphie left the safety of his newfound and secure resting spot and headed toward the building on the northern end of the island. Ralphie expected that in this moment that indecision was horrible. The challenge was all about making snap judgments and living or dying with them. So, he walked through the twilight hours of Day Six in the challenge with the hope of winning the Pandemonium Challenge.

If it was a trap, then Ralphie imagined he would extricate himself from the trap and turn the table on the trapper. The trap only worked if the hunted were unaware, Ralphie figured. He was aware and prepared for the worse.

He was headed to a trap. "They get you one way or another," Ralphie thought as he reached the edge of the building with the fire. Bring the moths to the flame, as it were.

Ralphie walked around the building for nearly an hour before entering. He was surprised that there were no nets that fell from the roof or booby traps as Ralphie kept to the walls of the building, looking for anyone to attack. No one attacked. Ralphie found a dark corner and hid in it. He watched and waited.

The first bully to appear after Ralphie was Emmett Carson. Upon seeing Emmett Carson, Ralphie pulled the burper that he had taken off David Rogers at the sky bridge. He held the burper in his hand. If things were different, Ralphie thought, it would have been easy to draw down on Emmett Carson and unload the clip into the First Gen tough. Emmett Carson deserved it, Ralphie thought.

If anyone in the challenge needed to be cheesed it was Emmett Carson. Yet, Ralphie watched as Emmett Carson circled the space where the fire burned from an exposed pipe. Ralphie looked down the front sight of the burper and thought of pulling the trigger and ending Emmett Carson. As he aimed the burper Ralphie thought that Emmett Carson did not deserve to be cheesed so easily.

"So, this is it?"

Ralphie stepped out of the shadows and Emmett Carson lifted his burper and aimed it at the Miller. Ralphie had his burper aimed and ready as he stepped across the space, headed toward the low burning fire. Emmett Carson cut his dark eyes at Ralphie and smirked. He looked at Ralphie as if he were a bug.

The two combatants paced around the fire, guns at the ready. Ralphie did not want to read anything into Emmett's posture but it looked as if six days of the challenge had worn the First Gen ruffian down, just a bit. Ralphie, on the other hand, knew that he did not have the spring in his step that he had started with five days before. He was bruised and battered and worse for wear after six days in the challenge.

"This your trap, Miller?"

"Nope," Ralphie admitted still holding his burper on the muscular Carson.

"So, who put this together?"

"Don't know," Ralphie admitted.

Emmett kept his burper aimed at Ralphie. The First Gen nodded. He studied Ralphie for a moment.

"Are you going to shoot?"

"I'm still deciding," Ralphie lied.

Emmett eyes widened in dramatic surprise. He let his jaw drop, all the while holding the burper level and at Ralphie's heart.

Ralphie took a breath and decided if he was to die, he would die with a clear conscience.

"You have been a maggot-pie to me since the first day that I met you, and I never did anything to you. I didn't talk bad about you. I didn't pile on when others talked bad about you. But you went out of your way to find and harass me and make my life hard."

"What? What are you going on about," Emmett sneered, looking at Ralphie as if he had grown another head. "What? Am I supposed to get all sensitive, all of a sudden, because some Miller knob decides that life ain't fair?"

"No, you're supposed to realize that being a maggot-pie all the time has consequences."

"Consequences?"

"Yeah, Juan, consequences."

Emmett winced at the insult and smirked.

"You heard of karma?" Ralphie asked. "It's coming."

Emmett Carson scoffed. He lowered his gun. Ralphie lowered his gun as well.

"You ain't trying to cheese me? You ain't trying to ex me? Suppose you trying to bore me to death with this gleeky nonsense?"

"You're a jackass, Emmett. You tried to break me, when I was younger."

"What are you talking about, numb nuts?"

"Remember when you and your idiot friends locked me in the dumpster? Remember when you and your boys ran me off the bike path because I wasn't a Gen?"

"Who remembers or cares about crap like that?"

"I do."

Emmett Carson nodded and winced as he did. He placed a big brown hand against his jaw. "You insane?" Emmett concluded.

"How come?"

"Because we were kids. We were kidding. We were screwing around. It didn't mean squat. It's what kids do to kids they don't know. No one cares about stupid crap like that."

"It wasn't kid stuff. It was mean and cruel, and you should have known better."

"What do you want me to say: I'm sorry?" Emmett Carson looked at Ralphie with open contempt. "I'm not," Emmett Carson smirked.

Ralphie knew that Emmett Carson was not going to apologize. He did not feel that Ralphie deserved an apology. More importantly, Emmett did not think that he had done anything deserving an apology.

Yet, Ralphie persisted.

"You know I might have let all the other stuff go if you had tried to be nice at least one time. You were a thorn in my side that I could not reach to remove," Ralphie stated.

"This conversation is boring?"

"You and your boys humiliated me. That's not right," Ralphie growled.

Emmett scoffed.

"There was no reason to puncture my bike tire or throw rocks at me," Ralphie noted, painfully.

"There was a reason, wrench turner. There's always a reason."

Ralphie stopped. He listened, directly interested in what Emmett Carson was going to say.

"For me, it was simple. You're a Miller in our compound thinking you could fit in with us. First Gens protect First Gens." Emmett Carson paused, thinking. "We didn't invite you to the compound. We didn't want you in the compound. Might not have cared or paid attention if you hadn't got close to … my girl."

Ralphie listened to Emmett Carson and all that he said except the last words were noise. He let what Emmett Carson said sink in and without thought narrowed his eyes to look at the First Gen rude boy from a different point of view.

"Bailey?"

"Bailey is *my* girl. She been my girl since I can remember. She's not supposed to be friends, with….to like you."

Ralphie was suddenly confused.

"You and Bailey?" Ralphie said. The idea was so ludicrous. "Is that what this is all about?"

"Isn't that what everything is about?"

Ralphie shook his head; hoping to understand what Emmett was saying. "You crazy," Ralphie asked. "I've known you and Bailey since I was seven, thanks to my dad and his work." Ralphie paused. "I like her, but not like that."

"You like to call people maggot-pies, but you are the biggest pie of maggots of all." Emmett Carson gritted his teeth, angry suddenly. Emmett Carson was struggling.

Ralphie listened to the words Emmett Carson uttered. He listened and was surprised that he was having this conversation with Emmett Carson. First Jax. Now Emmett. He all of a sudden had no words.

"I thought…Bailey was my girl," Emmett Carson droned on. "I mean, we went to the same Ed facility since before we were teens. We knew the same people."

Ralphie listened speechless. Ralphie listened not knowing what to say.

"I asked her to our Valentine's Day school dance," Emmett pointed out. Emmett continued talking but Ralphie did not hear or care what Emmett was saying suddenly. He was working out a mental puzzle. Had he missed the signs that Bailey had been sending out?

When he had left the First Gen complex to return back to the Miller compound with his parents Bailey had given him a hug and crooned: "Stay in contact." Everyone said that. She was just being nice.

A week later, after his move back to the Miller compound, he and Bailey were video chatting and she was just talking about her day and he was talking about his day. Everyone did that. That was normal. There was nothing odd about that.

Once a week, Ralphie met and saw Bailey and they hugged. They were friends. Friends hugged. Friends stayed in contact. None of this was abnormal.

He said: "Hey" to Bailey at the Gathering Center, but that was casual. There were no expectations. Ralphie liked going to the Gathering Center. Ralphie liked seeing Bailey when she was there. They never arranged the meetings. They just usually saw each other there.

When Bailey joined the Remains debate league, she found herself at the Foundry debating against Foundry students. Ralphie went to the debates and found Bailey. Again, in his mind, that was just friends being friendly. He was supportive of his friend.

Then the challenge happened. Bailey told him that she was thinking about registering. Ralphie thought the idea was interesting.

Ralphie saw Emmett Carson looking at him with a look that said that he wanted to cut off his head with that samurai sword on his back.

"I thought about flatlining you when I saw you in the challenge. But I didn't want Bailey to think that I was being petty."

"So," Ralphie began only to stop.

"So, Bailey doesn't want me to be a caveman," Emmett pouted. "Her words."

All those moments coalesced in Ralphie's head and he realized that Bailey did not like him like a friend. The idea hit Ralphie like an unexpected slap in the face. Ralphie grinned at the idea of being liked by Bailey.

"So, you can't cheese me?"

"Something like that," Emmett spat. "Think that I can't end you if there are others to go after. But if it's just you and me then it's okay to term you, for some reason."

Ralphie listened. His world was suddenly turned ninety degrees to the right. He was seeing things different.

"At 2400 hours, here is the eighth and final report for Day Six of the Pandemonium Challenge: There are only four contestants that remain in the challenge. The Pandemonium Challenge wishes to remind all of the loss of the following contestants from the last three hours: Destiny Fontaine has been removed from the Twenty-Third Pandemonium Challenge."

"But, why did you come to the challenge?"

"Hell, lug nut, the challenge is all about becoming legendary. Everyone wants to be legendary," Emmett boomed. "Everyone."

Ralphie nodded.

"I came here, tonight, to fight but since it's just you, it's not worth it without Bailey being here," Emmett paused. He looked around. He listened. Then he added: "Think I want to get a little rest before things go all sideways," Emmett confessed. He added: "Well, whoever did this I don't want to make it too easy. I am going to leave and find some place to sack out, by myself. Tomorrow, today, whenever I see you again, Miller, things will be real different." Emmett added, "I'll tell Bailey that you know the deal. So, the next time that we meet Bailey or no, no more Mister Nice Guy."

"Suppose so," Ralphie reluctantly agreed.

"Think it would be better if Bailey saw you, before I dead you, to realize who is better for her," Emmett said with a wide grin.

"Better?"

"Yeah, foot-licker," Emmett spat. "Every girl needs a protector. They may act like they don't, but they all want someone that is going to punch someone in the mouth when the time comes."

Ralphie bristled at Emmett's logic. He took a moment and chose not to point out his error. Emmett had proven that he did not like correction.

"This don't make us cool. I still am thinking about deading you, ice box dead, just not tonight."

"I appreciate that," Ralphie stated.

Emmett bent down and picked up a small rock and tossed it at Ralphie.

Ralphie bent and tried to shield himself from the unexpected attack. He turned back and looked where the Cro-Magnon teen had stood and breathed a sigh of relief and noted that he had thrown the rock to distract him. Emmett Carson had disappeared.

Ralphie looked around the empty space. The fire still burned. Emmett Carson had disappeared. Ralphie was once again the only person in the great space.

He pushed into the shadows. Once in the shadows Ralphie found an opening in the warehouse structure and stepped out and into the darkness. He looked left and then right and moved as quietly as possible away from the structure where he had encountered Emmett Carson.

Back at the two-story building Ralphie had booby-trapped the teen Miller did a quick scan of the building. Once checking the building Ralphie sat in the dark and thought about what Emmett Carson had told him. Ralphie shook his head. *"Bailey liked Emmett? Emmett liked Bailey, was more like it. Emmett and Bailey were probably friends when they were kids,"* Ralphie thought. "*Emmett got a crush,*" Ralphie figured. "*Bailey being Bailey, she was not even aware of Emmett's crush. Emmett is crushing on Bailey and then I arrive. Now, Bailey sees me and I'm all brand new and different, because I'm not Emmett. Bailey relaxes, smiles, laughs and likes me,*" Ralphie thought.

It was a lot to take in. It did not make sense, but it did make sense simultaneously. Suddenly, his head hurt. Ralphie snapped out of his musings of who liked who and when.

Chapter Nineteen.

Day Seven.

Day Seven, Ralphie, bruised and battered, sat in his safe spot and waited for something to happen. It was the final day of the Pandemonium Challenge and something had to happen. There was no way around, the fifteen-year-old Ralphie thought. Everything before had led to this moment and day. So, the inevitable end, the finish of the Pandemonium Challenge, the conclusion of the seven days on Pandemonium Island was, now, just hours away.

Ralphie sat in the dark and had to admit that he did not know how it would end. He only hoped to see the end of the Twenty-Third Pandemonium Challenge. In the back of his mind he wanted to make it to the final two. Of course, Ralphie wanted to win the Twenty-Third Pandemonium Challenge, but that idea seemed so far-fetched.

That thought had to have been in the minds of the twenty-two others that had come out on top at the end of the previous Pandemonium Challenges. They had to doubt that they would win. They had to have the same thought, the day that they woke up and realized that it was just a handful of hours to the end of the challenge. Ralphie, believed of the hundreds that had fought to make it to the last day they had to wonder if they would survive. Ralphie mused that he was just like the twenty-two others suddenly, except that he had not finished the challenge or won.

Only twenty-two had figured out a way to conquer all those that stood before them in that quest for the title of champion. Twenty-two had become Pandemonium Challenge winners. He did not know all their names. He only knew the last ten winners but not specifics.

There was Hank Aaron Price who had run out of lead pills and beaten his opponent to death with a crowbar to win the challenge.

There was Jamaica Henrietta Kincaid who had fought throughout the challenge and nearly died a dozen times to come out, miraculously, as one of the last three to fight for the championship.

Howard Hewitt Reed was an underdog that few gave odds to make it more than three days on the island. Howard Hewitt Reed had come upon a crossbow and destroyed everyone foolish enough to cross her path.

Denzel Washington Hudson, the first Boomer to make it to the final day booby-trapped a structure that ultimately gutted two of the final three bullies, leaving just one unsuspecting Trad to face the wild child.

Oprah Winfrey Johnson won the challenge by pretending to be cock roached. Oprah Winfrey Johnson was a human possum. Anytime someone approached her, she played dead and when the person passed Oprah Winfrey jumped up and stabbed the unsuspecting rascal in the back. It was not fair play but nothing in the Pandemonium Challenge resembled fair play.

James Baldwin Valentine was in the most chaotic challenge. Somehow nearly a dozen combatants made it to the last day. In those waning hours half a dozen murkers were ended. The last six rowdies faced off and decided to go medieval. At the end, James Baldwin Valentine remained.

Regina King Brown appeared on the sixth day and most thought that Regina King Brown would be ended before the seventh day. Regina King Brown had scavenged an incredible arsenal for the last day of the challenge. He won using a cutlass.

Hannibal Morgan Nelson was the last Miller to win the challenge. Hannibal Nelson had a building in the Foundry named after him. He was a legend. He was the Miller that everyone in the Foundry dreamed of being if they went to the challenge. Hannibal Nelson had proven that he was the best stickler and the fiercest competitor in the challenge that year.

Samuel Jackson Booker gained the challenge championship by dropping a brick wall on the last opponent.

Stuart Scott Somers won the Twenty-First Pandemonium Challenge with the use of a baseball bat.

The Twenty-Second Pandemonium Challenge was won by a Boomer by the name of Wesley Snipes Crane. Crane played possum and drop kicked a curious maniac out of a second story window.

It amazed Ralphie that he recalled, in such detail, the exploits of so many in the challenge. He knew some information, but nothing like Jax or others.

He sipped water from the water bladder inside his solar backpack and toyed with one of his last protein bars. The mornings in the challenge were quiet. They had become quieter as the numbers decreased. The gunfire that sounded like firecrackers in the first few days of the challenge were now non-existent. Whoever had a gun was conserving his/her bullets, Ralphie figured.

He had a burper, thanks to the psychotic David Rogers, and on Day Seven Ralphie examined it for the second time since he had grabbed it on the sky bridge. The burper was an old-time Walther PPK. It was a small burper compared to the giant cannons he had seen some carrying. But the way that Ralphie saw it the burper could be used because empty or filled everyone still believed that it spit death. That was all that mattered.

Ralphie went through his backpack and noted that he still had two cans of Jolt Cola. Ralphie felt his skin goose flesh at the sight of the Jolt Colas. He shivered thinking of drinking two of the double caffeine cans of soda.

Jax and Zeke were the first to find the Jolt Colas, Ralphie remembered. This was the second or third day, Ralphie recalled. They knew everything about anything related to the challenge.

"Jolt Cola was created in 1985 by CJ Rapp. They went out of business in 2009. They returned in 2017 and were very popular with gamers and night owls."

"Why do you know all that information," Ralphie had asked.

"It seems important."

"Do you remember the slogan," Zeke asked, testing Jax.

"All the sugar. Twice the caffeine," Zeke and Jax had howled simultaneously, laughing like schoolgirls.

Ralphie could only shake his head in his memories. They were the weirdest friends he had. They were the only friends he had in the challenge. As Ralphie played the challenge over in his head, he knew that he did not consider Dame or Isaac Moore or Gina or Maddy as enemies. They were Millers. Ralphie knew that there were others that he would not target first, and in the challenge that was friendship. He liked Bailey. They were allies. Everyone else he knew but did not consider friends. They were expendable.

"Why they give us those drinks," Ralphie had asked.

"Why they have the challenge? It's entertainment, man, I suppose," Jax responded.

After removing the Jolt Colas and lessening the load in his backpack Ralphie decided to scan his digital map reader and see if anyone had their camera on. Ralphie was not having any luck on body cameras when he noticed that there was a video that had been recorded that he had not watched.

Less than sixty minutes after the fourth announcement Ralphie was alerted of an active body camera and found himself in his safe spot watching the body camera footage of Campbell Henderson. He watched the following:

The video on the camera was moving slowly forward. There were wooden beams throughout the interior of the structure. It was at least two-stories and wide. Shadows fell across the entirety of the structure.

"You know that my father took me to a field a long time ago, before he shut down, and I loved it. He said that we were hunters or hunted. When my family heard that my father had taken me hunting, they acted like he had taken me to a dog fight or something," Campbell Henderson explained, reloading her double-barreled blaster. "I just never got that. I mean, we eat meat. We eat fish. The cows don't just die of natural causes and then we stumble onto them. The fish aren't suicidal or anything. We have to sneak up on 'em and end them. So, hunting and deading are essential to living." She paused. "Ending others is a part of life. We need to eat. We have to eat. There are those that say that ending is wrong. I say: Scrap that. We all like chicken. We all eat chicken. No one eating chicken considers themselves chicken exterminators. It's something that has to happen. The same with the challenge. It isn't good or bad. It is just a part of the Remains." Campbell Henderson giggled. "It's necessary."

Campbell Henderson slow walked across the quiet space of the shadowy interior of the building. Shafts of light sliced through the interior giving the interior a tranquil appearance. The body cam focus shifted as Campbell Henderson turned a corner taking in the dimness of the space.

The steady cam took in the corner of the warehouse near the entrance of the building. The body cam swung wildly around and there in the background, in silhouette, was the small figure standing defiantly by a pile of stacked pipes. The camera focused and tightened to make out the form of the petite girl who had two Kama blades in her hands, as protection. There stood Bailey dressed in hooded sweatshirt, jeans and combat boots.

The live video perspective shifted to Bailey's body cam and there was a bit of jostling about as Bailey shifted her Kama blades to one hand and seemed to be looking around for another weapon she might use against the heavily armed Campbell Henderson. The same camera shot gave a better perspective of Campbell Henderson. The tall and athletic girl with long legs and wild curly black hair parted on the side of her triangular head was holding her shotgun under her arm like she was duck hunting.

The body camera switched again and back to Campbell Henderson and took in Bailey Beaumont as she jumped up from her hiding spot. Bailey Beaumont's camera perspective was all jittery. She swung and in the right side of the camera Ralphie noticed that Bailey was holding something in her hand. In another moment, Ralphie made out the thing in the small girl's hand was a broken piece of brick. The brick flashed across the screen as Bailey threw the brick toward Campbell Henderson.

The tight camera perspective switched and suddenly was falling back and toward the ground, as if cartwheeling. The camera bounced twice and settled. The perspective was suddenly from the ground up. In the distance the camera lens took in Bailey Beaumont as she ran into the darkness and disappeared.

The camera view shifted again to hear the heavy breathing of a surprised Bailey when Campbell Henderson had not fired the shotgun and cut her down. Bailey turned around curious. She looked into the maw of the warehouse that Ralphie recognized from the outside. It was the warehouse Ralphie had imagined was a trap and where Emmett and he had cleared the air and the First Gen had divulged that Bailey liked him.

Ralphie watched the body cam footage with intense interest. Ralphie watched Bailey's body camera footage and right away knew that she should not stop or more importantly look back, but she was standing there in front of the warehouse and not running away.

"Are you crazy," Ralphie breathed in his hide out. "Don't do it. Don't go back inside. You're out. Just leave. Going back is never a good option."

As Ralphie intoned that, against Ralphie's pleadings Bailey re-entered the place where she had nearly been cheesed. It was not a thought that made sense to Ralphie, logically, but for some reason he watched the girl that liked him walk back into the shadowy structure. Bailey moved cautiously and retraced her steps only to find an unconscious Campbell Henderson.

Bailey Beaumont cautiously returned to Campbell's side to find that her random throw had hit Campbell in the head. The body camera that was filming showed Bailey step to Campbell with two unusual weapons that looked like spiked knives. For the first time Ralphie was surprised at Bailey. He had expected the First Gen to have a different weapon. He had imagined a short sword or gun but not the pair of spiked knives.

The First Gen toed Campbell Henderson and Ralphie imagined that the psychotic girl was playing a game of opossum. Ralphie imagined that Campbell was just waiting for Bailey to get close enough to spring into action and gut his newly minted crush. But Campbell Henderson did not move. Bailey smiled and exhaled loudly. Bailey's smile broadened as she looked at Campbell Henderson's shotgun lying just inches from the girl that had threatened to blast her, head off but had fallen instead. The chunk of brick that Bailey had thrown lay bloody next to Campbell.

Campbell Henderson was breathing but unconscious. Bailey kicked the shotgun out of harm's way and bent down and pulled the shoelaces out of Campbell's boots. With the shoelaces Bailey secured Campbell's hands and then secured Campbell to a metal pole that was attached to something that had been railing or pipes of the building. Bailey kicked the shotgun even further out of Campbell's reach. Bailey took a moment and unimaginably did not gut, shish kabob or dead the defenseless girl but unexpectedly ran out of the warehouse.

Ralphie turned off his digital map reader and climbed to his feet and looked out the window and saw nothing. He twisted his lips, thinking. Should he go? Should he wait? Ralphie looked again and suddenly saw Bailey running across the street. He took a step toward the exit and street and was about to call out to her, but before he could, she was gone.

The Miller fifteen-year-old tried to figure out where the First Gen had gone. He looked back to his hiding place and back to the top of the street where Bailey had just run. Ralphie returned to his hideout. Slipping his newly acquired sword and sheath over his back and grabbing his backpack Ralphie was about to try and find Bailey when he saw her, all finger braids and cuteness, running from the structure a few doors from the trap warehouse with Emmett Carson in tow.

Ralphie padded to the top of the street, silently. He watched as the pair ran down the street as if they had something important to do. Ralphie followed behind at a discreet distance. The pair ran to the trap building just a block from where Ralphie had been hiding. They entered, never looking back to see Ralphie following.

Ralphie entered and found the strangest situation imaginable. Emmett Carson was standing there with his samurai sword strapped across his back like some samurai badass. Ralphie noticed that Emmett had a short sword in his hand. Bailey was standing over the pie-faced girl that Ralphie had seen before. She was a long legged caramel skinned girl with a bandage on her head.

"So, what do you want to do?"

Bailey did not answer.

"Your boyfriend wants to know if you want to cheese me or if you want him to do it," Campbell smiled thinly.

"Emmett," Bailey exclaimed looking from Campbell to Emmett.

"Well," Emmett shrugged.

"You are one cold piece," Ralphie admitted, stepping out of the shadows of the building holding his croquet mallet parallel to the ground.

"Oh, this just got good," Campbell Henderson turned, hearing Ralphie's voice and grinning from ear to ear.

Emmett tightened the grip on his short sword.

"If I had been evil, I could have cheesed all three of you," Ralphie mused lifting his croquet mallet. Of course, he was not that despicable. Ralphie entered and watched as the First Gen bully cut his eyes toward Ralphie and back to the seated Campbell Henderson. Emmett hoisted the short sword above his shoulder, menacingly. Emmett did not seem too concerned about Ralphie.

"Ralphie?"

Ralphie nodded to Bailey. He noted her big fawn eyes studying him. He saw her slight smile.

"You and me got unfinished business," Emmett interrupted.

Ralphie nodded refocusing on Emmett.

Bailey stepped between Emmett and Ralphie.

"You doing this now?"

"Bee, if not now, when?"

Ralphie smirked at Emmett's response.

"You should let them fight," Campbell Henderson stated.

"This is the challenge," Emmett continued.

"Yeah, but— "

"This," Emmett pointed at Ralphie. "This has been a long time coming. It's just that we're in the challenge. It's time."

"This looks like the showdown," Campbell grinned like a brown skinned jack-o-lantern.

"Shut up," Bailey growled, looking at Campbell through angry eyes.

Ralphie listened and watched the exchange between Emmett and Bailey.

"You got your situation," Emmett noted, looking at Campbell Henderson tied to the pole. "I got mine." Emmett gestured toward Ralphie and a more spacious part of the warehouse.

Emmett took a step toward Ralphie. Ralphie studied Emmett.

"Come on," Emmett said.

Ralphie followed silently, cautiously.

Once in the open space, Ralphie tensed, prepared to fight.

Emmett raised a hand, cautioning Ralphie.

"No games?"

"No games," Ralphie confessed.

Emmett pointed to a broken beam to the left of Ralphie. Somehow the beam had been broken in two pieces as if someone had been able to cut through the three-foot-thick wooden beam.

"What gives?"

"Termites? Wood rot? Don't know," Emmett Carson admitted.

"Surprised that this place is still standing," Ralphie said looking at the rotting wood beams.

"It's all just a death trap," Emmett Carson noted.

"It's a death trap, seriously," Ralphie smirked.

"Over there," Emmett directed, pointing to another open space.

Looking at the space that Emmett pointed to, Ralphie shook his head and pointed toward the building he had been in the night before. It was only across a patch of weed choked grass.

"More room," Ralphie sneered.

The two stopped in front of the building.

"You sure?"

Emmett frowned. "Yeah, why?" Emmett reached behind his back and removed his burper. Ralphie studied Emmett as he smiled broadly and casually aimed the burper at Ralphie. He looked around and placed the burper on a broken piece of masonry that seemed to be a part of the ruins of a foundation.

"Don't know if you can make it that far," Ralphie joked mirthlessly.

The bully scowled.

"You don't look 100%," Ralphie noted.

"Scut that," Emmett growled.

"Your funeral," Ralphie jested, spinning his croquet mallet in his hands.

Ralphie painfully shrugged off his backpack, leaving his samurai sword strapped across his back, diagonally.

"You hurt?"

"No," Ralphie lied, studying Emmett and noticing that the fifteen-year-old had a scratch across his cheek and a cut across his chin. Emmett was standing but he was babying his right ankle, for some reason.

"You wrench head," Emmett snorted. "It's your funeral."

Ralphie sneered at Emmett's repetition.

"You say anything original?"

Emmett looked at Ralphie as if he could bash him at the moment.

"You hurt?"

"No," Emmett sneered, watching Ralphie. The pair had been through the ringer. They were both bruised and beaten after seven days in the challenge.

"You get an oowie?"

Ralphie blinked at the second person to use that word to describe someone being hurt. He scoffed at the word and the question.

The two boys stared at each other. Neither sat. Ralphie gripped and twisted his croquet mallet. Emmett Carson was twirling his short sword.

"This is all bad for you, Miller."

"I have a name," Ralphie pointed out, lifting his croquet mallet off his shoulder.

"Yeah, suppose you do, but it don't matter anymore," Emmett smiled mischievously an evil perfect smile. He had his short sword in his hand and looked pretty confident with the blade. Emmett was maybe ten feet away from Ralphie.

"We'll see about that," Ralphie quipped, watching the short sword.

The First Gen bully stepped forward and began to run toward Ralphie. Ralphie automatically backed up and prepared for the sword attack as Emmett feigned to run to the left only to stop and attack primarily on the right. The attack was quick and almost fatal except that Ralphie was no slouch at fighting. He fended off Emmett's initial attacks, but they drove the smaller Ralphie from the structure. They appeared on the exterior of the building glaring at each other.

Emmett attacked again and Ralphie deftly fended off all efforts to impale, filet or decapitate him. Emmett started an attack only to stop. They had come to a standstill.

The bigger Carson sidestepped to the structure where Bailey and Campbell had been and backed into the shadowy interior only to pop out and jump back into the shadows again. Ralphie watched as Emmett toyed with him. Ralphie impatient, dove into the shadowy interior and slammed hard into a rotting beam and bounced off of the I-beam as flecks of wood danced in the air. On the ground and slightly stunned Ralphie jumped back to his feet before Emmett could attack. His right shoulder stung with the pain of the beam's impact. Ralphie closed his eyes to the pain, for an instant, and it was just long enough for Emmett to slash his cheek with the short sword, in an attempt to decapitate him.

Ralphie spun out of the arc of the short sword as Emmett Carson pressed his attack. Ralphie created distance with his croquet mallet, making the First Gen bully stop and hesitate for a second. In that second, Ralphie recovered.

The First Gen pushed against Ralphie and his croquet mallet and with a twist of his wrist Emmett was standing few feet back from Ralphie, reassessing his attack. Emmett narrowed his dark eyes, studying the croquet mallet. He stared at the nicked and chipped mallet and shaft curiously. He had chopped and attempted to break the mallet to no avail.

"How?"

"You got tricks, I got mine," Ralphie smiled mischievously. Ralphie took a step back and raised the croquet mallet over his right shoulder, evilly. "I been all over this island." He slid his left foot forward and brought the mallet level with his hip. "I did a little improvement on the original design. Added some metal inside the shaft a few nights ago when I was in one of those metal structures. The mallet's head I replaced, two days ago."

The First Gen bully did not respond. He did not know what to say.

Ralphie smiled broadly at being able to silence the cocky and talkative Emmett Carson.

"Okay, that's surprising," Emmett admitted, recovering from the shock of Ralphie's reveal. "But you got tricks. Don't be surprised when you are lying dead on the floor."

Ralphie seemed perturbed at Emmett's logic. He opened his mouth to correct him only to nod, watching as Emmett lifted his short sword even with his left shoulder. Ralphie studied Emmett. The bigger boy seemed like a tank. Gigantic. Invulnerable. Deadly.

Emmett attacked. His attack, after Ralphie's reveal of his alteration of his croquet mallet, started with an overhead chop with the short sword. The First Gen was strong. Ralphie imagined that Emmett Carson was used to physically overwhelming his opponents but against Ralphie he found the overhead attacks were futile. He was fast but not as fast as Ralphie. Ralphie did not wilt. Instead, Ralphie parried the attacks expertly.

Ralphie did not speak. He tried to control his breathing. He knew that the fight was not going to be won in these first few moments, no matter what Emmett Carson imagined.

The Miller challenger stood there unmoving, uncut and prepared for war. Ralphie studied Emmett with cool brown eyes. He tried not to give away any emotion or thoughts.

"Damn, wrench boy," Emmett sneered.

The fifteen-year-old Miller listened to Emmett Carson's breathing. The first attack, outside of the structure, had been intense and Ralphie expected it. He knew people like Emmett. Emmett expected to break Ralphie down in the first attack if not finish him off, injure him, and pick him apart.

Ralphie was prepared and ready for Emmett. Ralphie did not panic. He seemed to be prepared for the spinning short sword attack more than the first assault.

Emmett moved fluidly from the roundhouse attack and finding no entry tried to look for another opening. Ralphie parried Emmett's attacks as if they were more routine than a series of spontaneous attacks.

The First Gen paused, in between his fury of attacks, and for the first time Ralphie could hear the bigger boy breathing a little heavier than before. Ralphie could not help but smile.

"What you smiling at," Emmett snarled.

For a long moment the two measured one another. Ralphie watched and listened. He knew that Emmett could not attack even if he wanted to and that encouraged Ralphie.

Emmett recovered and was the first to move and pull another short sword from behind his back. Ralphie, in response, allowed the croquet mallet to easily descend to his right side. Emmett attacked, but even slower than before, and used the blades like drumsticks to beat against the parrying croquet mallet.

Ralphie parried the attacks and cut his eyes to the First Gen's breathing as Emmett redoubled his efforts as if this was the pivotal moment. Ralphie fought his fears as Emmett Carson's attacks shook him to his core. The attack was fierce and furious. All the while Ralphie tried to watch the attacks of Emmett.

During the attack, Ralphie took a few steps back and watched as Emmett paused and then stepped forward, emboldened. As had been the case, throughout the challenge, Ralphie learned that feigning retreat usually led to an opening that was usually not visible face-to-face. Emmett, encouraged by a simple step back by Ralphie; rushed forward in an attempt to make a final attack.

Emmett moved forward and tried to remove Ralphie's head from his shoulders. Ralphie parried the attack and then and there and for the first-time attacked Emmett Carson. The croquet mallet swung around and hit Emmett Carson squarely on the kneecap.

The First Gen cartwheeled past Ralphie as his kneecap gave way. The First Gen right grabbed at his knee as he fell hard in the interior of the building, groaning in excruciating pain. It was the same building that Ralphie had slept in earlier.

Ralphie moved forward and noticed that the two short swords, Emmett had one second go, were sticking out of the ground on either side of the fifteen-year-old Miller. Emmett Carson moaned and grimaced as Ralphie, cut and leaking, stepped to the fallen First Gen. Ralphie smirked at the short swords not hitting him. It was a close call.

"I think you broke my knee," Emmett howled, holding his knee as if holding it would make it better.

"You can't break your knee, rat kisser," Ralphie corrected, frustrated with Emmett Carson. "I could break your kneecap. I can't break your knee."

"What? What?" The injured First Gen scowled. He looked at Ralphie like a wounded tiger. If he could get close, Ralphie knew Emmett might still be dangerous. "If you hadn't cheated, bolt tightener, I would have cut you in two," Emmett managed, tears streaking his cheeks suddenly as he complained, unable to do anything but hold his injured knee.

Ralphie shook his head at Emmett's words. He watched Emmett balled up in a fetal position and for the first time in the challenge giggled. Ralphie his mallet and paused.

He stared at the broken First Gen. The bastard. The rude boy. The monster. Yet, Ralphie hesitated.

"You cheated," the crippled teen moaned.

Ralphie looked at Emmett Carson incredulously. He chuckled.

"What you laughing at? You … Miller cheat," Emmett Carson groaned and rolled over unable to climb to his feet. Ralphie stepped off Emmett and considered leaving. He was just out of arm's reach. He tried to consider what he should do. Emmett had been a constant pain in Ralphie's ass.

Ralphie turned and began to limp away from the suddenly meaningless Emmett Carson.

"You running? You dirt under the nail coward? I didn't think you were yellow, Miller," Emmett teased, tears in his eyes.

Ralphie retrieved his backpack and limped toward the exit.

"You're an embarrassment to your line, you know? Your line is pretty much an embarrassment to the Remains," Emmett bleated sitting up, still holding his knee. He tried to climb to his feet, but his right leg collapsed under the weight of the effort.

"Sonuvabiscuit," the First Gen bully hissed.

Ralphie snorted at Emmett's inability to climb to his feet. He could not help but smile as he looked at the once intimidating and deadly Emmett Carson now as dangerous as a baby bird with a broken wing.

"Don't laugh at me, wrench turner. The First Gen line advanced robotics. We modernized the Remains." Emmett Carson gritted his teeth. "What have you or your line contributed to the Remains? Nothing. Sweat? Blood? Hell, every line has contributed that. The Millers are a joke."

Ralphie continued to the exit and turned. He fished inside his backpack and spun and aimed his bright orange flare gun at Emmett. Emmett froze for an instant. He studied the flare gun. He sneered. He chortled.

"What's that? A cartoon gun? For a cartoon boy?" Emmett sniggered from the ground where he sat.

Ralphie aimed the flare gun at Emmett and then redirected the barrel at the last moment. He fired the flare gun over Emmett's head. Emmett winced, naturally, and turned and watched as the flare went into a corner over his left shoulder.

"You missed Miller," Emmett crowed with a condescending smirk on his face.

Ralphie ducked down and waited.

Chapter Twenty.

End of Pandemonium Challenge?

The concussive blasts surprised Ralphie. He had expected an explosion. The handful of Molotov cocktails he had planted created a ball of fire that tore through the makeshift offices of a business long ago. The fireball tore through the two-story structure in a surprisingly intense fashion.

The heat and explosion formed a perfect exhaust chute for the fire to blow Ralphie out the structure he had slept in the night before. The fireball kicked Ralphie like an angry mule and in the blink of an eye he came tumbling out and into the weed and dirt patch between the building and the street.

Ralphie imagined a blast that would set part of the building on fire. He felt the heat wash over him as the first Molotov ignited and the flash of the first ignited the second and then the third Molotov cocktail. He had thought of the number of cocktails he had planted and could not recall the exact number. It could not have been more than half a dozen, Ralphie imagined.

Outside, Ralphie rolled over and checked to see if he were on fire. The intensity of the fire and heat made him do a double take. Already two robotic fire extinguisher systems were putting out the fire, Ralphie noticed. The systems, four micro robots, stationed in the roof of the structure, Ralphie noted, were all over the island, to ensure that no fire caused significant damage to the islands crumbling structures.

Thankfully, Ralphie mused, flipping over and pressing himself up and off the ground, he had avoided being burned alive. He climbed to his feet and laughed silently at the fact that he had not died at the hands of Emmett Carson, the First Gen bully. He looked around and noticed that his croquet mallet was missing. Had he left it in the structure? Ralphie twisted his lips on his dark chocolate face, thinking. He turned around and to his surprise there, unexpectedly, stood Bailey with his croquet mallet in her tiny brown hands.

"Ralphie, what did you do," Bailey yowled. "What did you do?"

Ralphie opened his mouth to reply and suddenly did not know how to answer the girl with braided buns standing in front of him, holding his croquet mallet. She was holding the croquet in both of her hands.

"You didn't have to," Bailey almost cried, only to trail off.

Ralphie rolled his dark eyes. He had no words for the First Gen girl he had practically grown up with. All he knew was just seconds ago he had avoided dying. He had survived a fireball. He had avoided dying, for a few moments.

"Didn't have to? You expected me to be gutted?"

Bailey did not respond.

"You thought that First Gen boy would be standing here?" Ralphie was suddenly annoyed.

"No," Bailey stumbled. "I just didn't think that--"

"I would survive?" Ralphie looked at Bailey accusingly.

Bailey shook her head.

He studied Bailey for a long moment silently. He looked back at the structure where he and Emmett Carson had battled. Ralphie pinched his brows, for a moment, and again opened his mouth only to silently limped past Bailey.

Ralphie reached out and grabbed at his challenge weapon that the First Gen had and Bailey, for a moment, resisted. Ralphie was a little surprised at Bailey's reaction.

"What," Ralphie asked.

Bailey shook her head, disappointed.

"You wanted me unarmed? Defenseless?"

Bailey shook her head no, in response.

A moment later Ralphie was holding the croquet mallet in his right hand, still an arm's length from Bailey.

"We could've ...," Bailey began and faltered.

Ralphie looked at Bailey out of the corner of his eye. Maybe it was because he had nearly died. Maybe it was because every part of his body hurt from his run in with Emmett. Ralphie was not sure but at that moment he found himself becoming angry at Bailey.

"This ... is not like that. This ... is life and death. It's your life. It's my life. It's my death. It's your death." Ralphie said, not wanting to fight with the prettiest girl in the Remains. He appeared flummoxed, frustrated. "This is *the* challenge, and everyone is against everyone. There are no ties. There are no do overs. We all have hard decisions to make. We don't get to ... stop and cry or say: "Things ain't fair." Things ain't fair. We don't get to wait until things get better or just leave. This is the last day and we got less than 24 hours to win or lose. There is no over time. It's you and me and," he paused. Ralphie was suddenly physically and mentally tired. He pointed in the direction of the building where everyone had been earlier. "Now, it's just you and me and that fool-born psycho in the other structure. In a minute, it's going to be just you and me. That's *the* challenge," Ralphie pointed out.

Bailey looked at Ralphie with an odd expression on her face and for the first time Ralphie paused.

"What? This news to you?" He paused. Ralphie studied Bailey out of the corner of his eye. He did not stop his stride. "What were you thinking? You and Emmett would finish hand-in-hand?" Ralphie studied the girl beside him, cautiously.

Fifteen-year-old Bailey walked silently alongside of Ralphie. She was within arm's reach. For the first time that day, Ralphie noticed how much smaller Bailey Beaumont was compared to him. She could not be five foot tall.

Bailey slowed just a little and his slowing was almost unnoticeable, but Ralphie was hyper vigilant, though tired. He tried to buoy his spirits by breathing deeper and deeper to regain some of his depleted oxygen from the fight and the fire.

As he walked Ralphie felt the uncomfortable dizziness of standing too quickly trying to wax or abate. All the while, Bailey seemed to sulk. She seemed lost in her own thoughts.

"You are blind, Ralphie," Bailey Beaumont concluded.

Ralphie thought of a million things to say but said nothing. He did not always give into defending himself against all attacks. Yet, he was aware and sensitive to Bailey's mood change. He walked on, thinking.

"You and Emmett were planning a double cross," Ralphie asked, knowing that teaming up was not out of the question in the challenge. He slit his eyes at Bailey questioningly. "Is that why you didn't bash her earlier?"

Bailey smiled mirthlessly at the question. "You say the stupidest things," she breathed. "She tried to bash me earlier. I don't know how that works out to a double cross." Bailey paused and twisted her lips on her nearly lineless face. She unexpectedly grinned. "Why would I need to team up? Think I need to be with someone to win? I could take you by myself," the petite First Gen announced and reached behind her back and pulled out a pair of num-chuks. The two pieces of wood attached by a length of chain were suddenly in the girl's hand. Bailey slowly spun the num-chuks at her right side, like an expert.

Ralphie smiled and then smirked at Bailey and her confidence with the num-chuks. If it had been anyone else, he might have thought they might crush his skull in. Yet, as the First Gen beauty twirled the num-chuks Ralphie did not alter his step or feel in danger.

"Come on," Ralphie insisted, suddenly smiling despite his fatigue. "You ain't going to cave in my bean," Ralphie stated. "If you were that would have happened when you learned that I blew up Emmett."

Bailey Beaumont puckered her lips, as if she was about to spit but said nothing.

"Maybe, I got this all backwards," the Miller challenger said. "We are in the challenge. We are the last ones. So, we get to decide on how this ends."

Bailey circled Ralphie. Ralphie watched the First Gen with the num-chuks and as she half-heartedly attacked, he deftly swung the croquet mallet and twisted the shaft with just enough force to wrench the num-chuks out of Bailey's hands. Ralphie pulled down hard and disarmed the dangerous girl. He swept the num-chuks back toward the burning building. Bailey paused and for an instant seemed to hesitate.

"You thinking of going to get 'em?" Ralphie said looking back in the direction of the num-chuks. He shook his head. "How you make me something like this and then want to bash my brains in?" Ralphie asked raising his wrist toward Bailey and showing her the handmade bracelet she had made him.

Bailey Beaumont lowered her eyes. She seemed cowed. The First Gen did not respond.

"I don't get it," Ralphie breathed. Ralphie stopped in the weed patch between the two structures. He turned on Bailey and tried to muster up enough anger to hurt the only girl he knew for more than half his life. Ralphie squinted and screwed up his face for a moment, only to shake the idea from his head.

Bailey considered Ralphie. She smiled despite Ralphie's anger and frustration. The First Gen girl dressed in a hoody, jeans and combat boots still was close and in arm's reach.

"Why do you have that?"

"I don't know, I sort of like it."

Ralphie looked at Bailey wordlessly. He examined her and spoke after a minute. "You and me," Ralphie began. "You and me, we have to fight. That's our only choice. There's no Emmett. There won't be Campbell to get in the way. If you want this to end now, then we can." Ralphie took a breath. "I don't." Ralphie inhaled. "I wouldn't have minded going mano-y-mano with anyone else," he trailed off.

Bailey smiled mischievously and effortlessly reached behind her back again and pulled out a three-pronged weapon that Ralphie had seen in Kung Fu movies on videos.

"Bailey, I don't want us to end, this way," Ralphie admitted looking at the Kung Fu weapon and pointing to her and back to himself.

"What chose we got," Bailey asked.

Ralphie turned on Bailey and looked at her for a long moment. Bailey hesitated. She seemed surprised. Bailey tightened her grip on the strange weapon in her hand.

"You know that this is the challenge too," Ralphie gestured to Bailey and back to himself. "Yesterday, Emmett told me that he hated me because you liked me. Now, you are acting like you want to shish kabob me. If you want to gut me, I suppose that's going to happen." He paused, he seemed drained.

"I just want to hold onto the idea that you like me for a few more hours before things go oblong."

"I don't like you," Bailey protested. She, the girl he liked, changed in front of him. She had been so determined and resigned, an instant ago, Ralphie thought. She now seemed embarrassed or shocked or something else.

"Yeah, I know you don't like me, and I don't like you and we don't have feelings for each other." He shook his head, feeling incredibly exasperated. This girl, Bailey Beaumont, suddenly had the capacity to frustrate and anger Ralphie just as easily as her smile made him courageous. Was this affection? Was this something more. Ralphie shook those thoughts from his mind, for the moment. "If we had tons of time that would be okay. We could figure it out. You could pretend. I could pretend. But we don't have tons of time. We just got now. In a moment, you are going to try and flatline me. I might have to bash in the brains of the only girl I knew, and I have ever had feelings for," Ralphie paused. "It's a tough day."

Bailey smiled at Ralphie's words.

"Remember, we decided to give each other a pass, even though you just tried to Hong Kong Phooey me with those num-chuks."

"I wasn't serious," Bailey admitted.

Ralphie smirked. He wanted to laugh. Bailey had the ability to make him smile in the darkest moments.

"I'm serious," Bailey said, with her weapon in her hand.

Ralphie shook his head. "If you don't gut me, we going to figure it out, when this is over?" He paused. "If, being the operative word."

Bailey nodded and smiled again.

"If it has to be between you and me, then so be it. Right now, though, let's hold off on flatlining each other 'til we handle Campbell." Ralphie again paused. He ached all over. He had just fought Emmett Carson and nearly been blown up. He continued. "Let me hold onto the moment of you liking me, and you knowing that I like you, even if you don't like me like I like you and you knowing that I like you like this." Ralphie paused, thinking. "We can figure out who likes who or doesn't like who after we deal with one more nutcase and let the chips fall where they may."

Bailey pouted. She looked disappointed. Ralphie smirked. They were suddenly at the edge of the structure and searching for an entrance.

"If you want to dead me, then dead me." Ralphie did not expect Bailey to take him up on his offer. He thought he knew the Frist Gen pretty well. He added, "I'm going to untie Campbell and give her one last chance. That... seems...sporting."

"Sporting? What is sporting about the challenge," Bailey queried.

"Okay, it might not be sporting. I meant compassionate. I don't know. I'm just doing what everyone does in the challenge; trying to win."

"You confusing," Bailey admitted.

"I don't know about that. We don't have to let the challenge beat us, here." Ralphie pointed to his temple painfully. "We fight. We fight to win. We fight to be the champion," Ralphie blurted remembering Robert Nesta's mural. "We don't decide. The only real choices we have are in the game. We all deserve a chance. You had the chance to gut her. You didn't. Now, it's my chance to give her a chance. My choice. The challenge ain't easy. It ain't supposed to be." Ralphie heard the words that he was saying and suddenly he felt like his father was talking instead of him.

Bailey still had her Sai in hand. Ralphie looked at Bailey and turned to enter the structure.

"Bailey," Ralphie stopped and looked at the small girl with the spray of freckles across the bridge of her nose and round cheeks and smiled despite all that had happened. Bailey was beautiful and for a moment Ralphie thought that all he wanted was to be with her forever. She looked at Ralphie with those big fawn eyes.

"I'm a Miller. In the compound that I come from, I'm not better than anyone, not in the world I live in. The biggest difference in the compound is that I'm in the challenge." Ralphie shook his head. "Every Miller that goes to the challenge is expected to work hard and try and win. That is just GP."

Bailey stopped next to the Miller challenger who was bruised and broken. Ralphie looked and Bailey was beside him. He smiled at her closeness. He was not afraid, even though he knew that she had a weapon that could dead him. He hesitated.

"You're wrong."

"You are the second person to tell me that I was wrong," Ralphie asserted, annoyed.

"Well, you are--"

"Wrong about what?"

"There's more," Bailey contested.

"What more is there?"

Bailey and Ralphie stopped a little less than a foot apart. Ralphie reached out and Bailey did not recoil. Ralphie took a deep breath.

"What do you want?"

Ralphie shrugged his shoulders in answer. Bailey looked at Ralphie with those endless delicate and big doe eyes. His head began to swim. He was suddenly falling.

"I suppose I want to just enjoy a couple of minutes with you before we try and gut each other?"

"Before we gut each other." The girl took two steps forward and Ralphie stepped forward as well and they were hugging. Ralphie breathed Bailey in. He held his mallet in his right hand and then let it fall behind Bailey soundlessly. Her hair played against Ralphie's cheek and chin.

In that embrace Ralphie smelled the honey suckle smell of Bailey's curly red and brown hair that was in two braided buns. Her skin, her neck, smelled like warm cocoa butter and fresh baked bread. Ralphie held onto Bailey as if she were life itself. It was as if Ralphie was re-energized in the embrace of the First Gen beauty.

The embrace, which seemed to last forever, ended and the electric moment between Bailey and Ralphie lingered. Ralphie leaned in and gave Bailey a kiss. Their lips touched and Ralphie held the First Gen beauty in his aching arms and did not want to let go. Bailey melted, giving Ralphie an embrace. For Ralphie the kiss lasted for a very long time.

The two separated. Bailey was studying Ralphie with a smile. Ralphie did not know what to do with himself. Bailey smiled. Ralphie smiled, awkwardly, not knowing what to do with his hands and feet.

"We better go and deal with Campbell," Bailey smiled awkwardly, as Ralphie made eyes at her.

"Yeah. Yeah," Ralphie admitted, suddenly focused. Ralphie looked around and saw his croquet mallet and retrieved it.

Bailey moved with Ralphie toward the structure. Ralphie smiled awkwardly trying to watch Bailey out of the corner of his eye as he walked.

"You can look at me," Bailey quipped.

"I am looking at you."

"Things don't have to be weird." Bailey snickered. She was all of a sudden playful.

"You like weird," Ralphie joked.

Bailey smiled.

"Do you believe all the stuff you said earlier?"

Ralphie shrugged. "Yeah, I suppose."

They were weaving through the interior of the structure. Ralphie noticed that he was shivering. He felt cold for some unknown reason. He touched the back of his head and felt a sore spot near his ear. It was sore to the touch. Bailey was talking but Ralphie had missed something.

Bailey smiled.

Before Bailey could speak Campbell Henderson crowed.

"What? The love triangle broke? The doofus is done," Campbell cooed twisting on the ground. Campbell smiled broadly. "You shut 'em down? You ended that fool. I didn't like how he acted when Black Barbie and him were talking. He wanted to cheese me and not give me a chance. I could tell."

"Campbell, can you shut up," Bailey shouted.

Ralphie was cut and leaking and suddenly struggling to stand.

"What time is it?"

"I didn't hear the fifth announcement. So, it can't be past 1500 hours," Campbell Henderson taunted, trying to get to her feet. "We still have time to cheese each other. All I need is for one of you to untie me. Just want a fair fight. I ain't asking for anything more than that. I don't even need a weapon."

"Ralphie, think about this," Bailey pleaded.

"What? Is she going soft?"

Ralphie cut his dark eyes toward Campbell.

"We in the ninth inning, baby girl, we have to finish this, win or lose."

"Campbell," Ralphie suggested, blinking and trying to focus.

"Your boy got cockroached trying to be all Billy Bad Ass and whatnot. Now, it's just us three. Come on, untie me. Give me a fighting chance. That's all I'm asking."

"Campbell, can you just take it down a notch, for a second," Ralphie advised, feeling the dimness of the space slowly spinning as Campbell spoke.

"What? Keep your eye on the prize, Miller. Your line nearly won a couple of years ago." Campbell paused. She craned her neck for a better vantage. "You okay? You ain't looking too good."

"We got plenty of time here."

"We got just enough time to figure out things," Campbell smiled. "Untie me. Give me a fighting chance."

Ralphie looked at Bailey and then to Campbell.

"I think—"

Bailey and Campbell listened as Ralphie was not one to say much.

"Man, we have to take our lives in our own hands. This is not a sit on the side lines kind of thing. We have to take action," Campbell continued.

"Ralphie, we still have time."

"Look, you two can fight about how much time is left all you want," Campbell Henderson advised. "Just untie me."

Ralphie turned from Bailey to Campbell and suddenly felt the floor shift under his feet. He reached out and found the solidness of one of the splintered beams of the structures.

"Your boy don't look too good, Barbie," Campbell pointed out. "What were you two doing?"

Ralphie rested against the beam in the structure. He leaned on the beam and tried to examine it through blurry eyes. He held onto his right shoulder and suddenly felt that he could not stay on his feet. He took a deep breath and dug deep to speak.

"I think that we don't have—."

His words were swallowed by the sound of the cracking of the wood beam Ralphie was leaning against. The beam he rested against gave way and the one beam tapped three other beams that dramatically endangered the structural integrity of the entire structure.

Ralphie fell back and toward the ground as the roof came hurtling toward him. He was slammed to the floor by the beam that came crashing down and only had enough time to see Bailey lose her footing and slip into a cloud of dust and debris.

In that terrifying moment Ralphie looked from Bailey to the left to see the ever-smiling Campbell Henderson be swallowed by the gaping maw that yawned in the floor that suddenly gave way and opened to the Acid Bay. The building fell inward. Half of the building was gone, then and there.

The dust cloud rose one hundred feet into the air. It took nearly ten minutes for the dust to settle and for Ralphie to find that though he was in the midst of the collapse there were islands of structure that remained attached to Pandemonium island. It was an island tic-tac-toe game where the marked spaces remained, and the unmarked spaces had fallen into the Acid Bay.

Ralphie somehow held onto a network of pipes that were exposed in the collapse. He painfully climbed out of the dust and debris and sinkhole. Reaching the part of the island that had not fallen into the Acid Bay he breathed a sigh of relief and exhausted found himself on his back breathing and looking up at the slate gray sky. He only rested long enough to check that he was not impaled by anything from the wreckage of the building.

He slowly climbed to his feet and instantly felt a jagged pain in his left side. He grimaced. Ralphie bent over bruised and cut in half a dozen places and studied the building that had only recently fallen down around him. He was having a difficult time just inhaling. Every time he inhaled his left side felt as if it were going to ignite and burst into flame.

The battered survivor crawled out covered in dust and tried to determine the extent of his injuries. His left arm was numb. He could not for all his strength lift it. He noticed that he was covered in the silt of the imploded building. He had to look a sight. Ralphie shook that thought from his mind. He felt and saw that he had his backpack still. His croquet mallet was gone. The samurai sword that had been on his back was gone as well.

In moments, mere seconds, he had lost everything. He had leaned against a beam and everything had gone black. Ralphie thinned his dark eyes. Where was Bailey? Where was the First Gen? She was close to him.

She might have escaped, he figured. He looked around him, hoping that Bailey would be standing with her hand on her hip, a smirk on her face and brighter than the sun. After a quick scan Ralphie did not see Bailey.

Was he supposed to look for her? No one is responsible for anyone in the challenge, he recalled Jax saying. This is the challenge. No one can be responsible for anyone, especially in the challenge. Yet, Ralphie hesitated. He longed to find and be with Bailey. Despite the pain and hurt Ralphie stumbled through the wreckage.

He was scanning the debris of the building and finding nothing but broken pipes, glass, and wood. Here and there the odd piece of steel stood. A card table remained miraculously untouched. There was a stairway and steps rising from the debris toward a non-existent second story, standing in the midst of the ruins.

The Miller challenger that had survived to the last day tried to recover just long enough to regain his strength. He had seen Campbell Henderson disappear in the sinkhole and Acid Bay below. Yet, he was not sure of the fate of Bailey Beaumont. He leaned against a pile of rubble and thought that the easiest thing for him to do would be to crawl away and win the challenge. Something nagged at him.

While he tried to figure out the nagging feeling, he was revived when he thought that he heard a voice, only to find that the sound was the settling of the wreckage upon itself. He searched the wreckage for thirty minutes and told himself that if he didn't find Bailey she was never going to be found. He moved rocks and pipes and rubble.

"Bailey," Ralphie called his voice raw and dry. He found the hydration tube of his backpack and sipped at the water bladder.

At his deadline he gave his search another ten minutes and then another ten minutes.

"Bailey," Ralphie called and straight away his right side felt as if he had been stabbed by a truck. He closed his eyes to the pain. Ralphie had to stop. He had to regain his strength that was suddenly drained from him with the simple effort of trying to scream. He took a Deep breath and then another one. He fought through the pain of inhaling and exhaling.

He whimpered despite his personal belief that he was impervious to pain. He cried and wiped the tears from his eyes as the pain subsided, just a little. He prayed for strength.

At some point, after the building collapsed, Ralphie spotted Bailey's finger. Seeing her finger electrified Ralphie. It invigorated him. He scrambled to her finger and slowly, methodically began the process of digging Bailey out from the rubble.

Time became measured brick by brick and piece of rubble by piece of rubble. Small, medium and large wires, rocks and blocks of concrete around Bailey's buried form was all that Ralphie focused on. Everything before that discovery fell away and Ralphie only saw what a building had been and its interior and the debris and rubble that separated him from retrieving Bailey.

Ralphie carefully and painstakingly dug with his cut hands until he was able to free Bailey's hand then arm then shoulder from the rubble over her. Finally, after he thought he would never be able to free Bailey from the wreckage he was able to lift the small girl up, just a little.

After what seemed an eternity Ralphie was able to pull the broken and unconscious body of Bailey Beaumont from the rubble of the building that had nearly crushed the life out of the First Gen. He put a hand close to her nose and tried to determine if the girl was breathing. Ralphie had to bend down and look and listen to the slight rise and fall of the girl's chest and faint breathing to reassure himself that Bailey was breathing.

He was drained emotionally and physically. Yet, he kept his focus and wiped the dirt and dust from her face and moved her as gently as possible, with one arm, from the pile of rubble that had been the structure that the last day of the challenge had come to a head.

In all that time Bailey never spoke. She was cut and leaking and thankfully unconscious. Ralphie was no doctor but her injuries looked bad. He needed to get her medical assistance. He needed to help Bailey.

He sat and rested hoping that Bailey would live. The sun was setting as Ralphie thought of a million things that he wanted to do, but all of them ended with him staying by Bailey's side and caring for the unconscious First Gen.

Sometime in between the rescue and his falling in and out of consciousness, from exhaustion, he heard the sound of boots on the rocks near him. He was fully alert and trying to ascertain what was going on around him. The sun was low on the horizon and reddening the rooftops of the lower buildings on the island when Ralphie peered into the slightly dim day that was turning to night.

Ralphie tensed.

"We have survivors," a deep bass voice sounded.

Ralphie looked in the direction of the voice and saw a red beam. That beam doubled and doubled again. Suddenly, there were six beams aimed toward Ralphie.

Six enforcers appeared. They all were dressed in their paramilitary black matte uniforms, helmets, face guards, gloves and combat boots. Behind them strode a thin framed enforcer dressed all in black but without a helmet. He wore a beret.

"Sit rep," barked the enforcer wearing the beret. He had a mustache and goatee. His hair was short cropped against his long face.

"Looks like we have two here, sir. We are not getting any other heat signatures," announced the enforcer holding an assault rifle and on the side of the rifle sat a square device that looked to be about four inches wide.

The five others had fanned out and created a perimeter around the wreckage. They seemed very organized and trained. The men, Ralphie noticed, did not appear to be the enforcers that he was used to seeing in the Remains. They had no numbers over their hearts like the numbers did everywhere that Ralphie had been in the Remains. There was a nameplate but instead of a name was what looked like a QR code.

"Who are you guys?"

The enforcer closest to Ralphie bent down and placed a gloved hand on Ralphie's shoulder. Ralphie did not struggle against the enforcer knowing that was futile.

"Relax, we're the good guys. We're taking you off this crazy rock," the enforcer reported, and the words suddenly created more questions than answers for Ralphie. Ralphie looked at the nameplate over the enforcers heart and there were old calculator numbers there.

"Are there any others?"

Ralphie opened and closed his mouth, wordlessly, his voice seemed to fail him.

"Need a medic," 7734 called back to the group, and one of the group members detached from securing the perimeter and moved toward Ralphie and Bailey. The enforcer that stepped up was shorter than 7734 but thicker around the neck. He flipped up his face guard and Ralphie noticed that the enforcer had a wicked scar that cut diagonally across his right cheek.

"This here's Allen," 7734 announced from behind his face guard. "He'll take good care of you." He patted Ralphie on the shoulder and stood up. Ralphie was suddenly face-to-face with Allen, the enforcer.

Allen nodded and leaned in. He had stubble on his cocoa–colored cheeks and looked to be old. There were wrinkles in the corners of his light brown eyes.

"Okay, you look like you dislocated that shoulder there, junior," Allen diagnosed. "You will be all right." Allen took Ralphie's free hand and placed it under his elbow. "Hold that right there while I check on your friend."

The enforcer wearing a beret stepped forward.

7734 stood at attention.

"Is there any others?"

"Kid says that it's just him and the girl. We did a cursory scan already, sir, should we do another sweep?"

Ralphie widened his eyes, trying to understand the question. Another sweep? As Ralphie was trying to understand the idea there was movement from the edge of the enforcers.

Behind the seven enforcers, came four more enforcers holding assault rifles. In the midst of the four enforcers walked Ella Buchanan, the Shaker who had been in the Pandemonium Challenge for two days before being extricated. She was dressed in a blue leather motorcycle jacket, yellow T-shirt, jeans and yellow combat boots. She looked like she should have been doing a photo shoot for toothpaste or burpers and poison pills.

The enforcer closest to Ella, 1134 watched Ralphie like a man watches a rabid dog. He was not wearing a helmet either. As far as Ralphie could tell only two of the eleven enforcers were without helmet.

"What the froth--," Ralphie finally was able to say.

"Hey, you're Ralphie, right?" Ella Buchanan smiled one of those perfect white smiles of the rich and powerful. The enforcer closest to her never took his eyes off Ralphie, his hand on his sidearm.

Ella Buchanan was this cocoa beauty with a wide smile and big eyes. She was pretty and smart and rich, Ralphie nodded. Ella looked at Ralphie and Bailey and turned to the enforcer who still had his hand on his sidearm.

"Thomas, is this it?"

Thomas, the enforcer nodded.

Ella pouted. She took a moment and looked around her and then pushed past Ralphie to Allen and Bailey. She looked back to the enforcers and signaled to two of them. A pair of enforcers moved past Ralphie. The two other enforcers waited near Ralphie.

"How is she?"

"She's breathing but needs some medical attention, quick, fast and in a hurry."

"Well, that's why we're here. Get them to the copter. We need to get off this island as soon as possible."

"Roger that."

Ella Buchanan smelled like roses, Ralphie thought absently as he watched the enforcers lift Bailey and place her on a stretcher and walk her away. He was lifted as well and put on a stretcher as well. Two enforcers carried him away from the ruins of the structure.

Allen, the enforcer medic, followed along close to Bailey. The first enforcer that had talked to Ralphie was near. The enforcers moved quickly from the destruction of the building and through the deserted streets. Ella Buchanan appeared by Ralphie's side.

"What--"

"It's okay, Builder," Ella Buchanan advised as the convoy of armed men and women walked toward a three-story structure just a few hundred yards from the ruins that Ralphie had been digging in for hours. Ella showing off her perfect white teeth placed a small hand on Ralphie's hand. "It's over. I came back to make sure that not everyone had to die."

"But--," Ralphie attempted.

"The Remains doesn't want you to die. At least, not this way. At least, not today," Ella Fitzgerald Buchanan confided. The convoy climbed up a flight of stairs. They climbed up three flights of stairs and were suddenly on the rooftop of one of the buildings on the island.

On the roof sat a bright yellow helicopter waiting, its rotors spinning and washing the roof in the slight breeze of the slow turning blades. The lead enforcer waved the enforcers and Ella Buchanan toward the waiting stealth helicopter.

Ralphie could see Cosson Hall to the right. The sky bridge would be to the north, Ralphie calculated. The robo-spiders would begin hiding and recharging, Ralphie thought absently.

"Welcome aboard. We are the first three to leave the island alive," Ella Buchanan announced. "I wanted to save more but I could only negotiate the final four."

Assisted by the enforcers Ralphie cut and bruised and leaking was lifted into the interior of the stealth helicopter.

"We are ready," announced Thomas, the enforcer. Ella Buchanan nodded. She sat next to the gruff Thomas.

"Vamoose, muchacho," Thomas announced and tapped the helicopter pilot and the pilot nodded.

The doctor was seated next to Bailey. She was still unconscious but breathing. Allen was assisting. He had taken off his helmet and gloves.

Ralphie looked around the helicopter and the effort tired him. Somehow, at some time someone had put a splint on his arm and a sling. 7734, the enforcer that had been the first to Ralphie at the rubble pile was seated near the fifteen-year-old boy. He and everyone in the helicopter had their helmets off. There were some hardened men and women.

"Is she okay?"

"I think she's seen better days. But I think for now, she's fine. We gave her a sedative. She needs to rest. We'll check her when we land," 7734 stated and for the first time Ralphie noticed that 7734 had a square chin and three cuts across his forehead.

The helicopter rose into the air in a slow and methodic whoosh of air. The engines were dampened. There was no real sound as the helicopter took to the air and after one hundred feet banked eastward and back toward the Remains.

"You said you negotiated for the final four," Ralphie breathed.

"Yes, I couldn't get permission to leave until there were four challengers remaining. By the time we got here there were only two of you left."

Ralphie nodded.

"It took me going to the challenge to convince my father that I was serious," Ella Buchanan explained to Ralphie.

"Serious, about what?"

"Stopping the challenge."

Ralphie looked confused.

"The challenge isn't fair, Ralphie," Ella stated surrounded by enforcers.

"Wait. I thought the enforcers were a part of the challenge?"

"These are the Innovators enforcers. They protect the Innovators. They are our own private little army."

"What?"

"They protect the Innovators. My father sent them to get you and Bailey."

"How?"

"Sometimes it's who you know. Sometimes it's what you know. Sometimes it's a little of both," Ella Buchanan jested.

"I don't under--."

"There is nothing to explain. The challenge is barbaric. There are some that think that it should be abolished. There are others that want to see the men and women that put it on imprisoned. We have so many other things to worry about in the Remains and outside of the walls. But we are spending so much money worrying about who's going to win the Pandemonium Challenge."

Ralphie listened and suddenly felt confused.

"Wait. What are you trying to do?"

"Ralphie, things can't stay the same. Things have to change."

"Who is going to change things?"

Two of the enforcers sat close to Ralphie. Bailey lay silently just a few feet from Ralphie.

"I think that someone has to step up and make a change. Today, that is me. Tomorrow, it could be you."

"Why me? Why us?"

"Why not?"

Ralphie thought of asking another question but he did not think that Ella Buchanan would answer. She was an Innovator. Their lives were all but planned out. He was a Miller. He was born and raised to be a worker.

"What's going to happen to us now?"

Ella Buchanan did not respond. She moved back toward the front, suddenly uninterested in talking with Ralphie.

Ralphie thought for a moment to ask his question again. He instead looked around the interior of the helicopter and the hard men and women, the private enforcers of the Innovators, that made up a private army in the Remains. Ralphie rubbed his head and that simple action caused him incredible pain. He took a few short breaths and tried to think how he and Bailey had survived out of all the others.

The medics bandaged Ralphie. He would live. The realization that he would live overwhelmed Ralphie suddenly. He sat up and looked again at the blinking lights and intricate technology in the helicopter. It was more spacious than he imagined.

Tears pooled in his eyes. He was alive and so many that had started out with him were not. Gone were Jax, Zeke, Tee, Maddy, Ant, Dame, Gina and all the others. Some would be missed. Some deserved the end they brought on themselves. Ralphie tried not to concentrate on the negatives.

Ralphie knew that he must look like an Egyptian mummy with all the bandages. The bandages covered his hurts and cuts but could not hide all he had done in the challenge. Ralphie had done things that he did not imagine he was capable of. He had zapped nearly half a dozen in the challenge.

He looked out the doorway of the helicopter and imagined life in the Remains. He would return to the Remains and be a legend. Ralphie would return to the Foundry and hug his mother and father and baby sister. He was alive. He had survived the challenge. He and Bailey had survived the challenge.

They might name a building after him. They might name a park after him. In the back of his mind, Ralphie thought, the Millers might erect a statue to Ralphie's success at the Twenty-Third Pandemonium Challenge.

"You thinking about what's going to happen when you get back to the Remains," asked the square chinned enforcer. Ralphie looked up and into the eyes of the enforcer with the three cuts across his sloping forehead.

Ralphie nodded.

"Well, the way I see it, this goes one of two ways. You two land and you are heroes. Or you two land and you are criminals."

Ralphie listened and twisted his lips as if he had tasted something sour. "Why criminals?"

7734 smiled a smile that seemed to be much less about amusement than anything else. "The Remains bets on the challenge. Someone made a lot of money with this move. Someone, whoever bet that you and the girl would not die on the seventh day made bank." 7734 paused. "Someone who sees this move as a total long shot is going to be mad about that."

"But that's not our fault," Ralphie pointed out.

"Don't matter. Someone has to take the blame. The Innovators are untouchable. So, it falls on you or the girl's line. Me, I'm banking on you and the Millers taking the heat."

Ralphie pursed his lips. He struggled for a moment. It seemed as if he might say something but chose against it.

7734 turned away with a wry smile and Ralphie found himself looking down again at the handmade bracelet that Bailey had made for him. He looked past the bracelet to the tops of his basketball sneakers. There were specks of blood on his shoes. The blood reminded him of all that he had been through.

He closed his eyes to the memories of the challenge. There were things that he did not want to talk about. Yet, Ralphie knew that the part that made the challenge interesting was the post-interviews of winners. Everyone who interviewed challenge winners wanted to know the same answers to the same questions. Did you regret anything? Would you do things differently? What are you going to do now? What does returning to the Remains mean to you? With all the deaths you have seen do you think that you can return to the Remains and be a "normal" citizen?

Ralphie tried to think of the answers to the questions that the interviews would ask him and Bailey. He did not know if he could answer all the questions. All he knew was that he had survived. He had survived and that was enough, for now.

He had lost friends and that thought made his chest tighten. Ralphie wiped at his eyes and took a deep breath. Ralphie thought, if he was going to be a criminal then every challenge winner was a criminal. Ralphie disagreed with 7734, the Innovator guard. He would be seen as a celebrity in the Remains. He would be legendary.

As the helicopter cut through the darkening sky Ralphie looked out of the open door as the orange and purple surface of the deadly water flashed by. Ralphie looked down and onto the dangerous and unpredictable surface of the Acid Bay and wondered what life would be like now that he was returning to the Remains.